Comes the Dark

"Michael Prescott delivers a harrowing thriller of the first order. His characters are flesh-and-blood real, the atmosphere's intense, and the plot races along unceasingly."
—Jeffery Deaver, *New York Times* bestselling author

"Prescott effectively captures the pain experienced by his characters and how it leads them to terrifying acts of desperation."   —*Publishers Weekly*

"A first-class thriller. . . . Prescott's smooth writing propels readers. . . . First-rate!"   —*The Arizona Daily Star*

Also by Michael Prescott

NEXT VICTIM
LAST BREATH
THE SHADOW HUNTER
STEALING FACES
COMES THE DARK

Published by New American Library

MICHAEL PRESCOTT

IN DARK
PLACES

AN ONYX BOOK

ONYX
Published by New American Library, a division of
Penguin Group (USA) Inc., 375 Hudson Street,
New York, New York 10014, U.S.A.
Penguin Books Ltd, 80 Strand,
London WC2R 0RL, England
Penguin Books Australia Ltd, 250 Camberwell Road,
Camberwell, Victoria 3124, Australia
Penguin Books Canada Ltd, 10 Alcorn Avenue,
Toronto, Ontario, Canada M4V 3B2
Penguin Books (N.Z.) Ltd, Cnr Rosedale and Airborne Roads,
Albany, Auckland 1310, New Zealand

Penguin Books Ltd, Registered Offices:
80 Strand, London WC2R 0RL, England

First published by Onyx, an imprint of New American Library,
a division of Penguin Group (USA) Inc.

First Printing, February 2004
10 9 8 7 6 5 4 3 2 1

PUBLISHER'S NOTE
This is a work of fiction. Names, characters, places, and incidents either are the
product of the author's imagination or are used fictitiously, and any resemblance
to actual persons, living or dead, business establishments, events, or locales is
entirely coincidental.

Thou hast laid me in the lowest pit,
In dark places, in the deeps.

—Psalm 88

Prologue

I know who you are.

That thought beat inside her in time with the steady rhythm of her heart. That thought gripped her with hard, cold fingers and wouldn't let go.

I know who you are. I know who you are.

At first she hadn't known. She'd assumed he was just some random sicko. He would rape her and let her go. Or maybe he wanted money, a ransom. Her parents weren't rich, but they lived the lifestyle of the wealthy, in a house they couldn't afford, in an exclusive neighborhood that was too upscale for them. They were social climbers, joining country clubs and playing golf at charity events, acting like big shots, never letting on that they paid for their fun with a second mortgage and endless loans from both sides of the family.

He might have mistaken image for reality. He might have thought she was rich. But she didn't believe it. She'd thought rape was more likely. She knew she had a hot body, the kind that turned older guys on. She'd seen plenty of men in their thirties or even older stopping to check her out as she walked home from school. Once, a good-looking guy in a Mercedes convertible had tried to pick her up. She'd told him she wasn't legal, and he'd said he hadn't cared. She'd walked away, secretly pleased.

So, yeah, it had seemed pretty likely that the creep who had her now was just another desperate, dirty old man. Except she wasn't sure he was so old. In the glimpse she'd gotten, he hadn't looked much older than Jason, her classmate Sasha's boyfriend, who worked in an accounting firm and was twenty-five.

If all he wanted to do was screw, she could handle it. She'd lost her virginity three years ago, when she was fourteen. She'd been with four boys since, five if she counted Nelson Samovar, who'd been so nervous he hadn't been able to get off. Sex held no mysteries for her. She would let the creep do whatever he wanted. She just hoped he would use a condom. There were diseases to worry about.

But he hadn't raped her. And that was when she'd begun to get scared.

If he didn't want money, and he didn't want sex . . .

Then why had he snatched her off the street at gunpoint, hustling her into the back of his parked van? Why had he taped her wrists and ankles, sealed her mouth with a punctured tennis ball and more tape, driven her out of the city? Why had he left her alone in the rear of the van, long after the engine had stopped and the last daylight had faded behind the flower-patterned curtains over the windows?

She didn't pay much attention to the news—it was all so boring and stupid—but she knew about the other high school girls who'd disappeared in Los Angeles over the past year. None of them had come from her school or her neighborhood. There was no reason for her to connect those crimes with the driver of the van.

But if it was the same guy . . .

There had been four victims, or maybe five; she couldn't remember. Two were still missing. The other two—or three, whatever—had been found. Their bodies, anyway, left in different places in the Mojave Desert. He had kidnapped them and killed them. She didn't recall what method he'd used. A gun, she thought. Probably a gun.

When the thought first occurred to her, she told herself it couldn't be true. Then she admitted it was possible—but unlikely. It seemed to become more plausible as time passed and she lay on the van's carpeted floor, twisting her ankles and wrists, chuffing against the gag. At some point, imperceptibly, it passed from being just an idea to a certainty.

I know who you are.

And what you're going to do.

Now the world outside the van was fully dark. Must be eight o'clock or later. Her parents would have reported her missing. The police would be looking for her. She might be mentioned on the news. She wondered when her friends would hear about it and what they would say. Were cell phones ringing all over Bel Air even now? Were Sasha and Taylor and Tabitha all relaying the scary news?

Damn, she was afraid. Seventeen was way too young to be dead.

She'd heard no noise from up front for hours. Had he forgotten she was even here? Maybe he was just crazy enough—

The van creaked.

She stiffened.

Another creak as the vehicle shifted on its springs. The driver's door opened with a soft snap. She heard a crunch of shoes alighting on sand or gravel.

He was getting out of the front seat. After all this time, sitting in silence, he was making his move.

She twisted onto her side, flexing her wrists against the tape, her breath explosive in her nostrils.

The van's rear door swung open. She craned her neck and saw movement behind her, his shadowy form. Then he was on top of her, and for a moment she thought he really was a rapist, after all.

But he made no move to assault her. He simply peeled the tape away from her mouth.

"Spit it out," he said.

She coughed out the tennis ball and heard it drop on the floor. She kept coughing for a long time.

"What's your name?" he asked when she was through.

"Jessica. Jessica Bender."

"Bender." A chuckle. "You a contortionist?"

She had heard every possible joke about her name, but here and now she couldn't process humor. "What?"

"Never mind. How old are you, Jessie Bender?"

"Seventeen."

"Nice-lookin' piece of ass, ain't you?"

She didn't know how to answer that.

"Yeah, you're a looker." His voice was oddly mellow and slow. "Well, I'm real sorry I had to give you a scare. We're heading home now."

"Home?"

"Your home, I mean. I'm taking you back. Worked out an arrangement with your folks. Just business, is all."

He leaned close when he spoke the last words. She smelled a strong medicinal odor. Liquor. He'd been drinking.

"Oh," she said.

"Get you back to beautiful Bel Air in no time. You'll be bouncing on your daddy's knee and hugging your favorite teddy bear."

Something sharp glinted in the dark. She drew back.

"Don't be a scaredy-cat, Jessie Bender," he said in that slowed-down voice. He cut through the tape around her ankles. "How you supposed to walk if you're all trussed up like a Christmas turkey? Now let's get a move on."

He stood and pulled her to her feet. She had the impression he was strong—strong enough to make any attempt at fighting back a futile exercise, even if her wrists hadn't still been bound behind her back.

"Where are we going?" she asked as he hoisted her out of the van.

"My car. Parked on the other side of the road. Can't take the van. Boys in blue may be looking for it."

Darkness lay all around, huge and silent under a starry sky. They were somewhere in the Mojave where the developers had not yet reached. The air was warm and dry, and as he led her forward, their shoes made soft scuffing noises on the hard-packed soil.

"What kind of arrangement?" she asked.

"With your folks? Let's just say your daddy owed some money to certain people, and I had to hold on to you until he decided to pay up."

"Oh."

"Like I said, business."

"Yes." She let a moment pass. "So how come you didn't know my name?"

"They only tell me what I need to know."

"Uh-huh."

It was a pretty good story, but there were two big holes in it. First, although her father liked to live above his means, he wasn't stupid enough to get involved with the kind of people who would abduct his daughter and hold her as collateral. And second, she had been listening in the van the whole time. There had been no phone conversations, no radio transmissions. So how could any kind of deal have been arranged?

There was no deal. There was no car parked on the other side of the road. There would be no trip back into town.

I know who you are. I know who you are. I know who you are.

"I know who you are." She said it aloud.

Beside her, the steady pace of his footfalls faltered. "How's that?"

"You're him. You're the one who . . . who kills high school girls."

He said nothing. They came to the road, a strip of blacktop bordered by yucca plants and spiny cactus. There was no traffic anywhere. No billboards, lampposts, buildings. She hadn't known that any part of California could be so empty.

"That's who you are," she pressed. "Right?"

"Right," he said.

So it was confirmed. No doubt anymore.

She lowered her head, afraid to speak.

"You're smart," he said. "Smarter than the others."

She cleared her throat. "The other five?"

"Four. There've been four."

"I couldn't remember. I'll make five, then." She heard her voice from far away.

"You'll make five," he agreed.

She wondered if she could talk him out of it. Probably not. The others must have tried, but maybe they'd gotten all hysterical. She knew he wouldn't respond to tears and screams. Logic might reach him. It was possible.

"You don't really want to do this," she said as they crossed the road. "If you did, you wouldn't have to get drunk to go through with it."

"Is that so?"

"You got drunk because part of you wants to let me go."

He coughed up a dull chuckle. "Yeah, right."

"I'm serious."

"You're dead." He said it without emotion, as a statement of fact. "You were dead the minute I grabbed you. You're dead now. That's not gonna change. Get used to it."

They arrived at the other side of the road. She knew that nothing she said could touch him.

He led her into the brush. A few yards from the road, he stopped walking. The flat desert extended in all directions under the moonless sky.

She looked down and saw a gun in his hand. He must have had it tucked in the waistband of his pants. Some kind of handgun, small and shiny.

He saw her staring at the gun, and he smiled. "You scared, Jessie?"

She had been afraid for so many hours that she had almost stopped noticing.

"Yes."

He lifted the gun. "Close your eyes."

She tried one more time. "You don't have to do this."

"Close your eyes."

"Can't we talk about it?"

"Close your eyes."

"I can do things for you." It was her last gambit, one that she knew was hopeless even before it was tried. "I'm not a virgin. I can make you feel good."

"Close your eyes."

"Please."

"Close your eyes."

Because there was nothing left for her to say or do, Jessica closed her eyes. And waited.

She didn't have to wait long.

Chapter One

"Granola bars," Meg said without enthusiasm when she entered the kitchen, her blond hair freshly washed and pulled back with a purple scrunchie. "I hope they're not peanut butter again."

Robin Cameron had sworn over and over that she would start serving her daughter nutritious breakfasts, but in the usual frantic effort to get Meg ready for school and get herself ready for work, she hadn't seemed to find the time.

"We used up the peanut butter ones on Friday." Robin tried to sound upbeat. "These are cookies 'n' cream."

"Dessert for breakfast. Does this still count as the most important meal of the day?"

"Never complain about getting your daily sugar fix. When you're older, you'll learn that the regular intake of highly sweetened snack foods is the key to happiness."

"That's the slogan of the American Dental Association, isn't it?"

"If they know what's good for business, it is. Look, granola bars aren't any worse for you than those honey-frosted cocoa puffs, or whatever they were, that your dad used to buy for you in Santa Barbara. You practically lived on those."

Meg looked up from smoothing the wrinkles out of her

gray-and-white uniform. "Mom, that was, like, a million years ago."

"That's a bit of an exaggeration. I don't think your father and I were actually married during the Ice Age."

"I don't know. Things got pretty chilly."

Robin couldn't argue with that. The marriage had been failing for years before it was finally put out of its misery.

"Anyway," Meg added, "sugar makes me break out."

"That's a myth."

"It is?"

"For the purposes of this conversation, yes." Robin placed two unwrapped granola bars on Meg's plate. "As a medical practitioner licensed in the state of California, I can assure you that millions of commuters subsist on this healthful and satisfying breakfast fare every day. They survive. So will you."

"I wish I could believe that," Meg said, but she ate the bars. "How about you?" she asked through a mouthful of oats. "Aren't you going to savor the joys of your own cooking? By the way, mentally, I put 'cooking' in quotes."

"Thanks for sharing that. I'll eat mine at the office."

"You'll probably stop at some gourmet restaurant after you drop me at school. You'll have eggs Benedict and croissants. This whole granola bar runaround is just a scam."

"My secret's out." Robin sat down at the table. "Get all your homework done?"

"Yeah, it was easy. Just had to write a report on *Catcher in the Rye*."

"Thumbs-up or -down?"

"The book was okay. I couldn't relate to Holden Caulfield as much as I was supposed to."

Robin took this as a good sign. "As I recall, he was a pretty mixed-up young man."

"He's alienated, I guess. That's a popular theme, isn't it?"

Robin made a quick literary survey, from *The Odyssey* to *Hamlet* to every modern book, movie, and TV series about suburban angst and disaffected youth. "Always."

"Hey, didn't they used to call people in your line of work alienists?"

"Way back when. The term referred to Freudian psycho-analysts more than to us cognitive-behavioral types."

Meg seemed uninterested in the distinction. "Alien-ation," she said a little too casually. "That's a bad thing, isn't it? To be cut off from society?"

Robin eyed her with suspicion. "I have a feeling you're going somewhere with this."

"Not really. It's just that, well, people who go to an ex-clusive private school are kind of alienated, wouldn't you say?"

"Nice try."

Meg wouldn't be deterred so easily. "The uniform alone is enough to make you feel alienated." She plucked at the white blouse. "No normal person dresses like this."

"You're a perfectly normal person. And Gainesburg is a perfectly normal high school. Not to mention one of the best schools in the city."

"There are plenty of good public schools. Magnet schools. They take the best and the brightest. Namely me."

"The Gainesburg School also takes the best and the brightest."

"They take anyone who can afford the tuition. Speaking of which, how do we afford it, anyway?"

"I sneak out at night and sell my body on Hollywood Boulevard."

"LA psychiatrist by day, Hollywood hooker by night. See, if I went to public school, you could give up your sor-did double life."

"Is wearing a uniform really that onerous?"

"It's not just the uniform. It's the whole Gainesburg at-mosphere. It's, like, a whole different world. Not part of the city at all."

"That's the idea."

"It feels isolated."

"It's supposed to feel isolated. The whole point of going there is to be isolated."

"So alienation is bad, but isolation is good?"

Robin sighed. Teenage sophistry was a powerful thing. "It depends on what you're being isolated from. In this case, yes, it's good."

"Why? What's so scary out there?"

"Do you ever read the newspaper?"

"Do you?"

"I would if I had more time. And if I did, I would read about gang shootings, drug overdoses, teenage pregnancies—"

"I'm not going to get pregnant or take drugs just because I go to a public school. You don't trust me. That's what this is really all about."

"Meg, you'll have a better chance of getting into a good college if you have Gainesburg on your application."

"I'll get into a good college anyway."

"You have friends at Gainesburg."

"I can make friends anyplace. Will you at least consider a magnet school?"

It would be easy to lie and put the issue to rest, at least temporarily. But Robin made a conscious effort never to lie to her daughter. She had not lied during the divorce or the painful months of relocation and readjustment that followed, and she wouldn't start now.

"I feel better having you in Gainesburg," she said. "Sorry."

"It's for my own good, right?"

"Partly. It's also for my own good. My peace of mind."

Meg showed a sly smile. "You know, even Gainesburg students get into trouble sometimes."

"But you won't. Will you?"

She deflated. "I'll never get the chance."

That's the way I like it, Robin thought. "Get your book-bag, and I'll set the alarm."

Their two-story, three-bedroom condo had come equipped with a security system, a major selling point in

Robin's estimation. Meg chided her for her obsession with the alarm, but Robin was taking no chances.

West Los Angeles was a safe neighborhood by local standards, but within the last month there had been a break-in down the street, an armed robbery at a jewelry store two blocks away, and shots fired from a moving car on a Saturday night.

It wasn't that safe, no matter what people believed.

No place in this city was safe.

That thought stayed with Robin as she picked up Meg's friend Jamie, who carpooled with Meg, then drove them both to the private school on Barrington Avenue. She waved good-bye and hit the freeway, her Saab speeding east toward downtown, the CD player on. The disk on the tray was Bach's Brandenburg Concerto No. 4, the rich tones pumping through the dashboard speakers.

She wondered if she was too hard on Meg. But exiting the freeway, entering the wasteland of a burned-out neighborhood, she saw the ugliness and desperation of the city. It might seem exotic to her daughter, like the backdrop to a music video on MTV, but there was nothing exotic about drive-bys and drug deals. Nothing exotic about the patients she treated or their life stories, many of which had gone wrong in their teenage years when they'd fallen in with bad company and started making bad choices. She intended to shield Meg from that. And if her daughter thought she was overprotective . . . well, too bad.

Although the day was mild, with highs expected only in the seventies—seasonable for LA in the middle of May—she kept her windows up, the AC on. The closed windows, like the enveloping cocoon of music, were her way of holding the outside world at bay.

She had spent the last two years in Los Angeles, a city of transients, a place of people lingering nowhere, always on the move. But in the neighborhoods around her now, there was no place to go. The people here were transients who

stayed put, or maybe it would be less paradoxical to say that
their travels had been circumscribed by the narrow dimen-
sions of their lives—from slum apartment to prison cell,
from motel room to abortion clinic, from desolation to
degradation. There were people here, less than twenty miles
inland, who had never seen the ocean. There were people
here, a bus ride away from downtown LA and one of the
largest public libraries in the country, who had never read a
book.

She passed from the remains of a residential district into
an industrial section, largely deserted, the businesses gone.
Around her stood bleak commercial structures—warehouses and windowless brick buildings bearing faded signs
with words like *Packing* and *Processing*.

Idling at a stoplight, she noticed two teenagers staring at
her from a street corner. She'd seen hundreds of young men
like them on the streets of LA. Even the details were familiar—the baseball caps pulled low over their foreheads, the
black sweatshirts, the oversize baggy pants. Every day, after
leaving the comparative safety of the freeway, she drove
past these young men or others like them. It wasn't just this
part of town. They were everywhere in this city.

She looked away, afraid that her gaze might be miscon-
strued as a challenge. The music continued, but she couldn't
focus on it—not when her first session with Alan Brand was
scheduled for one o'clock. It was an appointment she'd been
anticipating all week, ever since she'd received the go-ahead
from Deputy Chief Wagner, her liaison with the LAPD.

She remembered Wagner asking why she was so gung ho
to poke around in a cop's psyche.

"What I'm gung ho about," she'd explained, "is the
chance to show how effective my method of treatment can
be. But I need a more diverse pool of patients than the inmates of the county jail."

It hadn't been easy to get the LAPD on board. She had
put months of effort into securing a police officer as a patient, invested hundreds of hours in writing and rewriting

proposals, meeting with the police brass, working her way through the tiers of bureaucracy. She had lost nights and weekends. She had lost sleep.

And now everything was signed and delivered, and she finally had the approval she needed. She had permission to use one police officer, just one, as a test subject. If she didn't get results with Sergeant Brand, she wouldn't be given a second chance. So she *would* get results, starting today.

It was taking a long time for the light to change. Maybe she should just run the red. The intersection was empty of traffic. She didn't like to break the law, but—

A heavy thump, a crunching sound.

Glass pellets sprayed her lap.

She whirled in her seat in time to see the crowbar's second impact against the window on the driver's side. The remaining fringe of safety glass was swept away in a shower of glittering crumbs, and then a hand reached through the window frame and unlocked the door.

It was the two young men she'd seen a moment ago. The nearer one had the crowbar.

The CD kept playing, the concerto bursting from the speakers.

A sharp rap on the windshield. Her eyes cut in the direction of the noise. She saw a gun, a large steel-frame pistol, held sideways, movie-style.

"Outta the car, bitch!" the one with the crowbar screamed over the music.

His voice was higher than she'd expected, almost a girl's voice. Distantly she wondered how young he really was.

"Okay," she said. "You can have it. You can have the car."

"Get *out*!"

"I am." But she wasn't, because she couldn't seem to unhook her seat belt, couldn't get her shaking fingers around the buckle.

"Get the fuck out!"

Finally she popped open the buckle, and the lap belt and shoulder belt slid away, freeing her.

"I'm coming," she said, "I'm coming."

Something hit the windshield. The spot in front of her face shivered into a meshwork of fractures, bending inward but not crumbling, held in place by the thin layer of plastic embedded in the safety glass.

It was the second thug, the one with the pistol. He'd delivered a hard swat to the glass with the gun barrel.

The first one grabbed her by the shoulder, hauled her out of her seat. She looked into his face, his eyes. Wild eyes—he was high on something—pupils dilated, the whites bloodshot.

His voice was a whisper. "Gonna mess you up, kitty cat."

In that moment she knew they didn't want only the car. They wanted her. They were going to hurt her, kill her.

She bent her left leg at the knee and kicked at the one with the crowbar, catching him in the stomach, surprising him. He let go of her, and she ducked back into her seat, bending low, and slammed her foot on the gas.

There was another smack against the windshield—the assailant with the gun must have hit it again—and then the Saab's front end thudded into him and knocked him reeling. She powered forward while a nasty scraping noise rasped along the rear of the car.

The intersection was still empty of traffic. She tore through it and around the corner, slamming the door shut as she took the turn, keeping her head down out of some unsuspected combat instinct. A block away she cut into the parking lot behind the building where she worked, pulling alongside a huge sport-utility vehicle that concealed her from the street. With a shaking hand she shut off the CD player.

There was a cell phone in her purse. She ought to call the police. But she couldn't do it right now. She had to know if they were still after her.

They had been out for blood. That was certain. Any possible doubt had been removed by that second impact to the windshield. It had not been another strike by a blunt object. It had been a gunshot, one that had punctured the glass with a neat round hole, surprisingly small. The bullet itself was lodged in the headrest of the driver's seat. If she hadn't ducked . . .

"But you did," she told herself. "So it's okay."

A lie. There was nothing okay about any of this. Since when had a morning drive to work become an exercise in survival?

She waited another couple of minutes, the Saab's engine idling, gearshift thrown into reverse. If the two men—boys, they were boys—appeared, she was ready to back out of the parking space at top speed.

But they hadn't pursued her. How could they, when they were on foot? They had no way of knowing where she worked, no way of knowing she was still in the neighborhood. They had given up on her, moved on to another victim, easier prey.

She shut off the engine and got out of the car. Her knees briefly failed, and she had to lean against the open door. The scraping noise she'd heard as she sped away had been the sound of the crowbar leaving a long, ugly groove in the trunk lid. A parting gift from the lead attacker.

Gonna mess you up, kitty cat.

She could ask the obvious question—*Why me?*—but she already knew the equally obvious answer. There was nothing personal about it. She was not any special target. They had simply spotted her, a woman alone in an expensive car, a Saab 9-5 sedan, and they'd decided to make their move. They would have beaten her or raped her or killed her because she had money and they didn't, or because she took too long to comply with their orders, or because it would be fun.

Just kids. Two of them. How many more were out there? And how many other kids, a few years younger, would be following in their footsteps?

You can't save the world, Robin, her mother used to say. She had always answered, *You can try.*

She restarted her car and parked in her reserved space. When she was ready, she took the cell phone from her purse and called 911.

Chapter Two

During the next hour, two squad cars patrolled the neighborhood in search of young males matching the descriptions she'd given the 911 operator, while a third patrol unit was dispatched to take her statement and examine the Saab. One officer took photos of the damage with a pocket camera. His partner dug the expended round out of the headrest and bagged it as evidence.

"Shouldn't a forensics team do that?" Robin asked.

Both cops looked at her as if she'd been watching too many crime dramas on TV. They were in their late twenties, a decade younger than she was, trim and tanned with buzz-cut hair and dark glasses.

"Dr. Cameron," the first cop said, "there are two or three hundred incidents per day in this division. If we brought out the crime-scene guys for every violent crime, they'd never get anything done."

"This isn't just any violent crime. It's attempted murder."

"Just be glad it was an unsuccessful attempt. You know, it's not worth losing your life to protect your vehicle."

"I told you, I was trying to cooperate, but they didn't give me enough time. I think they were on something. Amphetamines or cocaine."

"Unfortunately most of the lowlifes around here are high most of the time, so that doesn't exactly narrow it down."

"If you want my advice," the second cop added, "move your office to a better neighborhood. You're in a real bad section here, Doctor. VFW territory."

"VFW?"

The cop looked uncomfortable. "Never mind. Just an expression. Thing is, you're too close to downtown. Why not move to West LA or the Valley?"

"I need to be near downtown. That's where many of my clients come from."

"They live downtown?"

"They live in the county jail."

The two patrolmen exchanged a glance, and then the first one got it.

"Oh—you're *that* doctor."

"Right."

"The psychiatrist. The one who works with cons."

"That's me."

"Didn't you get an award from the city or something?" He seemed impressed.

She tried not to show her pride at being recognized. "A few months ago, yes. For my work with prisoners."

"You try to rehabilitate them by putting wires in their heads."

"Something like that."

"Huh." His tone changed. Suddenly he was accusatory. "Well, lemme ask you—you think the two jackers who tried to pop you today can be rehabbed?"

She held her ground. "I think anybody can be rehabilitated."

"Do they deserve to be?"

"Everyone deserves a chance in life."

"How about their victims? What kind of chance did they get?"

"There would be fewer victims if we could reduce the recidivism rate."

"The work you do just gives the system an excuse to put these pukes back on the street."

"In most cases they're going to be back on the street anyway. The only question is whether they leave prison reformed or more dangerous than before."

"So you'd try to reform the gangbangers that tried to clip you today?"

"I would."

He shook his head. "It'll never work. Some people are just scum. They never change."

"I hope to prove you wrong."

"You need to learn more about the bad guys, Doctor."

Her voice was low. "I already know more than you might think."

They told her that a detective would be in touch within forty-eight hours—more or less—and that she might be asked to look at mug shots of known offenders whose MOs fit the crime.

"You're sure you don't require medical attention?" the lead cop asked for the second or third time that morning, before climbing back into the squad car.

"I'm okay." She managed a smile. "A stiff drink wouldn't hurt."

"All right, Doctor. Well, you keep working to make the streets safe your way, and we'll keep doing it our way. Maybe together we can fix things so your morning commute isn't so stressful in the future."

The patrol car pulled away, giving a little bloop of its siren as a parting salute.

She stared after it, trying not to think about the rampant, random violence of this city. There was crime in Santa Barbara, but not like this. Meg was always saying she wanted to go to public school. No way.

Robin went back inside the building and wandered through her office suite. Well, *suite* might be overstating it a little. She had a small waiting room with a pile of magazines that were nearly current, and a second, larger room that served as her office, with an adjoining kitchenette. She had no receptionist or assistant. Voice mail was adequate for handling her routine calls when she couldn't get to a phone. In emergencies, her patients were instructed to call her cell phone number, which was printed on her business cards. She always carried the phone or kept it close.

Yes, she'd taken pains to prepare for her patients' emergencies, but she'd given little thought to an emergency of her own.

The prospect of dying didn't frighten her unduly. What worried her was what she would leave behind.

If she had died today, Meg would be alone.

Not technically alone. Dan would take her. She would go back to Santa Barbara, back to the house in the hills where she had grown up. But Dan was too irresponsible, too wrapped up in himself to take much interest in raising his fifteen-year-old daughter. Meg would be left to fend for herself, and she wasn't ready for that. She was not as grown up as she liked to think.

Robin shook her head, brushing off these thoughts. Nothing had happened to her. There was no reason to worry. She was fine. Meg was fine. Everything was fine.

Sure it was.

Chapter Three

Justin Gray lay on his bunk, gazing at the ceiling of his cell in the high-power ward of Twin Towers, where the K-10s were lodged. K-10s—the keep-away prisoners, the baddest of the bad. Some were bunking here for their own protection. They were the child rapists, the kid killers, the suspected snitches, all the ones marked for the big chill by their fellow inmates. Others were here because they were just plain old-fashioned dangerous motherfuckers, too damn scary to be put anywhere else.

Gray fit into both categories. He knew there were plenty of Twin Towers residents who would have been happy to slip a shiv between his shoulder blades. He also knew none of them would dare to try.

He didn't mind his K-10 status. It came with certain perks. A bright yellow jumpsuit, flashier than the standard orange duds worn by most inmates. And a private dorm— the authorities couldn't bunk two K-10s together or one of them would end up dead.

The downside was that the guards watched you twenty-four fucking hours a day. Deputy Dawgs, Gray called them, in honor of the old-time cartoon character he'd watched in reruns when he was growing up. Goddamn screws never let you out of your cage, not even for exercise. Hell, the high-power ward didn't even have a recreation yard. No common room, either, which meant no poker games, no trades of candy and cigs, no socializing or casual bullshitting or swapping jokes. Showers were allowed once every other day. The tiny cell was bare of anything except a cot, a combination sink and toilet, a phone that allowed collect calls only, and a TV mounted in the wall. There was nothing to do but sit on your rack and watch the tube and stroke your dick whenever a nice set of jugs came on the screen.

There was one bitch in a car commercial who was so damn fine, she'd stiffened Gray's hog for a week. He'd gotten a regular love jones for that slut. Fucked her a million times in his dreams, missionary style, doggie style, in the mouth, up the ass, every which way but loose. Fun times.

Yeah, sure. Meanwhile, out in the real world she was giving lube jobs to TV producers, and he was stuck in a glass box feeling his own wood. He was twenty-eight years old, for Christ's sake. He ought to be out on the town, kissing the girls and making 'em cry, sowing all those wild oats of his. Instead his girlfriend was a thirty-second apparition on a picture tube. Life fucking sucked sometimes.

Still, it could be worse. Lockup in County was a vacation compared with a stay in a state pen. And a state pen, some maximum-security shithole like Pelican Bay, was where Gray should have been by now.

He'd been convicted four months ago. Once sentenced, inmates were typically transferred to the state system as fast as County could spit them out. Gray, however, was still enjoying the dubious delights of life in Second City, as the county jail system was called in reference to the sheer size of its population.

He was here for one reason only: Dr. Robin Cameron. She had been his ticket to an extended stay in County.

Gray swung down from the bunk and lowered himself to the floor, where he snapped off a half dozen one-armed push-ups. He didn't need the exercise, just wanted to use up some nervous energy. No exercise gear was allowed in his cell, but he'd learned to stay in shape with a daily regimen of sit-ups, push-ups, and isometric exercises.

Under the yellow jumpsuit he was all lean muscle and taut skin decorated with a half dozen tattoos. Three of them—skull, scorpion, and spiderweb—were jailhouse tats, applied by his cellmate a few years ago, when he'd done a deuce upstate for auto theft. The prison tats were jet-black and crude as hell, but jailbirds couldn't be choosy.

Then there were the other three tattoos, larger, more detailed, and inked originally in full color, though with the passage of time they'd faded to a uniform blue. Those tats had been applied professionally by a guy named Ernesto at a tat shop called Wild Ink in Hollywood. Ernesto was a regular fucking artist, and he'd done some of his best work on Gray.

There was a big-ass crocodile swimming across Gray's shoulder blades, and a knife with a bloody blade on his left biceps, and the *pièce de* friggin' *résistance*, a tombstone punched into the hard knobs of his abdominal muscles above the navel. The stone bore his own name, Justin Hanover Gray, and his date of birth, January 22, 1975, and—what pleased him most—his date of death. Ernesto had selected March 15, 2001, saying, "Beware the Ides of March, *vato*," in a theatrical whisper.

Well, Gray was still here, more than two years after his personal doomsday.

He wondered how much more time he would have before he checked out. Years, probably. He'd never been one of those live-fast-die-young dudes. He intended to stick around.

The tats weren't the only form of body art he'd indulged in. Over the past twelve years, starting at age sixteen, he'd pierced his earlobes, lower lip, chin, and navel. The jewelry was all gone now, confiscated by the Dawgs, and some of the holes were closing up. But once he was out, he would get pretty again. He liked to look good for his ladies. And he liked the process of decorating his flesh, feeling the hot pain of the needle, seeing the deep purple bruise blossom against his pale, almost pasty skin. He had what the doctors called a high threshold of pain, and he enjoyed testing his limits, seeing how much he could take.

Maybe that was why he could handle the isolation and constant scrutiny of the high-power ward. It was another test of his strength, another initiation and rite of passage. He had proved he could take whatever the system could throw at him. He could survive, even in this shit palace. Even in the Reptile House.

That was his private name for the place. Twin Towers was the official designation for this newest correctional facility of the Los Angeles County Sheriff's Department, situated in downtown LA, across the street from Men's Central Jail. Because Men's Central was old and prone to overcrowding, Twin Towers had been built to take in the excess prisoners. It was named for the two eight-story buildings that housed four thousand homeboys, druggies, and skanks who'd run afoul of the boys in blue.

But to him, it would always be the Reptile House. That was how he'd thought of it since his arrival. He remembered emerging from the elevator, flanked by deputy sheriffs, trudging through the POD—prisoners on display—area. To his left, the smoky, tinted windows of the POD control booth; to his right, his new neighbors—gang *pachucos* and syndicate greaseballs and mass killers, all on display in their separate cages. No iron bars here, only sheets of reinforced, soundproofed, impact-resistant glass. Behind each transparent wall a man lay on his rack or paced in his cage or stared at the TV. Every face was blank, every eye glazed.

Seeing those cages from the outside, Gray was reminded of childhood trips to the zoo. His favorite part of those trips had been the submersion in the cool darkness of the reptile house.

Rectangles of glass. Copperheads, rattlers, vipers, each in its private habitat. The cages brightly lit, glowing in the dimness of the exhibit room. Lines of the curious passing by, noses pressed close, hands squeaking on the glass, eyes staring at these dangerous, sequestered things.

That was what he'd thought of, and that was where he now lived. He was a king cobra behind glass.

After a while, the eight-by-ten glass box had started to get to him, so he'd claimed he was sick, even forced himself to puke a few times—the old finger down the gullet had done the trick. He'd hoped to be transferred to the medical ward. At least it would mean a change of scenery and maybe a shot at some conversation. Privacy was okay, but it got old.

But he'd been disappointed. The doctor had come to him, bearing a panoply of medical gear on a cart. Gray was treated right in his cell, while two deputies looked on. The doctor had given him some pills.

That was when he realized there was no getting out of the Reptile House. No way he could stop being a display behind glass, not even for one day or one hour.

Until the offer from Dr. Robin.

He called her that, sometimes—Dr. Robin, like that bitchy shrink on the radio, Dr. Laura. He knew she didn't like it, so he kept it up.

Two months ago she had visited him in an interview room here on the eighth floor. Two hacks—their names were Paulie and Roger, better Deputy Dawgs than most—had escorted him on a rare trip out of his cage and down the hall. She had been waiting, seated at a table.

Despite the presence of the two deputies, she'd been nervous. He could see the fear in her pursed lips and flickering eyes. He had a feel for fear, other people's fear. He might not be a Rhodes scholar or a creative genius or even a good dancer, but he knew about fear, knew things nobody could learn in any school.

Paulie read her apprehension also. "Don't you worry about a thing, Doc. We got this boy covered as per usual."

"He looks at us cross-eyed, we put him on the floor," Roger added.

"I know," she said with a faltering smile. No doubt she appreciated the reassurance, but it was clear she would have felt better if the two deputies had been armed. The guards in the control booth could break out guns and riot gear in a crisis, but the men by her side wore empty holsters.

While Dr. Robin Cameron introduced herself, Gray sat down, facing her across the table. A woman—a real live woman in the flesh—was a rare thing in his world, and he took the time to appreciate the sweet little titties under her blouse, the long neck and strong, don't-fuck-with-me chin. She was maybe five foot six, a head shorter than Gray himself. Her eyes were brown, like her hair, chestnut hair brushed straight and cut to shoulder length. Nice hair, soft, catching glints of sun through the narrow window of the room.

She was in her late thirties. No wrinkles yet except a few laugh lines around the eyes, a feature he had always found attractive in women.

"You're a psychologist?" he asked her.

"Psychiatrist."

"MD? You look too young to be any kind of doctor."

"I'm thirty-nine. I've been practicing psychiatry for thirteen years."

"Married?"

"That's none of your business."

"No wedding ring. You a dyke?"

"Justin—"

"Right, right, I'm outta line. Thing is, locked up in here, I forget how to talk to a lady. Lemme guess. You *were* married. Now you're divorced. Spent too much time on your work. Hubby got frustrated, started fooling around—"

"We're not here to talk about me."

He was pretty sure he'd nailed it—maybe not right on the money, but close enough to get her undies in a twist.

He didn't pay much attention to the early part of her spiel. But when she started talking about the need to treat him at her office, she caught his interest.

"How often would I go there?"

"Two days a week for as long as the program lasts."

"What would you do to me?"

"It's not a question of doing anything to you, Justin. I'm interested in helping people like you."

"What sort of people would that be?"

"Violent criminals. That's what you are, isn't it? Unless you're going to tell me you're innocent."

"Shit, no. I'm guilty as sin. I'm just surprised it took 'em so damn long to nab me. How exactly are you gonna help me?"

"I think criminal tendencies can often be traced to unresolved traumas and the effects of post-traumatic stress."

"Post-what?"

"It's like shell shock, combat fatigue."

"Ain't never been in combat."

"For some people, just growing up is like being in a war zone."

Gray thought about his old man and chuckled. "Got that right."

"And they never get over it."

"Blame it all on Mommy and Daddy, that your angle? I can hack it. Feels better than blaming myself."

"I'm not talking about blame. I'm talking about subtle psychological effects that last for years and influence your adult behavior. Effects that make you more violent than other people, less able to channel your rage, less capable of self-restraint."

"You think that describes me?"

"I think that's why you're locked up. Am I wrong?"

He conceded the point with a lift of his shoulders. "So what can you do about it?"

"There's a new approach to treating the psychological effects of trauma. It involves passing a magnetic current through the two sides of the brain in an alternating rhythm—"

"Brain surgery?"

"Nothing invasive. No surgery. It's an outpatient procedure performed in my office. You'll wear an appliance equipped with electromagnetic coils. The coils produce the magnetic field."

"But no cutting me open."

"Correct. The field passes right through your skull. It inhibits certain neurons—brain cells. Prevents them from firing. By controlling the current, I can control which cells are shut off. I can vary the level of activity in your brain from one area to another."

"You invent this shit?"

"No, it's a technique that's being tried in various procedures around the world. Still experimental in the U.S. A variation of it, called transcranial stimulation, has been used to treat depression with some success. I believe I'm the first to employ transcranial inhibition for therapeutic purposes—certainly as a treatment for recidivist tendencies."

"Use smaller words. I'm not a college man."

"The procedure can help you control your anger. It can enable you to resolve old conflicts that are still rendering you dysfunctional. In doing so, it can gradually make you less likely to commit crimes in the future. At least, that's my hope. I've had success in earlier trials."

"I'm not your first guinea pig?"

"There have been three other experimental subjects."

"Cons?"

"Yes."

"Killers?"

"They committed lesser crimes."

"Not like me, then."

"Not as severely afflicted, no."

He allowed himself a smirk. "That what I am? Afflicted?" He didn't wait for her answer. "So you're hitting the big time now, huh? You're in the high-power ward."

"I know where I am, Justin. And where you are."

"First time on the eighth floor?"

"That's right."

"It's the floor reserved for guys with severe mental disorders. That's what they told me when they brought me here. Severe mental disorders—those exact words."

"Those words strike me as accurate."

"You think I'm a straight maniac, is that it?"

"You murdered five teenage girls, didn't you?"

"Five they know about."

"Shot them in the head, dumped their bodies in the desert."

"You've been reading up on me. I'm flattered."

"Under the circumstances, I'd say 'straight maniac' is an accurate description."

Gray nodded. "Just checking. It's been a while since I had an expert opinion. Now I got a news flash for you, Doc. I'm serving five consecutive life sentences, which means I'll be up for parole around the time I've been dead a hundred years."

"That's not news."

"So why rehabilitate me? What's the point? Even if you clockwork-orange me into a model citizen, I'm not going nowhere."

"The point is to show that it can be done. If it works for you, it will work for others who do have a shot at parole."

"You really want to put men like me back on the street?"

"Not men like you. Men who used to be like you." She glanced around. "What's the alternative? Build more places like this, warehouse more and more people, forever?"

"Hey, you don't gotta sell me on prison reform." He leaned forward on the bunk. "But I want to be up front with you. I don't think you'll have much luck with me. I'm a tough fucking nut to crack."

"I'll take that as a challenge."

He had known she would take it that way. And he had known she would like a challenge. However fearful she might be, there was something else in her—something hard and determined.

Finally she asked if he would participate. He made her

wait, though he'd never had the least doubt of what he would say.

"What the hell," he said at last. "Sign me up."

Naturally he didn't give a rat's ass about any experimental therapy. He didn't want to resolve his inner conflicts or become a better man. That was all bullshit.

What mattered to him was simply the chance to get out of his cage. To escape from the ward, feel the sun on his face, see the city streets as he was driven to Dr. Robin Cameron's office.

It wasn't living, but it was closer than anything Twin Towers had to offer.

That, at least, had been his original rationale for signing up. Recently he'd come up with an even better idea.

Freedom. Permanent freedom.

In another twenty-four hours, if everything went as planned, he would be out of the Reptile House for good.

Chapter Four

Deputy Chief Richard Hammond rarely arrived at his office before ten A.M. As he'd explained to Lieutenant Banner—who served, unofficially and contrary to department policy, as his personal media liaison—there was no point in showing up earlier unless he was booked on one of the local morning shows. When that was the case, he liked to be interviewed at his desk so viewers could see him on the job. For use on such occasions he reserved his full dress uniform, the same one he wore to funerals and news conferences. The uniform was cleaned and pressed after its every deployment, and was kept in a garment bag near the front of his closet at home.

At the moment Hammond was not wearing his dress blues or anything else. Naked, he straddled his wife in their four-poster bed, trying not to let his mind wander as he performed his marital duties. Lately Ellyn had put on weight, mostly around the hips, and he had trouble still seeing her as the svelte young debutante he'd married.

Hammond himself had not gained a pound since he was twenty-one. He could have fit easily into the uniform he'd worn as a probationer, cruising the streets of Harbor Division in 1977. He liked to see himself in the mirror, his abs tight, arms and legs hard with packed muscle.

His weight-control policy was part of a broader program of career advancement. Promotion to the department's top post was rarely offered to a man who had let himself go. There had been one exception, Willie Williams, brought in from Philadelphia to replace Daryl Gates in 1992, but Williams was the exception that proved the rule. The rank and file instantly despised him. The man was grossly obese, reeking of cologne, bedecked with gold jewelry, an embarrassment to the force. He hadn't lasted long, and Hammond knew the same mistake would not be made again. In the LAPD, as in LA itself, image counted. The man who would be chief of police — COP, in the department's curiously apropos acronym — must look the part.

It was a part for which Hammond had been rehearsing throughout the past ten years, during his rapid ascension from captain of a neighborhood station to assistant commander of Metro Division to deputy chief in charge of the vast Operations-Central Bureau. And when the current chief made a political misstep — and he would, he would — and had to be replaced, Hammond intended to see his own name at the top of a very short list.

Maybe it was this thought that finally got him off. He arched his back with a groan and released himself into Ellyn, then withdrew and rolled over beside her. He was sweating hard — putting out for her had become more difficult because of her damn weight problem — but she, he noticed, had barely stirred.

Hope it was good for you, too, he thought irritably.

Hell, he was doing his part. Love, honor, obey, and pay regular conjugal visits — wasn't that how the vows went? If he was no longer the world's most inspired lover, maybe she ought to take the hint and cut down on the chocolate-chip ice cream.

"Well," he said, rising to get dressed, "duty calls."

It occurred to him that he could have said the same thing before getting into bed with his wife.

*   *   *

A half hour later, he was riding to work in the backseat of a department sedan, his driver negotiating the traffic on the 405 Freeway. He had worn his regular uniform, not his dress blues. No media availabilities were scheduled for today.

He knew that his adjutant, a competent lieutenant by the name of Lewinsky, would already be at his desk. He called his office, and Lewinsky answered.

"What's on tap?" Hammond asked.

"Meeting with Deputy Chief Drummer and Deputy Chief Raynard at eleven hundred."

"I remember. Anything new on the streets?"

"Been pretty quiet. Hey, you know that shrink who treats cons? Dr. Robin What's-her-name? She got carjacked this morning."

"Maybe she'll start to reconsider the value of rehabilitating career recidivists. Especially if her car comes back in pieces."

"Well, she didn't actually lose the vehicle."

Hammond hated imprecision. "I thought you said it was a carjacking."

"Attempted carjacking, I should've said. Couple of bangers, it sounds like. She resisted."

"Did she? Was she hurt?"

"Just shook up, I guess."

"What, the jackers weren't armed?"

"They were armed. Let's see here—crowbar and a handgun. One shot fired. It missed her."

"She takes on two gangbangers, one of whom is capping off rounds, and all she gets is shook up?"

"Lucky lady, huh?"

"She should play the lottery. Officially I have to register my displeasure, since—officially—the department does not encourage civilians to stand up to their assailants. Fighting bad guys is best left to the professionals, et cetera, et cetera."

"But unofficially?"

"I hope she kicked some butt. But don't quote me on that."

Hammond ended the call and stared out the window at the blur of smog and speed. He had seen Dr. Robin Cameron on a few occasions. He remembered her trim figure and slender, suntanned legs. Now it turned out she was a bit of a street fighter. Quite a surprise. He didn't know too many Ph.D.s who could hold out against a pair of armed and dangerous homeboys. There must be more to her than he'd thought. He wondered what she was like in the sack.

Better than Ellyn, he was sure. But lately, that wasn't saying much.

Chapter Five

It was one-seventeen, and he still hadn't shown up.

Robin was beginning to think Sgt. Alan Brand of the LAPD had blown her off, and she didn't like that idea.

After the carjacking attempt she had canceled all her morning appointments. But her one-o'clock with Brand had remained on her schedule. It would take more than a near-death experience for her to postpone her first session with him.

And now he was the one standing her up. She had already called his home and his cell phone. No answer at either number. It was possible he'd been delayed by work or by traffic—traffic was always a valid excuse in Los Angeles—but she didn't think so.

Her gaze cut to the clock on the office wall. One-eighteen.

Most likely he just didn't want to be here. Most cops weren't enamored of the profession of psychology. It was alien to their world. They thought it was safer not to look inside themselves, not to ask too many questions. To open up their emotions felt dangerous; there was no telling where it might lead. Better to drown all doubts and fears in alcohol and adrenaline—drink away the bad feelings, or chase them off with some cops-and-robbers action. If they really needed to talk, they would share what they felt with another cop, one of their own, someone who wore the badge and knew the job, not with some head doctor whose only contact with the criminal world came from books and university courses—or so they thought.

And especially not with a woman doctor. No way a woman could understand them. Many of these guys had never had a deep, lasting relationship with a woman. They turned to women for sex, but they relied on their buddies for comfort.

The clock ticked. One-nineteen.

He should have been here at one. No, earlier—she'd asked him to arrive a little before the hour so he could complete the necessary paperwork. She remembered his sigh over the phone as he echoed, "Paperwork." It was the voice of a man who'd filled out too many forms.

A nice voice, she'd thought at the time. Mellow, tugged down into a low register by world-weariness. A man with that kind of voice might be cynical and tired, but he would not be empty inside. She had looked forward to meeting him.

She was still looking forward to it now—at one-twenty in the afternoon.

For a second time she called his cell number. No answer.

She wasn't going to pace her office aimlessly for the rest of the hour. She intended to have a session with this man. If he wouldn't come to her, she would go to him.

Quickly she walked through the waiting room, out into the hall, locking the door behind her. The hall door afforded access to the lot behind the building, where her battered Saab was still parked. She climbed into the car, wincing at the bullet hole and the spiderweb of fractures in the windshield.

Sgt. Alan Brand worked out of the Newton Area station. She looked it up in a city map book, then pulled out of her reserved space, heading east, avoiding the street where the attack had taken place.

Not that the other streets were any safer. Her office was

a few blocks from MacArthur Park, which had once been a place for family picnics and was now the disputed territory of three rival gangs. A bad neighborhood, as the patrol officers had said. VFW—whatever that meant.

She found herself clutching the steering wheel with both fists, aware of the rush of air through the glassless frame of the driver's-side window. She kept the CD player off. She was not in the mood for Bach, and besides, she wanted to maintain full alertness.

She hooked onto Hoover Street, heading south, and tried Brand's cell phone a third time without success. Then she left messages for the two other patients with appointments for this afternoon, asking them to reschedule. They were paying customers, and Brand was a freebie, but it didn't matter—she had to have the session with Brand.

Hoover Street took her down to the USC campus. She turned left onto Jefferson Boulevard, passing through a neighborhood of shotgun flats, liquor stores, and boarded-up minimalls. Knots of young people congregated on street corners or against walls tattooed with graffiti. She found herself wishing she could roll up her window.

Conventional thinking was that the graffiti vandals and the other antisocial elements here, or anywhere, suffered from a deficiency of self-esteem. As a proactive measure, from preschool onward, kids were indoctrinated in the dogma of their own unassailable self-worth. Yet they kept turning into taggers and dealers and killers anyway.

It was her view that a lack of self-esteem had little to do with criminal tendencies. The typical inmate in the county jail had sky-high self-esteem. He saw himself as superior to most of the population. He believed he was smarter than the police—never mind that they had caught him—and more adventurous than the workaday civilians he characterized unkindly as clones, drones, or "normals."

Felons could not be talked out of this attitude, or preached out of it, or medicated out of it. They had to be reached on a deeper level—the level of neural programming itself, the hardwiring of their mental circuitry. It was the only way.

If it worked, she reminded herself. *If*.

At the corner of Jefferson and Central Avenue, the police station came into view. She pulled into the parking lot. She felt safe here, she thought—but when she got out of her car, a shudder of panic quivered through her, and she turned, quickly scanning her surroundings for danger. There was none.

Damn, what was the matter with her?

Then she smiled at herself. Of all people, she ought to know the symptoms of post-traumatic stress disorder. This morning's fight-or-flight response had been burned into her neural circuitry. It would keep recurring at unexpected times. Meanwhile, she would seek to dissociate from the symptoms by rationalizing and intellectualizing the event— just as she was doing now.

"Physician," she murmured, "heal thyself."

The lobby of the station house was crowded with civilians and uniformed officers. One man in a jacket and tie, in earnest conversation with a crying woman, looked at Robin as she entered. She felt his stare and looked back, wondering if he was a victim, a witness, or a plainclothes cop.

People waited in line at the desk. When it was her turn to speak to the desk officer, she asked if she could speak with Sergeant Brand.

"Brand's not here," the officer said without glancing up from a stack of papers.

"Is he expected back soon?"

"He's not *here*. Not on duty."

Robin didn't get it. The appointment had been set up during Brand's normal working hours. "Are you sure?"

The officer flicked a glance at her. "Can *I* help you?"

She doubted it. "Who's in charge here?"

"The WC is Lieutenant Wolper." WC—watch commander.

"I'd like to speak with him."

"He's pretty busy, ma'am."

She held her ground. "I need to discuss something with him. It's urgent."

The cop shrugged, eager to be rid of her, and gave her directions to the lieutenant's office. Robin proceeded down a hall lined with corkboards displaying memos and notices. Fluorescent light panels buzzed overhead. Coffee stains spotted the carpet.

Lieutenant Wolper was protected from distractions by a civilian assistant, a heavyset, grim-faced woman with a butch haircut. Robin introduced herself, drawing a frown from the assistant. She didn't take it personally. The woman seemed like the type who frowned a lot.

"The lieutenant is on the phone. Have a seat."

Robin doubted this story. She had the feeling that the assistant merely wanted to show who was in charge. It was a power play, but Robin didn't care. She sat and waited. She would wait all day if she had to.

Noises echoed from other parts of the station—drunken shouts, laughter, slamming doors. Men and women in uniform passed through the hall, gear rattling on Sam Browne belts, radios crackling with cross talk.

None of it was unfamiliar to her. Though she had never been inside this station, she had spent time in many similar environments. The atmosphere was always the same. A police station, a county jail, a state prison—such places had been part of her life throughout her childhood, until the age of ten, when they took her father away for the last time.

She wasn't surprised when he was taken. He had gone to jail several times before. The other kids in Mrs. Allen's homeroom teased her about it, said she had a dad who was a jailbird and a crazy man. They said her dad had held up a liquor store and beaten the proprietor over the head with a baseball bat even after he'd cleaned out the cash register. They said her dad had driven a car off a bridge and down an embankment during his failed getaway from another robbery. They said her dad was a drunken loser who got into fights in bars. She couldn't dispute any of this. It was all true.

The next-to-last time her dad had gone away, Robin had asked her mother if he would ever get out. She'd been almost disappointed to hear that he would. Life was easier when her dad wasn't around. Not easier in the financial sense—not with her mom struggling to pay the bills and raise a ten-year-old daughter on her own. But easier emotionally. When her dad was around, the little house where they lived on the outskirts of Phoenix, in the fast-growing suburb of Paradise Valley, was hot with tension and the certainty of violence. Her dad had never lashed out at her, but he'd whupped Robin's mom plenty of times. Whupped her—that was what he called it when he got angry and took his fists to her face and backside. Sometimes he was drunk when he did it, but mostly he was just pissed off. He got mad all the time for no good reason. The TV picture was snowy, there was an overdue electric bill, his supper was too cold, his beer was too warm—any little thing was enough to get him riled, and for the next few days her mom would wear layers of makeup and long-sleeved shirts—in the desert, in summer, in one-hundred-degree heat.

So Robin wasn't surprised when the police came and took her dad away. The timing might have been better. It was Christmas Eve, after all, and this year they had a tree and presents and everything. Some of the relatives were there—Aunt Mazie from Denver, her mom's parents from San Diego, an aunt and uncle who'd driven up from Tucson—and naturally they made a fuss when the cops snapped the handcuffs on. Well, most of them did, though her grandparents sat quietly and watched with sad, knowing faces. Her mom begged the cops not to take him tonight, but her begging had a hollow sound, as if it were a script she had memorized for the occasion. Nobody listened to her. Then the police car was gone, not even bothering to run its siren or flash its emergency lights, and the huddle of family was left behind in uncomfortable silence.

"It's hard for you," Aunt Mazie said to Robin at one point.

She shook her head and said with a child's bluntness, "What's hard is when he gets out."

They all told her she didn't mean that, and she agreed, but secretly everyone knew she had meant every word.

Her mother served the Christmas ham. Nobody looked at the empty chair at the head of the table as the ham was sliced and doled out on the best china.

When the meal was done and the presents were unwrapped, Robin retreated to her room, and there, alone, she cried. She knew she was crying for her father, but she didn't know why. He was a bad man and only got what he deserved. That was the hard logic she couldn't argue with. And yet . . .

Yet there was a deeper truth she sometimes sensed. Her father was not always mean and dangerous and crazy. She remembered how he'd read from *Treasure Island* all night long when she had the flu, how she'd fallen asleep to his voice and awakened to find him still in her bedroom, watching her, the book shut in his lap. There had been other moments like that—a hug, a shared secret, a special gift perhaps purchased with stolen money, but purchased for her—moments when a different man had been her father, a man who did not carry her father's load of rage.

That man was real. He existed. But most of the time he was buried inside a shell of crazed violence. It was the shell of her father who did the bad things. It was the shell who deserved to be carted off to prison. And the prison could have that part of him. But why did it have to take the other part?

In her room that night, as on other nights, she pressed her palms together and prayed. Her prayer was simple. "Give him back to us," she whispered up at the moon hanging in her window. "Give him back."

The real man, she meant. The man trapped inside the shell.

But he never did come back. A week later, on New Year's

Eve, her father was killed in a disturbance at the county jail, where he had been housed awaiting trial for armed robbery and auto theft. Some inmates had attacked a guard. Other guards had broken out shotguns. The details were unclear, but at the end of it, her father and two other prisoners were dead.

Robin had stopped praying after that. She hadn't prayed again for a long time.

"Robin Cameron?"

She looked up, startled out of her memories, and saw the man from the lobby who'd been watching her. A big man, tall and heavyset. "That's right."

"The psychiatrist, right?"

She stood, preferring to face him at eye level, but even standing, she was a head shorter than he was. "Yes," she said.

"Bill Tomlinson. Detective. I work the homicide table around here." He extended his hand, and she took it, feeling his strong grip.

"What can I do for you, Detective?"

"I saw you come in. Recognized you from that awards shindig a while back." The statement was innocuous enough, but she sensed an undertone of tension. "I wanted to talk to you, if you've got a minute."

"About?"

"Sergeant Brand."

"I can't discuss—"

"Your patients. Right. I know. The privilege thing, like attorney-client. But Brand's not your patient yet, am I right?"

"I can't confirm anything about his status, even whether I am or am not treating him."

He chuckled. "You're like the White House. Can't confirm or deny. Got it. But you can listen while I talk, right?"

"I suppose so."

"Look, I don't know Brand real well, but I see him

around, work with him. He's a good man, Doctor. He's been through a lot."

"I'm sure he has."

"Been treated like crap by the department, too. You know they gave him only two days off after the shooting? Two days of stress release; then he's back on the job. That seem fair to you?"

"No. But that's something you'd have to take up with the appropriate authorities."

"Oh, I'm just venting some steam. I could go on all day about the way they treat us." He shrugged away the topic. "But that's not the point. What you need to know is how they're treating *you*."

"Me?"

"You want my opinion, Dr. Cameron, they're setting you up. I think you've gotten a raw deal here."

"How so?"

"Look. Brand is a good cop. But he's . . . unsociable, I suppose is the word. Not antisocial, you understand. Just unsociable. He's not somebody who opens up. He's not a talker, and he doesn't want anybody's help. He'll be fighting you every step of the way."

Robin said nothing.

"The higher-ups selected Brand," Tomlinson went on, "because they knew he would be uncooperative. They want you to fail. You hear what I'm saying?"

"I'm surprised you're so interested in my welfare."

"I just don't like the games they play. I don't like to see them screwing you over when you're just trying to help out. If I were you, I'd go back to the brass and tell them you want a better candidate. Somebody who'll work with you, not against you. Somebody you've got a chance with. Because with Brand, you've got no chance at all."

"Maybe I enjoy a challenge."

"He's not a challenge. He's a brick wall."

"I'll take it under advisement. Thank you for your concern."

"Just trying to be helpful. You keep in mind what I said. Don't let them play you. They will, if they think they can."

He pantomimed a tip of his hat to her, an old-fashioned gesture made more quaint by the fact that he was, of course, hatless.

She watched Tomlinson walk away, while wondering what that had been about. Perhaps he really was trying to help. Perhaps something else was going on.

Whatever his reasons, she wasn't going to be deterred. She would find Brand and she would work with him, whether anyone wanted her to or not.

Chapter Six

Roy Wolper was having a bad day.

He sat at his desk in his uniform, ramrod stiff, his black hair brushed back from his high forehead. As always he felt strong and vigorous and vital and not at all like a dinosaur, which was what he was.

A dinosaur in the new LAPD, anyway. He jogged four miles every day, ate only lean meat and fresh vegetables. There was no flab on him. He was steel hard, his body a carefully tended machine.

Cindy, his wife—ex-wife—had thought he was a fitness fanatic. She hadn't complained about it in bed, as he recalled, but at other times she seemed almost embarrassed by his dedication to health and strength. But then she had been unhappy with everything about him by the end. When they divorced two years ago, there had been nothing to hold them together—except Zach, of course.

At first there had been no more than the usual conflict between ex-spouses, the usual wrangling over weekend custody. Then this attention deficit thing had started. Some doctor had decided that Zach's Cs and C-minuses were the result of a learning disability that required therapy and special schooling, both of which required extra money, which Wolper didn't have. For the past six months Cindy had been on his case nightly, at first requesting and then demanding more child support. Now she was talking about taking legal action.

And the thing was, he wasn't holding out on her. He had never held out on her. He had been loyal to his son, giving him whatever he needed, fighting with Cindy to spend more time with him. Now she was treating him like the villain, insisting he cough up money he didn't have so she could treat a problem that might not even be a problem.

What did shrinks know, anyway? According to them, every kid who was restless in school needed Ritalin, and any kid who wasn't a straight A student had a learning disorder. The thing sounded like a scam, and Cindy had fallen for it, and now she was threatening to take him to court.

Wolper sighed. He hated and distrusted shrinks. He had never believed in any of that psychiatric voodoo. It was crap, an employment program for the unemployables churned out by this society in increasingly large numbers. He knew all about the unemployables, more and more of whom were showing up in blue uniforms as proud members of the new LAPD.

Not the LAPD he'd started out in. Not the LAPD of Daryl Gates, who had run the department in the 1980s and made it into a slick paramilitary force. He remembered the physical-fitness requirements when he joined up—jump a wall, drag a 160-pound dummy, execute pull-ups, chin-ups, run a mile. Nothing like that for today's applicants. They were asked to balance on a teeter-totter, for Christ's sake. They had to pedal a stationary bike, skip between lines like kids on a playground.

Gates was gone, and so was his vision of the department. The new LAPD was all sensitivity training and community outreach and diversity. It was an equal opportunity employer that invited women into the ranks even though they couldn't meet the physical standards established for men. The solution was to lower the standards for everyone. So what if a cop lacked the upper body strength to scale a fence or subdue a suspect? Playing political games was what the department was all about. Bullshit had been elevated to a science. Wolper hated all of it.

Now political correctness was invading his personal life. *Damn.*

And yet . . . suppose the doctor was right. Suppose Zach really did need the meds, the counseling, the special ed. If so, then it didn't matter whether Wolper had the money or not. He would have to provide it. He could not let his son down.

Fourteen years in the patrol side of the LAPD, working the roughest divisions, had left Lt. Roy Wolper with few ideals, but loyalty to one's own flesh and blood was a credo he would not violate.

He took a sip of coffee and spat it back into the mug. Some idiot had percolated a pot of water through a batch of used coffee grounds. And since he had his own coffeemaker here in the office, and he was the only one who used it, he knew the identity of the idiot in question—namely, himself. The stuff tasted like bilgewater.

He took out the rubber ball he used to work off tension and started squeezing it in his left fist. God, what a crappy day. Lately all his days were like this. He'd taken to spending more time at the bar down the street at EOW—end of watch, the close of his business day. He'd never been all that sociable with his fellow officers, but now he preferred to hoist a few with the boys if the alternative was to go home to a ringing telephone and another shakedown by his ex.

He knew he ought to chill out, but it was hard to stay calm where his livelihood was concerned. Money was a bitch. A marriage killer, a friendship killer. Often a literal killer. Most of the shit going down on the streets was about money—the lack of it, the craving for it, the worship of it.

He squeezed the ball harder.

This morning, at five A.M., even before he'd left for the start of the day watch, Cindy had been on the phone to him, telling him that she would have to take Zach out of therapy if she didn't get enough cash to cover the last three sessions.

At two hundred bucks a pop, the sessions weren't cheap, and insurance paid almost none of it. Wolper had ended up telling her that Dr. Hacker—that was his actual name, Hacker—was a fraud and a con man, and she was being taken for a ride. He'd slammed down the phone and left his house before she could call back.

Best thing to do was not to think about it—any of it. He would stay fit and keep a low profile. He knew he would rise no higher in this politicized bureaucracy. If Gates were still running the show, Wolper might have been a deputy chief by now. Instead the newest deputy chief was that pansy Hammond—same age as Wolper, but much less experienced on the street. Hammond wasn't even the worst of them. A lot of these other guys—the new recruits and the veterans who liked the new administration better than the old—were pure politicos who'd never made a righteous bust in their lives, cowards who ran the other way when bullets flew.

When the whole department consisted of affirmative-action hires and civil-service bureaucrats and ass kissers, where would this city be? Wolper knew the answer to that one. Up shit creek, that's where. The public was too dumb to care, and the politicians encouraged the trend, seeing an advantage in a police department they could control. Everything was heading that way, and here was Lt. Roy Wolper, the last dinosaur mired in his own personal tar pit.

Well, he'd put in fourteen years. Another six, and he would cash out. Until then he would be a rock. Rock hard, rock solid, rock steady.

"Rock on," he said to himself, and smiled.

His assistant stuck her head into the office, interrupting his thoughts. "Lieutenant, there's a Dr. Cameron to see you."

Oh, hell. Another shrink. And one who, like Dr. Hacker, seemed committed to making his life a continuing pain in the ass. He took out his annoyance on the squeeze ball, crushing it flat.

"Send her in," he said evenly.

He caught his assistant's blink of surprise and realized he

wouldn't have been expected to know that Dr. Cameron was a woman. The doctor had never been to his office before. They had never met anywhere, in fact. But he knew about her. She was part of the whole Brand situation.

The office door opened again, and Robin Cameron entered. He took a second to look her over. She seemed younger than he'd expected, and there was an air of calm determination about her. He wasn't sure he liked that.

"Please have a seat, Doctor. I assume this is regarding Sergeant Brand."

She took the chair in front of his desk. "That's right."

"Didn't show up for his appointment, did he?"

Her eyebrows lifted. "How did you know?"

Wolper sighed. "I've known Sergeant Brand for a lot of years. I have a pretty good idea how he'll behave."

"He was supposed to see me at one. Never arrived. I called his home number and his cell phone. No answer."

"He's off today. Guess he's not answering his phone."

"He's off? I was led to understand that he would be scheduled for therapy during his normal working hours."

"Called in sick." He kept his tone neutral.

"Did he?"

"That's right."

"So he's ill."

Wolper hesitated. "I said he called in sick. The actual state of his health is another matter."

"Meaning?"

"It's not the first time he's taken a sick day since . . ."

"Since the shooting."

"Bingo." Wolper winced at himself. Cops were always saying *bingo* in the movies. He wished he hadn't picked up the habit.

"You're telling me Sergeant Brand hasn't been coming in for work?"

"Not reliably. Not like he used to."

"So you don't think he's sick."

"I'm not a doctor. I guess that would be your diagnosis to make."

"It's hard for me to render a diagnosis when I can't find the patient."

"I guess that's true. Sorry. Wish I could help."

"But you can't?"

Wolper spread his hands. "If he's not there and he's not answering his phone . . ."

She leaned forward in her chair. "You wouldn't happen to have any idea where Sergeant Brand goes on his sick days?"

"How could I?"

"You said you've known him for years. You know how he'll behave, you told me."

"That doesn't mean I keep tabs on his whereabouts."

"Why do I have the feeling you're holding out on me?"

Wolper tried a smile. "You sound like a cop interrogating a suspect."

She didn't smile back. "I'm just a doctor trying to get some information. I think you can help me. Why won't you?"

A moment passed as he squeezed the ball a few times and considered several responses. "Let me be honest with you, Doctor. I'm not too happy about the idea of Brand's participation in this program of yours. Using the same treatment on cops that you've been using on criminals . . . it doesn't sit well with me."

"The only connection is the nature of the syndrome. Post-traumatic stress doesn't discriminate between good guys and bad."

"That's not how the media will see it. They'll jump all over this. You know the angle they'll play up—cops who are so shell-shocked, they're one step away from being hardened cons themselves. The department doesn't need that kind of publicity. We've gotten enough black eyes over the last few years as it is."

"Black eyes? I guess that's one way to put it."

He knew what she meant. Since the Rodney King arrest, there had been an unbroken string of public relations disasters for the LAPD—the riots of '92, the O. J. Simpson debacle, the succession of failed chiefs, and the overshadowing scandal of the antigang cops in Rampart Division, who had turned into a drug-dealing gang themselves.

"How would you put it?" he asked, though he really didn't care.

"According to the Christopher Commission report—"

"The Christopher Commission report was a politically motivated smear job."

"Was Rampart a smear?"

"The Rampart scandal was blown out of proportion. It was a few bad cops. The department overreacted, and the media jumped all over the story."

"But you don't deny there were abuses, that people were framed by their arresting officers, that cocaine was stolen out of evidence rooms, that police officers perjured themselves—"

"What is this, a *Sixty Minutes* interview?"

She took a breath. "Sorry. We're getting offtrack. The point is, the media need never know about this. My work with my patients is completely confidential."

"Nothing is confidential in this town." Wolper rubbed his forehead. "Ever since the orders came down from Parker Center, I've known this was going to be a pain in the ass. Brand doesn't want to cooperate, most of his fellow officers agree with him, and I get to play the bad guy, the enforcer."

"All you're enforcing is an opportunity for Sergeant Brand to get better."

"That's not how the rank and file see it."

"No? Why not?"

Wolper leaned back in his chair. "Brand's a street cop. He never wanted to be anything else. Some guys get into this work to be civil servants. They put in their twenty years, then cash out. They hate the street. They'll take a desk job as soon as it comes up. No one ever got killed riding a desk. It's nice and safe back here. We call them pogues."

"Pogues?"

"Pogues. I don't know where the term comes from, but it means a commanding officer—lieutenant, captain—who knows all about paperwork and has zero street IQ. Not exactly admired by the rank and file. Brand's never aspired to a desk job. He's only happy when he's pushing a black-and-white, chasing the radio. It's what he lives for. He has no wife, no kids, nothing at all outside the job."

"Doesn't sound like a very well adjusted personality, does he?"

Wolper fought back his irritation. "My point is, he's the kind of cop that other cops respect. Any officer who's ever worked with him trusts Brand to watch his back—or take a bullet for him if necessary. Men like Brand are the guts of this police force. We've already lost too many of them to early retirement or transfers to other cities. We can't afford to lose any more."

"That's a nice speech, Lieutenant. But the fact is, you've already lost Brand, haven't you? He's not showing up for work. He's showing other symptoms of post-traumatic stress also. I know. I've talked with the psychiatrist who's been treating him. If he's as important to the department as you say, then you ought to want him to get over this problem that's keeping him off the job."

"I do want him to get over it."

"Then why are you shielding him from me?"

He flattened the squeeze ball again. "I'm not shielding anybody."

"That's not how it looks from here."

Wolper took a moment to compose a reply. "Being a cop . . . it's a lot like joining a fraternity. We all go through the same initiation, the same hazing. We earn our street degree. We look out for each other."

"You're supposed to look out for the public."

"We do that also. The two aren't mutually exclusive."

"Aren't they?"

He knew she was thinking of the scandals. Baiting him.

He was tired of being on the defensive with this woman. He set aside the squeeze ball and stared her down.

"Look, if Brand needs to work off his emotional baggage by doing some things I wouldn't do, hanging out in places I wouldn't go—" He stopped.

"What places?"

Damn. He hadn't meant to say that much. "Even if I told you, Doctor, you wouldn't want to go there. Take my word for it."

"What places?" she asked again.

"I have no idea. I was speaking hypothetically."

"No, you weren't."

"Let's just say I was." He showed her a hard smile.

"Let's just say I'll go over your head to Deputy Chief Wagner. If he asks you, maybe you'll give a straight answer."

So she was playing hardball. Great.

Wolper had gotten himself cornered. He could give her a phony address, but what would that accomplish? She would only come back to hassle him again. And if he kept putting her off, she would put Wagner on the case. That was all he goddamn needed—a deputy chief breathing down his neck.

He drummed his fingers on the desk for a long moment, then picked up a plain index card and wrote on it in block letters. He almost handed it to her, but hesitated. He really did not want her to have this information. If she knew what was good for her, she wouldn't want it, either.

"Going here is not a good idea, Dr. Cameron. Believe me."

"Bad neighborhood?"

"As a matter of fact, yes."

"VFW?"

He was surprised she knew the term, and even more surprised she'd used it. "Definitely. But that's not the only reason. It's the nature of the establishment itself. To be blunt, I can't vouch for your personal safety."

She wasn't backing down. "Are you going to give me the address or not?"

Reluctantly he surrendered the card.

"You're putting yourself in danger if you go," he said.

"Maybe you'd like to accompany me."

"Can't do that, I'm afraid. It's off my beat. Besides . . . I shouldn't be seen there."

Something flickered in her eyes, and he knew she'd understood why he filled out the index card in capitals instead of his normal, identifiable handwriting.

"And if anyone asks how I got the address . . .?" she began.

"You never received it from me."

"I'll keep that in mind. So you think I can find him at this address?"

"Can't guarantee it. But it's your best shot."

She stood. "Thanks for your help. By the way, what exactly does VFW stand for?"

"I thought you knew."

"I don't. It's just something I picked up."

"Well . . . not everything about the LAPD is politically correct, even today. It stands for 'very few whites.'"

"I see."

"Shocked?" He allowed himself to smile at her.

"It takes more than that to shock me, Lieutenant Wolper. Thanks again for your help."

She left, shutting the door. Wolper stared after her.

She wasn't quite what he'd expected. He had imagined someone more timid. Instead she was stubborn and tough. Maybe not as tough as she wanted to appear, but tough enough.

He might have made a mistake telling her Brand's whereabouts. But he hadn't believed she would be crazy enough to go there. Even now, he couldn't believe it. When she saw the neighborhood, she would back off.

At least, he hoped she would.

Chapter Seven

Wolper had been right about one thing, Robin decided. It *was* a bad neighborhood.

But he was wrong if he thought she'd turn back.

She guided the Saab deeper into the maze of streets that ran parallel to Imperial Highway, heading east, toward Watts. The fractured windshield and blown-out side window and dented trunk were not out of place here. She actually welcomed the damage. It helped her fit in.

After leaving the police station, she'd continued south on Central Avenue, past Florence Avenue. It was at the corner of Florence and Normandie, about a half mile away, that the 1992 riots had erupted. She hadn't lived in LA then. She had watched the news coverage from the home she and Dan had shared in Santa Barbara, until four-year-old Meg had wandered in to ask what was going on. Then Robin had switched to a cartoon show.

She had always tried to protect her daughter. But if that was true, why had she brought Meg here, to a city of random carjackings and drive-bys, a city that seemed to be losing its mind?

The address Wolper had given her was near the intersection of Imperial Highway and Compton Avenue. The spot was six miles south of the Newton Area station, but that distance was deceptive. If Newton was a borderland, this was enemy territory, one that a middle-class white woman with an expensive car and a postgraduate degree was not expected to enter.

She didn't know which gangs fought over this turf, but she could see their markings on every wall and fence and trash bin, the loops and squiggles of spray paint visible everywhere, even on the boles of drooping, sickly palm trees. The thump of rap music pounded from boom boxes set on curbs and from the radios of jacked-up cars, cruising the streets. Most of the people were dressed in black, and she wondered about that at first, until she realized that it was dangerous to wear colors on gang turf. Although it was a school day, kids lounged on street corners and in vacant lots and alleys, wearing loose T-shirts and do-rags, watching her roll past with suspicious eyes.

Every pair of eyes was a flashback to this morning's attack, the thump of the crowbar, the crunch of glass. . . .

Not too late to turn back, she reminded herself.

She kept going. The address wasn't far now.

She thought of how narrowly she had escaped this kind of poverty after her father died in jail. Her mother had worked two jobs to keep up the mortgage payments.

If they'd lost their home, if they'd had to move to a neighborhood like this, would it have changed her? She already had a father who was a felon. Throw in an environment seemingly designed to breed criminals, and what would have been the result? She liked to believe she could have maintained her sense of self even under that kind of pressure. But she couldn't be sure. What dictated the direction of a human life? Nature, nurture, free will, destiny? What was the formula, or was life too complex to be expressed as a formula?

She shook her head. If there was an answer to that question, she wouldn't find it here, now.

She continued driving east, deeper into Watts. Part of her wanted to be angry at Brand for putting her through this ordeal, but she couldn't entirely blame him. He had been given no choice about taking part in the program. In the LAPD, a troubled officer could be ordered to undergo any form of counseling. Being sent to the bank, it was called, because the LAPD's Behavioral Sciences unit, where the psychologists worked, was housed above a bank in Chinatown. To be sent to the bank was to face the possible closing of one's account—the end of a career.

Brand had been spending a lot of time at the bank. His new course of treatment was only an extension of the mandated therapy he'd been receiving from Dr. Alvin, one of the Behavioral Sciences shrinks. When Alvin had failed to make progress, Brand's case had been labeled treatment-refractory, suitable for experimental intervention. And now he was required to see a new doctor for a therapeutic technique that the patrol cops this morning had characterized as "putting wires in their heads."

No wonder Sergeant Brand was resistant to the idea. He didn't seem like the docile type, anyway. From Alvin's briefing, she knew that Brand had grown up in Pico Rivera, a tough, blue-collar town south of LA. He had been in the department for fourteen years, working the high-crime districts of Southwest, Rampart, and now Newton. His ID photo showed a man with rough-hewn features and a thick neck starting to wrinkle into a double chin. His eyes were dark and hard to read under the heavy tufts of his eyebrows. His head was shaved at the sides, his hair thin and short like black bristles on top. He looked older than his age, forty-one.

Not a man who could be pushed around, she thought. And also not a man who would be easily traumatized. But a fatal shooting was enough to traumatize anyone, especially given the fact that Sergeant Brand had never fired his gun on duty before the night of February 9, three months ago.

That night had changed him. Brand had become a different man. Now, facing a new form of therapy, he was scared, and he was hiding. But not for much longer. She would find him, and in the end, she hoped, he would thank her for it.

The address she was seeking was one-half of a duplex on a cul-de-sac—not a reassuring location, since it afforded no easy escape route. Bungalows and small apartment buildings curved around an oval patch of dead grass that had been a small park. The park's swing set was broken, its seesaw overgrown with weeds. No kids played there. Liquor bottles and cigarette packs lined the sandy verge of the play area.

Robin studied the duplex, two stories high, the ground-floor windows barred, the upper-story windows mostly boarded up. An air conditioner chugged in one window, dripping condensation. Cars were parked around the cul-de-sac, taking up most of the curb space, and more cars rested on the narrow front and side lawns of the duplex. Something was going on inside. She heard no music or voices, but the cars told her of a large gathering of people.

"This is crazy," she whispered as she sat behind the wheel of the Saab, double-parked on the street, staring at the house.

The smart thing was to drive off, hit the freeway, and keep calling Brand's cell phone until he answered. If he never did, she could report him to his superiors.

But then Brand would be even more hostile to her for having squealed on him, and the LAPD brass would have cause to reconsider greenlighting the treatment program. She could hear Deputy Chief Wagner now: "If you can't handle the challenge of establishing a rapport with one of our officers, Dr. Cameron, maybe we'd better reevaluate the whole idea."

She wouldn't let that happen. If Brand was in this house, she would find him.

She got out of the Saab and locked it, activating the alarm, which might offer some protection even with a busted window. Quickly she approached the house, checking her purse to confirm that her cell phone was inside and turned on. It would probably be her only lifeline once she was inside.

The two front doors of the duplex were closed. A hand-scrawled, misspelled sign on one of them read GO ARROND BACK, the same message repeated underneath in Spanish.

She threaded her way between the parked cars on the side lawn and came to a small, fenced backyard, empty except for two preschoolers squatting in the grass and examining a crowd of ants. Neither child looked up as she found the open rear door.

Inside, there was a great deal of noise, all of it electronic in origin—TV sets blaring different channels in different rooms, a radio competing with the din. She saw a man with a shaved head and a bodybuilder's physique lounging on a sofa with a dazed look on his face. He was no more interested in her than the children had been.

Moving into the kitchen, she heard voices—live voices, not TV and radio chatter. She found an open door to a stairway leading down into a cellar. People were down there, a lot of them. She stepped onto the staircase.

"Who the fuck are you?"

She turned. The bodybuilder had come out of his daze. He stood at the other end of the kitchen, staring her down. She noticed something strapped to his left arm and was dismayed to see that it was a knife.

"I'm looking for someone," she said over the noise of a TV on the kitchen counter, tuned to a game show.

"The fuck you are. You don't know nobody here. You ain't never been here before."

There was only one way to play this, and that was to bluff.

"You're right," she snapped. "I've never been to this shithole, and you can bet I'm not coming back. I just came to find Brand. He down there?"

"Fuck, I don't gotta tell you nothing."

"Is he down there?"

She knew there were several possible outcomes to this

conversation. She could be ejected from this house, or she could be beaten up or raped, or she could be allowed to proceed. An odd feeling of calm came over her as she understood that the decision was out of her hands. She could only wait and see what the man with the knife would do.

"Yeah," he said after a long moment. "Brand's here. You his woman?"

"I'm his friend."

"Friend." The man smiled, showing a gold tooth. "Yeah, right."

He left the kitchen. Robin took a breath and went down the stairs into a large cellar, the ceiling overlaid with plumbing pipes, bare lightbulbs shining down amid the meshwork of conduits, illuminating a noisy, jostling crowd. Most of the cellar's occupants were men, a mixture of ages and races, nearly all of them wearing dirty overalls or ragged jeans, a few in business suits. The scattered women were young or trying to look young, with big hair and silicone breasts and collagen lips.

Robin wished she had worn different clothes. Her blue skirt and white blouse were all wrong for this place. In jeans and a sweatshirt she might have looked less conspicuous. As it was, she had to hope she didn't draw too much attention in the dim light and the pressing crowd.

She moved through the room, still not sure what was going on. She heard two men arguing, their voices raised.

"He's a fuckin' land shark, gonna have that pussy piece of shit for lunch."

"Bullshit. He ain't got game enough for Driver."

"Driver's fucked up. Last time took too much out of him. He's meat."

"C-note says he pulls an upset."

"You're on, asshole."

Had to be a fight coming up. Like that movie, the one with Brad Pitt, *Fight Club*. But where was the boxing ring? There ought to be a raised platform, but she saw nothing but a crush of people pressing everywhere.

Most of the heads were turned away from her. She side-stepped along the back of the crowd, her back against the cellar wall. She saw nobody who looked like Brand. To really scope out the crowd, she would have to move forward into the thick of it, where she could see the men's faces.

She took a breath and pushed into the mass of bodies.

The first thing she noticed was the reek of sweat all around her, the smell of men jammed together in a hot, airless place. Then there was the heightened volume of noise, a hundred voices yelling at once in an unintelligible roar. An elbow jabbed her shoulder. A careless hand brushed the nape of her neck. She heard someone shouting that the last bets were being taken. Somebody else was calling Rambo a motherfuckin' coward while the man next to him protested, "Rambo ain't no coward; Rambo got *cojones*; you better believe he's one badass *hombre*." Two other men yelled at each other in Spanish, waving fistfuls of cash. A woman with peroxide blond hair that clashed with her dark complexion caught Robin's eye and gave her a wink, as if they were girlfriends sharing a joke.

Still no Brand. Maybe Wolper and the bodybuilder were both wrong, and he wasn't here.

She had maneuvered her way near the front of the crowd now. A curved metal railing came into view. Men were leaning against it, gazing down, while others craned their necks for a better view.

It was some kind of recessed arena, about twelve feet in diameter, probably too small for two men to fight in. A cock-fighting ring, perhaps. Were Rambo and Driver two roosters? She'd never heard a chicken described as a badass *hombre*. Then again, this was LA. Any form of insanity was possible.

Officer Brand, she wondered, *where are you?*

She was jostled from behind by a crew of guys straining to get closer to the arena. The impact pushed her sideways into a narrow gap between two men at the railing. "Hey, sister," one of them said. His face was shiny with perspiration, and there was a long scar stitched like a seam down the side of his neck.

She was saved from deciding how to reply by a stentorian voice that broke through the babble. "No more wagers taken."

Robin looked down into the arena. It was a circular depression in the cellar floor, four feet deep, possibly the remains of an artesian well. Sawdust, strewn over the floor of the pit, was dark with dried blood and a few blotches of fresh blood, glossy and vivid.

Rambo and Driver were in the pit, facing each other, each one held by his owner, who knelt outside the ring and reached through the railing. They were not roosters. They were dogs.

One animal was a pit bull. The other one, larger, looked like a mastiff, a crossbreed engineered for power and viciousness. Both were scarred from other battles. They were suited up for combat, wearing studded chest protectors and leather collars. Their tails and ears had been cropped so an opponent would have nothing to grab hold of. They glared at each other with programmed malice, every muscle stiff with tension.

"Let 'em go," boomed the voice of whoever ran this show, and instantly the two owners released their grips on the dogs.

The mastiff struck first, lunging at the pit bull and seeking to lock its large jaws over the smaller dog's throat. The pit bull dodged the attack and barreled into the mastiff, slashing a deep gash in its foreleg. Then the two animals were all over each other in a fury of snarls and bites and kicking legs.

There was new blood on the sawdust, and more blood painting the walls of the arena in a spatter pattern. Robin looked down and saw flecks of red on her blouse.

She wanted to turn away, but the press of men against her back pinned her to the railing. She shut her eyes. Everyone was screaming now, even the other women in the room. The voices blended into a chaos of curses and exhortations to kill: "Go for the neck," "Get his eyes," "Cut him again," "Cripple him," "Maim him," "*Maim the fucker.*"

Her head hurt. Bright lights flashed behind her closed eyelids. As an undertone to the shrieks and howls of the crowd, she heard the savage struggling of the dogs. No barks, no whimpers, only the tearing of flesh and the awful, relentless gnarling and the snapping of jaws.

"Get him, Rambo; kill that cocksucker! Kill him!"

"Fight back, God damn it! Driver, you dumb piece of shit, you're only good for bait!"

Rambo was winning, it seemed. Despite herself, she opened her eyes and saw the pit bull's teeth buried in the mastiff's neck, below its collar. The mastiff, unable to defend itself with its jaws, was slashing and scrabbling at the pit bull with both forelegs, fighting to tear itself loose, inflicting deep cuts across the pit bull's back, but the smaller dog hung on, blindly tenacious, smelling blood.

"God, somebody stop this," Robin whispered, her voice lost in the uproar.

The mastiff dropped to its knees. It shook its head feebly, delivered a few more perfunctory cuts to the pit bull's side, then slumped on the floor of the arena, its limbs shivering in a lake of maroon blood. The pit bull, Rambo, held on to the mastiff's neck until the twitching had stopped and the bleeding ebbed. By then there was space around the railing, as the winners collected money from the house and from the various side bets that had sprung up.

Rambo's owner, or handler, or trainer—whatever he was called—stepped into the pit and tended to his dog. The man responsible for Driver stripped the collar and chest protector from the carcass, leaving the dog where it lay, a torn and wasted thing, its throat open, limbs askew, fur stiff with drying blood.

Robin finally had the space behind her to turn aside. She stood drawing deep breaths and fighting the pull of nausea. And then she saw him.

Brand.

Across the room, near the cellar stairs, wearing a black button-down shirt and black pants.

And laughing as he collected a wad of cash. He'd backed the right combatant, evidently. The mastiff's death had paid off for him.

"You son of a *bitch*," Robin said aloud, startling a man next to her, who thought the comment was directed at him.

She slipped through the dispersing crowd and closed in on Brand as he pocketed his winnings.

"Alan Brand," she said, getting in his face.

"Who the hell . . .?" But then he knew. Somehow he knew, though they had never been introduced.

"Oh, shit," Brand said.

"Sorry to spoil your fun."

"Shit," he repeated. He seemed slow to react, less intelligent than she'd expected. Maybe it was more than a love of the streets that had kept him from advancing higher in the ranks.

"You forgot your appointment," she said.

He presented a stupid smile apparently intended to charm her. "I didn't forget. Had more important things to do."

"So I see."

"Hey, sorry about that. We'll reschedule."

"That's not necessary."

"You mean you're giving up on me?"

"I mean you're doing your session today."

He blinked, processing this statement and finally producing a startled response. "Now?"

"Yes. Now."

"I don't think so."

"I do. Or we'll see how your superiors feel about the kind of entertainment you enjoy."

He puffed up, a man defending his rights. "What I do in my off time—"

"Watching dog fights is a misdemeanor, Sergeant."

"You gonna arrest me?" He said it with a sneer.

"I'm going to report you."

"Go ahead."

"But not to Wolper or anyone at Newton. I'll go over their heads. I'll bring it up with Deputy Chief Wagner."

"Your fucking angel in the department. The dickwad that approved this half-assed psychiatric bullshit."

"I doubt he'd appreciate being characterized that way."

"How'd you get him on your side? A little mouth action? Oral report? You give his baton a few good licks?"

"Stop being an asshole."

His flippancy abruptly vanished. "You're fucking serious, aren't you? You'd rat me out to the D-chief?"

"I'm calling him right now—unless you follow me back to my office for our first session."

"You're a regular ball buster, aren't you?"

"Is that a yes?"

"God damn it," Brand said, and he headed up the stairs.

Chapter Eight

She watched Brand's eyes tick nervously as his gaze shifted around the office. Possibly he'd been expecting a mad scientist's laboratory or a chamber of horrors, but all he saw was a large room furnished with the plush sofa he was sitting on, and an assortment of thickly cushioned chairs. A desk and a file cabinet occupied one corner of the room. Framed diplomas and other credentials hung on the walls. Sunlight trickled through curtains rustling in the breeze of the central air-conditioning. The floor was carpeted. A potted fern stood near the doorway to the kitchenette.

All very normal. She hoped Brand took some reassurance from that fact.

He didn't seem to—maybe because of one other chair in the room. It had metal arms and a straight back. Wires ran from it to a bank of computer consoles and heart and brain monitors. Nestled among this gear was the MBI appliance, a metallic cap sprouting wires.

Brand's gaze kept coming back to the appliance. His hands twitched in his lap.

She had produced waivers for him to sign. So far he had merely stared at them, his face grim.

"Before we get started," Robin said, "I want to explain a little about the theory behind my work." She tapped an illustration on the wall. "As they say in those public service spots, this is your brain."

Sometimes she got a smile out of a patient with that line, but not this time.

"See this almond-shaped structure just above the brain stem? It's called the amygdala. A primitive part of the brain, responsible for tying together the data that come in from your sense organs. Sight, sound, smell—they all meet here. The amygdala not only puts all this incoming information together, it also instantly applies a kind of nonverbal value judgment. Dangerous or safe—those are the two main judgments it hands down. And it does all this before your conscious mind, operating in the neocortex, has even received the data. Do you see the implications?"

"The only implication I see is that I'm stuck in this office when I've got a hundred better things to do."

"The implication," she persevered, "is that you can perceive something as dangerous or upsetting before your conscious mind has analyzed it. Phobias work this way. A person who's phobic about dogs may react in terror to a little Pekingese. Rationally he knows a lapdog isn't dangerous, but the amygdala has already registered a threat. The same is true of any persistent, irrational fear. Telling yourself to be logical or trying to exercise willpower doesn't work. The fear exists on a lower level than logic or will."

Brand showed a glimmer of interest. "So how do you fight it?"

"You have to reprogram the brain so it stops responding in a counterproductive manner. Basically, the core experience that frightened you is frozen, incompletely processed, so it keeps coming back. Any stimulus that reminds you of the core event will trigger the same automatic fear response. But suppose you could reexperience the event, this time without amygdaloid arousal—relive the trauma, but process it correctly so the memory is properly evaluated and stored. Then you would stop overreacting to subsequent stimuli. You could view your earlier trauma with objectivity and perspective. And you wouldn't be a prisoner of your memories anymore."

"And you can do this?"

"I've been successful in other cases."

"How? By strapping that thing"—he pointed to the appliance—"on my head so my brain gets zapped with electricity?"

"There's no zapping involved."

"That's not what I heard."

"Heard from whom?"

"Well . . . there are, you know, rumors around the department about what you do."

"Rumors aren't always your best source of information. Still, you're partly right." She walked over to the appliance and picked it up. "I will be asking you to wear this."

"The helmet?"

"I call it the appliance. But it doesn't send out an electric charge. It uses magnets." She turned the device over. "As you can see, the inside of the appliance is lined with about fifty figure-eight electromagnetic coils. Each coil produces a fluctuating magnetic field that can pulse at speeds ranging from one cycle per second to sixty cycles per second. Low frequencies work best, so in our session the fields will be running at one hertz, one cycle per second. These magnetic fields produce local electrical currents in the brain tissue. PTSD is characterized by increased blood flow in the right frontal and paralimbic structures, so that's where the fields will be activated. With me so far?"

"I guess so. Not all of the coils will be on?"

"Only the ones targeting the relevant brain structures. There will be about fifteen superposed fields generated by the coil array."

"Sounds like a lot of juice. I'm not too keen on getting brain cancer."

"The overall field strength will be lower than that of an MRI scanner. There's no danger. You may feel a slight contraction of your facial muscles, sort of like your forehead is being pulled taut. While the procedure is going on, you may experience blind spots in your vision, owing to inhibition of the occipital area."

"Great. You're making me blind."

"Afterward, you may experience a mild headache. And that's it."

"Come on, Doctor. Nothing's that safe. Even aspirin bottles have all kinds of warnings on them."

"The process *is* safe, Alan. The only possible complication is the risk of seizure."

"Seizure?"

She held up her hand. "A risk that will be minimized by maintaining a maximum field intensity of only eighty percent motor threshold."

"Say again?"

"If the magnetic field were at one hundred percent of motor threshold, there's a chance that your motor cortex would induce involuntary muscle movements. As long as the field is below that threshold, you'll be fine. I've used this therapeutic technique repeatedly over the past year without any complications."

She didn't add that she kept anticonvulsants on hand for emergencies. Some patients took comfort in that thought. She was sure Brand wouldn't be one of them.

"This technique of yours," Brand said. "Has it got a name?"

"I call it MBI, short for Magnetic Bilateral Inhibition. The magnetic part you already understand. Bilateral means that the fields will fluctuate from one side of the brain to the other. This enhances communication between the left and right hemispheres of the brain. It gets the two sides in sync. So that's what bilateral means. Which leaves inhibition."

"I thought inhibitions were supposed to be bad."

"It's a technical term. The magnetic fields are of such low frequency that, instead of stimulating neural activity, they'll selectively block it by disrupting neuronal firing."

"You're shutting off my brain?"

"The MBI appliance will temporarily inhibit some of your higher brain activities."

"Jesus . . ."

"It's no different from undergoing hypnosis. The higher brain structures responsible for critical thinking and self-censorship will be sidelined for the time being."

He seemed considerably more uneasy. "I don't think I want to be hypnotized."

"That's only an analogy." Men like Brand were always leery of any loss of control.

"Gotta be honest with you, Doctor. This isn't sounding like something I'm gonna do."

"You think heading back to the dogfights is the answer?"

"It's better than having some kind of magnetic lobotomy. Save that for the cons. Use them as lab rats, not me."

"You're here because the results I've obtained with convicts are good enough to offer hope for other people suffering the aftereffects of trauma."

"I'm not suffering any goddamned aftereffects."

"That's not what Dr. Alvin says. He tells me you've been experiencing chronic stress, nightmares, irritability, hypervigilance, and flashbacks."

"Look, I'm a cop. Every cop has nightmares. Irritable? Shit, you try working these streets, dealing with the hookers and the homeboys, and see if you don't get irritable."

"And the flashbacks?"

"They're getting better."

"The chronic stress? The back pain, neck pain?"

"Gives me an excuse for a massage. Believe me, Doctor, everybody should have my problems. I can show myself out."

He made a move to stand up. Her voice stopped him.

"Alan, I don't want to be confrontational. But the fact is, you have been directed by your superiors to come here because they are concerned about your psychological welfare. And so am I. You're clearly in denial about your problems. You skipped our appointment, and you've been skipping work. Your career is in jeopardy. You need help, whether or not you want it. And you're going to get my help—whether or not you want it."

Brand stared at her for the space of several heartbeats, and she stared back, refusing to turn away from his gaze. Then with a resigned wave of his hand, he settled back on the couch.

"So you use magnets to bilaterally, uh, inhibit my brain. That about the size of it?"

"Close enough. Once you're in a relaxed state, you'll be asked to process the target incident."

"You talk like a goddamned bureaucrat, you know that?"

"Sorry. You're right; it's jargon. I just mean you'll relive the experience."

"The shooting?"

She nodded. "You'll go through it step by step and narrate it to me."

"Under hypnosis . . ."

"In a related state. I know it can be difficult reexperiencing the trauma. But by doing it, you'll gain a new perspective on the event. Its emotional colorations will be minimized. You'll be able to reevaluate what happened from a noncritical standpoint. And I believe the flashbacks, the stress, and the other problems will be dramatically reduced."

He was silent, fidgeting.

"Alan?"

"You're not giving me any choice, are you? I mean, you want me to be informed so I can sign these papers, but I have to sign. If I don't, I'm going against the department."

"I'm sorry if you feel pressured—"

"Cornered is more like it. And you don't give a shit, as long as you can do your precious research."

Even the prisoners she'd worked with—even Justin Gray—had not been so openly hostile. "I honestly do want to help you, Alan."

"Great. Let's get started then." He scrawled his signature

on the waiver documents. "Come on, rewire my brain and make me healthy."

Normally she would use the initial session to take a detailed history, run some baseline medical and psychological tests, and determine if there were any physical problems that might complicate the procedure. But Dr. Alvin had already acquired that information, which she had reviewed, and she didn't want to postpone the use of MBI until the second session. She was well aware that if Brand remained uncooperative, there might not be a second session. Her best chance of winning him over was to show him how painless the technique really was.

At her request, he moved to the straight-back chair—the MBI chair, as she called it. Two plastic straps with metal buckles dangled from the armrests. "You going to strap me in?" he asked warily.

"Those are for some of my patients from County. Since I don't like having the deputies in the room when I work, the patient has to be restrained."

She began attaching small adhesive electrodes to his exposed skin. The electrodes would allow her to monitor his brain function, heart rate, and muscular tension on parallel readouts on the computer screen.

"You work with some badass characters, I hear."

She smiled. "They're not as badass as they used to be."

"Yeah? Even Justin Gray?"

"I didn't think his participation in the program was public knowledge."

"Public—maybe not. But word gets out in the department. If you can turn that crazy son of a bitch around, you're a miracle worker."

"I do what I can," she said. She began taking the EEG, ECG, and EMG readings, then lowered the MBI appliance onto Brand's head while he sat stiffly, his shoulders hunched, fists gripping the armrests, like a prisoner in an electric chair.

She spent a moment reprogramming the appliance. Before each session she liked to make subtle adjustments in the hope of optimizing the field exposure protocol. When she was ready, she pulled down a window shade, shut the door to the waiting room, and turned off the overhead light.

"What's with the darkness?" Brand asked. "You planning to run a seance while I'm under?"

"The treatment is directed primarily at the back of the brain, where the occipital region is located. That's the part of your brain that processes visual information. Bright light can interfere with the neuronal inhibition."

"Interfere how?"

"You'll be entering a relaxed state characterized by an alpha brain-wave rhythm. Perception of light could trigger a startle response that would shift your rhythm to beta."

"In other words, I'd wake up."

"You won't be asleep. You'll just be relaxed."

"Hypnotized," he said uneasily.

"Relaxed. The way you'd feel if you were meditating."

"Yeah, that's something I do a lot." He punctuated the comment with a snort. "How much will I remember once I come to?"

"That varies. There's nothing in the MBI procedure per se that would induce amnesia. However, because we're dealing with painful memories, you may find yourself reluctant to bring them to conscious awareness. The mind has many strategies of dissociation—of suppressing material it finds disturbing or threatening. I've had patients who recall all the details of a session the very first time, and others who didn't remember much until we had worked together for weeks."

"So I could tell you stuff and not even remember that I said it?"

"Initially, that's possible. Our goal is for you to come to grips with the memories consciously, but that may take time."

He pushed down on the armrests, as if about to rise from

the chair. "Look, I've already come to grips with the damn memories, okay?"

She laid a hand on his shoulder. "If that were true, you wouldn't be skipping work to watch two animals tear each other apart."

He sank back down. "Okay, okay."

"Now there's one more piece of equipment you need to wear. The coils," Robin said, "produce a loud clicking noise, loud enough to cause hearing damage. As a precaution, both of us will use noise-canceling headphones and we'll speak into these headset microphones, which broadcast on a walkie-talkie frequency. The equipment is shielded to prevent any magnetic interference. I'll hear you on my headphones; you'll hear me on yours."

"This goddamn high-tech stuff," Brand grumbled.

"It's for our own safety. The coils can be as loud as one hundred twenty decibels."

She attached his transceiver headset and her own, then pulled the swivel chair away from the desk and parked it alongside Brand, within reach of the MBI gear. She sat down.

"All right, Alan," she said softly into her stalk microphone, using the calming voice that came naturally to her at the start of a procedure. "I'm turning on the appliance. You'll feel a slight tingle in your scalp."

"Fire away," Brand said, trying for bravado. His voice came through her headset clearly.

She flicked a switch, and the fifteen preselected coils started ticking.

"Everything okay?" she asked over the muffled background noise.

"I guess."

"Just relax now. You'll be entering a quiet, peaceful state of mind. Imagine yourself in the woods, resting on the grass with your back against a tree. It's shady and cool. Birds are singing. You feel peaceful and utterly at ease. Sleepy . . . Are you sleepy, Alan?"

"Sleepy." His voice was a monotone, hollow and distant.

Both the EEG and the rhythm of his breathing confirmed that he had entered the alpha state, the twilight realm between sleep and waking. The MBI's suppression of his higher cortical functions had acted like a powerful hypnotic suggestion, dissipating his nervous tension. His eyes were closing. The muscles of the eyelids were unaffected by the appliance's motor inhibition.

"All right now, Alan. I'm going to guide you out of the woods and into a memory from your past. We're going back to the night when Eddie Valdez was shot."

Brand shook his head slowly. "No."

"It'll be okay, Alan."

"No." Stronger.

She hesitated. Such resistance even in the trance state was unusual. She tried a different approach.

"Here's what we'll do. We'll go back to that night, the night Eddie Valdez died, but you won't have to go through it the way you did before. Instead, you can stand outside the scene and watch as it happens. Just stand and watch from a distance, like watching a movie. Is that okay?"

Brand was silent.

"Alan. Is it okay if you just watch?"

"I can watch. . . ."

"Then that's what we'll do. Remember, it's only a memory, and you're just watching it. You can get away from it at any time just by asking me to make it go away. Do you understand?"

"Yes."

"Nothing can hurt you. You're perfectly safe. All right?"

"Yes."

"I want you to go to the memory of that night. I want you to remember the parking garage. Can you see it?"

"I see it."

"Tell me what you see."

"It's dark. Cars everywhere. Parked cars."

"Is anyone there?"

"There's two. Two in the shadows."

"One of them is Eddie Valdez?"

"It's Eddie, yeah."

"And the other is"—*you*, she almost said—"the police officer. Right?"

Brand made a soft noise like a groan.

"Alan, it's not you. It's someone you're watching. A police officer. That's all."

"Cop," he murmured.

"Do you see him with Valdez?"

"I see him."

She released a breath of relief. They were past that hurdle. "Tell me what's happening."

"They're talking."

Talking? She hadn't expected that. "Tell me what they say."

"The cop . . . okay, the cop, he's saying Eddie seems nervous. Says Eddie wouldn't be planning to fuck with him, would he?"

"And what does Eddie say?"

"He says no way. He says, 'You and me, we're tight, bro.' " Brand had slipped into an approximation of the dead man's voice.

"And the policeman?"

"He says that's good. Because if Eddie ever does get a hard-on to try fucking with him, it won't end well. And Eddie, he's scared, he says he knows that. He's not fuckin' with nobody. He's playing it straight. He's got . . . he's got . . ."

"Yes?" Robin prompted. "What has Eddie got?"

"He's got the money—this month's cash."

A chill rode Robin's shoulders, and suddenly Brand's reluctance to participate in the procedure took on a new coloration. "The money?" she said.

"What he owes. He pays on the first Saturday of every month. Right here in the parking garage."

"Pays for what?"

"It's a patch."

She didn't understand, but she preferred not to interrupt the narrative flow. "Go on. What happens next?"

"Eddie brings out the money. Thick wad, wrapped in wax paper, all taped up. Looks like a fat deli sandwich. Makes me hungry when I see it. I didn't have lunch that day—"

"Not you. You're the observer, Alan. You're only watching. Tell me about the two men, Eddie and the cop."

"The cop takes the money, puts it in his coat. It doesn't print too bad against the material. Nobody will notice it there."

Robin let a moment pass. Suddenly she wished she had tape-recorded this session. What Brand was confessing—if it was a confession . . .

"And then?" she prompted.

"The cop starts to walk away. But he stops, turns back, still wants to know why Eddie's nervous. Something's not right. He thinks Eddie's playing him."

"Yes?"

"So he takes out the package, opens it. There's not enough. There's fifty-dollar bills on the outside of the wad, but inside it's all singles. And Eddie, he's shitting his pants now, and he says he can explain. He's just a little short, he says. But that's gotta be bullshit. The Gs have been banging and dealing all over the hood. Their fucking revenues are going up every month. No way the Gs are short on cash."

She wasn't clear if he was recounting his thoughts or his conversation. "Is that what the cop says?" she asked, but Brand, caught up in the narrative, no longer heard.

"Eddie says it's not the Gs who are short. It's him. Him personally. He fucked up, he says. They gave him the full payment, like always. He lost it." Brand slipped into Eddie's voice again. " 'Motherfucking dogfights, man.' "

Then Brand's own voice, hard and clipped. " 'You gambled the money on some fucking dog?'

" 'It was stupid, okay? They told me I couldn't lose.'

" 'They were wrong, *paquito*. You lost big-time.' "

He fell silent.

"What happens, Alan?" she asked. "Alan?"

"Bang."

Brand spoke the word with sudden vehemence, loud in Robin's headset. She jumped a little.

"One round in the face. Asshole crumbles. He's twitching, jittering.

"You backed the wrong dog, Eddie," Brand said.

Robin wasn't sure if he was repeating what he'd said then or commenting on what he saw now. She licked her lips, fighting the dryness in her mouth.

"What are you—I mean, what's the cop going to do now?" she asked. "How can he get away with it?"

A cynical smile formed on Brand's lips. "Oh, he'll get away with it. All he's gotta do is plant a throwdown on Eddie, an old three-eighty wheel gun he's got. Then call in an officer-involved shooting, finesse the shooting review. No sweat."

He was wrong about that part, at least. His face was bathed in a sheen of perspiration.

Robin got up from her chair and expelled a shaky breath. "All right, Alan. I want you to leave that memory now, leave it and rest. Don't think about it. Don't think about anything. Just rest."

Chapter Nine

She and Brand spoke little after he regained alertness. He seemed dazed, uneasy. She wasn't sure how much he remembered of what he'd told her. It was common for patients to be unsure of exactly what they had experienced while in the trance state. And she didn't think it would be wise to press him on the details and possibly jog his memory.

"As a rule," she said briskly, "we don't make much progress in an initial session, but if you're willing to work with me, we can go deeper and retrieve more details next time."

This was safely general and, she hoped, would convince him that he'd said nothing incriminating.

Brand just nodded. He pressed a hand to his forehead.

"A slight headache may persist for a while. Aspirin will take care of it."

This raised a wispy smile. "Take two aspirin and call you in the morning?"

"Call me anytime. I'm always available if you need to talk about . . . anything." She handed him her card, which gave her cell phone number and office address, but not her home address, of course. Her residence was unlisted, and she was suddenly glad about that—although a cop could find it anyway, couldn't he?

"Thanks, Doctor." He palmed the card without looking at it.

She led him through the empty waiting room into the hall. As he was leaving, he turned to her with a puzzled look.

"Did I say . . . Did I . . . ?"

She waited, her breath held.

Then he shook his head. "Never mind."

"The session went very smoothly, Alan, but you can't expect significant results the first time. This was more of an introduction to the process."

"Introduction. Yeah."

"Can I expect you to show up for your next appointment?"

"I'll be here," Brand said, but he didn't sound sure.

He left the building, exiting into the parking lot at the rear. Robin returned to her office and locked the door.

She was trembling. Maybe not quite so badly as after the carjacking attempt. Still, this seemed to be her day of living dangerously.

If Brand had been on the take, had shot that man in cold blood, execution style, with no possible justification . . .

Then he was a stone-cold killer, and he would surely not be reluctant to kill anyone who stumbled onto his secret.

But he'd taken no action toward her. Perhaps because he was too dazed to act. Or because he didn't recall what he'd said. Or because he wasn't a killer at all.

It was possible. No therapeutic technique was infallible. The MBI procedure could dredge up repressed material, long-forgotten abuse, memories blocked by some self-protective action of the subconscious, but sometimes it could also manufacture false memories, stories that seemed real but were only elaborate fantasies.

She had not personally encountered this problem before. As far as she knew, all the memories recovered from her other patients were genuine. This one might be, as well.

If it was . . .

Then she knew why Brand had been so resistant, why he

had skipped his appointment, why he'd become more nervous when the topic of entering a trance had come up. And perhaps why he'd been showing the apparent symptoms of post-traumatic stress in the first place.

Edginess, impaired concentration, panic episodes could all be produced by a stress disorder . . . or by guilt. If not guilt, then fear of getting caught.

She paced, trying to decide what to do. Go to Deputy Chief Wagner? Physician-patient confidentiality did not apply to cases in which a crime had been committed. In fact, she was legally obligated to report what she'd learned. But if it was a false memory, she would be incriminating an innocent man. And even if the memory was accurate, it would be her word against his—and the police were never eager to turn against one of their own.

The alternative was to wait it out, see if the same material resurfaced in subsequent sessions, maybe get his confession on tape. But suppose he was guilty. He might come after her.

Maybe it would have been better if she hadn't been so damn stubborn about tracking this man down. Maybe she shouldn't have gone to Wolper and made him give her Brand's whereabouts.

She stopped pacing.

Wolper. She could talk to him. He'd already made it clear that he wanted to protect Brand. He wouldn't go running to the higher-ups without good reason. At the same time, he'd been willing to help her when she asked. And he might know enough about the shooting to judge whether or not Brand's remembered version of the event was plausible.

It was a place to start, anyway. She looked up the number of the Newton Area station and called, asking for Lieutenant Wolper. After some delay she was transferred to an unpleasant female voice she recognized as that of Wolper's civilian assistant. The day watch ended at three, she was told. The lieutenant was gone for the day.

"I need to speak with him. Can you give me a number where he can be reached?"

"It's not possible for me to give out that information."

"Then it looks like I'll have to go straight to Deputy Chief Wagner. He's not going to be happy to be distracted by a matter the lieutenant could have handled—if I'd been able to find him."

A tick of silence on the line, then a sigh. "I can give you his cell number."

Robin took down the information and called that number. Wolper answered. "Look, Doctor," he said when she'd identified herself, "if you still can't find Brand, I don't know what more I can—"

"I found him. We had our first session."

"Hallelujah. So what's the problem?"

"Something came up. I can't talk about it over the phone. I . . . I . . . need to see you."

"If you wanted a date that bad, you could've just asked."

"Lieutenant—"

"Okay, okay, just a joke. This can't wait, I take it?"

"No."

"You know Patsy's All-American?"

"Say again?"

"It's a coffee shop, corner of Santa Monica and La Brea. I'm sort of a regular. They make good burgers. What do you say we meet there about five-thirty?"

"That's fine. Thank you, Lieu—" But he'd already hung up.

She checked the clock. Four-fifteen. There would be no time for her to go home before heading to the coffee shop. And she might not be home in time for dinner.

She dialed her home number. Meg should have been home from school an hour ago—she and Jamie were driven home by Jamie's mother in the afternoon.

She got through to Meg on the third ring.

"Hey, Mom. What's up?"

"Looks like I'm going to be late tonight."

"Now that's unusual." Sarcasm, a favorite weapon of the long-suffering high school student.

"I know I've been busy lately," Robin said, "what with the research project coming on top of my regular client list. But it won't last much longer. And you know it's important to me."

"I get it. No problem."

"The thing is, there was a . . . complication with one of my patients. I need to talk to someone about it. It may take a while."

"Mom, I can handle being on my own."

"There's still some of that Chinese food in the fridge."

"I'll reheat it. My microwave skills are improving daily."

"I'm sorry about this. I shouldn't be *too* late."

"Take your time. I'm okay. Like the man said, everything's copacetic."

"Don't say that." She felt a stab of some emotion that was either anger or fear. "Don't use *his* words."

"It was only a joke."

"I'm serious, Meg."

"Okay, Mom. Okay."

Robin took a breath. "Sorry. I'm a little wound up."

"Well, you can chill. Feeble attempt at humor, that's all it was. Uh, you know I'm going over to Jamie's later?"

"That's tonight?"

"Yeah. Monday."

"Right, right. Not till seven-thirty, though?"

"Uh-huh."

"Don't worry; I'll be home in time to drive you there."

"If you get held up or something, I can take the bus."

"A city bus? I don't think so."

"We live in West LA, Mom. There's, like, no crime in this part of town."

"There's crime in every part of town. I *will* be home in time to drive you, and you will *not* take the bus. Is that clear?"

"You're kind of paranoid, you know that?"

"I'm a parent. A certain degree of paranoia is normal and healthy."

"You learn that in shrink school?"

Robin shut her eyes. "I learned it in life."

Chapter Ten

Megan Cameron hung up, shaking her head. She wasn't sure what it was about her mom. She was always worrying about not being there for her daughter, not spending enough time at home, all that stuff.

Probably it was overcompensation. Some single-parent guilt trip. Maybe her mom thought Meg blamed her for the divorce. Which she didn't. Nor had she ever tried to play one parent against the other, or ever suggested that she'd rather live with Dan.

That was how she thought of him—as Dan, never as her father. He hadn't been around enough to be a father.

He was an artist, probably a good one—at least everybody seemed to think he was good, and his paintings, which were more like mixed-media collages, were displayed in galleries around Santa Barbara. Rich people paid major bucks to buy his originals and his limited-edition lithographs. He had even worked as a designer for a big hotel chain, flying around the country to supervise the decoration of lobbies and luxury suites.

He was talented, maybe a genius. He just wasn't a father.

He had unlimited time to devote to his projects. He could work in his studio, a converted guesthouse at the back of the property they'd owned, for forty-eight hours straight. He could go without eating or sleeping or bathing. When he got inspired, he got wild and frazzled. His creative spells weren't much different from an alcoholic's drinking jags.

Okay, that wasn't fair. Her father produced works of art. He wasn't some drunk on a lost weekend. But the point was, he might as well have been, because it didn't make any difference whether he was creating a new canvas or sleeping off a bender. Either way, he wasn't there for her, or for her mom either.

And then on one of his trips—it might have been the hotel gig, or some out-of-state gallery opening—he met a woman with the laughably chichi name of Cassandra, and he started fucking her, and, of course, before long Robin found out. There was yelling, followed by weeks of tense silence, until finally her mom came to Meg's room one night to tell her the marriage was over.

That was two years ago, when Meg was thirteen. Once the divorce was finalized, she and her mom moved from Santa Barbara to LA. Robin claimed there were better career prospects in a bigger city, but Meg knew she just wanted to get away from the memories and start over.

Dan visited occasionally, acting from a sense of duty to his daughter—an extremely weak sense of duty, seeing as how he saw her only two or three times a year. It wasn't like Santa Barbara was a million miles away. Apparently a two-hour drive was too big an effort for a busy creative genius to make.

She had no problems living with her mom. She just wished Robin would stop worrying so much and start treating her like an adult.

She sighed, studying herself in the bedroom mirror. She had changed out of her despised school uniform into jeans and a T-shirt. A long fall of blond hair framed her suntanned face. Despite her protests about granola bars for breakfast, she had so far avoided any major breakouts of acne, and she'd shaken off her baby fat last year. She was frequently mistaken for an eighteen-year-old. Visiting the USC campus, she had passed for a freshman.

She was, for all practical purposes, an adult. Everyone but her mom saw it.

The intercom buzzed.

Her reflection frowned with a who-could-this-be expression. UPS or FedEx, maybe.

She left her bedroom, went downstairs into the foyer where the intercom control was located, and keyed the microphone. "Yes?"

"Guess who?" a familiar voice said.

She didn't answer. She couldn't believe he was here. He had never come to her home.

"You there?" the voice crackled.

Still without reply, she pressed the button that unlatched the front gate. Then she opened the door and watched him stroll through the courtyard of the condominium complex. He was wearing a business suit, as usual.

"Get inside," she hissed. "Hurry up!"

He obeyed, but with a wry smile that mocked her worries. When he was in the condo and the door was closed, she turned to him, speechless.

"Surprised?" he said with a smile that showed that the question was rhetorical.

"What are you doing here?"

"Visiting you."

"That's really stupid, Gabe. Robin—"

"Is at work."

"Somebody could *see* you."

"They're all at work, too."

"No, they're not. Some of them are retired or they work at home. They could be looking out the window—"

"They still wouldn't see me. I'm invisible when I want to be." He fluttered his hand in a magician's wave. "I cast no shadow."

"Be serious. There are rules. We can't screw around like this."

"I thought screwing around was the whole point." He pulled her into his arms and soothed her with a kiss. "Don't fret, Meg. Nobody saw anything. This is LA. Nobody ever sees anything."

Meg sighed, relenting. "I guess you're right. I mean, I don't want to get all uptight. One paranoid obsessive in the family is enough."

"Meaning?"

"Robin." She always referred to her mom that way in conversations with Gabe. It just sounded more adult. "She's kind of overprotective."

"That's a parent's prerogative."

"You sound just like her."

"I'd better quit before I get in any deeper. So is there anything to drink in this dump?"

She punched him lightly on the arm for the "dump" remark, then led him into the kitchen, where he opened the fridge and helped himself to a bottle of beer.

"Hey," she asked, "you have any kids?"

He twisted off the bottle cap. "What makes you ask?"

"That stuff you said about being a parent."

"That stuff was just something to say. Didn't mean anything."

She noticed he hadn't answered her question. No surprise there. Gabe never told her anything about his personal life. He didn't wear a wedding ring, so she liked to think he wasn't married. He could be taking it off, though.

All she knew about him was that he was in law enforcement. Could be LAPD or Sheriff's Department or FBI. He'd never even told her his age, though she guessed he was about forty. She couldn't press him for the information since, after all, they both knew that age didn't matter. That was the whole basis of their relationship. If age mattered, she ought to be seeing one of her classmates. But her classmates didn't interest her. She couldn't talk to them, couldn't relate to them at all. They treated her like a girl. With Gabe, it was different. With him, she was a woman.

A memory floated back to her. Her own words, spoken defiantly. *You kill women.*

And his answer: *No. I kill girls—like you.*

"Jerk," she whispered.

"What was that?" Gabe looked up from his beer.

"Just . . . thinking of someone."

"Should I be jealous?" His smile told her that the idea was a joke. For a moment she wished she could make him jealous. She could invent a suitor, see how Gabe reacted. But she'd never been any good at games like that.

"No," she said. "It was this guy I met one time at Robin's office. This psychopath."

"You don't have to be a psychopath to see a psychiatrist."

Gabe handed her the beer bottle. She hesitated, then drank from it.

"I know that. This guy was, though. He's a serial killer. The one who killed high school girls. Justin Gray."

"Robin's trying to rehabilitate *him*?"

"Seems like a long shot, huh?"

"The longest. How the hell did you meet him, anyway?"

She took another swallow of beer. "It was about a month ago. I got out of school early, hitched a ride with a friend. He dropped me at her office. I thought she'd be happy to see me, but she, like, freaked. Wanted to get me out of there before the guy arrived. She called a cab, but he got there first. They brought him in a prison van. In handcuffs, with armed guards and everything. And he saw me."

"He say anything to you?"

"Nothing much."

This was untrue. They had exchanged more than a few words in the waiting room of Robin's office, the killer named Justin Gray staring down at her from his height of six foot one.

"Well," he'd said with a cool smile, "what've we got here? Catholic schoolgirl on a field trip?"

The words had angered her. Without thinking, she snapped, "Shut up. You don't know me."

"I know the type."

"Well, I know *your* type."

"Meg—" her mom began, then stopped herself. Clearly she hadn't wanted Gray to know her daughter's name.

"Meg, huh?" Gray said. "Short for Margaret? Marjorie?"

She ignored the question. "You don't scare me. I know all about you."

"Bullshit. You don't know nothing. I ain't exactly bed-time-story material for little girls."

"You're Justin Gray."

"Hey, you do know me. Cool. It's always nice to be recognized by a fan."

"You're a psycho. And you'll always be a psycho. I don't care what my mom does for you."

"That's enough," Robin cut in.

"Your mom?" Gray smiled. "Hey, what d'you know? Can't believe I missed the family resemblance. Here I thought you were just another screwed-up Angeleno getting her head shrunk."

"Take him inside," Robin said to the deputies.

"Stand aside, miss," one of the deputies told Meg, but she stood her ground, blocking their path.

"I don't need my head shrunk," she said staunchly. "I'm not crazy. You are. You kill women."

"No. I kill girls—like you."

Her mom tugged at her. "Get out of the way."

"They weren't like me," she told Gray. "I would've killed you if you'd ever touched me."

Gray smiled at Robin. "She's a spitfire. I could have some big fun with her."

"*Shut up!*" Robin yelled, losing it. She pulled Meg away, and the deputies led Gray forward, into the office.

"Don't sweat it, Doc." Gray hadn't lost his smile. "Everything's copacetic."

Meg had never heard that word in conversation before, and she had been forbidden to use it ever since.

"So what's he like?" Gabe asked, leaning on the kitchen counter.

Meg shrugged. "Nutcase."

"Some of these guys can be pretty charming."

"Not him."

"He scare you?"

"No."

"It's okay to be scared, Meg."

"He didn't scare me. He pissed me off."

Gabe laughed. "Justin Gray pissed you off."

"Like I said, he's a jerk. Would've liked to—"

"What?"

"I don't know, punch his face."

"I'm not sure I see you as the warrior-princess type."

"I was thinking more along the lines of vampire slayer."

"I don't see you that way either."

"How do you see me?" She felt her mouth slide into a seductive smile. She wasn't used to drinking beer. It was going to her head.

"I see you"—he came forward and draped his arms around her waist—"as a beautiful and sensitive young woman who shouldn't let a creep like Justin Gray get under her skin."

There was that word she loved to hear him say. *Woman.* She was a woman, whether her mother realized it or not.

A thought occurred to her. "Were you part of the serial-killer task force?"

"Maybe I was, maybe I wasn't. I can tell you about the case, though, if you want to hear it."

"I do."

"On second thought, it might give you bad dreams."

"I don't get bad dreams."

"Well, you know the basics, I guess. Like how he specialized in abducting and killing teenage girls."

"How did he . . . do it?"

"Kill them? Execution style. Single gunshot to the head. Twenty-two-caliber round, mashed up so badly when it penetrated the skull that you couldn't even make a ballistics match. Death was instant. Cerebral pulpefaction, the coroner calls it. Midbrain disruption. Those are fancy ways of saying that the slug turned the victim's brain to ground chuck. Bang, lights out. She never even saw it coming."

It chilled her to hear him speak of murder so coolly, but she supposed all cops were like that. "At least it was quick," she said.

"At the end, sure. But he kept them prisoner for a while, about four, five hours usually, before the big sendoff."

"Did he . . . rape them?"

"Nah. No penetration."

"So what did he do with the girl during the four hours?"

"He's never said. Talked to her, maybe. Or maybe he just let her sweat. Big fun, huh? The clock's ticking, she's waiting, praying, and the time just crawls by."

She wasn't sure she wanted to hear any more, but if she asked him to stop, it would be a display of weakness. She never allowed herself to be weak around him.

"Why did he do it?" she asked. "Just for kicks?"

"If you want to know his motive, you're asking the wrong person. Even the shrinks can't figure out a serial killer. Well, maybe your mom can."

"Maybe I'll ask her."

"You should. I'll bet she's got a theory. Shrinks always have theories. And your mom's pretty sharp. She might have a handle on Justin Gray."

He reached out and touched Meg's long blond hair, stroked it.

"Bet he thinks about you in his cell," Gabe whispered.

"Stop. . . ."

He drew back, studying her face. "Whoops. I shouldn't have said that—any of it. It's got you all worked up."

"I'm okay."

"You don't need to hear about that kind of craziness."

"I think I could use some craziness in my life. My boring, predictable, sheltered, overprotected life." She smiled up at him. "You know, as long as you're here and we've got the place to ourselves . . ."

"You're not worried about Robin?"

"She's a workaholic. Obsessive-compulsive type. Goes along with her paranoia. Won't be home till after dinner."

"She seeing Justin Gray today? That why she's working late?"

"No, today's Monday. She sees him on Tuesdays and Thursdays. She must have some other thing going on. She's always busy, you know. Always on the go."

"She should learn to loosen up." He kissed her. "Have some fun. Enjoy life." He kissed her again. "Stop and smell the coffee."

Meg giggled. "She really should. She doesn't know what she's missing. You know, my room's just upstairs."

"I'd like to see your room."

"I thought you would."

They left the kitchen together. Meg thought she'd been wrong to ask him if he had kids. His private life was his business. She didn't need to know anything about it. She didn't even need to know his last name.

Gabe was enough. It was the name of an angel. Wasn't it?

Chapter Eleven

The sun was drifting lower in the western sky, caught in a mesh of utility lines and billboards, when Robin found Wolper in the coffee shop at Santa Monica and La Brea. Across the street, a jacked-up Monte Carlo had skidded over the curb and plowed through one wall of a comic-book shop. Copies of *Batman* and *Spider-Man* and *Wonder Woman* were scattered on the sidewalk, the four-color pages flapping in the breeze. A crew of young boys loitered at the edge of the crime scene, surreptitiously collecting the comics.

Wolper was seated in a window booth. Without his uniform, wearing a turtleneck and jeans, he looked like a different man, but she noticed that he was still squeezing the rubber ball in his left hand.

"I hope I didn't keep you waiting," she said as she took the bench seat opposite him. "I had trouble finding a place to park."

"No problem. I got here just a couple minutes ago."

She nodded toward the window. "It's a real mess out there."

He shrugged. "No serious injuries."

"I take it you talked to the officers at the scene."

"I checked in for a second. Force of habit."

"Was the driver drunk?"

"Just a moron. He was changing a tape in his cassette player. Took his eyes off the road."

"Hopefully he'll lose his license."

"Even if he does, he'll keep driving. Half the people in LA drive unlicensed."

She looked out the window at the small crowd of on-lookers. "I'm surprised there weren't more witnesses."

"There were a million wits. They all ran off. Illegal aliens. Afraid we'll turn 'em in to INS. Which we wouldn't, but they don't trust us. It's getting so the only wits we can count on are the panhandlers and the pallet guys."

"Pallet guys?"

"You know those wooden crates they ship things in? You can break them down into pallets, sell them for reuse. You see guys hauling them around in shopping carts. Pallet guys. Anyway, they'll stick around and talk. Never show up to testify in court, but this thing won't get to court anyway. Too many higher priorities. Too much insanity in this city." He gave her a look. "You have a kid?"

The question, coming out of nowhere, surprised her. "A daughter. Fifteen."

"Fifteen? What did you do, get married at age twelve?"

She shrugged off the compliment. "I'm thirty-nine. I had Meg when I was in med school."

"Isn't med school tough enough without raising a baby?"

"You'd think so, wouldn't you? It wasn't exactly planned. I had my life all worked out. Four years of premed. Five years of med school, hospital internship for one year, three years to a master's in psychiatry, two-year psychiatric residency, private practice by age thirty-two."

"I'll bet you stayed on schedule, even with a kid."

"Well . . . yes. I'm kind of determined once I set my mind on something."

"I noticed."

"Why did you ask if I had a child?"

"Because I've got one, too. A son, Zachary, twelve years old. I don't see him as much as I'd like—my wife and I split up. But whenever I get to spend a night or a weekend with Zach, I think about this city. The insanity here. More and more of it every day. I think about that—and what it might do to him."

"I know what you mean."

"You worry about your daughter, huh?"

"Too much. All the time."

"The curse of parenthood. You bring them into the world, and then you can't let go, even when they want us to. It would be easier if I was there more often, but you know how it is in a divorce. Well, maybe you don't."

"I do, actually. My husband—ex—is up in Santa Barbara, creating art."

"Art? He make a living at it?"

"A surprisingly good living."

"Hope he keeps up the child support."

"That's the one area where he's proven reliable."

"Good for him. A man should never abandon his own child. That's the worst thing he can do." Wolper smiled. "Listen to me. With all the crap I've seen, you wouldn't think a guy missing his support payments is the worst crime I could think of." He shook his head. "You didn't come here to talk about this."

"Not really."

"So what exactly is the problem, Doctor?"

She hesitated. "How much do you know about the Eddie Valdez shooting?"

"I know it was thoroughly reviewed by the OIS team— that's short for officer-involved shooting. Brand's actions were found to be within use-of-force guidelines."

"But there was no witness to the shooting, correct? There was only Brand's account of what happened."

"There was ballistics evidence," Wolper said carefully.

"Lieutenant, what is a patch?"

It was his turn to hesitate. "A patch . . . well, it's a cop's take of the bad guys' take. A payoff to look the other way while crimes are committed. I need to know why you're asking me this."

She ignored him. "Who are the Gs?"

"Drug gang in our division. Gs is short for Gangstas. The San Pedro Street Gangstas is what they call themselves. What the hell did Brand tell you?"

"More than he intended. The technique I use has a way of releasing a person's inhibitions."

"Like truth serum?"

"There's no such thing as truth serum, but this procedure may be a pretty close equivalent."

"You're saying he witnessed a payoff?"

"I'm saying he *received* a payoff, then shot Valdez when he came up short."

"That's ridiculous."

"It's what he told me."

"There has to be a mistake."

"There may be. I can't be sure Brand's story was true. That's what we need to find out. Tell me about the shooting."

A waitress interrupted them, delivering menus. Wolper gave back the menus, unexamined, and ordered two cheeseburgers, two Cokes. "You're not a vegetarian, are you?" he asked Robin belatedly.

"Cheeseburger is fine."

"Okay. The shooting. Sergeant Brand was riding in his unit, alone—"

"Shouldn't he ride with a partner?"

"Sergeants don't have partners. They function in a supervisory capacity. As a matter of fact, Brand was on his way back from supervising a crime scene."

"Isn't that the watch commander's job?"

"Brand had the watch that night. The lieutenant—not me—was off."

"All right. So he's heading back to the station . . ."

"When he sees Valdez enter a parking garage on foot, going down the ramp. Right away Brand is suspicious.

Valdez is known in the neighborhood. He's been picked up for ripping off car stereos, boosting vehicles, and being an all-around pain in the ass."

"Was he a member of the San Pedro Street Gangstas?"

"Good question. We never made him as a G, and the coroner didn't find any gang tats on him."

"So he wasn't?"

"He could've been a wanna-be, or someone they used as an errand boy. But he had no gang ties we know of, and there was no gang presence at his funeral. Far as we know, he was just a small-time street criminal."

"And Brand saw him going into a parking garage. What time was this?"

"Two hundred hours. Two A.M., I mean."

"I can translate. What happened next?"

"Brand calls it in on his radio. Says he's checking out a five-oh-three—possible auto theft."

"Did he request backup?"

"No."

"Isn't that unusual? Especially considering he was alone?"

"He may not have shown the best judgment. Like I told you yesterday, Brand is a street cop. He figures he gets paid to take chances. He's not one of these guys who sit behind a desk waiting to go twenty and out."

"So he's a cowboy."

"Christ, you're like a goddamned reporter putting words in my mouth." He shook his head. "Sorry, but I get tired of hearing good men called cowboys or vigilantes whenever they show any balls. Let's put it this way. When you call nine-one-one to report a hot prowl, do you want the cop who responds to wait around for backup or to suck it up and do his job?"

"I'm not trying to be confrontational, Lieutenant."

"Right. Whatever. Anyway, not calling for backup isn't cowboy stuff. It's Sergeant Brand's assessment of the threat level. He knows Valdez. He has him pegged as a knucklehead, a troublemaker, but not violent. If he catches Valdez boosting a tape deck, he can handle the arrest on his own."

"All right. Now Brand is in the garage."

"And he looks around for Valdez, but the asshole— sorry—the kid isn't visible. Brand thinks maybe Valdez has already gone to another level of the garage—it's one of those multistory things. Then he sees movement in a corner, and he heads toward it. He thinks Valdez is trying to bust into an SUV. He's wrong. Valdez heard Brand come down the ramp and he's waiting for Brand with a thirty-eight Special."

"A three-eighty wheel gun?"

"I'm surprised you know that term."

"Brand said that was the kind of gun he planted on Valdez after the fact."

"That doesn't prove anything."

"Did Valdez use a gun in any of his earlier crimes?"

"No, but it's not hard to believe he'd be carrying. Hell, everybody in Newton is carrying. Shootin' Newton, we call it. So Valdez makes a move on Brand—they struggle— Brand pops him at close range. Calls in a nine-ninety-eight. Requests the captain, the coroner, and a shooting team—all by the book. When units respond, they find Valdez dead of a single gunshot to the head, and Valdez's thirty-eight on the floor by his body."

"Case closed."

"No. Not case closed."

The waitress returned with their orders. They said nothing until she was gone. Then Wolper leaned forward, elbows on the table, his left hand furiously squeezing the rubber ball.

"There was a thorough investigation. Brand was put on leave, sent to Behavioral Sciences for trauma counseling. Ballistics came back clean. Tapes of his two radio calls were consistent with his story. He's a decorated veteran officer, and Eddie Valdez was street scum. There was no reason to doubt that it went down exactly like Brand said."

Robin sampled her cheeseburger. It *was* good. "And the gun? Did it belong to Valdez?"

"It couldn't be traced."

"Then Brand could have planted it, just as he said. It could have been a throwaway."

"Throwdown," Wolper corrected through a mouthful of burger. "Police officers don't carry those."

"Oh, come on."

"Not in my jurisdiction."

"How can anyone believe that, after Rampart?"

"We cleaned up the department since Rampart. We don't tolerate rogue cops. Even if we did, Al Brand isn't one of them."

"Then why did he say what he said in session?"

"I don't know. But I sure wouldn't convict a man on the basis of something he said while he was undergoing some kind of experimental therapy."

"Fair enough. And I admit there are legitimate questions. That's why I came to you."

"To me?"

"As opposed to Deputy Chief Wagner. He's the one I probably should be talking to, but I didn't want to do anything rash. I didn't want to risk damaging Sergeant Brand's career unnecessarily."

"You bring this to the top brass, you'd better know what the hell you're getting into. Brand can't be a bad cop. This stuff he said . . . it's gotta be a glitch or something. Faulty wiring, maybe. You had the thing set on high when it should've been medium."

"It's not a toaster, Lieutenant."

Wolper took a long, thoughtful swallow of soda. "Valdez was a righteous shooting. Had to be."

"I hope you're right," Robin said. "I really do."

"How's this? I'll take a look at the file on the Valdez shooting and see if there are any loose ends."

"You have access to the file?"

"I have access to somebody who can get me a copy. What do you say we meet tomorrow and go over it?"

"All right."

"Your office? Afternoon?"

"My last session is at three P.M. Should be over by four."

He looked worried. "Not Brand again?"

"No, you don't have to worry about that. It's just a nice, safe inmate from County."

"Okay."

"If you're so sure Brand is innocent, why were you afraid I'd be seeing him again?"

"In my line of work, you learn never to trust anybody one hundred percent. That may be why my wife left me. Lack of trust. It's that whole stupid intuition thing."

"Intuition?"

"My ex was always going on about that. How I didn't have any. Intuition, that is. How I think everything through in a straight line, A to B to C. No imagination. No feel for people or situations. That's what she said. What the hell, she was right."

"Do you think so?"

"Probably. Hell, I took the detective exam twice. Didn't pass. My opinion was that it was goddamned affirmative action. When you're a white male, it's not enough to score well. You've got to ace the test. But Cindy, my ex, said a detective needs to be intuitive, and I'm not."

"And you think she's right?"

"She could be. To be honest, I don't even know what she's talking about. Intuition—what the hell is that, anyway? It's just another word for guessing. Police work shouldn't be guesswork."

"Intuition involves more than—"

He waved her off and picked up the rubber ball again. "Yeah, yeah, I know. That's your thing, right? Look at a patient and just kind of sense what makes him tick. It's all head games."

"It's not a game."

"It's voodoo. Sorry, but that's how it looks to me."

"If you looked deeper, you might change your opinion."

"Changing my opinion isn't a real common occurrence with me."

Robin believed him. She said nothing.

"I've been around a while," Wolper went on, "and I know what's real and what isn't. The job you do . . . it's moonshine to me. I deal with facts, not feelings. If you can't touch it, smell it, taste it, what good is it? Getting a handle on feelings . . . it's like trying to grab a fistful of air."

She tried a smile. "At least nobody can accuse you of being one of those touchy-feely New Age guys."

"Yeah, that's one thing I've never been called."

"What would you like to be called? How would you like to be thought of?"

"Practical. A realist. I take things as they are."

"That approach works for you? You're comfortable with it?"

"I'm comfortable."

"Then why are you squeezing that ball?"

He looked at it as if surprised to see it in his grasp. "This thing? It's just a workout for my hand. Keeps the fingers strong . . ." He smiled. "Okay, that's a snow job. It's a way to release tension. Better than going out and getting drunk."

"Or going to the dogfights."

"That, too."

"You can't be happy that a sergeant in your station house is breaking the law, even if it is on his own time."

"I'm not happy. I just accept it. It's something Brand has to do—for now. It's a fact, and I'm a realist, like I said."

"It's realistic to let one of your men engage in self-destructive behavior?"

"Self-destructive." He snorted. "You sound like a documentary on PBS. The man is just blowing off steam."

"By watching two animals tear each other up?"

"Wouldn't be my choice. Makes me sick, to be truthful.

But if that's what he needs to get through the day, I'm not blowing the whistle on him."

"How'd you even know he was going there?"

"There aren't too many secrets in the department."

"That's pretty vague."

"You want specifics? All right. A house in Watts was raided a month ago for dogfights, and Brand was picked up along with the rest of the crowd. He called me, and I got the charges dropped. He told me he'd been going there a lot. He also told me he was going to stop."

"He lied."

"He weakened. Anyway, I'd heard that the fights had started up again in a new house, same neighborhood. When Brand didn't show up for work today, I had a feeling he would be there."

"Then why don't you get the fights shut down again?"

"It's out of my territory."

"That's not an answer."

"We have a thousand homicides a year in this city. You want me to focus on animal abuse? We've got our resources tapped out just trying to save human lives. Besides, if you shut those scum down, they'll just start up again in a week or a month. It's the way it is."

"Realism," Robin said tonelessly.

Wolper shrugged. "Welcome to LA."

They had finished their burgers, and they were all out of conversation. Both seemed to sense it.

"So," Wolper said, "four P.M. tomorrow, your office?"

"Let me give you the address."

"I already know it. I'm a cop, remember?" He smiled. "I find out things about people who interest me."

Robin pondered that remark as she drove away. It was just barely possible that Lieutenant Wolper was trying to get something going between them, one divorced single parent to another. She wasn't sure how she would feel about that.

There had been no romance in her life since her marriage

ended. She'd known she would have to restart her personal life eventually, but the prospect of enduring first dates and awkward kisses at the door was not appealing.

Well, no, that was a thin rationalization—a snow job, as Wolper would say. The truth was, she had been scared away from relationships by the failure of her marriage. She'd been afraid of repeating the same mistake.

In retrospect, her relationship with Dan had probably never had much of a chance. She had married him—it was now safe to admit this—chiefly because he was the opposite of her father. Yes, Daniel Cameron, the artist, a man who was gentle and sensitive and nonviolent and law-abiding, who would not desert her and leave her crying and alone. But then he had deserted her anyway, emotionally at least. Her efforts at self-protection had failed.

Robin shook her head. She was aware that in her work she was, in effect, trying to rehabilitate her father. That was obvious—cookbook Freud, as someone had once said. But was she trying to rehabilitate Dan, too? To symbolically resuscitate the corpse of their marriage?

She was probably overthinking things. She hoped so. She didn't want Dan to be controlling her life when he wasn't even part of it any longer.

Now she was planning to meet a man to discuss a police file on a shooting case. Not exactly an evening of dinner and dancing. And Wolper wasn't exactly the man she'd pictured as her beau. Too stiff, too righteous. He didn't respect what she did. He called it voodoo, moonshine. What he thought of as realism, she viewed as cynicism.

Not a good match for her. No way.

"No way," she said aloud, as if to confirm it to herself.

Chapter Twelve

Meg woke up at six-thirty and found herself alone in bed. Gabe had gone. Vaguely she remembered the brush of his lips on her cheek when he left. That was at least an hour ago.

No surprise. He never stuck around after sex. When they did it in the apartment he rented, he would find some excuse to get out as soon as possible. The few times they'd done it in the backseat of his sedan, he'd put the car in gear almost before he zipped up his pants. In and out, that was his style.

It was okay. She didn't expect him to hang around. It was enough just to have him for a short time each day. Sometimes during lunch break at school, when she would sneak off campus. Sometimes on the weekends, when she made an excuse to get out of the condo for an hour or two. And sometimes in the afternoon, when she claimed she was studying with her classmates or working on the school newspaper and would get a ride home from an older friend.

The game was dangerous. Her mom would freak if she found out. But the risk was worth it. She had become a whole new person since Gabe came into her life. She wasn't a kid anymore. She was a woman.

She had met Gabe at an awards dinner three months ago, in February. The dinner was big shindig in honor of outstanding members of the law-enforcement community, as well as a few civilians who'd made a contribution to the fight against crime. One of those civilians was Dr. Robin Cameron, who'd earned a plaque and a certificate for the first phase of her research into reducing recidivism. Robin had treated the event as a dreary chore, necessary to cement her good relations with the Sheriff's Department and to make new contacts in the LAPD. She had no interest in prizes or commendations, and she'd fretted over the brief acceptance speech she was expected to give. Public speaking was not one of her strong points.

Still, she had soldiered through the evening, with Meg seated beside her at the long table on the dais. At some point in the evening Meg had visited the ladies' room. On her way out, she'd met Gabe.

"You must be very proud of your mother," he'd said. She agreed that she was. "But you'd rather be someplace else?"

"Well, yeah."

"I don't blame you. So would I." He'd introduced himself as Gabe, not giving a last name. In his tuxedo, with a white carnation in the pocket, he looked dashing, like a movie star at a premiere, an impression enhanced by the tight, tanned planes of his face and the flash of his white teeth when he smiled.

They spoke briefly. She told him her name and answered a few other questions that she assumed he asked purely out of politeness. When she returned to the table she didn't mention the encounter to her mom. She wasn't sure why. It wasn't important enough to mention, she decided.

A few days later she found a message from Gabe in her e-mail in box. He had tracked down her e-mail address, using an Internet service that maintained a searchable database of Web users. He said he'd found her interesting and he wanted to chat with her via e-mail, if that was all right.

It seemed kind of weird. The guy was way older than she was. In his late thirties, maybe forty. Ancient! On the other hand, there was no harm in answering his e-mail. And at least he wasn't some loser, like the high school guys who were usually interested in her.

So she had begun a correspondence with Gabe. Topics of discussion were general at first. She talked about the boys at school who tried to impress her with their money or their cars. He talked about the pimps and dealers on the street who devoted their lives to the acquisition of material goods. They agreed that such superficial concerns only warped a person's perspective. What mattered was not what a person owned, but who that person was. Most people didn't understand this. They were shallow. She and Gabe connected on a deeper level.

After a month he asked if she would meet him for coffee at the Starbucks near her school. She said yes. And she still didn't tell her mom. Gabe was about as old as her father, after all. Her mom was conventional enough to care about stuff like that. Anyway, it was just coffee.

Then it was a kiss on a side street by Gabe's parked car, then a hectic half hour in the backseat when he stroked her breasts with his long, gentle fingers. A month ago it was a car ride to a studio apartment in the Wilshire district, near the tar pits, where he had unfolded the sofa to make a bed, and she had given herself to him.

It was her first time, and she wasn't sure she'd been very good at it, but in the weeks since, she had learned. She had let him teach her what men liked.

They never spoke of the future. She didn't know if there was a future for them. She was satisfied just to give him what he needed—

Footsteps downstairs. "Meg?"

Her mom had come home.

Quickly Meg straightened the bedsheets and threw on her clothes. She met her mother coming up the stairs. "Hey."

"There you are. You have dinner yet?"

"Uh, no, not yet." She wondered what had happened to the beer bottle Gabe had taken from the fridge. Was it still in the kitchen? Would her mom see it?

"It's nearly seven o'clock. You have to be at Jamie's in a half hour, remember?"

"Right. Sorry. I'll fix dinner now."

"No, I'll do it."

Meg didn't want her mom going into the kitchen. "Let me. You look tired."

"You noticed." Robin blew a stray hair away from her face. "Okay. The Chinese food is on the top shelf of the fridge."

"You want me to make some for you?"

"No, I already ate."

"Four-course meal at a five-star restaurant?"

"Burger at a coffee shop."

"Even better."

Meg hurried down the stairs, into the kitchen. A quick search proved that the beer bottle wasn't there. Gabe must have taken it when he left. He was in law enforcement. He knew better than to leave evidence at a scene.

But in the trash she found the bottle cap, clearly visible on top of a pile of discarded paper napkins. It was always the little things that got people caught.

She buried the bottle cap deeper in the garbage, then set to work microwaving dinner. Her hands, she noticed, were shaking. She felt like a criminal, which was wrong, really wrong. She had done nothing to be ashamed of. What was between her and Gabe . . . it was good; it was right. She was protecting Robin, that's all, because Robin couldn't handle it. Robin wouldn't understand.

No one would understand.

Chapter Thirteen

"I'll pick you up at ten," Robin said as she cleaned up after Meg's hurried dinner.

Meg showed her the pouty face she used when she was being treated unfairly. "I can get a ride from Jamie's sister. She's got her license now."

"Very reassuring. I'll be there at ten."

"You know, it's bad enough being dropped off by your mother. But being picked up by her—"

"Just think of me as your personal chauffeur. So why a party on a Monday night?"

"It's not a party. It's a study group for lit class."

"Sounds very academic."

"You know me, the junior scholar."

"Any boys participating in this educational effort?"

"Boys? Yuck. Seriously, no Y-chromosome types are allowed. It's a strictly double-X affair."

"You might want to rephrase that."

"What I'm saying is, it's a girl fest. Who knows, there might even be pillow fights."

"So you, uh, you're still not seeing anybody?"

"I guess you'd know if I were."

"It wouldn't kill you to be sociable with some of the boys in your class."

"I'm not interested in them. They're all so immature. They're just, you know, kids."

You're a kid, too, Robin thought, but she said nothing.

"Hey," Meg added with a glance at the clock, "we'd better take off, or I'll be late."

"I just need to close the windows so I can set the alarm."

"Why bother? It's a five-minute ride. Ten-minute round trip."

"Ten minutes is long enough for someone to break in." Someone like Brand.

Meg shook her head. "Wow. You weren't like this in Santa Barbara. You spend way too much time around criminals. It's making you crazy."

"Thanks for the diagnosis."

They set the alarm, locked up, and descended to the condo building's underground garage. Meg stopped short when she saw the Saab. "Oh, my God. Were you in an accident?"

"No, nothing like that."

"Why didn't you tell me about this?"

"I forgot." This excuse, lame was it was, happened to be true. With everything else that had taken place today, the damage to the car had slipped her mind.

"You forgot? What happened to it?"

"Vandals," Robin lied. "They broke the windows while I was at work."

"You mean they did this in the parking lot behind your building?"

"Afraid so."

Meg pondered the damage before reaching a decision. "I can't be seen in this car. It's a wreck."

"Think of it as retro."

"Mom, seriously . . ."

Robin wanted to ask Meg if she was really that worried about what her friends would think, but of course she knew the answer. Friends were your whole world when you were in high school.

"I'll park behind a tree," she said. "They'll never even see me."

"You swear?"

"Cross my heart and hope to never eat pizza again."

Tentatively Meg got into the car, treating it as if it were a giant bear trap poised to spring shut. Robin slid behind the wheel.

"You're going to get this fixed, right?" Meg pressed.

"No, I was planning to leave it this way. Gives the car some character, don't you think?"

Meg stared at her, aghast, then relaxed a little. "Oh, you're joking."

Robin started the engine. "What gave it away?"

"You must've been pissed when you saw the damage."

"Don't say pissed."

"Ticked off. Riled. Irked."

"That's better."

They pulled onto the street, heading north to Wilshire. The sun was lowering. Sunset was at seven-forty-five, twenty minutes from now.

"When did you start going all Miss Manners on me?" Meg asked.

"I've always been Miss Manners. Miss Manners is my alter ego."

"Right."

"Have you ever seen me eat with the wrong fork?"

"I've seen you eat takeout straight from the container with a plastic spork. I don't picture Miss Manners doing that."

"She does it. Just not in public." Robin turned right on Wilshire, blending into a smooth stream of traffic.

"So . . . did you see Justin Gray today?" Meg asked.

Robin frowned. The question had come out of nowhere. "Why ask about him?"

"Just curious."

"He's coming tomorrow. You know that. Tuesdays and Thursdays."

"Right, right." Meg looked out the window at the strip malls and fast-food joints. "It's weird."

"What is?"

"The stuff he did."

"Murdering girls? I'd say that qualifies as more than weird."

"The way he did it. Kidnapping them at random. And he didn't rape them or anything."

Robin wondered where Meg had picked up that detail. She had never been interested in following the news. "True."

"So if he didn't have anything personal against them, and he wasn't in it for sex, why'd he do it at all?"

"What's with this sudden interest in Justin Gray?"

"I was just wondering if you had any, you know, theory about it. Unless you're not up for the Grand Guignol stuff right now."

"I'm up for it, I guess. It's not Grand Guignol, anyway. It's sort of Freudian. Or Jungian. I don't know. Symbolic."

"I'm going to regret asking, aren't I?"

"Too late now." Robin composed her thoughts while the Saab idled at a stoplight. "The fact that he didn't know the girls personally was part of their appeal. It made it easier for him to objectify them, depersonalize them. He didn't want to see them as individual human beings. He wanted to see them as generic females. As femininity in the abstract. You with me?"

"I'm hanging on every word."

The light cycled to green. Robin glided through the intersection. "By killing them, he was finishing the job of dehumanization. He was—"

Meg finished. "Making them nonpersons."

"Yes. Exactly."

"Nonpersons—like him."

Robin was pleased. "You could end up as a shrink yourself, you know that?"

"No way. For me, it's either supermodel or research biochemist." She thought for a moment. "There's another way he's like the girls he killed. They were teenagers. So's he."

"He's twenty-eight."

"Not inside. Inside, he's still fifteen and probably all covered with pimples. That's why he's so obsessed with high school girls. He's still in high school. Emotionally, I mean. And I bet he always will be."

Robin felt a flush of painful pride. "Sometimes you're so smart, it's scary."

"I have a genius for a mother. Some of it had to rub off."

"I think you'll outgenius me by a long way before long."

"And Dan, too?"

"He's only a genius at selling himself."

"You believe that?"

"When it comes to your father, I don't know what to believe."

They reached Jamie's house on the outskirts of Westwood. Robin actually did pull up alongside a tree to hide the car.

"Ten o'clock," she reminded Meg.

"I got it. Jeez, you've got to get this car fixed tomorrow. It'll be, like, a total humiliation if anybody sees me in this thing."

"You'll survive."

"I'll never live it down. Make an appointment with a body shop, *please*?"

"I aim to serve."

"Cross your heart?"

"You only get one of those per day."

Meg nodded good-bye, then left the car and hurried up the walk to the bungalow's front door. Robin watched until she was safely inside, then pulled away, shaking her head.

Total humiliation, Meg had said. And she'd meant it, too. To be embarrassed in front of her peers was the worst fate she could imagine.

Nothing unusual about that. Her daughter had reached the stage of adolescence when the world centered on her.

Every problem was a crisis. Every decision was a turning point. Image was all-important. Her personal life was cosmic in scope and significance, and the rest of the world had shriveled to an afterthought.

This much was clear to Robin, not because she was a shrink, but because she had been fifteen herself not so very long ago—well, on second thought, it had been twenty-four years, more than a lifetime in Meg's eyes. Still, she remembered. Remembered the clash of fear and excitement whenever she contemplated the future, guessing at the path she would take, the obstacles she would face, wondering if she had the courage to run the race, or if she would stumble and fall like most of the adults around her. Remembered the moods that came and went like flashes of summer lightning, fluctuations of emotional voltage she herself couldn't explain. Remembered how much everything mattered—the right hairstyle, right clothes, right friends—and how she'd hated herself for caring so deeply about things that were so shallow. There was a painful immediacy to every momentary feeling. Any ripple of disappointment or pleasure became a surge of grief or joy.

Hormones explained some of it, but there was also the vertigo-inducing task of forming one's own character, the scary thrill of knowing that choices made now might echo down decades of regret.

And yet, nearly all of it was unnecessary. That was the secret Robin wished she could impart to her daughter. But it was not a secret to be shared. It was a lesson to be learned.

She wished she could hug Meg and say to her, *Life is not so hard. It's usually about as hard as we make it. We can't plan it out. We have much less control than we think. Mostly, things just happen, and if there's a reason, we don't know it at the time. But we don't have to know. It's not our job to do more than we can do. Life doesn't give us more than we can handle.*

But if she said all that, Meg wouldn't hear. She wasn't ready to hear. She was fifteen.

Chapter Fourteen

Brand lived in a bungalow in Hollywood. There were some nice parts of Hollywood that the tourists never saw, but his neighborhood wasn't one of them. The bungalow dated back to the 1920s and was said to be in the Craftsman style, whatever the hell that meant. When he'd bought it, the porch had been festooned with hanging plants that blossomed garishly in the spring. The plants were all dead now, killed by neglect, but he'd left them in their hanging baskets anyway.

He had made a few improvements to the place, but they were not of an aesthetic nature. He'd encircled the property with a perimeter fence, put bars on the windows, installed strong locks on the doors, and paid a monthly fee to a burglar alarm company. He would have liked to replace the carport with a garage—he didn't like leaving his car in plain sight, even if it was protected by the fence, and he especially didn't like leaving the carport empty, an advertisement that no one was home. But the expense was prohibitive. Anyway, in the ten years he'd lived here, he'd never been robbed, though most of his neighbors had.

Inside, he had made a halfhearted try at decorating, but had given up when the house was only partially furnished.

His rare visitors wrinkled their noses in a way indicative of a pervasive odor. If there was one, he was used to it.

His fridge was empty. His music collection was a decade out of date. There weren't many books on his shelves—he was more of a magazine reader. Lately he was inclined to sit and watch TV, the volume turned up loud enough to almost drown out the low boom of rap music from next door. That was what he'd been doing for most of the night. Funny thing—he couldn't even remember what he had watched.

At ten o'clock, impelled by a need to urinate, he wandered into the master bath. When he was done, he cranked the handle of the low-flow toilet and watched as it reluctantly emptied itself. He went on staring into the swirling water until the bowl had refilled. Finally he broke away, shaking his head.

Things like that had been happening to him lately. He would be mesmerized by the sound of static on the radio or the repetitive trill of a bird. Once, someone's car alarm had gone off down the street and he had listened for what must have been fifteen minutes, fascinated by its steady monotonous clangor.

What he needed was a drink. But he wasn't drinking, because he suspected that if he started to medicate himself with scotch, he would slide effortlessly into alcoholism. He didn't need that. He'd arrested enough boozehounds on the street. He was damned if he would become one of them.

He sure needed something, though. There was probably another dogfight going on at Billy Turro's place, but even he wasn't reckless enough to venture into a dead-end street in Watts after dark. It was dicey enough just going there in the daytime. He always packed two weapons when he went, his off-duty 9mm and a snub-nosed .32 in an ankle holster. The .32 was lighter than the .38 left near Eddie Valdez's dead, outstretched hand, and it was street-legal, unlike the .38, which had been treated with acid to burn off the serial numbers. A throwdown, untraceable.

Of course, the gun didn't need to be traced if he was going to spill everything to some damn shrink. . . .

He rubbed his head, wishing he could remember what he'd told her. Vaguely he recalled saying something about Valdez and the parking garage, but whether it was the truth or his cover story, he didn't know.

He had a bad feeling, though. It was based mainly on the way she'd been looking at him after the session. Like she was trying too hard to act normal. Like she was sizing him up, taking his measure. Or measuring him for a prison jump-suit, maybe.

Jail would be a death sentence. Cops didn't survive hard time. If he went down for Valdez, he was finished.

There was a half-empty bottle of scotch in the cupboard over the kitchen sink. He almost surrendered to the temptation to open it. Instead he found himself reaching for the phone. He called a familiar number and let it ring until Evelyn answered. "It's me," he said without further identification. "You free tonight?"

"Available—yes. Free—never."

"You know what I mean. Come on over. And bring that thing."

She arrived an hour later. She wore a raincoat and boots. When she opened the coat, she revealed black underwear. "Ta-da," she said with a smile.

He fucked her without ceremony, starting on the living room floor and proceeding down the hall into the bedroom. He did her doggie style, like always, watching the tattooed butterfly between her shoulder blades flutter as her shoulder muscles flexed. She was maybe thirty-five, but she worked out and stayed trim, maintaining the body of a college girl. Not that Brand had had many college girls. He'd attended a community college at night, working a delivery job during the day, a schedule that had left little time for partying.

Still, he liked to think of her as a college girl, one of those rich-bitch USC babes whose daddies gave them a Porsche for their eighteenth birthday. He thought about that as he turned her on her back and thrust his crotch into her face. She gave first-rate blow jobs. When he'd got his rocks off for a second time, he asked her about the thing.

"I got it, tiger," she said in that half-seductive, half-amused voice of hers. She retrieved her coat and produced a dildo from the pocket. He used it on her, pushing in hard and deep, making her wet all over again. She let out the usual noises, which might've been an act, but he hoped not. For the finale, she put the dildo in her mouth and faked another suction job while her nimble hands massaged his cock. He came all over her fingers, and she laughed. "Three times in one night—you're a stud."

Afterward she smoked a joint she'd brought with her, which he declined to share.

"You're a funny kind of cop," she said as she dressed to leave.

"Who said I was a cop?"

"I asked around."

"I'm surprised you came back."

"Your money's as good as anybody's."

He paid her five hundred dollars, which she carefully folded and slipped into her boot.

"I'll call you," he said for no reason as she left the house.

"Anytime, tiger."

He felt relaxed for the first time that day. He had problems, but they could be dealt with. He just had to figure out a plan. There was always a plan, always a way out. He would have to think, that's all.

Just think.

Chapter Fifteen

Midnight, and a phone was ringing.

Robin swam up out of sleep and groped for the phone on her nightstand, fumbling it off the cradle, pressing it to her ear. She heard a dial tone. Somewhere the ringing continued.

Her cell phone. In her purse, on the bureau.

She got up, blinking away the last tug of sleep, and found the phone. "Yes?"

What she heard in reply was a recording. "You have a collect call from an inmate at a California Department of Corrections facility. The name of the inmate is . . ." The recorded voice was replaced by the inmate's voice saying, "Justin Gray." The recorded message continued. "If you wish to accept, press . . ."

Robin needed a moment to process this information, then another moment to find the correct button on the lighted keypad.

Justin Gray's voice crackled over the earpiece.

"Yo, Doc Robin. How's tricks?"

"Justin, why are you calling me?"

"Why not? Always fun to shoot the breeze. Hope I didn't wake you."

"Shouldn't you be in your cell at this hour?"

"I'm in my cell at every hour. Got a jail phone in here. All the comforts of home. See, they gotta give me a phone, or my First Amendment rights would be violated. Us cons gotta have access to communication with the outside world—even us ultra–bad boys in the high-power ward. Besides, this way the hacks don't gotta drag their sorry asses out of the control booth and escort me out of my cell. They don't like to mess with me. I'm a dangerous individual."

"How did you get my cell phone number?"

"It's on your business card. I swiped one from your office a while back."

"You should be asleep."

"I don't sleep much. Night's the best time for me. It's so quiet and dark. I can move in the shadows. Silence 'n' violence, baby—what I live for."

"You're not moving in any shadows now, Justin."

"Got that right. But I still don't sleep much. Bad dreams, you know."

She was surprised to get a straightforward response. "Do you have bad dreams often?"

"They come and go."

"What do you dream about?"

"The ones I killed. The girls."

"What about them?"

"How they must've suffered. And how, you know, now that I'm in here . . ."

"Yes?"

"I'll never get to do it again. Really pisses me off."

She released a breath, angry at herself for having been suckered in. "Justin, I don't want you calling me."

"That's the sort of thing that could hurt my feelings. Mess me up, do all kinds of serious psychological damage."

"I'm serious. My patients call me to set up an emergency appointment, that's all. I don't do therapy over the phone."

"Don't flatter yourself, college girl. I'm not calling you for help. Just checking in, saying hi. It's what friends do."

"Not at midnight."

"If you're sleepy, maybe I can chat with Meg instead. I bet she's a night owl. Her and me got along real good, that time we met."

"Don't talk about her."

"I don't know, Doc. She's a fine piece of snatch, all right."

"Justin—"

"Hey, hey. Chill, Freud. Sorry if I offended. I guess it's wrong for me to be making crude remarks about a virginal young maiden. Except I got news for you, Doc. She ain't no virgin."

"I don't need to hear this."

"Hey, it's no bullshit. I can tell these things. Got a sixth sense about 'em."

"She's not even dating," Robin snapped.

"Not that you know about. I tell you true, Doc, these kids today start early. She's wettin' her whistle, all right. I bet she's gettin' more action than you."

"Be quiet."

"You think she's daisy fresh, never got her cherry popped? Fuck me, I can smell the jizz on her. She been doing the nasty, big-time. No surprise. She gets plenty of offers, for sure. Me, I'd like to bone her myself—"

"Shut up!" She took a breath, fighting for calm. "Did you call just to tell me this? What are you trying to do?"

"Me? I'm just performing a public service. What can I say? It's my nature to help people."

"Don't ever call me again. And I don't want to hear any more lies about Meg."

"You got it, Doc. Just keep your eyes shut tight. See no evil, right?"

"Stop it, Justin. Stop it."

"If Meg gets tired of whoever's dicking her now, send her my way. I'll show her what a real man can do."

Robin shut off the phone, then sat on the bed, shaking.

She shouldn't let him get to her like that. He was playing games, sick mind games, the kind he'd played when he was still at large. Now he was safely caged, but he could still use a telephone, still find a way to inflict pain on the world.

And she was trying to help him, make him better. She asked herself why.

"Because he's dysfunctional," she whispered.

Dysfunctional. Such a nice clinical term, so much more scientific and sanitized than other words she might have used. Words like *soulless . . . malevolent . . . evil.*

How much did she really believe in evil? Justin Gray was evil by any reasonable definition. Yet she treated him as someone with a disorder, someone to be cured. Then was there no evil, only illness? No morality, only the interaction of dopamine, serotonin, epinephrine?

She didn't know what she believed. She half suspected she didn't want to believe in evil, didn't want it to be real, because then her father . . . she would have to label him as . . .

She left the thought unfinished. The past wasn't the issue, anyway. It was the future that counted. A new method of treatment. Lowered rates of recidivism. A safer, saner society. Fewer victims. And an end to warehoused offenders, wasted lives.

Robin lay back in bed and closed her eyes.

New hope for people like her father—and their families. New lives. For that, she would endure Gray's games. She would endure anything.

Chapter Sixteen

Gray hung up, smiling, and climbed onto his rack, hands laced behind his head.

Now that had been some good, clean fun.

He'd never called the doc before, but tonight he was so goddamn jazzed, he had to work off his nervous tension somehow. And the best way to do it was with a little old-fashioned, all-American mind fucking.

That had been part of the sport all along. One of the best parts, always. He'd made it his trademark. He'd become known for the mind games he played on the parents of his victims.

Hours after one of his girls was dead, he would call her folks, using a stolen cell phone—a different phone each time. It had been fun, like making prank calls when he was a kid. Being drunk hadn't hurt. Typically he stayed wasted for a day or two after a kill, enjoying the buzz. And the conversations with the parents only made the high that much sweeter.

He could remember every word.

"I'm the one what took your baby girl, ma'am," he would say in a trailer-trash drawl. "And the thing is, I'm wondering if you had any preferences—y'know, as to where you'd like to pick her up."

"You're letting her go?"

"Oh, sorry. I meant where you want to pick up her body."

"Oh, God, please, please don't, she's a good girl, she's all we have."

"You're telling me you want the little bitch *alive*?"

"Please . . ."

" 'Cause I just assumed you were glad to be rid of her. No offense, but she's kind of a pain in the ass."

"Don't hurt her."

"Here I thought you'd be grateful to me for taking her off your hands. I was doing you a major favor. Now all of a sudden I'm the bad guy?"

"She's a good girl; everybody loves her—"

"If she's such a good girl, where'd she learn to give those high-quality blow jobs?"

"God, oh, dear God . . ."

"Sorry, must be some miscommunication. This ain't God you're talking to. My name's Willy. As in Free Willy. 'Cause I'm free and I intend to stay that way, and since your bitch daughter's seen my face . . ."

"She's all we have—"

"Then you better get started on another one. Biological clock's ticking, lady. Tick-tock. Tick-tock."

Some of his games were more elaborate. He would call the parents and playact as a concerned citizen, saying he'd found their daughter wandering down Olympic Boulevard, dazed but unharmed. Or he would be a doctor at UCLA Medical, reporting that their daughter had been brought to the emergency room. Or a reporter asking to confirm the rumor that their daughter had been picked up in San Diego, suffering from amnesia and sexual abuse.

He chuckled, remembering. He hadn't played that game in a year, but he'd picked the right time to get his groove back. With any luck, the doc would be up all night worrying. Tomorrow she'd be tired and distracted and pissed off. Hate would make her careless. It worked that way for people like her.

•

Not him, though.

Hate made him stronger, sharper, fiercer. Always had. Hate was what drove him.

His first session with Dr. Robin, she'd given him some bullshit test, and he'd scored high on the hostility index. No surprise. Hate had never been a four-letter word to him. Hate was strength, and fire, and taking no shit from anybody. Hate built him up, made him big, got him pumped. Hate was his rocket fuel, his adrenaline rush. Hate was like sex to him, an orgasm that lasted for hours, days, and got him off again and again. He was in love with hate.

And the doc wanted to cure him of that? Might as well snip off his balls. Without hate he would be a neutered puppy, a weak sister, a nobody.

Without hate, he could never have done even half the shit he'd pulled. And that would have been a damn shame. Everybody was always on his case, asking why he'd killed those girls. The answer was fucking obvious. He enjoyed the hell out of it.

The first kill hadn't been completely intentional. He'd snatched the girl with the vague idea of holding her for ransom. At least, he'd told himself that ransom was his motive, although he'd never fixed a dollar amount or worked out any means of collecting the money. Still, maybe he would have demanded ransom if the little bitch hadn't kept struggling in the back of his van. She'd squirmed, moaning behind the gag in her mouth, while he sat up front listening, until finally he couldn't stand the damn noise any longer. So he went back to tell her to shut up, and found that her blouse had come unbuttoned, exposing her fine round jumanjis for anyone to see. At the time he'd been sure she had undone the blouse on purpose, trying to come on to him, seduce him into dropping his guard. She was like that slut Delilah in the Bible—or was it Jezebel?—one of those old Bible whores who fucked with guys and played games with them and got them thinking with their dicks. Her trying to trick him that way . . . man, it had pissed him off royal. He'd taken her outside and put a bullet in her head without thinking twice about it.

Which was funny, because later, when he'd sobered up—he'd been wrecked out of his mind, like he always was when he pulled off dangerous shit—he'd realized the blouse had gotten unbuttoned by accident. She was just trying to loosen the duct tape on her wrists and ankles, that's all.

Yeah, he'd felt pretty stupid once his head cleared, but not so stupid that he hadn't gone out a couple months later and done it again.

It had been fun, was the thing. You took one of those stuck-up junior misses, and you scared the living shit out of her—literally, in one case; goddamned girl had pooped in her panties—and then you pumped a slug into her noggin, wham, bam, thank you, ma'am. And every time you thought about it or heard some blow-dried asshole talking it up on the news, you got good and hard all over again, and you could whack off till your arm was sore. Better yet, hook up with a gal on Western Avenue for the lay of your life—because it didn't matter how much of a skank she was or how many needle tracks she had on her arms, you could close your eyes and pretend she was little Miss Prom Queen, and that was all you needed to get off again and again and again in a series of blastoffs straight to the fucking moon.

That was the only sex he ever got out of the sport. He'd never raped his captives, not from any moral compunction, obviously, but because he had to get liquored up to do the kill, and when wasted, he couldn't perform. He was always too looped to get his johnson to cooperate.

Too bad for his girls. They never knew what they'd missed out on. Not that he cared. He got what he came for—the pure rush of the kill, the games and fantasies afterward. Another notch in his gun, another young lovely disposed of. Except they weren't lovelies to him. They weren't nothing but gashes, slits, coochies. Fur pies, bearded clams. Hot-boxes and honeypots. Gray chuckled, wondering how many words there were for that part of the female anatomy. Squirrels, muffs, jelly rolls . . .

He remembered the last time he'd seen his mother. "You talk like a damn nigger," she'd told him when he slipped into his ghetto slang. "Everybody talks like that on the street," he'd explained, but she wouldn't listen. "Like a damn nigger," she'd repeated, shaking her head.

She never heard him out. Just like when his dad used to hurt him, fuck him up—he'd tell her about it, and she wouldn't hear. It was like he was talking to a ghost.

Well, she was a ghost now. Dead for three years, dropped by a stroke. His dad was alone and getting drunk every night, pissing away his pension in a shithole apartment. All of which was fine as far as Justin was concerned. He didn't owe his old man a goddamned thing. Didn't owe nobody nothing, when you got right down to it. He was a self-made man through and through.

Of course, his mom had been right. He did talk like a nigger, but that was because on the street, and in stir, the jigs defined cool for the rest of the population. They set the trends. Gray didn't mind following trends, as long as he got some fun out of it. This whole serial-killer thing was a trend, a fad. Except for maybe Jack the Ripper, who the fuck had ever heard of a serial killer before, say, 1960 or thereabouts? Now they were as common as crabs on a crack whore. They were in style, and who was he to argue with the arbiters of popular taste?

Anyway, the whole gig had been some serious fun—until he got busted.

He always left the bodies where they fell, to be found by some hiker or park ranger. In two cases, they had never been found at all. Even after his arrest and conviction, when he told the authorities where to look, no remains were recovered. Coyotes and bobcats must have gotten there first, or maybe a flash flood or mudslide had swept the bodies away.

The trouble was that in one instance a body had been found too soon. By sheer bad luck, a motorist stopping to take a roadside pee had stumbled on the remains of Jessica Bender, his last victim, half-hidden in the brush. Because only a few hours had passed since the murder, the crime-scene nerds had been able to retrace Gray's steps and re-cover the tire marks left by his van. Worse, they had found a few flecks of paint where the van had scraped a yucca plant. The make, model, and color of the van were reported on the news. An overly observant neighbor of Gray's called the police hot line. Gray's prior convictions made him a plausible suspect. A search of his van uncovered hairs and fibers from his girls.

So here he was in a glass cage. All because some asshole couldn't wait to take a piss.

But tomorrow he would have a little surprise in store for the Deputy Dawgs. Something up his sleeve, so to speak.

Gray smiled, staring up at the ceiling of his cell.

In less than sixteen hours, he would be free—or he would be dead.

One way or the other, this was his last night in the Reptile House.

Chapter Seventeen

"Granola bars again?" Meg paused in the kitchen doorway, pretty in her gray-and-white uniform, exhaling a theatrical sigh.

Robin smiled at her as she finished rinsing yesterday's dishes. "But they're not cookies and cream this time. They're chocolate chip."

Reluctantly Meg took a seat at the table. "In some jurisdictions this constitutes child abuse."

"Aren't you the one who keeps reminding me you're not a child?"

"I'm a minor under the supervision of a parent or adult guardian. I have a right to a decent breakfast. I think there's something in the UN charter about it."

"Not the parts I read. Chow down."

Meg regarded the two unwrapped bars with mistrust. "Do you think we could afford a live-in cook? Someone whose only job is to prepare our food?"

"Quiet, the microwave might hear you. Drink your milk."

Meg obeyed, finishing all of her milk and half of her breakfast. "I'm done."

"There's a chocolate-chip granola bar left on your plate."

"Can't we just send it to India or China or someplace?"

"It would never survive the trip."

"You kidding?" Meg took a grudging bite. "These things could survive a nuclear war."

"At least there'll be something for the cockroaches to eat." Robin set the last of the plates in the rack and wiped her hands on a towel. "So have you managed to forget everything you committed to memory in your study group last night?"

"I retain some residual knowledge. I think it will last until I've handed in my test."

Robin sat opposite her at the kitchen table. "There's a chance I could be late again tonight."

Meg raised an eyebrow. "Another mystery dinner like last night?"

"What was mysterious about that?"

"Stopping for a hamburger when there's plenty of more-or-less edible food here in our fridge? Why would a person do that?"

"I was conferring with someone."

Both eyebrows went up. "A male someone?"

"A police officer."

"A *male* police officer?"

"Yes."

"A date."

"An informational get-together."

"Sounds very romantic."

"It was very informative."

"Did he kiss you?"

"Meg . . ."

"You didn't say no."

"There was no meeting of the lips."

"Was there a meeting of the minds?"

"Not really."

"But you're seeing him again tonight?"

"This afternoon. I'm not sure how late I'll be."

"I smell something developing here."

"There's nothing developing. Why are you so interested, anyway?"

"Hey, you're always on my case about meeting boys."

"Fair enough." The memory of Gray's late-night phone call came back, and Robin shifted in her seat. "Have you?"

"Have I what?"

"Met any?"

"I know lots of boys. Roughly fifty percent of the Gainesburg School's student population consists of boys."

"But none you're interested in?"

Meg seemed suddenly intent on finishing her granola bar. Her eyes didn't meet Robin's. "Nope."

Robin took a breath, hating herself for any suspicions she might feel, since Gray had planted them.

"Meg," she said slowly, "if you were involved in any kind of relationship . . . I mean, something serious . . . you'd tell me. Wouldn't you?"

Finally Meg looked up, a quizzical expression on her face. "Jeez, Mom. What do you think, I'm running around with a congressman or something?"

"I just meant . . ." Robin brushed aside the thought. She would not be manipulated by Gray's mind games. "Forget it."

Meg got up and came around the table, smiling. "Don't worry about me." She kissed Robin on the cheek. "I'm turning out okay—really. Everything's copa—" She caught herself. "I mean, everything's fine. My lifestyle is Ozzie and Harriet, not Thelma and Louise."

"Right. I got it. Go brush your teeth."

"Aw, I brushed 'em yesterday," Meg teased, and went up the stairs with a wave.

Robin sat at the table, feeling foolish and, perhaps irrationally, just a little bit concerned.

Chapter Eighteen

"Okay, Justin. Stand away from the door."

The voice of a Deputy Dawg, reaching him over the intercom. Gray swung off the cot and saw two guards standing outside the glass wall of his cage.

He keyed the intercom microphone. "What's happening, dudes?"

"You know what the fuck is happening. It's time for your trip to the vet."

"Ain't that tomorrow?"

"It's today. Step to the rear of the cell."

Gray retreated. He hoped they bought into his act. He didn't want the Dawgs to know how he'd been counting the hours throughout a sleepless night and a restless morning, when his last bowl of oatmeal mush had been pushed through the slot in the door. He'd been too goddamned nervous to eat, so he'd flushed the shit down the toilet. Same for lunch. He was wired, man. He was stoked. Now, finally, the time was here—two-thirty P.M. on Tuesday, May 13, his lucky day. His last day in Twin Towers.

The guards scoped him out, making sure he wasn't concealing some of his own pee or shit to toss at them. Some of the other no-hopers around here had pulled that stunt, but not Gray. To his way of thinking, it didn't make much sense

to pick a fight with the monkey-strong hillbillies they re-
cruited for this job. That was a fight he wasn't going to win.

The bolt on the cell door slid back. The guards entered,
watching him.

"You know the drill," one of them said.

Gray stripped. He felt no humiliation about it. He liked
showing off his tattoos. His whole body was a work of glo-
rious fucking art.

They made him bend over and cough. One of them
pushed a gloved hand up his asshole to probe for a shank.
Gray figured the goddamned Dawg was getting off on it.

When they were done, Gray pulled on his yellow jumpsuit. "Find anything interesting?" he asked the hack with the
rubber glove.

The guard told him to shut up.

"Just seems to me you guys have an unhealthy fixation
with my cornhole, you know? I gotta wonder what's up with
that."

This time both screws told him to shut up.

Like most of the deputies in Twin Towers, these two were
young, in their early twenties, just a few years younger than
Gray himself. Guard duty was assigned to new recruits to
the Sheriff's Department, who had to put in three years in
the jail system before they could go out on the streets.

They made a final check, looking inside his mouth like
amateur dentists. Then they clapped on the wrist manacles
and the leg shackles.

"Let's go, asshole," one of the guards snapped. "Don't
want you to be late for your distemper shot."

"Yes, sir," Gray said. *Yes, sir, you weak-ass, dumb-ass,
lame-ass, pussy-ass, bitch-ass, punk-ass, candy-ass, dick-
strokin' motherfucker, sir.*

They led him out of the cell and down the hall of the
prisoner-on-display area, past the row of glass cages and
the blank, staring faces inside. Gray took a last look at the
homeboys and assorted psychopaths preserved under glass.
He gave them a silent good-bye.

He and the screws left the POD and went through sliding steel-reinforced doors to an elevator, which dropped them to ground level. At the rear gate sally port, under the eye of a closed-circuit TV camera scanning overhead, another guard ran a wand over Gray's body. The inspection was completed without incident, and then the hydraulic lock on the exterior door was retracted by remote control, and Gray was outside, in the loading bay, where a Dodge van waited. Large groups of inmates rode a prison bus, but for special runs the van was big enough.

Everything depended on how he handled the next stage of the operation. If he fucked up, he would be finished before he even got started.

Just outside the door he stopped short, blinking at the May sky. "Man, that sun feels sweet."

One of the guards gave him a light shove from behind. "Move."

He stayed put. "Just lemme breathe in some of that LA smog. Shit, my lungs've been achin' for it."

The guard reacted the way Gray knew he would. He slammed Gray between the shoulder blades, driving him forward. "I said move!"

It all happened fast then. Gray got his shackled feet all tangled up and fell heavily on his stomach, shouting a curse. The hacks told him to stop dicking around and get up. Gray grabbed hold of a fire hydrant for support and boosted himself to his feet. He patted down his jumpsuit to smooth out the wrinkles and brush off the dirt. He was talking about police brutality and prison reform. The deputies weren't listening.

"You goddamn move when we tell you to," one of them said irritably. "Jesus."

The two Dawgs handed over their charge to a pair of transportation deputies. To Gray, they were indistinguishable from the first two guys. Something about their blue-and-gold duds made all these losers look the same.

Gray allowed himself to be caged in the rear of the van.

The transportation deputies climbed into the front. "What'll it be today?" the driver asked. "Me, I'm feelin' a little bit country."

He cranked up the stereo, tuned to a hillbilly station, and the van pulled away.

In the rear compartment, Gray brushed his manacled hands together, feeling the tool he had hidden under his sleeve.

It was a screwdriver, a small one, slender, seven inches long, rusty, dirty, the most beautiful thing Gray had ever seen. Ten days ago he'd found it, when he was riding in the prison van—either this van or another one just like it; like the Dawgs, the vans all looked the same. He'd noticed the screwie rolling on the floor near his shoes. How it had gotten there, he couldn't say. Maybe it had dropped out of a workman's toolkit while he was making repairs in the prisoner cage.

He had captured the screwie between his shoes, then slipped it under his sleeve when no one was looking. But he'd known there was no way to get it through the metal detector. So after being unloaded from the van, he had faked a stumble and dropped the screwie behind the fire hydrant. It had lain there ever since.

He had been patient. If he stumbled twice in a row, even the dumb-ass hayseed plowboys who pulled guard duty at Twin Towers might get suspicious. Ten days seemed long enough to ensure that the two deputies had forgotten all about his earlier mishap. Minutes ago, while getting to his feet and using the fire hydrant for support, he'd palmed the screwie and slipped it down his sleeve.

He took a look around. There was a large fish-eye mirror mounted behind him, which gave the Dawg riding shotgun a decent view of Gray. But the Dawg wasn't paying attention. He and the driver were involved in an intense conversation about the relative merits of NASCAR drivers.

"Tell you what," the driver was saying over the radio's

blare, "there hasn't been one of 'em worth a damn since Dale Earnhardt died."

"Not even Dale Junior? You telling me you don't like Dale Junior? Everybody loves Dale Junior."

"Dale Junior can kiss my spotted ass."

Couple of good ol' boys. One of them would be dead soon. Maybe both. Gray smiled at the prospect. He'd never killed a bona fide redneck. He was looking forward to it.

He slipped his right hand inside his left sleeve and carefully removed the screwdriver, positioning it between his second and third fingers, flat across his palm.

When he held his hand palm downward, the tool was invisible.

Up front the debate continued. "I'm just saying, okay, maybe he's not as good as his old man, but he's still pretty damn good."

"Hell, my grandma could drive better than him, and she's ninety-two years old and blind as a mole."

"I don't see how you can say that about Dale Junior. Everybody loves Dale Junior."

"Dale Junior can kiss my spotted . . ."

Gray separated his hands, placing one on each knee.

Step one and step two had been accomplished.

In Doc Robin's office he would finish the job.

Chapter Nineteen

"Hey, Dr. R." As he stepped into the waiting room, Gray showed the doc a big shit-eating grin, which he noticed she didn't return.

"Hello, Justin," she said coolly.

The two deputy dickwads hustled him through the waiting room, into the office. The doc followed. Gray gave her the eye over his shoulder.

"Gonna poke around inside my noggin some more? I keep telling you, there's nothing to find."

"I think we've found a great deal already."

"You're an optimist. You say my brain is half-full. Me, I say it's half-empty."

He was keeping up the patter, staying loose. Usually he liked to be a little blitzed when he pulled off dangerous shit like this, but right now he had some kind of major buzz going. Adrenaline or some goddamn thing.

The deputies removed his handcuffs and leg irons, standard procedure in the doc's office. She didn't want her patient all trussed up like a prize turkey. Still, he had to be kept under some restraint. The two hacks sat him down in the metal chair and belted his wrists to the armrests, cinching the metal buckles.

"It ain't enough I'm caged all the livelong day," he

groused. "Even when I'm out and about, I gotta be friggin' immobilized."

"It's for your own protection," the doc said.

"Yeah, right. Everything you fuckers do to me is for my own good. When you put that helmet on me and nose around in my brain, that's for my own good too."

"It will be, in the long run."

He was strapped in good and tight now. Deputies Dumb and Dumber seemed satisfied. "I'll be in the other room if you need me," one of them said.

Gray knew that the driver would sit in the van while his partner hung out in the waiting room. And he was pleased to see that Forrest Gump and his partner had kept their sidearms on their Sam Brownes, even while off-loading him. That was contrary to regulations—guns weren't supposed to be worn within reach of a prisoner—but he guessed the hacks were just too lazy or too butt-stupid to stow the guns like they were supposed to. That was good. He wanted the Dawg in the waiting room to be armed. There was no sport in icing an unarmed man.

When they were gone, and the office door was closed, the doc pulled up the swivel chair from her desk, setting it between his chair and the computer gear, and sat beside him. She was looking good today, he noticed, even if she was dressed in her standard ensemble, a beige suit jacket, a blouse in pastel blue, a pair of neatly laundered slacks, and sensible shoes. He wished she would wear a skirt. He was sure she had great legs. And he wouldn't have minded seeing her blouse unbuttoned a notch or two to reveal more of the smooth, tight skin below her collarbone.

"How are you feeling, Justin?"

"Footloose 'n' fancy-free." This was true.

"I'm serious. I need to monitor your progress."

"My progress? I live in a cage, Doc. Only progress I make is when I walk from my rack to the toilet and back again."

"I'm talking about progress inside."

"Yeah, I feel ya. Hamlet's kind of progress." He smiled at her incomprehension. "'I could be bounded in a nutshell and count myself a king of infinite space. . . .' Didn't think I knew that one, did you?"

"Honestly, no."

"First time I was in stir, my roommate got hold of a Shakespeare play. We took turns reading it. Wasn't *Hamlet*, though."

"Which one was it?"

"The one about the fairies."

"A Midsummer Night's Dream?"

"That's the one. Gotta say, I made one hell of a Titania."

"I'm sure you did." She rearranged some papers on her lap. "Well, let's get started."

"Don't you want to know the rest of the story?"

"Is there more?"

"Darn tootin'. I didn't say where I found *Hamlet*."

"Where?"

"It was in Susan Miller's backpack."

Her voice went cold. "I see."

Susan Miller was one of the five teenage girls Gray had killed.

"I went through her stuff," he went on blithely, "after I was done with her. Guess she was carrying it around for her English class. I figured I ought to read it, since I liked the one about the fairies. And I always try to further my education. We're a lot alike in that way, Dr. R."

"Are we?"

"Sure. You're furthering your education right now." He met and held her gaze. "By studying me."

She broke their eye contact. "We need to begin."

"You're the boss."

"We'll start with the inkblots."

He didn't like that. He wanted her to turn out the lights, start fiddling with the controls of her mind machine, quit looking at him. There was a chance she'd see what was hidden in his right hand.

"Fucking inkblots again?" He sighed noisily. "Damn, I was hoping you'd bring some more interesting pictures. Naked ladies, for instance."

"I don't have any pictures of naked ladies."

"Some cheesecake shots of you and your daughter would do."

Her saw her mouth tighten. "Justin—"

"I'm just talking, Doc. Little Meg Cameron . . . How old she be? Fifteen? Sixteen? That's a damn good age."

"We're not going to talk about this."

"Hope I didn't creep you out with my phone call. I just wanted you to know how much your daughter means to me. Some nights she's the only thing that keeps me going. . . ."

She got up, tossing the inkblot cards on her desk. Her hands were shaking. "All right, forget the preliminaries. We'll move on to the MBI."

Gray suppressed a smile. The doc wasn't the only one who could get inside a person's head and push their buttons. And he didn't need no fancy machine.

She attached the electrodes, pulled down the window shades, killed the overhead light, set the helmet on his head. First time he'd worn it, he thought it was heavy as a brick, but he was used to it now.

She put the headphones on him, like always. He wished he could hear some raucous metal tunes on these things and not just the doc's calm, comforting PA-system voice.

"Justin?" she said, the query coming over the phones. "Do you hear me?"

"Ten-four and roger that, big mama," he said in the general direction of the stalk mike protruding from the headset.

When she swiveled away from him to adjust the computer gear against the wall, he knew it was time to make his move.

Timing was critical. Once the helmet was switched on, he'd be unable to act. Those magnetic fields did something funny to his head, got him all messed up. It was like he wasn't even in the room anymore, like he was time-traveling or tripping on some really hard drugs. In the minute or two it would take her to make the final adjustments to the gear, he had to work himself free.

He twisted his right hand sideways, crooking it at the wrist, and guided the screwdriver toward the strap's metal buckle. The idea was to jam the screwie's blade under the tongue of the buckle and lever it up.

He glanced at the doc, still programming the machine. In their first session she'd explained to him that the helmet contained a whole bunch of magnetic coils. She could turn some of them off, turn others on, basically customize the helmet for each user. She liked to tweak the settings each time.

Gray eased the tip of the screwdriver under the buckle, and pushed up on the metal tongue.

"Okay. Ready to begin?"

He froze, waiting for the doc to notice the screwdriver in his hand. Luckily, the room was dark, illuminated only by the glow of the computer screens. Besides, she still hadn't looked at him. She was studying the readouts on the monitors.

"Justin? Ready?"

He needed to buy time, release the buckle.

"Hey, Doc, I'm sorry if I offended you a couple minutes ago." He tried again to pry open the buckle. "I was just, you know, playing."

"You're always playing, aren't you?" Her voice was flat.

"It's my nature. See, I—"

She cut him off. "Let's get started."

He wanted to say something more, but abruptly the helmet switched on.

He felt the familiar sensation of invisible claws hooking onto his scalp and dragging his forehead up under the helmet. There were blind spots in both of his eyes. The doc had explained that the voodoo current she passed through his noodle messed up his octopus area—not octopus . . . occipital . . . something like that.

His concentration began to fail. He was losing focus.

God damn it, he was so close.

He thought he could still do it, could still unbuckle the strap. He only had to hold on to awareness and self-control for another few seconds. He tensed his body, fighting the effects of the current.

"Justin? You seem to be resisting."

"Maybe I don't wanna be your play-toy no more, Doc."

His fingers jabbed the screwdriver against the buckle.

"You're not a toy, and this isn't a game. Now I want you to relax. Take deep, slow breaths."

The buckle shifted, coming partly undone. He strained to finish the job. But his fingers, damp with sweat, couldn't get purchase on the screwdriver.

"This isn't working," Robin said, still watching the screen. "Your muscular tension is high. So is your heart rate. I'm going to boost the appliance's output a little. That should induce relaxation."

"You're gonna force me to cooperate? How's that any different from tying me down for some of the old electric shock treatment?"

That stopped her. "I don't want you to feel I'm mistreating you."

"Well, I do." He'd gotten hold of the buckle at last. "I feel damn mistreated, Doc. I'm like Nicholson in *Cuckoo's Nest*, you know? I'm getting fuckin' lobotomized here."

The tongue of the buckle lifted another few degrees. One more good push, and he could snap it back, unhook himself.

"Actually," she said, "I don't think it will be necessary to adjust the output. You seem to be settling down."

He didn't know where the fuck she got that idea. His heart was still rabbiting in his chest.

He flexed his wrist, jamming the screwdriver against the metal tongue, and the buckle popped open.

His right hand was free.

The rest was easy. Just reach over and unbuckle his left wrist. Had to do it fast, before the doc had time to see what was going down. Even in the dark, she might see that his hand was loose. If she yelled, the hack in the waiting room would come running.

He tried to reach across his body with his free hand. . . .

Couldn't do it. Couldn't move.

Oh, hell. The doc had been right, after all. Goddamned machine was taking control of him. He'd fought it off as long as he could.

Now his head was going all ker-blooey, and his eyes were ticking back and forth like he was watching a Ping-Pong game. His hands felt warm and tingly, and his arms were a hundred yards long, his whole body stretching out like an elastic band.

He felt his fingers splay. The screwdriver dropped to the floor, its fall muffled by the carpet.

"Justin, can you hear me?"

The question reached him from far off. He forgot whose voice it was. His mother's, maybe. Or was it Susan Miller, the one with *Hamlet* in her backpack?

"Justin . . . ?"

No, it was the doc. He was in her office, and she was using him as her personal lab rat. There was something he'd been planning to do about that, but he couldn't remember. He was tired. . . .

"Justin?"

"Yeah." He heard himself answer, but it was like somebody else was talking and he was only eavesdropping.

"I want you to relax, Justin."

He *was* relaxed. He was limp.

"I want you to visit the beach. You know the spot I mean."

"I know."

In their first session he'd told her about a place up the coast, around Pismo Beach, where he'd stopped one time. It was so peaceful there.

"I want you to go there. Are you there, Justin?"

"I'm there. . . ."

He was, too. That was the weirdness of it. He was really fucking there. Oh, sure, part of him was still in a straight-back chair in an air-conditioned office, but another part of him was sitting cross-legged on the sand watching gulls swoop over the breaking waves. The air was misty, damp, but some sun was getting through. He breathed in the good salt smell of the ocean.

"Just sit on the beach and be at rest."

"At rest," he said, his voice merging with the sigh of the surf.

Something had been worrying him, but he no longer remembered what. Didn't matter anyhow. Nothing mattered.

It was a beautiful day at the beach. He was happy.

He was free.

Chapter Twenty

Robin let Gray adjust to the trancelike state initiated by the bilateral magnetic fields. In the dim light cast by the computer screens, she could see that his eyes were half-closed, his mouth agape. His breathing was slow and regular.

When she thought he was ready, she spoke to him again.

"All right, Justin. Now it's time to leave the beach."

"Like it here . . ." he murmured.

"I know you do, but we have work to do. I want you to go to your parents' apartment, the one on Pine Street. The place where you grew up."

When working with Brand, she had guided him to act as an observer. Gray, less resistant, could relive the experience directly.

"Okay."

"Are you there?"

He nodded.

"Last time, you told me that your father used to punish you. I want you to go to a time when you were punished. Can you do that?"

"Don't wanna."

"Can you?"

A long pause. "Yeah."

"Are you with your father now?"

"I'm with him. I'm with my old man."

"What's he doing?"

"Yelling."

"That's all? Just yelling?"

"He's got . . . it looks like . . . oh, hell, he's got his damn belt off."

"Does he hit you with the belt?"

Snort of derision. "I wish."

"What, then?"

"He uses it to tie me . . ."

"Tie you up?"

"Tie me to . . ."

"To what?"

"The radiator. He ties the belt 'round my waist, hooks it to the radiator. That's just for starters."

"What happens next?"

"My hand."

"What about your hand?"

"My left hand."

"What about your hand, Justin?"

"He puts it on the radiator. He's got his shirt off. It's wrapped over his hand like a glove. He grabs me by the wrist and . . ."

"He presses your hand to the hot radiator?"

Gray winced, feeling it now. "Hurts like a motherfucker. That's what I tell him, them exact words—hurts like a motherfucker."

"What happens when you say that?"

"He says, my old man says, 'Watch your mouth.' "

"And your hand . . .?"

"He's holding it down."

"What's he saying now?"

"He don't want me shoplifting again."

"What did you shoplift?"

"Don't remember."

She tried again. "What did you shoplift?"

"Some fuckbook. *Penthouse*, *Hustler*, some shit like that. Would've paid for it, but they won't sell it to you if you're not eighteen."

"How old are you?"

"Thirteen. Christ, my hand hurts."

"Is this the first time he's hurt you?"

"Fuck, no."

"First time with the radiator?"

"No."

She remembered something he'd said in a previous session. "You told me about a baseball bat. . . ."

"That's later. For taking his car without asking. He tries to bust my kneecaps. But he misses me, 'cause he's drunk."

She returned to the radiator incident. "Is he drunk now?"

"Maybe he's had a snort, I can't tell. Doesn't matter."

"Why doesn't it matter?"

"He's like this all the time. Drunk or sober, makes no difference."

"Has he let go of your hand?"

"By now . . . yeah."

"Badly burned?"

"Blisters all over."

"You've got serious burns."

"Damn straight."

"Does he take you to a doctor?"

"Not him. My mom does."

"Your mom?"

"To the ER. She tells 'em I was playing around the radiator. They bandage me up."

"What do you say about playing by the radiator?"

"I don't say shit."

"Nobody asks you?"

"Nobody cares."

"If they had asked—"

"I'd tell them, yeah, I was playing around. I'm a stupid kid. I hurt myself like kids do."

"Who are you protecting? Your dad?"

"Fuck him."

"Your mom?"

"Fuck her, too. She married the asshole."

"Who, then?"

"I don't know. I guess . . ."

"Yes?"

"You don't squeal. Not on family. Even when they treat you like shit. And anyway . . ."

"Yes?"

"I *did* shoplift the goddamn magazine."

"So you had it coming?"

"I don't know."

"Does your hand heal okay?"

"Pretty much. Thumb's a little fucked up. Nerve damage, maybe."

She let him rest for a minute or two. His breathing, which had grown rapid and shallow, slowed and deepened as he relaxed. She thought about what he'd told her and what it might mean. An idea occurred to her.

"Can we go to one more place?" she asked.

"What the hell." A smile touched the corners of his mouth. "Might as well rack up some frequent-flyer miles. . . ."

"You have a lot of tattoos, Justin."

"Ain't they pretty?"

"Some look professional."

"They are."

"Where'd you get them done?"

"Wild Ink."

"Where's that?"

"Hollywood. Ernesto works there. Ernesto's a fuckin' artist."

"Then that's where we'll go. We're in that tattoo parlor. You're in the chair, and Ernesto is working on you."

"Okay."

"Needle in your flesh. How does it feel?"

His shoulders lifted in a shrug. "Hurts."

"Hurts how? In what way?"

"Burns."

"Tell me what you're feeling right now."

"Needle going in. Hot wire in my skin. And . . ."

"Yes?"

"And I like it."

"Do you?"

"I like to feel the burn."

"Is that why you're at the tattoo parlor?"

"Yeah. Don't even want another goddamn tattoo. All I want is . . ."

"What?"

"The pain."

"Why do you want pain, Justin?"

"Makes me feel . . ."

"How does it make you feel?"

"Strong."

"Why?"

" 'Cause I can take it."

"Why do you have to take it?"

A slow shrug of his shoulders. "That's life."

"Life is pain?"

"Shit, yeah."

"Is that the way life should be?"

"It's the way it is."

"Is it fair? Or unfair?"

"It's life. Fair ain't got nothing to do with it."

"Your father mistreated you, Justin."

"I guess."

"He abused you."

"He fucked with me, yeah. So what? Everybody fucks with everybody."

"You were only a kid."

"So?"

"Is it wrong to hurt a kid?"

"I know where you're going, Doc. Fuck you."

She'd lost him.

She had hoped to make him see that his violence against teenage girls was, in part, a reaction to his own father's violence against him. It was the kind of insight that could be accepted more readily when the mind's defenses were lowered in the MBI trance. But he wouldn't go there. He wasn't ready.

"All right, Justin. Back to the beach. Rest a minute."

She wrote up her notes, using a pen with a built-in flashlight because she didn't want to turn on the room lights until he was out of his trance. After a short time she told him that he would be waking up. She powered down the MBI appliance, then checked the record of the session. Time: nineteen minutes. MBI at 80 percent motor threshold, 60 percent of the coils engaged.

Behind her, she heard Gray stir.

"How are you feeling?" she asked without turning.

"Woozy. What'd I say?"

"What do you remember?"

"I can never get a straight answer from you, can I, Doc?"

She saved the record of the session to a CD. "We talked about your father. He used to punish you. Burned your hand."

"Fuck, yeah. That's right."

He seemed to be shifting in his chair, unusually restless. Maybe the memory had disturbed him more than he'd let on.

She ejected the CD from the tray and slipped it into a plastic case. "What he did to you was wrong. He hurt you— and ever since, you've been hurting others and yourself."

She labeled the disk, using her flashlight pen.

"That's the way I like it," he said.

"Is it, Justin?"

"Yeah, Doc. It's what I live for."

Something in his voice made her swivel in her chair, turning toward him, and then there was a solid smack against the side of her head—a dazzle of light and delayed pain, and with curious detachment she had time to think that he was loose, he'd freed himself.

Another blow stunned her. She toppled backward off the chair onto the carpet, knowing she had to scream for help, but before she could, he pressed his hand over her mouth, and in the light of the flashlight pen she could see his face.

One last impact, his fist against her temple, a new eruption of brightness, and then a high humming wave carried her away.

Chapter Twenty-one

Robin had no idea how long she'd been out, a minute or an hour. When her eyes opened, she saw Gray leaning over her, a knife in his hand.

"Justin . . ."

"Hey, Doc. You banged your head something fierce."

"You're . . . out of the . . ."

"Straps? Well, yeah. Thanks to my buddy here." The knife flashed. It was long and shiny and looked like one of those knives used by assassins. What was the name? A stiletto.

And now it was held inches from her throat, and even in the dim light of the computer console she could see its leading edge slick with blood.

He read her thoughts. "Don't worry. Not gonna cut ya."

"No?" The word was thin and faint and distant.

"Just need your cooperation for a minute. Roll over."

"What?"

"On your belly."

She was frozen. She couldn't move.

Gray grabbed her shoulder, shoved her onto her side, and she remembered the deputy in the waiting room. She wanted to scream, but only a hoarse whisper escaped her throat. "Help . . ."

"He can't hear you, Doc. Believe me." She remembered the blood on the knife. "Just roll over and quit making things so friggin' difficult."

He flopped her on her belly, and she felt his hands on her back. She tensed up, her entire body rigid. Then he was stripping off the beige suit jacket she'd worn today.

"Got it. Thanks for your assistance."

She craned her neck, staring up at him as he shrugged on the jacket and buttoned it. The fit was tight across his wide shoulders, but the fabric didn't tear.

"Need something to hide my jailhouse rags," he said by way of explanation. "Already got the lower extremities covered."

For the first time she noticed that he was wearing a blue cap on his head and blue pants over his jumpsuit. Items from the deputy's uniform.

As he fastened the last button, it occurred to her that both of his hands were free, which meant he wasn't carrying the knife. Her gaze cut to the floor and there it was, a foot away, within reach if she dared to try for it. . . .

Too late. He snatched it up again.

"Interested in this?" He squatted, resting a knee on the small of her back, and drew the weapon close to her face. "Pretty, ain't it? A thing of beauty is a joy forever. Or so they tell me."

It was close now, so close she could see that it was not a stiletto, not a knife at all. It was a flathead screwdriver. The blood on it was glossy, dripping.

"Christ, I get pissed off at you sometimes," Gray said.

"You do?" She kept her tone neutral.

"The way you run me through my fucking paces, a rat in a maze. That's all I ever was to you. A lab rat."

She didn't dare challenge him by contesting what he said. "I'm sorry you felt that way," she whispered.

"You ain't sorry. You're just scared I'm gonna rip out your freaking throat." The screwdriver eased up against the soft underside of her chin. "It wouldn't be hard. . . ."

She waited.

"Who the fuck was he, anyway?" he asked.

The question was incomprehensible. "Who was . . . who?"

"Him. The jagoff that KO'd you. Mr. Cool."

She was lost. "Mr. Cool?"

"Well, I gotta admit, I thought it was pretty cool, the way he snuck up behind both of us and never made a peep. I mean, the shoes that dude was wearing—I gotta have 'em."

"I don't know what you mean."

"The guy that clocked you. What's the story there?"

"I thought . . . I . . ." She selected her words with care, conscious of the screwdriver testing her throat. "I thought you were the one who . . ."

"Brained you? Not sayin' I wouldn't have, but Mr. Cool beat me to the punch. The punch, ha, that's kinda funny."

"Yes. Funny."

The blade tickled her skin. "I don't hear you laughing."

"I guess the concussion robbed me of my sense of humor."

He grunted. "Petty theft. You saying you don't recollect Mr. Cool?"

"I'm sorry. I don't."

"You looked right at him. That pen thingamabob flashed a light in his face. You *had* to see him."

"I don't remember any of that."

"Bullshit."

"A lot of times a blow to the head will result in minor amnesia. Memory loss."

"Yeah, I know what amnesia is. So you're blaming your bad memory on the concussion, too?"

"It's the only explanation."

"You probably think I'm shittin' you."

"No, Justin, I don't." She kept her voice toneless.

"You think there never was no Mr. Cool. Right?"

"I didn't say that."

"You're thinking it. But you're wrong. I didn't mess you up. Didn't waste the Deputy Dawg neither."

"Okay."

"Mr. Cool must've iced him on the way in. Slit his throat nice and quiet. Silence 'n' violence. You got to respect that."

"Uh-huh."

"He was dead already, is what I'm saying. I didn't do him. He was lying there in the other room when I ran out."

She went along with his story because she had no choice. "Chasing Mr. Cool."

"Fuck, no. Being chased by him. Yeah, I tangled with him for a sec, but all I had was this fucking screwie. Who knows what hardware that cat was carrying? So I make a run for it into the waiting room. Then I see the deputy, and his piece is still in the holster. This piece here."

He drew a gun out of the waistband of his pants. Robin pulled in a shallow breath.

"I snatch it," Gray said, "and I come back inside. Figure the odds are evened up."

"I see."

"It's a shame you was asleep for all this. You missed the whole damn show."

"Sounds like it."

"We played cat-and-mouse in the shadows for a minute or so." He snorted. "Minute, hell—more like ten seconds, probably. Then Mr. Cool hightails it outta here."

"You scared him off."

Gray shrugged, snugging the gun in his pants again. "Maybe he just remembered he left something on the stove. So who was he?"

"I told you, I don't know."

"You got an enemies list that long? Doc, you been hanging out with the wrong people. Hey, you know what? I bet I saved your damn life. Bet he woulda sliced you open just like the Deputy Dawg if I hadn't furnished a distraction."

She wondered if he believed the story himself. He might have suffered a psychotic break. "That's true."

"Woulda gutted the heart out of you, I bet. Then found a way to pin it on me."

"Probably."

"No *probably* about it. I gave you life, Doc Robin. And what I giveth I can taketh away."

The blade nuzzled her throat like the snout of an animal. Robin held her breath.

"Nah," he said, withdrawing the weapon. "Sorry, Doc. You ain't my type. I like 'em young and nubile. You're too goddamn old."

He stood, then glanced around the office and found her purse. Digging through it, he extracted her wallet and a key chain.

"I'll be needing cash and a set of wheels. If you don't mind . . ." He checked the logo on the key chain. "Saab. Nice. I seen that one parked out back. The nine-five, right?"

"Right."

"I'll see it gets back to you in good condition. And by the way, when you talk to the cops, be sure to tell 'em I did you a good deed. Not that it'll matter none. I'm still gonna be America's Most Wanted." He grinned, as if pleased with the prospect. "Ta-ta."

He left the room, and she started breathing again.

Chapter Twenty-two

Gray was fighting back panic, an unfamiliar feeling for him—but then he'd never been a hunted animal before. His arrest last year had come without warning, and he'd spent all his time afterward in confinement. Now he was free, but the trick was to stay free. No fuckups, or he would be back in the Reptile House, then transferred to some state hellhole like Pelican Bay, and all his good times would end.

What he had to do was put some miles between himself and the office. Easy enough, once he was driving the doc's Saab, but it was parked in the lot behind the building, and the prison van was there too, with Forrest Gump nestled behind the wheel.

Gray opened the building's rear door and scouted the parking lot, considering his options. If he left this way, he'd be directly in the driver's line of sight. The doc's jacket and the deputy's cap and pants made him less conspicuous, but the Dawg was almost sure to recognize him if he looked in Gray's direction.

Maybe he wouldn't, though. Goober seemed to be reading a newspaper or some shit. Which was surprising, since Gray hadn't realized these deputy dipshits *could* read. The driver might not even look up. And if he did . . .

Gray could pop him. He had the dead hick's gun—a nice

hefty Beretta nine, a bigger piece than the deuce-deuce he used when he was snuffing cheerleaders. Maybe he could smoke the Gumpster before old Forrest had time to react. Still, he wasn't kidding himself. He wasn't exactly surgical with a piece. The odds weren't exactly on his side.

Well, whatever the motherfuck he did, he better do it fast. Doc Robin might already be shaking off the woozies and getting on the phone to 911.

He should've pulled the plug on that bitch when he had the chance. Wasn't sure why he hadn't. Could've snapped her neck while she was out cold, or raked a hole in her throat with the screwie.

Too late now. He had no time to go back and finish the job. No time to find another exit, either. His only hope was to go out the back door and get out of the hillbilly's line of sight before he was made.

He stuffed the gun into the waistband of his pants, under the jacket, then stepped outside. He resisted the instinct to keep his head down, instead looking boldly ahead like any other nine-to-five zombie who had a perfect constitutional right to be here. He never even glanced at the prison van or the brainless inbred fucker in the driver's seat.

Hands in his pockets, he crossed the parking lot, taking slow, even strides, a man in no hurry. At the other end of the lot he finally allowed himself a look at the van—not by turning his head, but by checking it out in a parked car's side-view mirror.

The Deputy Dawg was still sitting behind the wheel, head down, reading. He'd be reading his fucking termination notice soon.

"You're horse-fucked, Gomer," Gray muttered with a smile, "you dumb peckerwood piece of shit."

It had been too easy.

He remembered where Doc Robin parked her wheels. On previous occasions he'd noticed the shiny new Saab in a re-served space—a tight car, perfect for his getaway. He headed toward it at a fast walk, then slowed, shaking his head in consternation.

Shit, what the hell happened to his ride? It used to be so sweet and shiny. Now it was a fucking wreck. Windshield cracked, side window busted. He was disappointed in the doc. He'd expected her to take better care of her rig.

He turned off the car alarm with the remote control on the key ring, adjusted the driver's seat, then slipped inside and turned the key in the ignition switch. Quickly he backed out of the space. Once clear of the lot, he accelerated, speeding down a series of side streets until he felt safe.

He relaxed a little, allowing himself to enjoy the feel of the steering wheel and the responsiveness of the engine, pleasures he hadn't experienced in a year of incarceration.

The CD on the tray was some classical shit. That crap made his ears bleed. He ejected the disk and tossed it out the window, then dialed through the FM stations till he found some kick-ass rock 'n' roll. He pumped it loud, beating his hands on the steering wheel above the blare.

He was laughing. He was out of Twin Towers. He was on the loose and living large.

"Lock up your daughters, moms and dads," he said with a whoop of glee. "Justin Gray is back in town!"

Chapter Twenty-three

When Robin was sure Gray had left the office, she pushed herself into a sitting position, then rose upright. Two unsteady steps brought her to the phone on her desk. She assumed she would dial 911 and was surprised when her fingers speed-dialed the first number in the phone's memory.

Meg, she realized. She was calling Meg.

There had to be a good reason, but none occurred to her until Meg picked up on the third ring.

"Cameron residence."

"Meg, I want you out of the house right now."

"It's a condo, Mom, not a house, and why would I be out of it when I just got into it? Jamie's mom dropped me off, like, thirty seconds ago—"

"*Meg!*" The shout of anger surprised them both. "Shut up and listen to me. I want you to leave the house and go to Mrs. Grandy's and then call me from there. Call me at the office. Understand?"

The jollity was gone from Meg's voice. "What's happening?"

"Just do it."

"What if Mrs. Grandy's not home?"

"She's always home. If not, try Mr. Haver."

"The guy who works at home all day in his bathrobe? The guy who's always hitting on you—"

"That guy. Now leave the house. Right now. Don't stop to get changed and don't take another call. Just go. Have you got that?"

"Yes, Mom."

"I love you," Robin said, ending the call before her daughter could reply.

Now it was time to call 911, except first she had to put down the phone and bend over the wastebasket by the desk and throw up, voiding her stomach of lunch.

Lifting her head, she caught sight of the rectangle of waiting room carpet visible in the doorway, and on the carpet, an outstretched hand.

She forgot 911. Slowly she walked through her office to the doorway and looked down at the deputy on the floor, his face upturned to her. His throat had been opened to release a lake of arterial blood. His cap and pants were gone. Gray hadn't taken the shirt and jacket; they were ruined, splashed by red spray.

The man's expressionless face was hard to take, but somehow worse was the casual obscenity of his Jockey shorts and hairy legs.

She stared at the corpse for a long moment before remembering that he had a partner waiting in the prison van in the parking lot, only steps away.

The trip through the waiting room seemed endless, and then there was the longer trek down the hall to the rear door with the exit sign glowing overhead. All the while she was thinking of Gray on the loose with a gun—Gray, who had met Meg and never stopped speaking about her, and who now had Robin's wallet, containing her driver's license, which listed her home address—the place where Meg was now, unless she had already left.

Gray wouldn't go after her. Of course not. It would be too risky. It would be crazy.

And a man who killed teenage girls for sport would never do anything crazy, would he?

Robin reached the exit and flung open the door and then she was standing at the top of the steps, waving with both arms at the deputy in the van, like a castaway signaling a distant, vanishing plane.

Chapter Twenty-four

Hammond's cell phone buzzed as he was driving into West LA. The caller was Lewinsky. "Chief, we've got a situation."

"I'm on my way to the dentist, Carl."

"I know that, sir. But I think maybe you'd better have Tom drive you back here."

"Tom's not driving. I'm in my personal car."

"Okay."

"I don't use my department driver for personal business. You know that."

"Yes, sir. But—"

"I wouldn't want people thinking I'm abusing the office. There could be serious repercussions to any rumors like that."

"Yes, sir."

"Try to be more careful with what you say."

"Yes, sir. We *do* have a situation here, Chief."

Hammond sighed. "What is it? Some crack dealer suing the department for restraint of trade?"

"It's Justin Gray. The serial killer."

"I know who he is, Carl. I read the papers."

"He's escaped."

"What?"

"Gray has escaped."

"He busted out of Twin Towers? That place is a fortress."

"No, he was out on a special run. He was going to that shrink, you know."

"Robin Cameron."

"Yes, sir."

"The same Robin Cameron who was nearly carjacked yesterday? What is she, a one-woman crime magnet? Jesus." He took a breath before asking the obvious question. "Is she dead?"

"Gray roughed her up a little, that's all. But he killed one of the correction officers on escort duty."

"Cameron saw all this?"

"I guess so. I don't know the details. She's talking to some Rampart officers now."

"She's lucky to be alive. Gray isn't the type of guy to leave a witness. All right, I'm coming in, but it may take a while for me to get there, with the crosstown traffic at this hour. I want you ready with a complete rundown to bring me up to speed as soon as I walk in the door. And get out my spare uniform. I'm in civvies now. I want to be properly attired for the"—*cameras*, he almost said—"the investigation."

"Chief"—a new voice spoke up—"I don't know if that's a good idea."

It was Banner, Hammond's de facto public relations manager, although his official title was office coordinator, whatever that meant. Only the chief of police was authorized to have his own media handler.

"You don't want me wearing my uniform?" Hammond snapped.

"I don't want you getting involved in this case, period."

"And why is that?"

"This thing is a mess," Banner said. His voice faded in and out. He seemed to have been patched through on a cell. "It's too high-risk. There's no telling where this might go. I say palm it off on the Rampart guys or RHD."

"You lack vision, Phil." Hammond was smiling. "Where you see risk, I see opportunity."

"I'm just saying it could . . ." Fadeout.

"What? Didn't catch that. Where the hell are you calling from, anyway?"

"Halfway home. I mean, I figured if you were taking a half day for the dentist . . ."

Hammond got it now. "You'd kick back, too. How convenient."

"It's not like that. Caroline's in a music recital. I thought I could catch it. It's not like I see much of my family any other time."

"Whenever you want to be rotated back to Traffic, just say the word."

"No, sir. That wasn't what I meant at all."

"Good. Well, Helen will just have to videotape your daughter's performance. Turn your car around and come back to work. Read me?"

"Yes, sir. But I still say this course of action is unwise. It could backfire on us. It could undo all the hard work we've—I mean, the work *you've* done."

Hammond sighed. "Phil, I remember the Justin Gray case. He's a mutt. You ever see his jacket? He already did a two-year slide in Chino for auto theft, and he's got a bunch of small-time crap on his sheet."

"Even so—"

"Even so, nothing. He's a nobody, a sewer rat. Tattoos all over his body, pierced ears—hell, probably pierced *nipples*, for Christ's sake. Talks like a goddamn gangbanger. Hasn't got any better than a tenth-grade education . . ."

"I don't see what—"

"He's strictly small-time, is my point. Sure, he terrorized the city for a while, and sure, the media made him into the devil incarnate. That's what they always do with these idiots, make them bigger than life. But he's a loser, and the only reason it look so long to collar him is that he was working alone so there was nobody to drop a dime on him."

"Granted, but—"

"But nothing. We know who he is now. We know his name, his face, what he eats for breakfast. He can't run far. He can't hide. He is federally fucked. We'll nab him in a few hours—hopefully in time for the eleven-o'clock news. And when we do, guess who'll be running the press briefing?"

"It's dangerous, Chief."

"Faint heart never won fair lady. I'm coming in, and so are you, Lieutenant. Carl, you still there?"

"Yes, sir."

"You're actually in the office, I assume? Not phoning this in from Zuma Beach?"

"I'm at my post, sir," Lewinsky said with a mincing tone. Hammond could almost see the man's self-important smirk. He was a toady, but a reliable one.

"See if you can get in touch with my wife. If she's home, maybe we can messenger my dress blues to the office." The spare uniform he kept at work wasn't formal.

"Uh, yes, sir."

"On second thought, scratch that. Might be better if I'm not all decked out. I want to look like a working cop. Anyway, the public won't care what I'm wearing. All they'll care about is that a ruthless psychopath has been speedily recaptured, thanks to the outstanding work of those whose motto and duty is to protect and serve. Phil, you get that?"

"Got it, Chief."

"Use that in my remarks announcing Gray's arrest. I want a rough draft in an hour. Dictate into your microrecorder while you drive. Better do an alternate version announcing that he was killed resisting arrest, just in case."

"Yes, sir." Banner still sounded dubious.

"Hey, don't worry, be happy. You'll catch Candice's next recital."

"Caroline, sir."

"Right. In the meantime, we'll hook and book this asshole and look like heroes. Hell, if we play this right, I could be bumped up to the A-chief slot." Assistant chief was a higher rank than deputy chief. It was, in fact, only one step below the coveted COP position itself.

"I still say—" Banner began.

Hammond cut him off. "Don't sweat it. You're about to see the master in action, Phil. Just sit back, take notes, and enjoy the show."

Chapter Twenty-five

Wolper was out of breath and sweating hard when he emerged from his Mercury Sable and slammed the door.

"What the hell happened here?"

He addressed the question to two patrolmen standing at the rear entrance of the office building where Robin Cameron worked. They were only two of the patrol officers deployed here. A total of three squad cars were slant-parked nearby, along with the two rescue ambulances Wolper had followed into the lot. Four paramedics were exiting the RAs, carrying their gear into the building. There was also a prisoner transport van with Sheriff's Department markings. The driver wasn't in sight.

Wolper didn't expect to be recognized, since he was outside his territory, driving his personal car, and wearing civilian clothes—button-down shirt and a sport jacket. But one of the cops by the door knew him anyway. "Lieutenant?"

"In the flesh." He nodded to the cop's partner. "Lieutenant Wolper, Newton Area."

"You're a ways off your beat, sir," the first man said.

"I'm off duty, too. I'm about fifteen minutes late for a four-o'clock with Dr. Cameron." It occurred to him that an appointment with a shrink didn't sound too good. "Business meeting," he added.

"All right, sir." The cop sounded skeptical.

Wolper let it drop. "I drive in behind two RAs and see three LAPD squads and a sheriff's van. This have anything to do with Dr. Cameron?"

"Yes, sir."

"Figured as much." He pointed at the van. "One of her patients from County?"

"Not just any patient. It was Justin Gray."

Wolper blew out a long breath. "Is Dr. Cameron . . . ?"

"She's okay. Just shook up. Gray attacked her, knifed one of the transport deputies."

"How bad?"

"We called the RA, but truthfully, I think it's too late."

"And Gray? Please tell me he's not at large."

"I'm afraid so, Lieutenant."

Wolper spent a moment staring at the van. "The minute this gets out, we'll have a media circus. Who called it in?"

"The other deputy—the driver."

"He didn't put it on the radio, did he?" LAPD radios were digital and encrypted, immune from eavesdroppers, but the Sheriff's Department had not yet converted to digital communications. Anyone could listen in on their frequencies.

"He used the radio"—the other cop spoke for the first time—"but he never mentioned Gray. Just called in a four-fifteen and officer-down."

Wolper nodded. "Okay. Look, be careful what you say even on the police bands. I know these high-tech transmissions are supposed to be secure, but watch yourself anyway. Who's running the scene?"

"First officer is Bridges. Inside with his partner."

"He won't be running it for long. Robbery-Homicide's gonna be all over this one."

"Yeah, the WC said it was routed straight to RHD. Also said the brass were plenty interested."

"The brass won't go near this hornet's nest."

"Probably not," the first cop agreed. "Did you want to talk to Dr. Cameron?"

"If she's up to it. You call the other RA for her?"

"We called it, even though she said she didn't want one."

"She's an assault victim. She needs medical attention."

"Well, the medics are in with her now, but I think she's probably okay. She's tougher than she looks."

Wolper nodded, heading through the door. "I noticed."

He went down the hall and stepped inside the waiting room of Robin Cameron's office. One pair of paramedics worked on the deputy sheriff, starting an IV, checking for vitals. Wolper could tell, just by looking, that there would be no signs of life.

Spatter patterns of blood had doused the walls. Wolper had seen enough crime scenes to know that the forensic technicians could use the angle and trajectory of the blood spray to determine the victim's position when he was attacked. In this case, they would conclude that the deputy had been standing with his back to the interior office door. He had been seized from behind, his throat cut, the blood from the severed carotid artery spewing forward, leaving the killer largely untouched. When the blood flow eased, the deputy, expiring, had been lowered to the floor.

The medics slipped the deputy onto a gurney. Wolper took another look at the body. The man had lost his cap and pants, and his shoes had been removed and tossed aside. There was something tragicomic about the corpse lying on the stretcher, wearing only underwear and socks from the waist down. A large urine stain had spread over the man's Jockey shorts; his bladder had released when he died.

Respectfully, Wolper stood aside as the gurney was wheeled out into the hall. The EMTs couldn't call a death in the field, and no lawman present was going to declare a brother officer deceased.

Wolper shifted his attention to the doorway of the main office. Inside, the other two paramedics were arguing with Robin Cameron, seated on the couch. The doctor looked defiant, and the medics looked exhausted. Wolper knew that these guys worked twenty-four-hour shifts, frequently for several days at a stretch, catnapping in the fire station, never seeing their families. They had an average burnout of only eight years. Today was probably a slow day by the standards of this neighborhood. The first and fifteenth of the month were the busiest times, when paychecks and welfare money came in, allowing purchases of booze and drugs, which led to violence. Some medics wore handguns in Rampart and other bad parts of town—a strictly unofficial policy, but one that was overlooked by the higher-ups.

"Under the circumstances, Doctor," one EMT was saying, "we really would like to transport you to County-USC."

"No, thanks. I told you, I don't need a physical."

"Self-diagnosis is never a good idea."

"I like living dangerously."

She was legally within her rights to refuse treatment. As long as a patient was over the age of consent and was reasonably lucid, no one could forcibly impose medical care.

"Just let us check your reflexes, pupil dilation, run an EEG. . . ."

"I'm fine. Really. Sorry you were called out for nothing."

The men, grumbling, passed Wolper on their way out. Wolper hesitated, then entered the office, nodding a hello as he approached the couch.

"You sure about that decision?" he asked.

"Absolutely."

He stopped before her and took a long look at her face, studying the bruises left by the attack. A deep violet contusion on her left temple, and splotches of red on her cheek.

"He hit you in the face."

"A love tap."

"Love taps, plural. More than one."

"He's a very expressive person."

"You need to see a doctor . . . Doctor."

"It's nothing a little Tylenol won't fix."

"Did you lose consciousness?"

She seemed to hesitate. "He knocked me down, that's all. I guess he thought I blacked out."

"But you didn't?"

"No."

"Any confusion, memory loss?"

"I'm acquainted with the symptoms of head trauma, Lieutenant."

Wolper sat down beside her on the couch. "Why'd you say Gray thought you blacked out?"

"Because he claimed he'd never touched me. He must have thought I'd been unconscious and couldn't remember."

"He never touched you?"

"That's what he said."

"Then who beat you up?"

"Apparently it was the one-armed man. As in *The Fugitive*."

"Yeah, I got the reference."

"He seemed to want me to believe he'd saved me from harm. And that he never touched the deputy in the waiting room."

"He said that, too?"

"Claimed the other guy did it. Mr. Cool, Gray called him."

"Sounds like he's projecting. That's the kind of name he'd make up for himself. He probably sees himself as Mr. Cool."

Robin blinked. "That's very perceptive, Lieutenant."

"I may distrust shrinks, but I've picked up some of their lingo. I think I may know why Gray concocted that story."

"Feel free to share with the rest of the class."

"He'd just killed a law officer. That's a first for him. He knows the big-time heat that comes down on a cop killer. It might make him a big man in prison, but in the meantime it can make him a dead man. There is such a thing as street justice. I'm speaking unofficially, of course."

"Of course. So he blamed the killing on someone else?"

"That's my guess."

"In that case, he should have at least wiped the blood off the screwdriver. That was what he used to unbuckle the straps, I guess. And what he used . . . on the deputy."

"You got a good look at it?"

"He held it to my throat." She touched her neck self-consciously. "That's a little more up close and personal than I like to get with my patients."

Wolper frowned. "Doctor, I really think you should let me take you to a hospital. Even if there's no serious physical damage, an event like this can affect you in ways that—" He stopped himself. "I guess I'm not telling you anything new."

"I think I can recognize the signs of post-traumatic stress. If they develop, I'll get help. Right now I'm waiting for a phone call."

"From?"

"Meg. My daughter. I told her to leave our condo, stay with a neighbor. She's supposed to call me. I haven't heard anything. It's got me concerned."

"Why? I don't get it."

"It's a little paranoid, but Gray met her once. And he took my wallet. He'll know where I live."

"Doesn't seem so paranoid to me. Besides, a little paranoia is a good thing when you're a parent."

"That's what I keep telling Meg. I don't think she buys it."

Wolper caught the tremor in her voice. He took her hand. "She'll be okay, Doctor. Our boy's got other things to worry about right now."

"I hope so," she whispered.

Chapter Twenty-six

She should never have opened the door to him.

After the frantic phone call from her mom, Meg should have known something was wrong when someone knocked on her door. But the thing was, nobody could get into the courtyard of the condo building without being buzzed in at the gate. So she assumed—just *assumed*—that whoever was knocking was one of her neighbors. Vaguely she imagined that her mom had called Mrs. Grandy or Mr. Haver to check on her and make sure she left the condo promptly. It ticked her off that Robin wouldn't trust her, when she was getting ready to leave, gathering up her books and stuff so she could do her homework at Mrs. Grandy's.

Peeved, she opened the door without thinking, and he was there.

Not a neighbor. Not anyone who should have been able to get onto the property without authorization.

"Gabe?" she said, the word starting as a statement and lilting into a question.

"Hey, sweetie."

She was so surprised to see him, at first she didn't think to ask how he'd gotten through the gate. "You're not sup-posed to be here."

"Didn't we have this conversation yesterday?"

"I mean it. You can't . . . I mean, we can't . . ."

"Can't keep meeting like this?" He was smiling, trying to be funny, but somehow it wasn't quite coming off.

"You have to go."

"I just got here."

"I think my mom is coming home." In her excitement she forgot that she never called Robin her mom in Gabe's presence.

"Not likely. Your mother's a workaholic, remember?"

"No, something's going on today. She's all freaked about something. I'm not even supposed to be here. I'm supposed to be at a neighbor's. I'm going there now. And you're taking off."

"That's not very friendly, short stuff."

He had never called her by that particular term of endearment before, and she didn't care for it.

"I have to go. You do, too. Okay?"

"Take a ride with me."

"What?"

"Come on, take a ride. It's a nice day."

"Are you crazy? I just told you, my—Robin's on her way back. I can't go riding around with you."

"Sure, you can. Break the rules. Be a bad girl."

"Gabe, I'm sorry, but I'm going to a neighbor's apartment, and then I have to call Robin and find out what's got her so stressed. I'll talk to you later. You can e-mail me—"

"I don't think so."

She lost her patience. Gabe was standing in the doorway, blocking her exit. "Okay, don't e-mail me. Whatever. But I'm going."

"You *are* going. With me."

"I already said—"

"With me," he repeated, and she looked down and saw the gun that had appeared in his hand as if by a magic trick.

Her mind wasn't able to take in the reality of what her eyes saw. "What is this?"

"It's called a kidnapping, Meg. Which is appropriate, seeing as how you're a kid. A stupid, annoying kid."

The words shocked and hurt her almost as badly as the sight of the gun itself.

"What do you want?" she whispered.

"Guess you're not hearing too well today. I want you to take a ride with me. Will you do that? I'd advise you to say yes."

"Yes."

"Good girl. Now here's how we'll do this thing. You'll walk next to me through the courtyard, and you won't do anything dumb or you'll never make it to the front gate. Got it so far?"

"Yes." Her voice was low and far away.

"My car is parked down the street. We walk to it, and you get in on the driver's side. Slide over, with me next to you the whole time. You don't yell or run or fight me or do anything else that will get you killed. All right?"

"All right."

I thought you loved me, she wanted to say. *I thought we were soul mates.*

But she didn't say it, because she knew it would only make him laugh.

She did exactly what he said, trying nothing heroic, because any heroic gesture was sure to get her killed. She kept expecting him to explain, or at least to talk, to say something, but he seemed to have other things on his mind.

Even when the car pulled away from the curb and roared north to Wilshire, he remained silent, lodged behind the wheel, staring straight ahead, his gaze fixed in what soldiers called a thousand-mile stare. He might have been a dead man, or a man in a cataleptic trance. The only thing that proved he was alive and alert was the dull pressure of the gun against her ribs.

It was a handgun. She didn't know what kind—she didn't know anything about guns, had never wanted to know about them. She assumed it was loaded, and she assumed that if she tried to open the car door and throw herself out, it would blast a hole in her heart.

There was no realistic chance of leaping from the car anyway. He had made her fasten her seat belt before starting out. At the time, she had found it almost funny that he would care about her safety. Now she understood that safety had nothing to do with it. He wanted her strapped in so she couldn't escape without unbuckling herself. Jumping out of the car was a nonstarter.

The same held true of all the other maneuvers that ran through her head as the car shot onto the eastbound Santa Monica Freeway, rushing toward the downtown skyline. She imagined herself waiting until the car took an offramp and was idling at a stoplight, then rolling down her window and screaming for help. She imagined waiting until he forced her to get out somewhere, then wrestling the gun away. Or locking him out of the car and driving off, the keys conveniently still in the ignition.

Hopeless plans.

She couldn't outthink him, couldn't outrun him, couldn't do anything except let him take her wherever it was they were going.

She wished she could think of something to say, if only to show him she wasn't afraid, but her mind seemed to have frozen up.

"Guess I was too hard on you back there," Gabe said suddenly, breaking the long silence.

She didn't answer.

"Calling you a kid—that was out of line. I mean, sure, you're young, but that's some quality pussy you've got to offer."

She averted her face, afraid to let him see her sprinkle of tears.

"I've had other young ones like you. I gotta get 'em young and ripe. It's the only way to ensure the ultimate in, you know, fuckability. You're one of the best I've had. You go all-out, every time. You're so goddamned eager to please."

"Shut up," she whispered.

He took the exit for Vermont Avenue, slowing to thirty miles an hour. "I don't know what it is about high school girls these days," he said. "When I was growing up, they weren't like they are now. Girls of your generation— you're fucking Lolitas, all of you. Sex ed might have something to do with it; I don't know. Maybe there's something in the water. Whatever it is, I'm not complaining."

"I hate you." She spoke the words so softly, she didn't think he'd even heard.

"The only downside is that the law makes me a criminal just for doing what comes naturally. Fucking legal code is a hundred years out-of-date. This isn't the Victorian era, for Christ's sake. Girls today, they hit fourteen, fifteen, they aren't virgins. Well, of course, *you* were. I popped your cherry pretty damn good, didn't I, short stuff?"

She ground her jaws together.

"My point is, you were *ready*. Your motor was revving; you were primed. Hell, it would've been cruel *not* to do you. And if somebody was going to tax your ass, who should it be? Some dumb high school jock, or a *man*, an experienced man, who could guide you through it, teach you, ease you along?"

He turned to her, and she saw him smile.

"When you get down to it, I was doing you a favor. Helping you get a good start in life."

"Yeah," she whispered, "you're a saint."

He surprised her by laughing aloud. "Point taken. So I'm not exactly a candidate for humanitarian of the year. But I didn't do you any harm, either."

"Until you kidnapped me."

"That's different. That's business."

"Business? How?"

"Never mind how."

She looked away from him, out the window. She didn't

know this part of town. It was south of where her mom worked, not far from USC, but in an even worse neighborhood. She thought it must be South-Central. The streets were treeless and unpopulated, zoned for industrial use. Warehouses and salvage yards and big rambling buildings that might have been factories passed on both sides of the street. Nearly every building was encircled by a high chain-link fence topped with concertina wire. Graffiti bloomed on fire hydrants, alley walls, even parked cars. In the distance sirens sang out. Hearing them, Meg felt a rush of hope, which quickly faded as the sirens trailed off in another direction.

"They'll catch you," she said softly. "They'll know you did it."

"I don't think so. Nobody can connect me with you. I took all the necessary precautions. Never even told you my real name. No way I'm giving my name to a girl who could get me busted for statutory rape."

"I wouldn't have told anyone."

"I couldn't be sure of that, could I? You might blab to one of your pajama-party girlfriends. I couldn't risk it. Couldn't tell the truth about myself to some airhead cheerleader I was banging."

Airhead cheerleader. The words burned like acid. He chuckled as if he knew it.

"And here we are," he added.

They had arrived at a massive brick-and-stone building that seemed ancient, like some fortress from medieval times. It was vast, taking up most of a city block, its parking lot empty and forlorn. There was no sign over the entrance, and the few small windows had been boarded up. Another one of the ubiquitous security fences surrounded the building and its grounds.

"We can't get in there," Meg said. "It's closed off."

"O ye of little faith."

Gabe—or whatever his real name was—guided the car around to an alley at the side of the building, where a rear gate was secured by a rusty padlock. Gabe pressed the nose of the car against the gate, pushing it inward, straining against the chain that held it closed, until finally the chain snapped and the gate swung wide.

"Crappy security they got here," he said with a laugh.

He drove through and parked by the building.

"I'm getting out now," Gabe said. "I'm taking the keys. You could try locking yourself in the car, but I'll just unlock the door, and then I'll be mad. You could also try screaming for help. Does this look like a neighborhood where screaming for help would prove effective?"

"No," she said.

"You're very observant."

He left the car, walked around to the passenger side, and hustled her out, the gun held loosely in his hand.

"Now what?" she asked.

"We go in. This way."

The gun pointed toward a door in the building's brick wall, a few yards away. She approached it, her shoes crunching on broken glass and dead leaves.

"It's open. Just push."

She did. The door—a heavy door of solid metal—eased open with a groan. Beyond the threshold, there was dim, wavering light and a smell of age and rot. She stood motionless, afraid to go farther.

"Inside."

Her face felt hot, her head all stuffy, as if she'd just come down with the flu. She wasn't sure she could force her legs to move. They felt stiff and numb.

"Go," he ordered, shoving her from behind.

She stepped forward, into air heavy with dust motes. She heard rustlings from distant corners.

A whimper escaped her, and Gabe laughed.

"You said you wanted excitement in your life," he said. "Looks like you got your wish."

Chapter Twenty-seven

Robin checked her wristwatch for the thirtieth time. "Meg should have called by now."

"Whose apartment did you send her to?" Wolper asked.

"Mrs. Grandy. A neighbor in the building. Retired schoolteacher. I see her around all the time, but I don't know her phone number and I couldn't find it in the book. . . ."

"I'll get it for you."

"I told Meg that if Mrs. Grandy wasn't there, she should go to another neighbor, Mr. Haver. He works at home."

"I'll get that number, too."

Wolper took out his cell phone and made a call. While he was talking, Robin dared another look inside the waiting room. The deputy had been taken away, but the misshapen pool of blood remained, thick on the carpet. It troubled her that she could think of the man only as "the deputy." He had delivered Gray to her on many occasions, but she had never looked at his nameplate, never learned his name.

"Okay, Doctor." It was Wolper, handing her a sheet of paper with two phone numbers written on it. "Use my phone," he said. "We'll keep the office line clear for now."

She punched in the first number, praying to hear Meg's voice. But the person who answered was Mrs. Grandy. "No, dear," she said in response to Robin's question. "I haven't seen her."

"Were you out? Did you just get in?"

Mrs. Grandy chuckled. "You know me better than that. With my arthritis and my bad hip, how often do I go out? I've been here all day. Is anything the matter?"

"Everything's fine. Thank you." Her hand was shaking as she entered the second number. Wolper watched in concern.

"Mannie?" she said when Haver answered. "This is Robin." She cut short his reflexive attempt at small talk. "Is Meg there?" She was not. "You haven't seen her?" He had not. He offered to go to her apartment and ring the doorbell. Robin almost said yes, but she couldn't drag another person into this. "No, it's okay, Mannie. Thanks." She hung up and looked at Wolper. "Not there. She's not there."

"Calm down. Call your home phone. Maybe she hasn't even left yet. In the meantime I'll have West LA send a squad car."

She made the call while Wolper talked to a uniformed officer, who got on his radio. The phone in her condo rang four times before the answering machine clicked on. Meg had recorded the message: "Cameron residence. Mother-and-daughter psychiatric consulting services available at an exorbitant fee." Then a beep.

"Meg, if you're there, pick up. Meg? Meg, pick up, please."

No answer. Robin ended the call.

"Patrol unit's on the way," Wolper said. "They have permission to enter the premises?"

"Yes, of course."

"That's what I told them. How long ago did Gray leave?"

"Twenty-five, thirty minutes."

"I doubt that's enough time to get across town."

"It's a straight shot on the freeway."

"The freeway's always jammed at this hour."

"Almost always. Maybe today he got lucky."

"Even if he did, you told Meg to exit the apartment."

"What if she didn't listen?"

"Why wouldn't she?"

"She's always on my case about being overprotective. And I didn't have time to explain what was going on. She may have thought I was being hysterical."

"You don't strike me as the hysterical type."

"Tell that to my daughter. I probably *am* overprotective, honestly. She's always telling me not to worry so much. Maybe she decided to ignore my phone call."

"Do you think she would do that?"

"No. But . . . where *is* she?"

"He hasn't got your daughter, Robin."

She didn't answer. She rose from the couch and paced the office, flicking glances at her wristwatch.

"What's taking so long? Shouldn't they have called in by now?"

"There's about a ten-minute response time," Wolper said.

She went on pacing, her heart beating in counterpoint to the ragged rhythm of her steps.

Her head throbbed. She had told the paramedics she was fine. She had assured Wolper that she hadn't blacked out. She'd lied. She was not fine. She had been struck on the head and had lost consciousness for an indeterminate time period. She was suffering from a headache, intermittent blurred vision, and amnesia—the moments before her injury were a blank. All of these were symptoms of concussion. She could be bleeding intracranially. But she refused to submit to an exam, because an exam would lead to hospitalization, and she could not be hospitalized right now. She couldn't sit still for a CT scan. Not until she knew about Meg.

Her mind went back to the young buzz-cut officers watching her from behind shaded lenses, asking her if she believed that the gang members who attacked her deserved rehabilitation. She'd said everyone deserved a chance. But where to draw the line? She had wanted to help Gray, but maybe she had only helped him to get loose. And now maybe he had Meg.

She could handle anything that affected no one but her. But if Gray had Meg . . . if he killed her . . .

Gray had already murdered a deputy, and now he might be running through his old, familiar MO—the drive to the desert, the slow crawl of hours, then the bullet to the brain. He had done it five times before, and now he could be repeating the same stereotyped behavior pattern, replaying the well-worn tape.

One of the uniformed cops, whose name, she had learned, was Beecher, stepped into the office, rover radio in hand. "A-forty-three's at the residence. They found the front gate jimmied open."

Robin sank onto the couch. "Oh, God."

"Why would he need to force the gate?" Wolper asked. "He took your keys."

"My car keys. Not the house keys. That's a separate set."

Beecher was listening as the dispatcher relayed communications from the West LA unit. Robin heard only screeches and squawks, but apparently the noise was intelligible to the patrol officer. "They've found the door to the unit ajar. They're going in."

She bit back a moan. There was an endless period of silence before the radio crackled again. "The unit is empty. No sign of your daughter, Dr. Cameron."

The words seemed hollow and unreal, like a line of dialogue in a movie.

"Was there a struggle?" she heard herself ask.

Beecher shook his head. "They haven't reported any indications of violence."

"They should talk to the neighbors," Robin said dully. "One of them may have seen something, heard something."

"They will, Doctor. That's standard procedure."

Standard. But there was nothing standard about any of this. She felt her control slipping.

She sank onto the couch, her lower body going numb.

Years ago, on a trip to Oregon, she'd been caught in a snowstorm while driving through the Cascade Mountains, and her tires had lost traction on the icy road. The sickening sense of the road surface sliding out from under her, the car yawing toward the guardrail, the steering wheel useless in her hands . . . that was what she felt now, as her world and her life spun away.

Some kind of barely repressed hysteria hiccuped inside her, threatening to break out in a flood of screams and sobs. She pressed down on it with the full force of her self-control, refusing to fall apart when Meg was in danger and needed her. Later there would be time for helplessness, but not now.

"Dr. Cameron?" Wolper's voice, from far away. "Robin?"

She didn't answer.

Her daughter was gone.

Chapter Twenty-eight

"Inside," Gabe said again, as Meg hesitated on the threshold of the doorway.

When she didn't react, he hustled her through the door, into a large open space lit by narrow windows and skylights high overhead. In the middle of the room were two long conveyor belts, rusted and useless. Crates tied shut with twine were scattered around the dust-caked concrete-floored room like islands in a gray sea. Doorways at the far end of the room hinted at side passages that perhaps branched into a warren of halls and offices, lavatories and lunchrooms, all the places used by the employees who were now only ghosts.

"What kind of place is this?" she breathed.

"Bottling plant. Some soft drink—Dr Pepper, maybe. Shut down in the seventies, around the time this whole part of town was going belly-up. Been stripped of everything valuable."

"How did you know about it?"

"Years ago when I'd just started working patrol, we got a DB call here." He smiled at her incomprehension. "DB— short for dead body."

"Oh."

"Some bum had been squatting in here. OD'd or stroked

out or something. Other vagrants found the body. I remembered it because the dead guy had been here a long time. Seemed like a good place to stash a body."

Is that what I am? Meg wondered. *A body?*

"So you really are a cop," she whispered.

"Real as steel. Were you starting to doubt it?"

"I'd like to think a cop wouldn't . . ."

"Commit the occasional felony? Sweet meat, you got a lot of growing up to do."

"Will I get the chance to do it?"

He didn't answer. She hadn't thought he would.

In silence he led her across the cavernous room to a metal door in the far corner. When he opened it, the feeble daylight from the windows and skylights illuminated a flight of stairs, descending into darkness.

"Go down," Gabe said.

Meg looked at him. "No."

"It's only for a little while." He shifted the gun in his hand, just enough for her to become aware of it. "I need to stash you somewhere."

"You'll kill me down there."

"It's a holding area, that's all." He gestured with the gun. "Now go down."

"Please," Meg said.

"I don't have time to argue. Get the fuck down there. Do it."

There was no pity in his face, no memory of affection.

Heart pounding, she reached out for the metal handrail and made her way down the staircase with Gabe at her back. The treads were steel, and there were no risers, only gaps between the treads that threatened to catch her foot and pitch her forward into blackness.

At the bottom she turned to look at him. He was right behind her, smiling. "Give me your hand," he said.

"My hand?" she said blankly.

He grabbed her left hand, not asking again. Something

glinted in the semidarkness. Handcuffs. He fastened one cuff to her wrist, the other to the handrail at hip level.

"Sit tight," he said. "I'll be back for you. That's a promise."

He mounted the stairs. She reached for him with her free hand. "Please, Gabe . . ."

He laughed, shrugging free of her. "That's not even my name, you dumb bitch."

She watched him climb to the top, becoming a silhouette against the daylight. She expected him to look down, say something more, acknowledge her in some way, but he just closed the door. Darkness slammed down like an anvil.

She hugged the handrail, listening as his footfalls receded into silence.

Alone. She was alone in this place, this basement in a deserted bottling plant.

She rattled her cuffed wrist uselessly against the handrail and tried not to cry. She prided herself on not being a crier, and normally she wasn't, but these circumstances weren't normal, and she decided she could cut herself a break.

She cried because she was alone and scared, and because she would probably die soon, and because Gabe had called her an immature kid and worse things, and because she wanted to be out of here, home and safe, and she wanted her mom.

Not Robin, not anymore.

Her mom.

Chapter Twenty-nine

The offices of the OCB, Operations-Central Bureau, were located in the Central Facilities Building on Sixth Street in downtown LA, a spot conveniently close to Parker Center, LAPD headquarters, where Hammond intended to work someday.

He let his adjutant follow him into his office and shut the door. His uniform hung in the closet, clean and unwrinkled, where Lewinsky had placed it after removing it from Hammond's locker. He took down the hanger.

"Give me the overview," he said, unbuttoning his shirt.

"Gray escaped from custody at Cameron's office in Rampart. He stole her car and fled the scene."

"Armed?"

"He took the dead deputy's service piece."

"Deputy shouldn't have been carrying when the prisoner was offloaded from the felony bus anyway."

"Van," Lewinsky said. "It was a van. And no, he shouldn't have been carrying, but according to his partner, he was."

"Why wasn't Gray in leg irons, handcuffs?"

"Apparently Cameron had insisted on minimal restraints."

"Stupid bitch. He should've offed her. Don't quote me on that."

"No, sir." Lewinsky looked away as Hammond pulled off his pants.

"Any witnesses report which direction Gray was headed in?"

"No, but we caught one break. Because of that carjack attempt yesterday, Cameron's Saab is visibly damaged. It'll be easy to spot."

"Gray will ditch the Saab as soon as possible, if he hasn't already. We got ASTRO flying?"

"Choppers are up."

"Area cars?"

"Alerts have gone out to all patrol units, and of course we've dispatched BOLOs to the sheriff's office and all municipal PDs."

"CHP too? Orange County? Riverside?"

Lewinsky turned as Hammond buttoned up his uniform shirt. "The whole Southland."

Hammond paused in his sartorial duties and stood thinking for a moment.

"We need to put in place a general tactical alert."

He resumed dressing.

"A tac alert?" Lewinsky was bewildered. A general tactical alert was ordinarily reserved for situations in which there was imminent danger of civil unrest.

"You heard what I said. All LAPD divisions on alert. Switch to twelve-and-twelves. We'll have to go through the chief, obviously, but he'll be amenable."

"You expect this guy to start a riot?"

"I expect the department not to get caught with its pants down." He glanced at his bare legs. "So to speak. We need to be prepared for every eventuality. More important, we need to *look* prepared."

"Yes, sir."

"It's called covering your ass, Carl," Hammond said as he pulled on his blue trousers.

"Yes, sir."

"Now where do we expect the son of a bitch to go?"

"I've been on the horn to the RHD dicks who bagged him. They say he might go back to Culver City, his old neighborhood."

"Culver PD get a lookout?"

"Extra squads on the street. Plainclothes guys undercover outside Gray's former residence."

"Former residence." Hammond fastened his tie. Like all police neckties it was the snap-on kind, chosen because in a struggle it could not be used to choke the officer. "What is it, a fucking flophouse?"

"Low-rent apartment building. Courtyard with a pool, circa 1950."

"He won't go back there. He's no genius, but he's not shooting to be the punch line of one of those world's-stupidest-criminal jokes. How about Cameron's office building?"

"Sir?"

"It's within the realm of possibility that the Saab theft was misdirection. Gray may never have left the damn building."

"The car is gone."

"The car could be driven by an accomplice."

"Serial killers usually work alone."

"Except for the twenty-five percent who work in pairs. I want that building thoroughly cleared. Office to office, floor by floor, a clean sweep. Bastard could be hiding in there, figuring it's the last place we'd look."

"Yes, sir."

"You think that's crazy?" Hammond shrugged on his jacket. "It may be. But let me ask you this. Why did Gray leave Cameron alive? He's a stone killer, but he leaves her breathing. Why?"

Lewinsky flexed his brow, a sign of deep thought. "Because she's in on it?" he ventured. "Like, his secret lover or something?"

"Jesus, no. What do you think this is, a movie of the week? Maybe he left her alive because he wanted her to report that he'd taken her car. He wanted us chasing that Saab."

"You think so?"

Hammond sighed, strapping on his equipment belt. "Of course not. The guy is a mope. He can't think that far ahead."

Lewinsky was thoroughly confused. "Then . . . why search Cameron's building?"

"Once again, it's called covering our asses, Carl. Come on, this isn't graduate school. It's the goddamned basics." Hammond holstered his Beretta and secured his side-handle baton. "Who's at the crime scene, anyway?"

"Two or three Rampart units. Watch commander just got there. Oh, and Wolper."

"Wolper?" Hammond glanced up. "Why? It's not even his area."

"I'm not clear on that, sir."

"Hell. I've never liked that son of a bitch. You know he started off as a probationer in South-Central? I was his training officer."

"I know, sir."

"He was all right on the street, but he was always making trouble with admin. Late with his paperwork, sloppy with his logs. Didn't seem to grasp the importance of the managerial side."

"Or the political side," Lewinsky ventured.

"That, too. The man has a tin ear for politics. He's too damn sure of himself—that's the problem. He doesn't think he can learn from anyone else."

"Including his TO?"

"I may have taught him a few things."

"I'm sure you did, sir." Lewinsky cleared his throat. "Forgive me for asking an obvious question."

"I wouldn't expect anything else from you, Carl."

"Yes, well, I was just wondering . . . We've got Rampart searching the office building even though we know Gray's not there. And Culver watching his old digs even though we know he won't go there. And everybody's looking for the Saab, even though he's probably ditched it."

"Right."

"So we're covered. I get it. But the thing is, how do we actually, you know, *find* him?"

"We wait for him to fuck up." Hammond inspected himself in the mirror. "He will. He's a loser. Losers lose. It's all they know how to do."

"Yes, sir," Lewinsky said, not sounding entirely convinced.

Hammond was about to give him a lecture on the virtues of positive thinking when the door opened and Banner, the traffic cop turned publicist, walked in. "New development," he said. "It looks like Gray's got Cameron's daughter. Snatched her out of their condo in Brentwood."

Hammond blew out a long, slow breath.

"They're sure it's him?" Lewinsky asked.

Banner shrugged. "Who else could it be? He got the address off Cameron's DL."

"Shit," Lewinsky said.

Hammond found this observation less than astute, but he didn't pause to comment on it. "I want the condo crime scene routed straight to RHD. We don't need West LA dicks fucking around over there." He looked at Banner. "Gray takes them into the desert, right?"

"That's the MO."

"We need Sheriff's to set up roadblocks on desert roads. Need choppers in the air over the Mojave. If he snatched her this fast, he may not have had time to switch cars, so they need to look for the Saab."

"Guess we don't need the search of the office building after all," Lewinsky said.

"Wrong. Gray could still be using an accomplice. He wasn't actually seen grabbing the girl, was he?"

"No wits so far," Banner said.

"Then we make no assumptions. We cover every angle. I'll make the calls while we're on the road. Let's go."

"Where?"

"Cameron's office. The initial crime scene." He glanced at Banner. "Media on top of this yet?"

"We're still in denial mode."

"That's fine—officially. Unofficially, I wouldn't be un-happy if Channel Four shows up at the Rampart site."

"Another exclusive for Susy Chen?"

"Why not? She always gives us good press."

Lewinsky objected. "I think Rampart's been keeping the location secret. Cameron's still there. They don't want her facing a media circus when she leaves."

"Fuck her. She can handle a few cameras in her face. Crying mother in distress—that's good footage. Am I right, Phil?"

Banner nodded uneasily. "Sure thing, Chief."

"Call Chen. If she goes there, the rest of the news vul-tures will follow. I want coverage."

"Chief," Lewinsky said, "I hope you're balling that woman. Otherwise she's getting a lot of help for free."

"I'm a married man," Hammond snapped, noting dis-tantly that he'd neglected to say *happily married*. "Just call her. We need cameras."

"We'll get 'em," Banner promised.

"Good. Let's move." Hammond straightened his collar. "Nothing's worse than being all dressed up with nowhere to go."

Chapter Thirty

Wolper sat with Robin Cameron while reports came in from West LA. Unit 8-Adam-43 had been joined by a secondary unit, A-41. The condo had been secured as a crime scene. Neighbors were being interviewed.

At some point, the Rampart patrol sergeant who'd arrived at the office informed Wolper that Deputy Chief Hammond was taking command of the investigation. Wolper greeted this news with raised eyebrows. He and the sergeant both knew it was unusual for an administrator—a pogue—to get directly involved in a high-profile, high-risk case. "He must have his reasons," the sergeant said.

Wolper nodded. "That he must."

It was after five o'clock when Hammond made his appearance. He strode into the waiting room, surrounded by Rampart Division patrol officers and his own entourage of driver, adjutant, and press-relations flack. The flack was actually a traffic officer who had been reassigned to Hammond's office by some bureaucratic ruse that Wolper didn't comprehend. The D-chief was a one-man media event. Every time he announced some piddling change of policy or addressed a meeting of the Kiwanis club, the local media knew about it.

Wolper stepped into the room with an extended hand. "Chief."

Hammond ignored the hand. He eyed Wolper's civilian clothes. "Out of uniform, Lieutenant?"

"Off duty, sir."

"And a few miles outside Newton Area," Hammond observed. "Any particular reason you should be here?"

"I know the victim."

"Personal friend?"

"Personal acquaintance."

"She's unhurt, I take it."

"So she tells me."

"You have doubts?"

"I think she got bonked on the head a little harder than she's letting on."

"Then she should be in a hospital. We can't have this woman keeling over when she's in our care. That's not the kind of thing that looks good."

Hammond knew all about looking good, as did the PR flack, who was nodding vigorously.

"I don't think she's in any danger of keeling over," Wolper said. "Anyway, we have bigger issues to deal with. You've heard about her daughter?"

"I've heard, but I don't understand how the hell it happened. As soon as Gray's escape from custody was reported, there should have been a squad car at Cameron's home address."

"She called her daughter immediately and told her to leave the premises."

"Apparently that wasn't good enough," Hammond's adjutant, Lewinsky, put in with a shit-eating smile.

Wolper knew and heartily disliked Lewinsky, a drone whose sycophantic personality and regrettably topical name had given rise to a variety of suck-up jokes. He said nothing.

Hammond shook his head. "What a goddamned mess. How did Gray even know about the girl?"

"As I understand it," Wolper said, "he met her once."

"*Met* her? What is this woman running, a tea party for felons?"

"Sir, if you could keep your voice down . . . She's in the next room."

Hammond grunted. "Fucking mess. Makes me wish I wasn't involved."

"Do you have to be, sir?"

Hammond exchanged a glance with his adjutant, and Wolper could practically hear him saying to Lewinsky, *You see the kind of insubordination and stupidity I have to put up with?*

"It's my bureau. I'm handling it. I asked for the responsibility."

It was true enough that Operations-Central Bureau had jurisdiction. Central, the busiest of the four geographical bureaus of the LAPD, comprised four territorial areas, including Rampart, where Robin Cameron's office was located. Because the crime had occurred on his turf, Hammond, as commanding officer, bore ultimate responsibility for the investigation.

Still, he could have palmed off the job of running the manhunt on the bureau's assistant CO or someone lower in the chain of command. The fact that Hammond was here meant that the deputy chief genuinely wanted to be part of the action. Wolper figured he knew why.

"Has the media got wind of this yet?" he asked innocently.

"Not to my knowledge," the PR man–cum–traffic cop said.

That had to be a lie. It would take a division of Army Rangers to keep Deputy Chief Hammond away from the TV cameras on a case like this.

"So Dr. Cameron is in there?" Hammond said quietly. "Coherent? Lucid? I need to get a statement from her."

"She just found out her kid is missing. I think she's all talked out for the moment."

"We don't exactly have the luxury of time."

"Let me take her downtown, get her settled in an interview room, and then I'll talk to her."

Hammond regarded Wolper with suspicion. "Are you under the impression you have an official role to play in this investigation, Lieutenant?"

"She knows me, sir. She trusts me. She'll be open with me."

Hammond hesitated for a long moment. "Get her downtown; then we'll decide how to handle the interview."

"I really think it's best if I—"

"You know, *I* really think it's best if you follow orders, Lieutenant. Now how about you? Don't *you* think that's best?"

Lewinsky was smirking. Wolper wanted to clock him. "Yes, sir."

"Glad we understand each other." Hammond drifted away to speak with the Rampart patrol personnel.

Lewinsky and Banner lingered. "You're in over your head, Wolper," Lewinsky said, his voice low and nasty. "Go back to running a station house."

Wolper smiled. "Better watch that mouth of yours, Monica. It could get you in trouble someday."

If the adjutant had an answer to that, Wolper didn't hear it. He was already pulling Banner aside.

"What's the story, Phil? Why'd the DC involve himself in a sensitive case like this?"

Banner frowned. "Fuck if I know. It was against my recommendations. But the chief's a difficult man to dissuade."

"Guess that doesn't make your job any easier."

"Goddamn right." He forced a shrug. "Hell, it'll work out."

"If it doesn't, you can always spin it so it did."

Banner looked past him. "Some things," he said softly, "you just can't spin."

Wolper followed Banner's gaze. "I hear that."

Through the office doorway, Robin Cameron was visible, seated on the sofa in a tight, huddled ball of pain.

Chapter Thirty-one

Gray knew he had to ditch the Saab and the stolen clothes if he wanted to keep a low profile. And right now, going lo-pro was the only way to go. He was a big dog, a major violator, armed and dangerous, and the local lawmen would be getting their shit hot over him in a major way. Every swinging dick in a blue uniform would be gunning for his ass.

In the mid-Wilshire district he found a thrift shop, a ratty little place that looked like it had been going out of business for the past twenty years. He browsed the store, picking out tan pants, a brown shirt, and a denim jacket that fit him, paying with cash he'd taken from the doc's purse. The local news was airing on a black-and-white TV set behind the counter, but there was no mention of his escape.

In an alley he changed clothes, discarding the deputy's pants and the doc's jacket in a trash bin, along with his yellow jumpsuit.

So far, so good. He'd gotten his mojo back. Now for a new beast to thrash around in.

He cruised the streets, staying within the speed limit, stopping at yellow lights. The last thing he needed was a traffic citation. Ordinarily he wouldn't give a shit about the patrol fairies who worked traffic detail, doing drunk stops and cutting tickets, but today he had to play it smart.

Not far from the thrift shop, he found a parking garage, where he abandoned the Saab in favor of a Firebird owned by some weak motherfucker who was stupid enough to leave the passenger door unlocked. The car was an old bucket, nothing special, but that was okay, because the newer ones were harder to steal.

He slipped into the car and checked to see if the owner had left the keys under the floor mat or behind the visor. No such luck. Didn't matter. It was all good.

He shoved the two front seats farther back—whoever drove this dune buggy was a midget—then slid into the passenger seat and braced his shoes against the driver's door. He wrested the steering wheel toward him as hard as possible and heard the crack of the steering lock.

Back in the driver's seat, he used his screwdriver to pry off the plastic cowling around the ignition keyhole. Inside the exposed hole were a half dozen multicolored wires. He pressed them together at random. The battery and ignition feeds connected, turning on the dashboard ignition lights. He touched the remaining wires to the two feeds until the engine turned over, then put the Firebird in gear and rolled.

In the glove compartment he found the parking stub. Nice of the dude to leave it for him. Gray paid the fee on his way out. The attendant never even looked at him. Real good security they had here.

The car had 92,000 miles on the odometer, but it handled fine, and nobody would be looking for him behind the wheel of a Firebird. There was only a tape player, not a CD deck, but the owner's taste in tunes was a lot better than Dr. Robin's. The cassette in the slot was Eminem. Gray cranked the volume.

He motored aimlessly, favoring side streets, watching the parked cars. On the outskirts of Inglewood he caught sight of another Firebird, blue like the one he'd boosted. The car sat at a curb in a neighborhood so empty of life that it might have been the set of one of those post-Armageddon movies where people were always getting into brawls over the last drum of gasoline or the last tin of pork 'n' beans. Gray parked behind the other car and got out. Using the screwdriver, he quickly swapped plates, then drove off, whistling.

Now even if the stolen Firebird was linked to him, the cops would be on the lookout for a car with a different license number. And if some patrol faggots happened to give the car he was driving the evil eye, the plates would run clean.

He'd got his swerve on, all right. He was staying cool, handling everything nice and smooth.

Now he needed to quarterback his next moves.

First things first. He needed more benjamins. There wasn't much cash in the doc's wallet, and he'd already spent some of it. He couldn't use her plastic—too easy to trace—so he'd have to jack some asshole at an ATM. Once he got paid, find a crib.

After that . . . well, shit, he'd been in stir a year. Had himself a major love jones. It was time to knock off a piece of ass. Find himself a booty house or some boulevard gash and do some serious pipe cleaning.

Wouldn't hurt to change his appearance, too. Dye his hair or shave himself bald or maybe grow one of those pussy goatees. Wear long-sleeved shirts to cover the tats on his arms.

Then lay low for a few days before beating feet out of town and starting over again in Seattle or Las Vegas—someplace big and growing, where a new arrival wouldn't stand out.

One thing was for goddamned certain: He wasn't going back to the joint. He was out, and he would stay out. Play it right, and he could keep going for years, moving from town to town, state to state. Before he was through, this whole country was gonna bow down to him.

By now it was nearly six o'clock. His escape must be all over the news. He ejected the Eminem cassette and dialed the radio to KFWB.

He was the top story. "I'm the man!" he yelled.

And they used his whole name, Justin Hanover Gray. He loved that. Three names, like fucking royalty. That was how the news reports always referred to him. He wished they'd given him a nickname, some kick-ass moniker like they gave that Ramirez guy—the Night Stalker, they called him. But he guessed they didn't do that shit no more. There'd been so goddamn many serial killers, all the good names had been taken. Maybe if he'd done something more creative with his girls—carved them up or something—he might've gotten a nickname. The LA Butcher. The Death Dealer. The Bitch Snuffer.

"Bitch Snuffer." He laughed aloud at that one. He was feeling very damn good.

Then he heard the details of the report, and his warm glow faded.

They were saying he'd attacked a psychiatrist who was working with him. That he'd killed a deputy. And that he had kidnapped the psychiatrist's teenage daughter.

Meg? They thought he had *Meg*?

Even the boys in blue couldn't get their facts that fucked up. It had to be some kind of game they were playing, some way to mess with his head. He couldn't see the point, but one thing was for sure—the doc was part of it. Her and the cops were spreading a bunch of bullshit about him, making him out to be a cop killer, which he wasn't, and a kidnapper, which he also wasn't—at least, not this time.

"Doc Robin's lying," he whispered. "Fuckin' *lying* about me."

The report was rebroadcast as he kept driving. He flipped to other stations, but the story never varied.

He was majorly vexed. Here he'd been feeling so fine, and then this shit had to come on the radio and harsh his mellow. Now he really wished he'd sliced her when he had the opportunity.

Here he'd gone out of his way to be civilized, to be a fucking gentleman, and she goes and starts screwing with him, making up shit. He didn't mind sucking heat for stuff he'd done, but he'd be goddamned if he had to take the rap for stuff he had nothing to do with.

"Motherfucker," he said. He repeated the word every few seconds, feeling angrier each time.

What he needed was a drink. He stopped at a liquor store and bought a six-pack of Coronas, cracked a brew, and drove on, thinking about Dr. Robin Cameron and her bitch daughter and what he'd like to do to them both.

Chapter Thirty-two

Two hours.

Robin sat in an interview room at Parker Center, the LAPD downtown headquarters, checking her watch and trying to understand how two hours could have passed since she'd ridden here in the backseat of a patrol car.

Time seemed to have become disjointed in some unaccountable way. At some moments she felt she'd been sitting for a lifetime in this uncomfortable straight-back chair, facing the mirror that obviously served as the window of an observation room next door. At other moments she had the impression that she'd just taken her seat, and no time whatsoever had passed.

The ticking hand of her wristwatch was her only contact with objective reality, and it told her that the time was seven-fifteen. She'd left her office 120 minutes ago. And Meg had been missing for roughly an hour before that.

One thought sustained her: Gray didn't kill them right away. He let his victims live for a while—a few hours—before he took their lives. And in all the previous cases there had never been any indication of rape or torture. That was something, anyway. Something to hold on to.

She wasn't sure how long she had sat unmoving on the sofa in her office, after learning that Meg was gone. What she remembered was Lieutenant Wolper's voice finally reaching her after what must have been many attempts.

"Dr. Cameron?"

"Yes," she'd said. "Yes, I understand."

She wasn't sure what she understood. Her own name, maybe.

"Doctor, we're going to need a detailed statement."

"I've already gone over what happened."

"We'll need you to go over it again."

"Why? How does that accomplish anything? How does it help Meg?"

"Any little fact or observation might be significant. Do you feel up to going to Parker Center?"

"I can go there." She could do whatever she had to do.

"Okay, I'll arrange it."

She stopped him as he started to walk away. "If your son were missing, you'd do everything to find him, wouldn't you? Everything possible."

"Of course."

"That's how I want you to treat this case. As if it were your son."

"I will. We all will."

Leaving the office building had been a nightmare—more accurately, a fragment of the ongoing nightmare her life had become. A crowd of TV and radio people had gathered in the parking lot. She kept her face down as Wolper and two uniformed officers escorted her past cameras and microphones. Questions were shouted. People were asking, How did she *feel*? She wanted to scream at them to shut up. She wanted to smash the camera lenses that were making her private tragedy into a show.

At Parker Center she had waited in this interview room, running her hands over the steel eyebolt secured to the scarred wooden table. The eyebolt, she supposed, was used for handcuffing prisoners. That was what she was—a prisoner, held captive by Justin Gray, her future dependent on the unpredictable workings of his mind.

When Wolper finally entered, carrying a portable tape recorder and a Styrofoam cup of water for her, he wore the tired, bemused look of a man who had won a bureaucratic battle. She imagined he'd had to fight to stay on the investigation. The case was a big one. A lot of people would want to be in on it. And Wolper was out of his territory and off duty, to boot. Still, he was the one who interviewed her. There probably were other people watching from behind the mirror, maybe even videotaping the session through the one-way glass, but she didn't care.

Wolper turned on the tape recorder and recited the date and time. He had her give her name, then led her gently through her session with Gray, the shutdown of the MBI gear, then the sudden movement in the shadows. She glossed over her period of unconsciousness, still afraid she would be sent to the hospital if anyone found out about that.

"When did Gray kill Deputy Rivers?" Wolper asked.

Rivers. So that was the man's name. "After he knocked me down."

"You didn't shout for help, alert him somehow?"

She compromised with the truth. "I was woozy, disoriented. It all happened very fast."

"Did you see him kill the deputy?"

"No, I was . . . stunned."

"When he returned to you, was he wearing the deputy's pants over his jumpsuit?"

"Yes."

"If he had time to change, you must've been woozy for a couple of minutes."

Guilt made her impatient. "I wasn't timing it with a stopwatch," she snapped.

"All right." He let it go. "So Gray came back to take your jacket."

"Yes."

"And your wallet and car keys."

"Yes."

"But he didn't hurt you."

"He threatened me. But no, he didn't do anything."

"Kind of weird, isn't it? I mean, he's just murdered Deputy Rivers in cold blood. Then he comes back into the office and treats you with kid gloves."

"If that's how you describe having a screwdriver held to your throat."

"My point is, he could have killed you. He didn't."

"So?"

"So maybe this therapy of yours has actually had some effect."

Oddly, this particular thought had never occurred to her.

"He killed the deputy," she said slowly, "and he's abducted Meg."

"He killed the deputy because he had to. It was kill or be killed. As for your daughter, we don't know what he's thinking or what he'll do. If he let you live, it could mean he's having second thoughts about killing. It could mean he'll hesitate before hurting Meg."

"I'd like to believe that."

"Did you feel you were making progress with him?"

"I thought so, but he wasn't exactly the type to share his feelings."

"Hostile?"

"Sarcastic. Manipulative. Not as hostile as . . ." *As Brand,* she nearly said. But it wouldn't be appropriate to discuss Brand's treatment here, especially if other cops were listening on the other side of the mirror.

Still, the thought lingered. Brand . . .

"Robin?" Wolper was watching her. "You okay?"

She shook off whatever idea had half formed in her mind. "I've gone over this enough," she said.

"Yeah, I think you have."

"So what do we do now?" she whispered.

"We wait," Wolper said.

He had been right about that. They sat together for a while, bound by awkward silence, until he found an excuse to leave. Then she'd been alone. From beyond the closed

door of the interview room came sounds of activity—footsteps, ringing phones, shouts, the slamming of doors and the
sizzle of radios. She registered these noises distantly, like
the confused memories of a dream.

Wolper returned twice with updates. The LAPD was
working with the Sheriff's Department to set up roadblocks
on desert roads near the previous crime scenes. All local
law-enforcement agencies had been alerted to look for the
Saab, for Gray, and for Meg. Hammond had gone public
with an official statement on the escape and the abduction,
though without mentioning Robin or Meg by name. Interviews of neighbors at the condo building had turned up
nothing, and no clues had been found at her home—no indication of when or how Meg had been kidnapped or when
she'd been taken.

There was nothing for Robin to do. But she couldn't just
sit here. The enforced inactivity would make her crazy.

She fished her cell phone out of her purse and called Mrs.
Grandy.

"Oh, dear, I've been talking to the police," the woman
said after Robin identified herself. "Is Meg . . .? Has something happened?"

"She's missing. She's been abducted."

"Oh, dear, dear . . ."

"You didn't see anything, I take it?" Robin knew Mrs.
Grandy spent a good deal of her time sitting by the window,
and she missed little of what went on in the courtyard below.

"Not a thing, I'm so sorry. I wasn't feeling well today,
and I was lying down for most of the day. That's what I told
the officers."

Robin had figured as much. There was no reason that
she would be able to obtain information the police had
overlooked. "Well, I just wanted to ask. If you remember
anything—"

"I wish I could help, dear. Has your husband been told
yet?"

Dan. Robin had forgotten about him. She felt a pang of guilt. "No. I'd better let him know."

"Is he still in town?"

"Still? He hasn't been in LA in months. He lives in Santa Barbara."

"Wasn't he here yesterday?"

Robin blinked. "Well, no. Not that I know of. What makes you say that?"

"I just assumed that's who Meg was with."

"When?"

"Yesterday afternoon."

"You're saying someone was with Meg yesterday?"

"Why, yes. A man came to visit. Nicely dressed, jacket and tie. I've never met your husband, of course, but I thought it must be him."

"So it wasn't a high school student? One of Meg's friends?"

"Oh, certainly not. This man was about forty, I'd say. Wasn't it your husband?"

"I don't think so. Did you get a look at him?"

"My eyes aren't what they used to be. He had dark hair. I noticed that much. I think he was tall. Taller than Meg, when they stood together in the doorway. And she's getting to be quite tall for her age."

Dan was blond and not very tall. It didn't sound like him. "Did you see anything else?"

"Not really. Meg let him in. They seemed to know each other. They were talking. I didn't see him leave. I take my tea in the afternoon, you know, so I may have been in the kitchen. . . ."

"Okay, Mrs. Grandy. Thanks."

"Should I have told this to the police? I didn't think—"

"No, I'll take care of it. The police may want to talk to you again. Thanks very much."

Robin ended the call and sat unmoving for a minute.

Meg had received a visitor yesterday afternoon. A tall man with dark hair, a man of about forty in a jacket and tie.

What the hell was that all about?

She didn't know. She couldn't think. Maybe it was Dan, making contact on the sly, and Mrs. Grandy had gotten the details wrong. But why would Meg neglect to mention a visit from her father? The two of them weren't close. It made no sense.

She could call Dan, tell him what had happened, feel him out. . . .

No, not yet. There was another call to make first.

She speed-dialed her home number. A man's voice answered. "Officer Pierce."

"This is Robin Cameron. It's my house you're in."

"Yes, ma'am?"

"I wonder if I could speak to whoever's in charge."

"The supervising detectives from RHD just got here. They're still being briefed by the first officer."

"Is there somebody, uh, working the scene? Gathering evidence?"

"You mean SID?"

She thought he'd said Sid. "If that's his name . . ."

"No, I mean SID." He spelled it out. "Scientific Investigation Division. The forensics guys. They're bagging and tagging."

"May I talk to one of them?"

"One moment." There was a pause, some faint conversation, then a new man's voice on the phone. "Dr. Cameron? This is Criminalist Gaines."

She was glad he knew she was a doctor. It might help him take her more seriously.

She reported what Mrs. Grandy had said. "I know we're all working on the assumption that Justin Gray took my daughter. And that's probably what happened. But . . ."

"You think this other man might have something to do with it?"

"It's possible."

"That's interesting," Gaines said. He pronounced the words slowly, as if tasting them.

"Is it?"

"There's no sign of forced entry. From what we can tell, your daughter let in the assailant voluntarily."

"I thought the security gate was disabled."

"It was, but there was no damage to the door of the unit."

"She wouldn't have opened up for Justin Gray. She'd met him. She knows what he looks like."

"Well, of course, she might have opened without looking through the peephole. Especially if she assumed that only a neighbor could get to the door without being buzzed in at the gate."

"Or this other man might have come back. If he visited her yesterday, why not today?"

"Are you sure it wasn't your ex-husband?"

"The description didn't match. And I don't think it's in character for Dan to do anything like this, or for Meg to see him behind my back."

Gaines grunted, a dubious noise suggesting that human character was not so predictable. "We'll have to check out your ex anyway."

"Do that. He needs to know what happened. But there's something else that occurred to me—another thing we could look into."

"I'm listening."

"You could read her diary." Robin felt cheap and low for suggesting it, but she couldn't worry about Meg's privacy now. "She keeps it in her room. In her bureau. Top drawer, I think."

"We haven't been in there yet."

"I think you'd better find it. If she was . . . involved in anything secretive, she might have mentioned it there."

"I'll do that, Doctor. And I'll have someone contact your ex-husband too. We've got your address book here. His number is in it, I assume."

"Yes. Let me give you a number where I can be reached."

"That's not necessary. You have caller ID. I already jotted down the number you're calling from. It's your cell phone."

"How'd you know that?"

"I had Officer Pierce check it against your phone records. You see, I had to be sure I was really talking to Robin Cameron, not a reporter."

Gaines was thorough. Robin was glad.

"Once I've looked at the diary," he said, "I'll get back to you."

He clicked off. She exhaled a long breath, relieved that he had listened and not merely brushed her off as a hysterical civilian.

There might be nothing in Meg's diary. But she had to be sure.

It was possible—just barely possible—that Gray didn't have Meg, after all. In which case the roadblocks in the desert, the alerts issued for a man and a girl together in a stolen Saab, and most of the other measures already taken would be ineffective. Gray wouldn't be replaying his MO, at least not yet, and not with Meg.

Then what *would* he be doing? Where would he go?

And who had taken her daughter?

Chapter Thirty-three

The sun was dropping lower, flooding Brand's bungalow with hot orange light. He sat in his armchair in the living room, eyes unfocused, staring into the glare.

He was fucked.

That was the long and short of it. He had turned over the situation in his mind, trying to determine exactly where he stood, and this was his conclusion.

Things could have worked out differently. If Cameron had died today . . .

But she hadn't. And now everything had come apart at the seams.

Idly he noticed that the TV's remote control was still in his hand. He'd been holding it ever since he clicked on the local news and watched the story develop. Attack on a psychiatrist, unnamed in the newscast. Abduction of the psychiatrist's daughter—her photo shown but name withheld. Serial killer on the loose. Deputy sheriff declared dead on arrival at the hospital ER. Huge dragnet being coordinated among municipal and county law-enforcement departments. Updates as they become available. Stay with Eyewitness News. . . .

He hadn't stayed with them. He had clicked off the TV

and stared at nothing while the day dragged toward night-fall.

Seriously fucked. That was pretty much all there was to say.

The phone rang. He let his gaze slide toward it. To answer, he would have to leave the chair and cross the room, a small room but one that now seemed immense, requiring a journey of heroic scope. He would let the answering machine get it. But after seven rings, he remembered that the machine was broken. Just another thing around the house he'd been meaning to fix.

On the tenth ring he roused himself and shambled across the room, blinking at the harsh, lurid light. He fumbled the handset off the cradle. "Yeah," he said.

"Where the fuck were you?" A familiar voice, one he didn't want to hear.

"Nowhere."

"You drunk?"

"Wish I was." He hadn't touched alcohol or food all day. "What the hell do you want?"

"Things have been clarified."

"What things?"

"Cameron doesn't know anything. We don't need the daughter anymore."

Brand frowned. "What do you mean, you don't need her?"

"You've got a job to do."

It took a moment for the words to make sense. "Me? No way. No motherfucking way."

"It's not like you've got a choice, Al."

His heart was beating fast, his grip on the phone suddenly unsteady. "I'm not killing any kid."

"She's in the boiler room of an old bottling works in South-Central. You can get there in twenty minutes."

"No *way.*"

"One shot to the head. Or the heart, your pick. She won't feel a thing."

"Why the fuck don't *you* do it?"

"I'm a little busy right now. The job falls to you. You're elected."

"I'm not doing the kid."

"You've got no choice, Al."

"Stop calling me Al like we're friends. I'm not doing any damn fourteen-year-old girl."

"She's fifteen. This is LA, the city of angels. Fifteen-year-olds die every day."

"Suck my dick. I'm not doing it."

He almost hung up, but the voice on the phone was still speaking, exerting a hold that was almost hypnotic.

"If you won't, I'll find someone else who will. The kid will be just as dead, and you'll have missed your chance to prove yourself."

"Just leave me out of it, God damn it."

A pause. "There's still the problem of Cameron herself."

Brand was confused. "You said she doesn't know anything."

"Not about this afternoon." The words came slowly, as if addressed to a child. "She still knows what you told her yesterday."

"Right, right." This was obvious. He should have remembered. Wasn't thinking clearly.

"You need to prove your loyalty, Al."

"I'm not listening to this."

"Look"—the voice was reasonable now, almost gentle— "I can understand not wanting to do the kid. I get it. No hard feelings about that. But Robin Cameron's all grown up. She's plenty old enough to die."

Brand shook his head slowly. "Shit."

"She's at Parker Center right now. My advice is to watch the parking exit. She has to leave eventually. When she does, I'll send you an SOS on your pager."

"Fuck you." His words were barely audible.

"Think about it, Al. You could do yourself a world of good if you play this right."

Silence, then a dial tone. Brand hung up, his hand shaking. He thought about the scotch in the kitchen cabinet. He thought about calling Evelyn, having her drop by for another roll on the carpet.

Instead, he threw on a windbreaker, holstered his off-duty gun, and left the house, heading for Parker Center.

Chapter Thirty-four

The door to the interview room opened. Robin looked up as Wolper came in.

"What's this about your neighbor?" he asked before she could speak.

His face was grim. She tried to deflect his irritation with a smile. "News travels fast."

"She saw some guy yesterday. Some guy with Meg?"

"Apparently."

"And when were you planning to let me in on this?"

"As soon as possible. I called—"

"I know who you called. You talked to a SID technician. Guess you didn't feel like going through channels, is that it?"

Channels. Her daughter was missing, and he was talking about channels. "What I felt like," she snapped, "was getting Meg back. I assume that's how you feel, too."

Wolper looked away. "I just wish you'd worked with me, gone through me."

"Why?"

"We can't have the investigation ranging all over the place. We need centralized command and control."

"This isn't an academic exercise. It's Meg's life."

"I understand that—"

"I did the first thing I could think of. Maybe I wasn't thinking clearly. Can you blame me?"

He sighed. "No. No, I can't." He sat opposite her. "You think this mystery man is a legitimate lead?"

"I don't know."

"It would be a hell of a coincidence, this guy taking Meg at the exact same time Gray makes his escape."

"I know. But coincidences happen."

"Not often."

"My daughter doesn't get kidnapped often, either."

"Fair enough, Doctor." He looked at her. "So what else is on your mind?"

"What do you mean?"

"There's something you want to talk about. I know the look. I've done enough interviews to know when somebody has something to say."

She nodded. "I've been thinking . . . suppose Gray doesn't have Meg. Then he won't be running to the desert or doing any of the other things we assumed."

"So what *would* he do?"

"That's the question. He's out on the street. Free again after twelve months. He's in a state somewhere between panic and exhilaration. He's gotten loose, but the whole city will be looking for him. He can hide anywhere—but he may not be safe. He's a free man and a hunted animal."

"Okay."

"So how does he feel?"

"Do we care?"

"We do if it helps tell us what action he might take."

"Granted. How *does* he feel?"

"Disoriented. Confused. Like he's riding a roller coaster—scared and thrilled at the same time. It's all happening so fast. He needs . . . he needs to slow it down, sort things out, clear his head. He needs to go someplace safe."

"No place is safe," Wolper said. "Not for him."

"Someplace that *feels* safe. Someplace he's familiar with."

"His old neighborhood? He lived in Culver City. Units are patrolling there."

"That's not it. He's too smart to go to his old address. Anyway, have you seen photos of his apartment? It was empty, almost unfurnished. No keepsakes, no pictures on the walls, nothing in the fridge. It wasn't home to him. It was just a place to crash."

"Then what *was* home?"

"His van, maybe."

"Impounded for evidence. He might boost another one."

She stood, paced. "No. I'm looking at this wrong. It's not home he wants. Home was a nightmare to him. It was the scene of abuse, torture. He never had a home. After the kind of adolescence he went through, he wouldn't want one."

"I'm crying for him."

"You don't understand. I'm not trying to feel for him. I'm trying to feel *with* him. To feel the way he feels right now . . . Whenever his father hurt him, he would leave home. He wasn't running away. He just needed space, distance."

"Where would he go?"

"As a kid, he gravitated toward seedy, crowded, urban areas."

"That covers pretty much all of LA."

"I mean really seedy, like a red-light district. He would hang out in pool halls, video arcades, tattoo parlors." She fixed her stare on Wolper. "Tattoos."

"What about them?"

"He started getting tattoos when he was a teenager. Later he moved on to body piercing and scarification. He likes to punish himself. He takes pleasure in having his skin pricked and bruised."

"All right, so—"

"He got some of his tattoos after he moved to LA. He even mentioned the place in today's session. He said the name. . . ."

"Robin, even if you remember the name, I doubt he's going into any tat parlor today."

"Wild Ink," she said. "That was it. The guy who applied the tattoos was Ernesto. Ernesto at Wild Ink. That's what he said."

"Okay. But—"

"I know, I know, he won't go there now. I understand that. But you're missing the point. That's the area where we should be looking. That's the neighborhood. That's his zone of comfort. It's where he feels safe."

"Unless he has Meg. Then he'll need to take her somewhere."

"Yes, probably. But if he doesn't have her . . ."

"Then finding him won't help us find her."

"It will narrow down the possibilities. Help us focus in the right direction. That's got to be worth something."

Wolper nodded slowly. "Give me a minute," he said, rising from the table. He left again. Robin wondered if he was looking up the address of Wild Ink or arranging for a psychiatric consult. He might think she had lost her mind. He could even be right. Then he was back.

"It's on Hollywood Boulevard, east of Highland. But there's no way he'll go there. He can't go walking the boulevard. A wanted man isn't going to expose himself to those crowds."

"You never know. It's irrational, but if he's motivated by old fears, he may revert to old patterns of behavior."

"I can have Hollywood Division keep an eye out—"

She shook her head. "We need to go there."

"Robin, I had to call in a few favors to handle this interview."

"I gathered as much. So what?"

"I have no official involvement in this case."

"Then you won't be breaking any rules by taking me to Hollywood."

"If Gray is there, it's the last place you ought to be."

"If he's there, it's where I *have* to be."

He studied her, thinking. "How sure are you of this?"

"I don't know. There's a chance I'm right. I can't compute the odds."

"It's a gut feeling. A hunch. Intuition. Right?"

"You could say that."

He seemed relieved to have pigeonholed the problem in a convenient category. "Then you can call my ex-wife about it. I'm not in the market for hunches."

He started to walk out the door. Robin grabbed his arm. "If you'd unbend for a minute, have an open mind . . ."

"An open mind is an empty mind."

Her patience had frayed. "You're very damn complacent, you know that?"

"Now you're actually starting to *sound* like my ex."

"I'm starting to relate to her. Look, we have to do something—"

"Chasing mirages isn't doing something. It's wasting time."

"You promised me you'd do everything possible."

"That doesn't include wild-goose chases after a red herring. Excuse the mixed metaphor."

She released his arm and picked up her phone. "All right, if you won't take me, I'll call a cab and go by myself."

"That's also not a good idea."

"Why not? Gray's not going to be there anyway. You told me so."

"Gray or no Gray, it's a dangerous neighborhood."

"Not as dangerous as the one you sent me into yesterday afternoon."

He looked embarrassed. "Yeah, well . . . I didn't think you'd have the stones to actually go."

"Then I guess you really don't have much intuition, do you?" She took a step past him. "Now I'm getting out of here—unless you plan to place me under arrest."

Wolper spread his hands. "All right."

"You're arresting me?"

"I'm driving you to Hollywood. Come on, Doctor."

Chapter Thirty-five

Hammond stood under the glare of portable arc lamps at the entrance to a mid-Wilshire parking garage, facing a bank of microphones from every local radio and TV news operation. Reporters stretched before him in a semicircle of faces and lenses. He imagined that he could see his reflection in each lens, and he wished again that he were wearing his dress blues.

Behind him was Captain Turkle, commanding officer of the Wilshire Area station, a man who plainly did not enjoy being upstaged. Hammond couldn't blame him. Turkle's people had done the work and made the connections, and now the deputy chief had swooped in to steal the glory. Life was unfair sometimes. But Hammond didn't feel too bad about it. He looked a lot better on camera than Turkle. He was better able to represent the department. And it was the department that mattered, not anybody's personal ambitions.

Yeah, right.

"The Saab was recovered at seven-thirty this evening," he was saying in a smooth, measured cadence. "A security guard at this garage was making his rounds when he saw the vehicle parked in a reserved space. He recognized the car and its license plate number from media reports. Because there was a possibility that the suspect was still in the garage, the building was immediately sealed off. LAPD's D Platoon—our SWAT unit—then executed a floor-by-floor search and determined that the garage was clear.

"Since the fugitive had abandoned the car at this location, he most likely obtained another vehicle from the same garage. A Pontiac Firebird had been reported stolen here earlier tonight. We believe it to be entirely possible that this Firebird was taken by the fugitive, Justin Hanover Gray. The vehicle is a 1995 model, blue . . ."

He recited the plate number, then gave out the number of the telephone tip line and thanked the public for their cooperation. Thanking the public was something you could never do often enough. Joe Six-pack, lounging on his sofa with a tub of microwaved popcorn in his lap, just loved to picture himself as part of the heroic fight against crime.

When Hammond was sure he had covered every fact and squeezed every possible advantage from this update, he magnanimously surrendered the spotlight to Captain Turkle, "who may have a few remarks to add."

Turkle, of course, had nothing to add and was reduced to reiterating Hammond's announcement and spouting vague generalities about law enforcement. The impression was left that Hammond was the man in command of the facts while Turkle was an empty suit hogging airtime. When the questions began, all of them were directed at Hammond, leaving Turkle to sulk in the background. It was beautiful.

"How confident are you in your ability to locate Gray?" Susy Chen asked. He caught her fleeting smile when their eyes met, maybe as a tacit recognition of the softball question she'd just pitched.

He knew that everybody thought he was fucking her. He wasn't. Theirs was a relationship of mutual convenience. He needed a reliable media conduit. She needed a reliable source.

"I have complete confidence in the professionalism and thoroughness of the Los Angeles Police Department," he said. "We will find the fugitive. He can run, but we'll hunt him down. He can hide, but we'll sniff him out."

There was a sound bite for the late local news.

"What precautions should the public be taking?" That was Henderson from the Fox affiliate. Hammond wondered if the man was even aware of the absurdity of the question. In a typical twenty-four-hour period there were five or six homicides in Los Angeles County. Hundreds of killers, thousands of them, were at large in the city and its environs at all times. Did the escape of one highly publicized bad guy change the odds that much?

Obviously he couldn't say any of that. "The public is advised to be alert and calm," he answered, the words coming by rote. "No citizen should take any action to approach or apprehend the suspect. Anyone with any information as to the whereabouts of Justin Hanover Gray is urged to call . . ."

He took a couple more questions and dismissed the reporters with the air of a man whose time was too valuable to waste.

Away from the media, he conferred with Lewinsky and Banner. "How'd I do?"

"Home run," Lewinsky offered.

That was predictable. He turned to Banner for a less obsequious response.

"You did good," Banner said. "The 'run and hide' line worked. They'll all use that. Some of them may lead with it."

"If I was so great, why do you look like you just buried your best friend?"

"I'm still not sold on this, Chief. You're doing great—*if* you find Gray—*and* if he doesn't commit some major mayhem in the meantime. But if the guy proves elusive . . ."

"He won't. As I said before, Gray's a mope. He hasn't got the brains to stay lost for long."

"Boosting another car showed some brains. He was a marked man in that Saab."

"Now he's a marked man in the Firebird."

"Unless he's already ditched it for a new ride."

"Phil, you're a pessimist. Have a little faith. I know what I'm doing. I will get Justin Gray." He turned to Lewinsky. "What's the latest on the manhunt?"

"We've got sheriff's choppers over the Mojave using infrared tracking gear. Foot patrols of deputies are watching desert locations with night-vision scopes. The sheriff is talking about bringing in the National Guard if Gray isn't found by morning."

"The National Guard? What for?"

"Searching the back roads for the girl's body."

"Won't be necessary. We'll have Gray in custody before then. He'll tell us where he left the girl. Unless," he added quickly, "we recover her with him, alive and unharmed."

"What are the odds of that?" Banner asked, looking troubled.

Hammond shrugged. "I don't know. It might be too late for her."

"You sound real broken up about it." Banner's sudden vehemence surprised Hammond. Then he remembered that the former traffic cop had a teenage daughter of his own. Candice or Catherine—something like that. The one with the music recital.

"We have to keep our personal feelings out of this," Hammond said. "We can't afford to get emotionally involved."

"Has that ever been a problem for you, Chief?"

Banner said it with just the slightest inflection of disgust. Hammond didn't like it. "Don't you think you should be working the media?" he asked. "We wouldn't want them to spin this story the wrong way."

Banner nodded, accepting his dismissal, and walked toward the milling cluster of reporters.

"He's an asshole," Lewinsky said. "If I were you, I'd have him back cutting tickets."

Hammond didn't answer that. He said quietly, "I do care about the girl. But we can't afford to lose our focus."

"Sure. I get it."

"When we find Gray, we'll make him take us to Megan Cameron."

"Right."

"We'll get her back. Maybe alive, maybe not. There's nothing we can do about that right now."

"I hear you, Chief," Lewinsky said.

Yes, Hammond thought. *You hear me. But do you believe me?*

He headed for his car, where his driver was watching highlights of the news conference on a portable TV. Through the open window his own voice was audible, saying, "He can run, but we'll hunt him down. He can hide . . ."

Hammond supposed he ought to hate himself for thinking it—but damn, that really was a good line.

Chapter Thirty-six

Wolper snapped off the car radio as Hammond finished his announcement. "That's something, anyway," he said.

Robin wished she could be optimistic, but she knew that finding the car was unimportant. She'd never expected Gray to hang on to the Saab. "They won't find him by looking for a car," she said quietly from the passenger seat. "There are ten million cars in this city."

"With every patrol unit in the county looking for that Firebird, there's a chance it'll be spotted."

"Long shot."

"Not as long a shot as this snipe hunt you've got going. No way this is going to pan out."

"Thanks for the prognostication."

"If Gray has your daughter, he's in the desert. If he doesn't, he's probably already made his way out of town. The farther he gets from LA, the less heat there'll be."

"That's if he's thinking logically. I'm guessing he's scared, rattled."

"Sociopaths are cool customers. Ice-cold, in fact. They don't get scared and desperate."

"They're not human, you mean?"

He squeezed the steering wheel as if it were a substitute

for his rubber ball. "Technically they're human. Just barely. They don't have the normal range of emotions. You know that. No empathy, no compassion."

She threw his own words back at him. "Then I guess they're *realists*, aren't they? They're *practical*." She took a breath. "Sorry. That was unfair. It's just . . . I hate it when anybody's humanity is denied. It's wrong. It's demeaning."

"Demeaning to them or to us?"

"To them *and* to us."

"You haven't seen what I've seen, Doctor. You haven't seen a body dumped in a trash bin with its arms and legs missing." She stiffened, fear flashing through her. He noticed. "Damn," he said. "I forgot for a minute—about your daughter."

"It's okay." She fought for self-control. She could not think about Meg now. Thinking about Meg would make her crazy. "And I know you've seen a lot. You've been around—isn't that how you put it last night?"

"Sounds like something I would say."

"But the thing is, I've been around, too, believe it or not. And I know there's more to these people than a rap sheet. Every one of them, even the worst, is somebody's son or husband or . . . father." She did her best not to stumble on the last word.

"Their victims were also somebody's loved ones," Wolper said.

"I know. It's wrong to lose sight of that. We have to keep all of it in our field of vision. We have to see the whole picture, all sides." But all she could see now was Meg. Meg in danger . . . in pain . . .

"We can't be omniscient," Wolper said.

"We can't be unfeeling, either."

He grunted, noncommittal. She decided not to pursue the subject. She had no strength to argue right now. It took all her focus to keep herself from screaming aloud.

"We're lucky Hammond's running the show," Wolper said. "As the brass go, he's not too bad."

"I had the impression he's a bit of a showboater."

"He likes getting his picture taken; that's for sure."

"Then why are we lucky to have him?"

"Because he can snap his fingers and make people jump. Hammond's on a fast track to the top of the department. He might be chief in a few years if he plays his cards right—and he's sure as hell played 'em right so far."

"I wish Deputy Chief Wagner were in charge."

"Your angel. Your sponsor."

"My liaison with the department," she corrected.

"Wagner wouldn't go near this case. He avoids risk. Stays away from anything messy. And if he was running things, he'd be too cautious to get anything done."

"Caution might be better than recklessness."

"Hammond isn't reckless. He's just ambitious and not afraid to show it. Joined the force at nineteen. Went to night school to earn his college degree, then got himself a master's. Worked his way up the ladder—Narcotics, undercover work, patrol, the whole nine yards. He's the same age as me, and he's sitting in the catbird seat. Makes me wonder what I did wrong."

"You're not doing anything wrong. You're doing your job."

Wolper gave the steering wheel another squeeze. "Sometimes it doesn't feel like enough."

"Is it you saying that—or your ex-wife?"

"Oh, no, you don't. You're not putting me on the couch."

"Occupational hazard. Sorry." She didn't want an impromptu therapy session with him anyway. She had other things on her mind.

"When I showed up for our appointment," Wolper said, "the Rampart guys thought I was there to get my head shrunk. The news will probably be all over the department by tomorrow."

Their appointment. Robin had forgotten about that. She forced herself to focus. "What did you come to tell me, anyhow?"

"About Brand?" He shrugged. "I looked at the file. The shooting looks clean to me. The review was thorough, no whitewash as far as I can tell. Brand's story was consistent with the physical evidence."

"But he told me a different story."

"Don't people say all kinds of things under hypnosis?"

"MBI isn't hypnosis."

"It's an altered state of consciousness. Can't the mind play tricks on a person—power of suggestion—like in all those child abuse cases that turned out to be bullshit?"

"It can happen," she admitted.

"Happens all the time, as I understand it. People are hypnotized and start talking about their past lives. How they used to stuff mummies or got their head chopped off in the French Revolution."

"Brand wasn't talking about a past life. He was talking about Eddie Valdez. And if he killed Valdez the way he said he did . . ." She stopped. A new thought occurred to her, a thought powerful enough to shut out the clamor of fear for her daughter.

"Yes?" Wolper prompted.

"Then he might have a motive to come after me."

"After you?"

"Gray said there was another man. Mr. Cool."

"Give me a break. You know that story of his was bullshit."

"Of course it was." She looked at Wolper. "Except . . . what if it wasn't?"

He took a moment to reply. When he did, his question surprised her. "You were hurt worse than you let on, weren't you?"

"What makes you say that?"

"Don't play dumb. You lost consciousness when he hit you."

She gave in. "How did you know?"

"If you hadn't, you'd know for sure if there was one man or two."

"Okay, you caught me. I didn't want to be sent to the ER, so I fibbed a little."

"A concussion is nothing to fool around with—as you ought to know, Doctor. How long were you out?"

"Long enough for Gray to kill the deputy and put on the dead man's pants, I guess."

"That could be a couple minutes. I'm taking you to Cedars-Sinai."

"No, you're not."

"God damn it, you're a doctor. You know how serious a head trauma can be."

"Yes, I do know. And I don't give a damn."

"Robin—"

"I don't care if I have a subdural hematoma. I don't care if I'm getting ready to throw a clot and stroke out. Meg is out there alone and in trouble, and until she's safe, I don't care what happens to me. It doesn't *matter*."

"All right, all right."

Robin pulled herself together. She could not afford to become hysterical—or to be seen that way. "Look," she said almost calmly, "suppose Gray was telling the truth. Suppose it was Brand who broke into my office, killed the deputy in the waiting room—"

"You saw blood on Gray's screwdriver, remember?"

"Even so, just suppose . . ."

"First we have a mystery man who just happens to abduct your daughter fifteen minutes after Gray escapes. Now we have Sergeant Brand killing a deputy and assaulting you and, what, trying to frame Gray for it? Are you aware of how insane this sounds?"

"I don't know. I . . ." She rubbed her head. "I guess it does."

"Brand was nowhere near your office. He's not a rogue cop, not a killer. I've worked with the guy for almost twenty years."

"But you still don't know him. No one does. Right?"

"Let's just concentrate on locating Gray. He's the one person we know we have to find."

Robin couldn't argue with that.

Her cell phone rang. Irrationally she imagined it was Meg, but the voice that greeted her belonged to the SID criminalist, Gaines.

"Dr. Cameron? I've reviewed the diary. Does the name Gabe mean anything to you?"

She searched her memory. "No, I don't think so."

"In her diary, your daughter makes reference to someone by that name."

"Just Gabe? No last name?"

"I'm afraid not. But there may be a way to obtain more information. There are allusions to communicating with Gabe via e-mail. What I'd like to do, with your permission, is examine the computer in her room. She may have left the e-mails on her hard drive."

"Go ahead. Do whatever you have to do."

"I'll let you know if anything turns up."

He was gone. She pocketed the phone.

"What was that all about?" Wolper asked.

"Crime-scene investigator. He wants to access Meg's computer."

"Who's Gabe? Your mystery man?"

"Someone Meg mentioned in her diary."

"A boy she's got a crush on. A friend from school."

"Probably." She didn't want to discuss it, and she didn't have to, because they were turning onto Hollywood Boulevard.

Periodic attempts were made to revive Hollywood, but the improvements never seemed to take hold. Robin stared out at porno theaters, strip clubs, bars, and knots of street people eyeing each other warily. The sun had vanished behind the buildings and billboards, and the streets were deep in shadow under the darkening sky.

She hated to think of Meg in a place like this—or in

someplace worse. And there were worse places in this city. There were shadow lands everywhere.

"There's the tattoo parlor." Wolper pointed at the garish sign over the storefront of Wild Ink. "Now where will *he* be?"

"Just keep cruising."

They crawled in slow traffic down the boulevard, heading west. When they passed Highland, the area perked up a little, becoming more of a tourist center, albeit a dingy one.

"You know," she said, "if we do find him—"

"We won't."

"But *if* we do . . . well, he's armed."

"So am I."

"Even off duty?"

"A cop in this town is never off duty." He opened his jacket briefly to give her a glimpse of a handgun holstered to his belt in the cross-draw position. "Feel better?"

"I do, actually. But I think we've gone too far. Let's go back. We need to travel farther east."

The area got worse in that direction. Robin thought Gray would gravitate toward the seediest stretch of the boulevard.

Wolper turned around, executing an illegal U at an intersection, cutting off a driver who gave him a long blast of horn.

"One advantage of being a cop," Wolper said. "You never worry about traffic tickets."

She didn't answer. She was studying the crowded sidewalks, the shop windows, the side streets.

They passed Wild Ink again and kept going, east of Las Palmas. Robin leaned forward in her seat. "Wait a minute. Here's a possibility."

She was looking at the flashing lights of a video arcade.

"Those places are for kids," Wolper said.

"Gray isn't much more than a kid himself. Arrested emotional and sexual and social development. Fixation on high school girls." The words came by rote. "But that's not the only reason to look inside. He used to hang out in arcades when he was growing up."

"He told you that?"

"When he got away from his folks, he would play pool or Pac-Man. Games." She heard the bitterness in that word. "He's always enjoyed games." She looked again at the arcade. "He could be in there."

"We'll give it a shot." Wolper steered the car into a red zone and put his badge on the dashboard, insurance against a ticket.

They got out. As she stood up, Robin was briefly dizzy with a rush of blood. She caught Wolper watching her as he locked the car.

"Must've been one hell of a shot to the cranium," he said.

"I'll live."

"Probably. But, Doctor—don't lie to me again. I don't like it."

He led her inside the arcade before she could answer.

Chapter Thirty-seven

Brand couldn't figure out what the hell they were up to.

It hadn't been easy following Wolper and Cameron when they left Parker Center. He'd been parked across the street from the building's underground garage, watching official and unofficial vehicles go in and out, when his beeper chirped with an SOS. Even so, he hadn't expected Cameron to be with Wolper, and he'd nearly missed seeing her in the passenger seat of Wolper's Mercury. He'd had to pull away from the curb to catch up with Wolper in the dense downtown traffic, staying two or three cars behind to avoid detection.

He thought maybe Wolper was taking Cameron to the hospital or to her home. Instead the car wended into Hollywood, cruising the boulevard and doubling back, as if in search of something.

Now the two of them had gone into a video arcade. Didn't make much sense, unless Cameron had decided that Justin Gray might be hanging out there. Gray was the target, after all. Cameron obviously hadn't seen or didn't remember who had knocked her out, so Gray was taking the blame.

It was funny, in a way—a serial killer getting pinned for a bum rap. As if the dumb son of a bitch didn't have enough on his résumé already. And even if he was taken alive and swore up and down that he hadn't done it, who would believe him?

Cameron had probably gotten it in her head that Gray would visit this arcade. She'd treated the guy and must think she had some kind of insight into his psyche.

Personally, Brand didn't buy the idea that anybody could understand Justin Gray. Some people were just freaks, plain and simple. There was no more point in trying to understand them than there would be in analyzing the motivations of a school of piranha. That was how he looked at it, anyway.

He shook his head, amused at himself as he locked up his Crown Victoria, parked down the street from Wolper's Mercury Sable. Look at him, Alan Brand, philosopher. Like he knew what the fuck he was talking about. And like any of it mattered anyhow.

What mattered was getting Robin Cameron alone.

It would be tricky. The problem was Wolper. He would be right at her side. Most likely the two of them wouldn't split up—not if they thought Gray might be in the vicinity.

Well, maybe he could arrange a diversion, something to draw Wolper away, if only for a few minutes. Or maybe he would just get lucky. Hell, he was due.

Brand approached the arcade, fingering the off-duty gun under his nylon windbreaker. A Beretta 9mm, identical to his duty pistol. He didn't believe in trying to adjust to a different weapon. In an emergency he would depend on instinct and reflex, and he needed a gun that felt like it was part of him, an extension of his own arm.

Probably he wouldn't have to use the gun tonight. There were other ways of handling this situation. Above all, he had to be smart. He knew he wasn't the sharpest tack on the bulletin board. He'd never been a straight-A student, or even straight-B. He'd barely made it through community college, and he knew he wouldn't ever rise higher in the ranks.

But he'd learned a thing or two about self-preservation. Survival—that was what it was all about. On the streets you learned about survival, or you didn't last long.

During his wait outside Parker Center, he had decided something. Whatever happened, he was going to survive this mess. He would do whatever was necessary. He was not going down.

Chapter Thirty-eight

Meg wished she smoked.

If she did, maybe she'd have a lighter, some way to penetrate the total blackness around her. She should have taken up smoking and stayed away from Gabe. She'd made a poor choice of vices. Of course, she hadn't thought of Gabe as a vice. She'd thought of him as the love of her life, who would never betray her. Now it was as if she'd awakened from a dream—a stupid, irrational dream.

When he'd called her an immature kid, he'd been right. Only an immature kid could have made the mistakes she'd made.

People always said you learned from your mistakes. But you couldn't learn much if your mistakes got you killed.

She had to stop thinking that way, stay positive.

Positive. Right. She was handcuffed to a metal railing in a lightless basement, waiting for a man she'd thought she loved to come back and murder her.

Okay, he hadn't specifically said he was going to murder her. But it seemed like a really safe bet.

Though she might not know his real name, she knew *him*. She knew his face. His . . . body. She knew he had been at the awards dinner for Robin. She knew he was a cop. She knew too much.

Yesterday she'd wondered what it had been like for Justin Gray's victims, waiting in the back of his van, knowing they would die but not knowing when. Well, now she knew.

Uselessly she rattled the handcuffs against the railing. Around her, in the dark, she heard rustling sounds. Small creatures, disturbed by the noise.

"Bunny rabbits," she whispered, forcing a smile.

She guessed there was some kind of justice to the way things had worked out. She'd broken every ethical rule her mom had drummed into her. She'd lied and gone sneaking around and had sex with a guy who was more than twice her age. And she'd thought she was so damn smart, so grown up, and that her mom, for all her brains and education, just didn't get it because she was too old to understand true love.

But it turned out that what Gabe felt for her wasn't love at all, but some kind of pathological sickness, which her mom would have understood completely because she worked with crazies every day. She would have pegged Gabe as a psycho right from the start. She would have seen the insanity in him, which Meg had entirely missed.

"So she's smart and I'm dumb," Meg whispered. "She's right and I'm wrong. Great. How does that help me get out of here?"

It didn't, of course. Nothing would. She was trapped, and she couldn't get free, and her life was over at the age of fifteen. . . .

Footsteps.

Upstairs.

He was back.

A wave of trembling shot through her like ice water. She tugged at the handcuffs, rattling the short chain again, chafing her wrist. A noise halfway between a moan and a wail started rising in her throat. She bit it back and waited.

The footsteps came closer.

She didn't want to think about what would come next, but she couldn't stop herself. Images ran through her head like movie clips. How many dramatized murders had she witnessed in the course of her life? A thousand? Ten thousand? It seemed as if every one of them was replaying itself in her memory—every shooting and stabbing, every death by fire or water or torture, every gangland hit and serial-killer slaying, all the ways there were to die. Which would be her way?

The footsteps stopped outside the cellar door.

Looking up, she saw a dim seam of light limning the door frame.

A flashlight. It must be dark outside by now. He needed a flashlight to find his way.

The flood of images coursed faster. She saw herself strangled, smothered, beaten to death. She flinched from blows that hadn't yet come. She was crying again, new tears joining the tracks of dried salt on her cheeks.

The door opened. The flashlight's glow was blinding after her long darkness. She had to look away.

"Megan?" A man's voice. Not Gabe's. This was someone else.

She was too startled to speak. The beam of the flashlight skittered around the room, illuminating the corners she'd never seen, the cinder-block walls and concrete floor, the stale rodent droppings and skeletons of mice and elaborate cobwebs and dust, before finding her at the bottom of the stairs.

"It's okay, Meg." A gentle voice. "Everything's okay. I'm a police officer."

She lifted her head into the glare. "Police?" she whispered.

He set the flashlight on the landing, its beam dimly lighting the room. He came down the stairs, a big man in a business suit, moving slowly, as if wary of scaring her. "That's right. I'm Detective Tomlinson."

"Detective Tomlinson?" She was repeating the man's words like an idiot.

"Right." He was nearly at the bottom of the staircase. "LAPD. Robbery-Homicide."

"How'd you find me?"

"Someone reported a suspicious car in the alley behind this factory. The vehicle matched one seen leaving your neighborhood at the time of your abduction. I checked it out."

"Alone?"

"We're a little shorthanded at the moment. There are a lot of people looking for you—and for Gray."

"Gray?"

"Justin Gray. The serial killer."

"He escaped?"

Tomlinson had reached her now. The glow of the flashlight on the landing outlined one side of his face as he smiled down from his greater height. "This afternoon."

That explained her mom's phone call, but it only made everything else more bewildering. Was it coincidence that Gabe had kidnapped her so soon after Justin Gray's escape? If it wasn't coincidence, then what was going on?

"None of this makes sense," she whispered.

"Don't try to sort it all out. You've been through a lot." He reached into the side pocket of his jacket. "Let me get those cuffs off, and we'll be out of here."

He produced something from his pocket. A key. It must be a handcuff key. In the feeble light of the flash on the landing, she couldn't be sure.

He reached for her. "I'll have that cuff unlocked in no time."

Under any other circumstances she would have let him do it. But one thought stopped her.

Gabe was a cop too.

She took a step back. "Let me see it."

"What?"

"The handcuff key."

He frowned, bewildered by her suspicion. "Sure, Meg. It's right here."

He raised his hand slowly—then in a sudden motion thrust it forward, aiming at the bare skin of her right arm. She jerked away from him, and he missed her, his fist brushing her skin. She retreated as far as the handcuff chain would allow.

She had seen the thing in his hand. Not a key.

A syringe.

"Gabe sent you"—her voice was thick and raw—"didn't he?"

Tomlinson dropped the act. All at once he was a different man, his gentleness gone. "Gabe?" He chuckled. "Is that what he's calling himself?"

"What's his real name? Who is he?"

He ignored the question.

"That son of a bitch," he said, "is going to get himself in trouble one of these days, tomcatting around. Then again"—his gaze moved over her—"for a sweet piece of ass like you, a man might be willing to risk some consequences."

She stared at the syringe. The tube was filled with brownish liquid. "What is that stuff?"

"You ever been high, sweet cheeks?" Tomlinson's eyes twinkled with something like merriment.

"No."

"Never? Not even pot?"

"I don't do drugs."

"I see. You're a good girl. All you do is suck cocks and spread your thighs." He grinned at her with evil amusement.

She asked again, "What is it?"

"Darling, what we got here"—he held up the syringe, letting it catch the light—"is good old horse. Hard candy. You know what I'm saying?"

"No."

He laughed. "You really are a babe in the woods. Heroin. That's what I've got. Highly illegal, class-A narcotic. Colombian smack, good stuff, very pure. It disappeared from an evidence room not long ago—one gram, enough to send you on a real bad trip. A one-way trip, I'm sorry to say."

She stared up into the hollows of his eyes, where the flashlight's glow didn't reach. "Why?"

He ignored her. "See, I could shoot you, but this way there's no bullet to trace."

She tried to back away, but she couldn't retreat any farther with the handcuffs pinning her down. He grasped her right arm.

"Just stay still, Meg. This won't take long."

He squirted a few drops of liquid from the syringe and aimed it at her bare arm.

"You got nice blue veins. I'm gonna mainline this shit. That'll make it fast. Lights out in a hurry." He smiled at her in the half-light of the flashlight beam. "It's a shame I've gotta waste such high-quality stuff."

The needle descended in a leisurely arc.

"And wasting you," he added, "that's a real shame, too."

Everything had slowed down. Her breath had stopped. Her vision had narrowed to a single point. She knew that she could let fear paralyze her, and then she would die, or she could fight and give herself a chance.

With a shriek of rage she wrenched her arm to the side. He was gripping it tight, but her skin, slick with sweat, slid through his fingers, and she pulled free.

He would expect her to draw back, huddle in fear. Instead she lunged at him, angling her hand downward, closing her fist over his crotch. She felt the soft sacks of his scrotum squishing between her fingers. She squeezed tight and twisted hard.

His voice rose an octave. *"Fuck!"*

He grabbed at her hand, a reflex action. She released his crotch and snatched the syringe away. She stabbed at his face. He dodged, not quite fast enough. The hypodermic punched into the side of his neck, her finger depressing the plunger, releasing a stream of brown fluid into his carotid artery.

A noise like an animal's howl broke from his mouth. He tore away, leaving a bloody gash in his neck. He lifted his arm to strike at her, and then his face went red and his breathing was suddenly hoarse and shallow.

Tomlinson fell to the floor and lay on his stomach, making crawling motions with his arms.

"Can't see. Can't . . ."

He couldn't speak anymore. He rose to one knee before collapsing in a shuddering pile. His respiration was quick and noisy and sounded strangely wet, as if his lungs were clogged.

Meg stared at him, the empty syringe still in her hand. She thought she had probably killed him. The reality of it hit her like a slap, and then she was screaming for help, screaming uncontrollably, knowing that no one could hear.

Chapter Thirty-nine

The arcade was bedlam.

With Wolper at her side, Robin maneuvered through the crashing noise, the tight squeeze of people, the stroboscopic glare of game machines. She hadn't been inside a place like this in years, and vaguely she'd been expecting pinball machines or close relatives of early video games like Frogger and Pac-Man. Instead she was surrounded by large screens filled with startlingly realistic action, enhanced by stereophonic sound effects at a painfully high volume. One game console displayed the view from a race car; another put its operator in a submarine; others re-created torchlit temples and jungle swamps. She saw karate kicks, balletic leaps ending in a blast of automatic weapons fire, wrestling moves that turned lethal with the sickening crunch of an adversary's neck. The enemies to be dispatched were sometimes aliens, dinosaurs, or ghouls, but most often they were human beings, ethnically neutral, indistinguishable from the good guys as far as she could tell. Maybe good versus evil wasn't the point anymore. Maybe there was no point.

Ninety percent of the game players were teens and most of them were boys. They had the cold, expressionless stares she had seen around the slot machines in Vegas, and they stood hunched forward in concentration, their fingers moving on the joysticks with virtuoso rapidity, like skilled hands sounding stops on a flute. The kids were mostly black and Latino, affecting the baggy-pants gangsta style. She wondered what they would think if they knew that a serial killer might be hanging out here. Would they be scared, appalled—or would they ask for his autograph? The girls he'd killed might be no more real to them than the animated figures being vaporized on their display screens. To them, Justin Gray might be the ultimate player.

But the kids didn't matter right now. What she focused on were the rare adults in the crowd. They were all males—she saw no females here older than nineteen—and they were a curious mixture of overweight guys with bad complexions and gaunt, hollow-eyed men who looked like junkies.

She didn't see Gray among them, but it was too soon to be sure. The arcade was huge, branching off into alcoves and nooks and specially themed rooms, and the lighting was inconstant and distracting, and the crowd was jammed into every corner, every inch of floor space.

She wondered how much time these people spent here, killing time—like the men crowded around the dogpit. Men like Brand. Maybe he'd been at the dogfights today.

Or maybe he'd been in her office, killing more than time.

Brand liked this place. It was raucous and crazy, and although no real action was going down, there was a strange excitement in watching the kids bent over video-game controls, matching their reflexes against a computer's speed. And it was noisy. That was good. Noise made good cover. If he did have to use his 9mm, the shot might go unheard.

He circled along the perimeter of the room, scoping the layout, keeping Wolper and Cameron in sight. Although he was a generation older than most of the game players, he didn't stand out too badly. The dark windbreaker helped him blend in—unlike Wolper's sport jacket over an open-collared dress shirt, or Cameron's buttoned-up blouse and stylish slacks. The two of them looked like nervous middle-class parents hunting down a truant teenager. Which wasn't far wrong, when you thought about it. Gray was the shrink's pet project, her baby, and he sure had gone missing today.

A yell of frustration from a player a few feet away startled him. He glared at the kid, who was too absorbed in pummeling the machine to notice. When he looked across the room, his quarries were gone, lost in the crowd.

He scanned the blur of faces and bodies, hoping to pick them out. He hoped they hadn't already left.

There. Entering a side room, still together.

They hadn't separated, which was a problem, but at least he still had Cameron in view.

She wouldn't get away. That was a promise he'd made to himself. He might have fucked up most things in his forty-one years, failed in more ways than he could stand to remember, stalled out in his career, given up any chance at marriage or family, ended up in a sad little sweatbox of a house in a shit neighborhood—he might have no future and no life, but tonight he had a mission to perform, and he wouldn't fail. No matter what, he was coming out of this a winner.

He touched the bulge of his gun under the windbreaker as he crossed the room, slowly closing in on Robin Cameron.

"Did Sergeant Brand call in sick today?" Robin asked Wolper.

"Yeah. But he wasn't at the dogfights."

She glanced at him, surprised that he'd touched on the subject occupying her thoughts. "How do you know?"

"We raided them. Well, not us. The Southeast Area troops."

"How'd that happen?"

"I made a call to their CO."

"You?"

He leaned closer, straining to be heard over the noise. "What you said yesterday got me thinking. You know, how

I knew the fights had started up again, and I hadn't stopped them."

"You did the right thing."

"They'll just start up again someplace else. Anyway, Brand wasn't nabbed."

"So if he wasn't at the dogfights, where was he?"

"Don't know."

"Wouldn't you like to find out?"

"I was thinking I might put the question to him later."

"Let's put the question to him now."

She took out her cell phone and dialed, maneuvering into a quieter area where she could hear Brand if he answered.

"You know his number?" Wolper asked.

"His cell phone number, yes. I called it half a dozen times yesterday."

"Like I said in the car, it's Gray we should be focused on."

Rationally she knew he was right. But as she'd told him, there was more to life than logic. Intuition had its place also, and her intuition was insisting that Sergeant Brand should not be ignored.

Five rings, and no one had picked up. She was about to end the call when she became aware of an echo in the ringing. No, not an echo. A second ring, this one coming from the crowd.

She peered into the sea of shadows, then saw him. "Look."

Wolper had his hand on his gun. "Gray?"

She shook her head. *"Brand."*

Brand was getting close, wondering how to get Wolper out of the way, when his phone started to ring in the pocket of his windbreaker.

He didn't want to answer it, but after five rings he started to worry about the noise. Then he saw that Robin Cameron had a cell phone to her ear, and somehow he knew she was calling him.

In that moment she raised her head and looked right at him.

Shit. He'd been made.

Wolper followed Robin's gaze. "What the hell is he doing here?"

"That's another thing we need to ask him."

He nodded. "We will." He took a step forward.

Brand broke into a run.

"Stay here. I'm going after him."

She didn't argue. Chasing a suspect was Wolper's business—and Brand was looking more like a suspect every minute.

She noticed that her cell phone was still ringing Brand's number. She ended the call, then gazed across the arcade. Brand and Wolper were both lost to sight.

The phone in her hand rang. Stupidly she thought it might be Brand. She took the call and held the phone close to her head, cupping her other ear against the background din. "Yes?"

"Why're you lyin' about me?"

The voice was slurred and distant, but she knew it at once.

"Justin?" she said.

Chapter Forty

Gray had a pretty good buzz going—nothing major, just enough to take the edge off after a long, hard day. That six-pack he'd picked up had hit the spot. After a year in stir, he'd worked up a serious thirst. He'd polished off four of the sixteen-ounce cans. Maybe five. He'd lost track. Shit, there was more where that came from.

Only trouble with beer was that it didn't stay with you very long. As his daddy used to say, you don't buy beer; you rent it. In compliance with his father's wisdom and his own biological needs, he was now standing at a urinal, reading the pathetic graffiti scratched into the men's-room wall.

Dumb racist epithets. Queer jokes and queer come-ons. Gangsta slang and other attempts at establishing street cred by obvious wanna-bes. All in all, just a mess of stupid crap written by peewee paintheads and fake-ass homeboys who spent more time wanking off than getting laid, teenage punks still squeezing their zits and wearing their puny hard-ons like badges of honor. This shit was just a goof to them.

Gray voided an amber stream and wondered how them fairies would like to meet a real man, a bona fucking fide major violator with blood on his hands.

A famous man. Or infamous, notorious, whatever the

fuck the right word was. He was all over the news, and everyone in this city was saying his name.

He didn't expect to be caught, though. He'd taken precautions. Okay, maybe he'd been a little more alert before he got those beers in him, and maybe the beers had even been a mistake. But he was pretty sure he'd covered his tracks well enough to keep the boys in blue off his back, at least for now.

He ought to be feeling fine. Trouble was, those bogus news stories still had him mighty peeved. Every time he thought about the lies and the games and the crap they were putting on the air, he got ticked off all over again.

"Motherfucker," he said as he finished peeing. He zipped up and left without washing his hands. Personal hygiene had never been his strong suit.

In the alcove outside the rest rooms, there was a pay phone.

He stopped, staring at the phone, thinking about the business card he'd swiped from the doc's office weeks ago. A card that listed her cell phone number. A number he remembered, having dialed it just last night.

He moved to the phone. If not for the beers, he wouldn't do this. He knew he ought to show more sense. But fuck it all, he hated being jerked around, and that sexless bitch of a shrink had been yanking his chain from day one.

He dropped coins into the slot and dialed.

"Motherfucker," he said again, with feeling, as the phone rang on the other end of the line.

The ringing stopped, and over a rush of background noise he heard the doc say, "Yes?"

"Why're you lyin' about me?"

"Justin?"

"I don't got enough on my record, you gotta add stuff I didn't do?" The noise intensified, obliterating her response. "Doc? You there?"

"I'm here."

"You at a nightclub or something?"

"I'm looking for you."

"Where?"

"Never mind that."

"Everybody else thinks I hightailed it for the Mojave, and you're trolling the clubs in Hollywood, I bet. Thinking outside the box. I like that. But I ain't dumb enough to go back to my home turf."

"It was worth a shot."

"Sure it was. You're smart, Doc. I like you—or I used to, till you started fibbing on me."

"Justin, where is she?"

"Your darling daughter? The one all the news reports say I kidnapped? I ain't got her. I never touched her."

"Justin, slow down—"

"Why? So you can have this call traced?"

"They can do an instant trace on most calls these days."

"Okay, now at least you're being honest. Truth is, I don't care about no trace. The boys in blue can't snatch me. I'm too quick for 'em. LA's finest show up, and I'm Swayze, I'm a ghost. Great thing about LA is, you can jump on a freeway anywhere. That's what makes this town the bank robbery capital of the world."

"What are you talking about?"

"It's a sucker's game, knocking over banks. They always get you on the security cameras. Besides, the cash is always traceable or rigged with those explosive doohickeys that blow red dye all over the place—"

"Where is my daughter?"

"Oh, we still jawing about her? Straight up, Doc Robin, I got no idea."

"You *took* her; you *have* her—"

"Wrong and wrong. She's probably out playing tea party with one of her little girlie friends."

"Do you want *me*? You can have me for her."

"That's downright noble. I'm getting all choked up; I really am. Look, if I had to guess, I'd say it's the other guy who's got her. The guy that clocked you."

"I'm not interested in your lies."

"No lie, Doc Robin. I told you true. You said you believed me."

"And *you* had a screwdriver against my throat."

"So you bullshitted me? Gotta say, I don't care for that. I'm real big on trust issues. Being a shrink, you should know."

"If you saw this other man, describe him."

"I told you, I couldn't see much with the lights so low. Fuck, you looked right at his face before he decked your ass. You flashed him with that penlight doodad."

"It's a good story, Justin."

"You're the one who's spreading lies, saying I attacked you, grabbed your girl."

"Stop it, just *stop it*. I won't let you play with my head. There was no other man. You knocked me out, and you stole my wallet so you could find Meg—"

"I copped the wallet because I wanted cash."

"You went to my home, you took her—"

"Doc, I'm a free man again. I got higher priorities than snatching the fruit of your womb."

"Please give . . ." Her voice faded.

"What's that? I can't hardly hear you."

"I said, please give her back."

"Can't give what I don't have. Hey, that ain't no club I'm hearing. Those are arcade noises."

"You used to hang out in video arcades. I took a chance you might be at one now."

"Did you, now? Smart thinking, Doc." He eased away from the pay phone, stretching the cord taut. "Tell you what. You and me, we put our heads together—we can solve this thing."

"What are you talking about?"

He peered out of the alcove, then smiled as he spotted what he was looking for. "You gotta have some idea who your enemies are. One of 'em is Mr. Cool. Hell, I bet you got somebody in mind already. Ex-boyfriend? Another patient?"

She hesitated. "I'm not going to talk about this."

He'd heard her pause after he said the word *patient*. "Sure, makes sense," he said. "You work with psychos all day long. Only a matter of time till one of 'em goes postal on you. Come on now, give it up. You got one patient in particular who'd be willing to engage in serious violence? Snuff a Deputy Dawg, decommission our favorite shrink?"

"There's someone who might have a motive. . . ."

"Motive's one thing. He got the *cojones* to do it?"

"He's killed before."

"Now we're getting somewhere. See, you and me make a great team. But I need details. It's the only way I can help you."

"Why would you want to help me?"

"That's a good question, Doc. No good reason, I guess."

"You're playing with me. More mind games."

"Scout's honor, I'm not."

"I still think you're the one I'm after."

"No, you don't. You're starting to figure out that things are more complicated. I'm not the bad guy here, not this time. Think about it. If I'd wanted your scalp, I could've gone brutal on you right in your office." He smiled. "Or for that matter, I could ice you right where you're standing— next to the Quake video game."

Gray chuckled as, yards across the main floor of the arcade, Robin Cameron's head jerked up in sudden fear.

"Yeah, Doc, that's right." He raised his voice in a singsong falsetto. "I . . . can . . . see . . . you."

Chapter Forty-one

Wolper caught up with Brand a few yards outside the arcade. He grabbed the sergeant by the shoulder and spun him around.

"What the fuck do you think you're doing?" Wolper shouted. "Why'd you cut and run when we saw you?"

"Guess I wasn't in the mood for company."

Wolper flung Brand backward onto the hood of somebody's Chevy. Brand put up an instinctive effort at resistance. Wolper slammed him down harder, denting the hood.

On the sidewalk a few people stopped to stare. Wolper threw open his jacket, revealing his 9mm. "Police business," he snapped.

That scattered the onlookers. Nobody wanted to get mixed up in any police action.

When he was satisfied that his audience was gone, Wolper opened the folds of Brand's windbreaker and withdrew the man's gun from its armpit holster.

"This your off-duty piece?" he asked.

"You know it is."

Wolper glanced at the gun in the ambient glow of street lamps and neon signs. Standard Beretta—the registration number had not been filed off or erased with acid. The piece was street legal and traceable.

"Stand up," he ordered.

"Come on, Roy, what the fuck is this?"

"Just stand up, God damn it."

Brand dismounted the hood of the Chevy with whatever dignity he could summon. Wolper turned him around to face the side of the car.

"Spread 'em."

"You're patting me down, for Christ's sake?"

Without answering, Wolper shoved Brand up against the car and proceeded to do a body search.

There was no other weapon. Brand would have had to strap it to his leg in an ankle holster or tuck it into his belt, or conceal it in one of the windbreaker's pockets, possibly a secret pocket sewn into the lining. Nothing was there.

"You're clean," Wolper said finally, giving the Beretta back to Brand.

"I'm a good little boy," Brand mumbled as he reholstered the gun.

Wolper looked him over with a wary, skeptical eye. "I don't know about that, Al. I really don't. Now I'll tell you what. You and myself are going to have a talk, and when we're done, we're going inside so you can explain yourself to Robin Cameron."

"I've got nothing to say to her," Brand muttered with the stubborn, sullen frown of a disgruntled child.

"You'll have plenty to say to her and to me. As far as you're concerned, the doctor is in." Wolper leaned close, watching Brand's eyes and trying to catch any scent of alcohol on his breath. "Whatever you're up to, Al, I don't like it. We're already dealing with one pain-in-the-ass SOB who likes to play games. We don't need another one. You get what I'm saying?"

Brand faced Wolper's gaze for a long moment without blinking. "No games," he said in a beaten voice. "I get it."

"I hope you do," Wolper told him. "For your sake, I hope you do."

Chapter Forty-two

"You told me," Robin said slowly, "you weren't dumb enough to come back to Hollywood."

Gray's voice crackled over the line. "Guess I'm dumber than I thought. Didn't come in here to play no games, though. Had to take the lizard for a walk."

"Lizard?"

"Use the head, is what I'm saying. Caught them arcade noises on the phone and tumbled to where you were. Eyeballed you straight off. What are the odds we'd both show up at the same place? It's fuckin' kismet. We're *meant* to be a team."

She looked around her, trying to spot him. He could be anywhere in the shifting, shadowy crowd. Could be sneaking up to kill her from behind . . .

"Doc, you're way too antsy. If I was in for some silence 'n' violence, wouldn't I have executed the game plan by now?"

She took a breath. "You have to turn yourself in."

"Not gonna happen."

"I'm here with a police officer."

"You're alone. I'm looking right at you."

"He left for a second, but he'll be back. He could return at any time—"

"Chill, Doc. Not that I don't enjoy hearing you pant into the telephone, but you're getting your dainties in a twist for no good reason. I got no hard-on for doing you harm. That's what I been trying to tell you. Hell, I'm on your side."

"How do you figure that?"

"I don't like being framed. And that's what went down today. Some asshole set me up. Hey, I'm willing to do the time for the crime, but it's gotta be my crime, not some other Joe's. I feel proprietary about my reputation."

There was a pause. "Justin, I want you to tell me again that you don't have my daughter."

"Doc, I sung that song already."

"I want to hear it again. No jokes, no wisecracks."

Slowly he said, "I ain't got her."

"You swear?"

"On a stack of Bibles and my mama's life."

"Your mother is dead."

"Figure of speech."

A moment passed as she considered everything she knew or thought she knew about Justin Gray.

"Okay," she said.

"You believe me?"

"Maybe."

"Well, it's a start. If you'd said yes, I'd've known you was lying. So what you gonna do now, Doc?"

"Find Meg."

"Sounds like a plan. Good luck with that."

"You said we could put our heads together. Maybe we can."

"You're bullshitting me again."

"If you were serious about what you said, prove it."

"How?"

"Let me see you."

"So you can throw a net on me. Put a spotlight on old Justin for your cop friend that's with you."

"If you want me to trust you, then *you* have to trust *me*."

A beat of silence passed, and she thought she'd lost him.

"Deal," he said. "Turn around. You wanna see me, you're looking the wrong way."

She turned, peering toward the rear of the arcade.

"See the sign for the toilets? Pan down, zoom in."

She spotted him on a pay phone near the rest rooms. He'd changed out of the clothes he'd stolen. He was looking directly at her.

"Ta-da," said the voice on the phone.

"Let me talk to you, Justin."

"What do you think we're doing?"

"Face-to-face. Up close. Let me get near you."

"More of this trust business?"

"Yes."

He crooked the phone under his chin and spread his arms in a gesture of resignation. "What the hey. Come on over."

Holding the cell phone to her ear, she moved out of the alcove and into the press of the crowd. He was repeatedly eclipsed by shifting faces and bodies, and each time she thought he'd vanished for good, but always he reemerged, still standing by the phone, watching her with a wary, quizzical look.

Why was she doing this? Why risk getting closer to him? She knew the answer. It was the same thing she'd told him last night—*I don't do therapy over the phone.*

To treat someone, she had to see him, watch his expression, his body language. She had to be close to his personal space.

"Don't get spooked, Justin," she said into the cell phone. "I'm almost there."

Over the crashing noise, she heard him snort. "I don't spook that easy."

The crowd thinned as she approached the hallway to the rest rooms. She could see Gray clearly now. Less than fifteen feet separated them.

"Whose blood was on the screwdriver?" she asked, speaking to him directly, not into the phone.

"Say what?"

"The screwdriver. It had blood on it. If you didn't kill the deputy, whose blood was it?"

"Mr. Cool's."

"You stabbed him?"

"Nicked him. In the arm. I told you we tussled."

"You didn't say anything about stabbing him."

"Wasn't hardly a stab. Shit, I got paper cuts worse 'n that."

She took another step toward him, narrowing the gap. "You understand why I have trouble believing you."

His shoulders lifted. "Yeah, I guess. But I could've iced you in your office. Shit, could've done it here, after I laid eyes on you. You're still breathing. That counts for something, don't it?"

She drew closer. "It counts."

He hung up the phone and stood staring at her from ten feet away. "Now what, Doc?"

"You talked about working together."

"I'm up for it. But you ain't never gonna work with me."

"Why not?"

"Ain't your style. You're a straight arrow. You don't pal around with a bad boy like me."

"If you think so, then why are you even talking to me?"

His brow wrinkled. "You shrinks ask good questions, you know? They teach that in shrink school?"

"Among other things. Why talk to me, Justin? Why call? What do you want?"

"I guess . . . I want you to believe me."

"Why does that matter? You're still a wanted man, whether you attacked me and the deputy or not."

"Right as rain on that one. Maybe I shouldn't care."

"Maybe you and I have more of a connection than you thought." She advanced again. "Maybe that's why it matters what I think of you."

"Don't go putting up a statue of yourself just yet, Doc. I'm a long way from cured, if that's what you're getting at."

"Maybe"—another step—"you're closer to a resolution of your problems than you want to admit."

He was five feet away, almost within reach. She could see his eyes. They flickered with new thoughts, new possibilities. She might be getting through to him.

"Know what I think?" Gray said. "I think it was a cop."

She stopped. "What?"

"Mr. Cool. I smell bacon."

"Why would you say that?"

"Who else knew you were brain-scannin' me between three and four this afternoon? It's not exactly public knowledge. This bozo had to know that shit if he was gonna pin the rap on me. There any reason the cops might be pissed at you?"

"There might be," she said cautiously.

"In that case, I wouldn't trust 'em to find Meg."

"We're only talking about one police officer."

"One guy?" His eyebrows lifted. "Your patient—he's a cop, is that it? You're branching out from us cons, going for a higher quality of clientele?"

"I can't talk about that."

"Yeah, he's a cop. And you figure he's working this thing alone?"

"Why wouldn't he be?"

"Somebody goes after you—and Meg disappears the same time? Sounds like a conspiracy to me."

"I don't believe in conspiracies."

"Hey, I don't believe in jock itch, but I still got it. If the cops are on your ass, you can't expect 'em to find Meg. They might be the ones that have her."

"I have to trust somebody."

"Sure you do. Trust me."

"You're a killer, Justin."

"But I ain't a cop. Tell me who you think might be doing this number on you and Meg. Give me a name. I'll do the rest."

"I can't work with you that way. But . . . but I *can* help you."

"You're missing the bus, Doc. *I'm* the one who can help *you*. And maybe I will, just out of the goodness of my—"

His gaze snapped past her, and his face changed.

"Fuck," Gray said, turning.

Robin looked back and saw Wolper and Brand emerging from the crowd, guns drawn.

She looked at Gray again, but he was already sprinting down the hall.

The two cops blew past her, chuffing air. She grabbed at Wolper, wanting to stop him, tell him how close she'd been to a breakthrough, but her fingers failed to close over his flapping sleeve, and then he was gone.

"Police, freeze!" he shouted as Gray dodged down a side hallway, out of sight.

He was gone. Wolper and Brand might catch him, but if they didn't . . .

Then Gray would remain at large. And he would never trust her again.

Chapter Forty-three

Wolper pulled out his cell phone and called 911, identifying himself as a police officer. "I'm in pursuit of the fugitive Justin Gray. Request patrol units at the corner of Hollywood and Cahuenga. Gray is inside the video arcade, rear of the building."

"Dispatching units now," the 911 operator said.

"Patch me through to Dispatch."

He and Brand rounded another corner and saw an exterior door swinging shut.

"Control," a new voice on the phone said, using the official term for the dispatchers' command center.

"Suspect has exited the building via a rear door. We need Air Support." A helicopter could keep Gray in view as long as he was outdoors.

The door opened on an alley. Wolper and Brand went through the doorway fast, ready to return fire if Gray started shooting. He didn't. He was already behind the wheel of the stolen Firebird, facing into the alley.

Wolper caught a blurred glimpse of Gray's face through the windshield before the headlights snapped on, blinding him. His gun was drawn, but he had no shot. He stared into a wash of bright light that concealed the driver in the glare.

He ran down the alley. The car's engine gunned, and

there was a bad moment when Wolper thought Gray might accelerate and run him down.

A skid of tires, and the car retreated out of the alley at high speed, fishtailing onto the street.

And it was gone.

"He's in a car," Wolper gasped into the cell phone as Brand reached his side. "Blue Firebird—'ninety-five, 'ninety-six model. Eastbound on Selma. Didn't get the plate number, but it's got to be the car he boosted when he dumped the Saab."

"We have two units on Selma," the dispatcher said. "They've been alerted."

"Stay on the line."

"What now?" Brand asked.

"We drive. Come on." Wolper led Brand out of the alley and around the corner to the side street where his Sable was parked. He saw Robin standing by the car.

"What are you doing here?"

"Waiting for you," she said. "I take it Gray got away."

"Not for long."

"I was starting to make a connection. If you hadn't spooked him—"

"Shut up," Wolper snapped. He wasn't in the mood. He unlocked the car and slid into the driver's seat, Brand riding shotgun. He was pulling away from the curb when he noticed Robin in the backseat.

"You can't come with us."

"You can't stop me."

Wolper sighed. That was probably true.

He steered into traffic, cutting east on Selma. With the cell phone pressed to his ear, he said, "Control, you still with me?"

"I'm here. Six-Adam-eight has spotted the vehicle."

"They're in pursuit," he told Brand. Into the phone he said, "Location?"

"Still on Selma—wait. He's just turned south on Bronson. Ran a red."

Wolper accelerated, knifing through traffic as he veered from lane to lane. He wished he had a siren or one of those bubble flashers, but the Sable was strictly his personal ride.

At Bronson he swung south. "Any word on Air Support?" he asked the dispatcher.

"Inbound. ETA five minutes."

In five minutes this could all be over. Justin Gray could be in custody—or dead.

"There," Brand said, pointing.

Ahead, the strobing light bar of a Hollywood patrol unit was visible. As Wolper watched, a second squad car pulled onto Bronson from a side street, siren caterwauling.

He still couldn't see the Firebird, but it had to be just beyond the two black-and-whites.

"Adam-eight is reporting that the license plate is wrong," the dispatcher said. "Doesn't match the stolen Firebird."

"He could've switched plates," Wolper said. "Can they make out the car's occupant?"

"They say driver is alone, hunched over the wheel."

"It's gotta be him."

Wolper had closed in on the nearest of the two squad cars. Just beyond the first car, the Firebird weaved across lanes as Gray fought for an opening in the traffic.

"Son of a bitch is panicking," he said with satisfaction.

"They can't kill him," Robin said from the backseat.

"What?"

"They have to take him alive. So he can tell us where Meg is."

The Firebird slewed onto the shoulder and barreled onto Fountain Avenue, westbound. The two squads followed, with Wolper right behind.

"He's trying to lose us," Wolper said. He shouted his location into the phone, even though he was sure the two Hollywood units were relaying the same information, then tossed a quick glance at Brand beside him. "Thrill of the hunt, huh, Al?"

"Absolutely. This puke thinks he can outrun the whole fucking police department."

"No chance. This is the end of the line for you, pal."

Gray hooked right onto Vine, then pulled a quick left onto a side street, De Longpre Avenue.

"Like a rat in a maze," Brand said. He glanced back at Robin. "Though I guess that's your department, Doctor."

Sudden brightness washed the street. A searchlight beam from a police chopper. Air Support had arrived.

"Got you now," Wolper breathed.

The blue Firebird struggled to escape the searchlight, taking street after street after street, seeking a way out.

The amplified voice of a cop in the lead patrol car ordered the driver to pull over. Gray ignored him.

Down the block, another black-and-white screamed into view, and Gray cut left onto Las Palmas, trying to outdistance this new enemy.

The third patrol car fell in behind the Sable. Bursts of color from the light bar pulsed over the car's interior, lighting up Wolper's hands, white-knuckled on the wheel.

Gray cut left again, cut right, cut left, never escaping the white circle of the chopper's beam. Another left, a right . . .

"He's fucked." Brand punctuated the comment with a fist pump.

Wolper saw what he meant and laughed. He braked the Sable. The three patrol cars stopped, slant-parked on the street.

It was a dead end.

The Firebird slowed as Gray realized his mistake. The street ended at the brick wall of an industrial building. Low-income homes flanked the cul-de-sac, some of their windows barred, others boarded up. A dog barked fitfully.

The Hollywood squad cars opened up, and patrol officers leaned out, bearing riot guns at port arms, shielded by the car doors. Standard felony-stop configuration. A voice on the lead car's PA system told the driver to exit his vehicle, keeping his hands in sight.

There was no response. The Firebird sat motionless in a puddle of light from the hovering chopper.

"Ten bucks says he makes a run for it," Brand said.

"There's nowhere to run," Robin whispered from the back.

"Guys like this always think they have one last chance. They don't know how to surrender peacefully."

"If he runs, they won't shoot him, will they?"

"He's not going to run," Wolper said. "Look at him. He's just sitting there."

"Pissing his pants, I bet," Brand said.

A long moment passed. The dog kept barking, and another joined it. One of the homeowners took a cautious step onto his front porch. A patrol car's siren burped a warning before the PA system ordered him to stay inside his residence. The man withdrew.

"So what happens now?" Robin asked.

"We wait him out." Wolper put the phone to his mouth again. "I guess you've heard the suspect is cornered."

"That's affirm."

"They scrambling a crisis team?"

"That'll be the D-chief's call. He's en route."

"Of course he is." Hammond wouldn't miss this action. "Okay, Control, I'll let you go. This is one you can tell your kids about." Wolper ended the call.

Robin leaned forward. "As long as we're just sitting here, I want to know what Sergeant Brand was doing in the arcade—and why he ran when we saw him."

Brand shifted in his seat. "I already explained all that to the lieutenant."

"Explain it to me." Her voice was hard.

"Okay." Brand sighed. "Here's the thing. I staked out Parker Center, and when you left the garage I followed you."

"Why?" Robin asked.

"I thought you might know something about Gray. He was your patient, after all."

"I don't understand."

"Everybody else was focusing on the desert areas, but you came into Hollywood. It was obvious you were looking for him. Why else would you come here? I thought you might have some kind of, you know, insight. An inside track, a hunch. Way things turned out, I guess you did."

Robin wasn't satisfied. "That still doesn't explain why you came after us."

"Doesn't it? Look, Dr. Cameron, my career's been going down the shitter ever since the Valdez shooting. People are saying I've lost it. They look at me funny. They treat me like a has-been. And maybe they're right. Hell, I been spending more time at the dogfights and the bars than on the job."

"I don't see what this has to do with—"

"With tailing you? I need a break. I need to get back in the game. Helping take down Gray would go a long way toward doing that. If you found him, I'd be there to assist in the collar. Then I'm not a burnout anymore."

"If that's true, why sneak around? Why not just accompany us?"

"You don't trust me, that's why. I'm not sure exactly what I said under hypnosis—"

"It's not hypnosis."

"Whatever. I'm not sure what I said, but you were giving me a look I didn't much like. The kind of look you'd give a rattlesnake. What the hell *did* I say, anyhow?"

"That's not something I can discuss right now."

"Right. Because you don't trust me. So I kept my distance. Figured I could help out if you spotted Gray. Or maybe I'd even spot him first."

"It's not even your job to make an arrest. You're off duty."

"So's Lieutenant Wolper. Cops make arrests when they're off duty. Hell, it makes an even better story. 'Off-duty cop nabs serial killer.' Let 'em try to call me a burnout after that."

Robin was silent for a moment. "Why did you run?" she asked finally.

"I panicked."

"Why?"

"I thought you got a glimpse of me. And I figured . . . well, if you were suspicious of me already, you'd be twice as suspicious if you thought I was sneaking up on you."

"You *were* sneaking up on us."

"I was just keeping you in sight, so I could be part of the action if you spotted Gray. I had to stay close or I would have lost you in that mob scene."

"This is what you told Lieutenant Wolper?"

"That's his story," Wolper said.

"And do you believe him?"

Wolper hesitated, looking at Brand beside him, Robin Cameron in the rearview mirror. "I've worked with Sergeant Brand for a lot of years. What he says makes sense, I guess. And I patted him down. He wasn't carrying."

"He's got a gun," Robin protested. "He had it out when you were chasing Gray."

"Like I told you," Wolper said patiently, "a cop always carries a gun, even off duty. Standard procedure. What I meant was, he wasn't carrying a gun he could use if he wanted to get away with something."

"Is that what you were looking for?" Brand asked. "A goddamn throwdown? Saturday Night Special with the serial number filed off?"

"I had to cover all the angles," Wolper said.

"Some fucking shrink plays head games with a mind machine, and now you're frisking me? Jesus, this really sucks."

"Shut up," Robin snapped. "You don't have a right to complain. By your own admission, you were following us. You skulk around in the shadows, then act like a victim when you get caught—"

"I wasn't skulking. I told you, I thought you might have a lead on Gray. Which you did. And here we are. We got him. So what's the problem?"

"The problem is, I don't *know* if he's the one who took my daughter. I don't *know* if he's the one who attacked me."

Brand turned in his seat. "You think I did that shit? What are you, fucking paranoid?"

"That's enough, Sergeant," Wolper cut in.

Brand ignored him. "Some shrink you are. You got your head so far up your own ass, you don't even know how to think straight when your kid's life is at stake—"

"*Enough*," Wolper said.

Brand settled back in his seat with an explosive sigh. "Fuck."

There was silence in the car and outside, broken finally by a squeal of tires as a new vehicle parked behind Wolper's Sable. He glanced at the side-view mirror and saw Deputy Chief Hammond getting out with his entourage.

"No more worries, people," Wolper said. "Here's our fearless leader now."

Chapter Forty-four

Hammond was feeling very good about things. He had taken a risk, and it had paid off. Cowards like Banner might hesitate, but Hammond hadn't risen in the ranks by playing it safe. Now Gray was cornered, and it was only a question of playing out the endgame.

En route to the scene, he'd put in a call to Susy Chen. She was on her way over, and where Susy went, the rest of the media would follow. He would have a lot of cameras and microphones recording his triumph. Tonight's success might be enough to secure him the chief's job when a replacement was sought.

He got out of his car, followed by Banner and Lewinsky. He found the first officer and received a briefing. The suspect's car was a blue Firebird of the right model year, with a single male occupant who was refusing to come out. The plate number was wrong for the stolen car; it had been traced to a resident of the Hyde Park area near Inglewood. Presumably, Gray had switched the plates, a common ploy. Inquiries had been made at the Hyde Park man's address, but he wasn't answering his phone. A Seventy-seventh Street Area unit had been dispatched to that address.

"All right," Hammond said, ignoring the Hollywood officer and addressing Lewinsky, "this is a crisis-team situation. We need SWAT on the scene, negotiators, traffic control, a comm team. If we're lucky, we can talk Gray out of the car in time for the eleven-o'clock news. If we're really lucky, he'll surrender at eleven on the dot and we'll lead the news with live coverage of his arrest."

On cue, a news chopper appeared in the night sky, competing with the Air Support unit for airspace.

"And if he opens fire and SWAT has to take him out?" Banner asked. "That won't look so good on TV."

"Won't it?" Hammond smiled. "Wasting a serial killer might get the ACLU crowd riled up, but I'll bet it goes down pretty smooth with Ma and Pa Six-pack. Of course," he added piously, "I hope it won't come to that. Now let's get going on that SWAT call-up."

"Chief," Lewinsky said, "that may not be necessary."

Hammond saw his adjutant staring past him. He followed Lewinsky's gaze to the end of the street, where the door on the driver's side of the Firebird had swung open.

"Hell," Hammond said. "Except for the chopper, there's not a single news crew here. I don't want just aerial shots. The bastard gave up too soon."

Slowly, Justin Gray emerged from the car, head lowered, hands raised. The hovering police helicopter pinned him in its searchlight.

The Firebird's passenger door opened. A second figure emerged into the glare.

"Who the hell is that?" Hammond said.

"Maybe it's the girl," Lewinsky offered. "The daughter. We got ourselves a twofer."

It was a girl, but not Megan Cameron. This girl had the skanky, strung-out look of a habitué of the street. Her hair was a frazzled pile, her arms skeletal and blotchy, her thin frame clad in a micromini and tank top. Everything about her said *whore*.

The driver lifted his dazed face into the light. He was not Justin Gray.

"God *damn* it," Hammond whispered.

He knew what had happened, of course. Some bozo from Hyde Park, the actual owner of the Firebird, had been cruising Selma Avenue, where the strawberries hung out ever since they'd been chased off Hollywood Boulevard. He'd picked up a hooker, and he'd been driving her somewhere, maybe to a motel, when a squad car had fallen in behind them. The john had panicked and tried to flee, leading Hollywood's finest on a pointless chase.

"I don't get it," Banner said. "The patrol units reported the driver alone in the vehicle. No passenger."

Hammond understood that part, too. "She was bending low."

"Keeping out of sight?"

"Giving him head."

Banner took this in. "During the chase? That's pretty impressive. I mean, you've got to admire that kind of focus."

"Shut up, Phil."

The driver and his passenger were on the pavement, being patted down and handcuffed by patrol officers. The hooker was laughing. The john looked like he was about to throw up.

"It's not a problem, Chief," Lewinsky said. "We're not any worse off than we were before."

The KNBC news van bearing Susy Chen turned the corner at that moment. There would be others.

"We're not, are we?" Hammond shook his head in gathering fury. "Every station will lead with this. Cops let a serial killer slip through their fingers while they nab a perv with a party girl."

"It's a setback, is all," Lewinsky said with exasperating optimism.

"It's a fuckup. And I'm the one who has to take the blame." He caught Banner flashing an I-told-you-so look and answered it with a cold glare. "Phil, start working the Channel Four crew. Put the best spin on this. I'll make a statement once the rest of the TV assholes show up."

Only TV mattered. Radio and newspapers were strictly minor-league ball.

"Got it, Chief. Meanwhile, you gonna get some background on the driver?"

"Fuck the driver. I want to talk to Wolper. I want to know what in Christ's name went on here."

Hammond stalked toward Wolper's Sable, Lewinsky trailing him like an eager puppy.

Chapter Forty-five

Robin got out of the car along with Wolper and Brand as the deputy chief approached. By now it was obvious that the pursuit had been a mistake. The wrong car had been followed. Gray had slipped away. She wasn't sure how she felt about that. She ought to want him apprehended—but part of her, oddly, was relieved.

Her worst fear had been that Gray would die in a shoot-out resisting arrest. Then she might never find Meg, never know what had really happened today. That possibility was too painful to consider.

"All right," Hammond said to Wolper and Brand, while Robin lingered close by. "I want to know what the hell happened here."

"We spotted Gray in a video arcade," Wolper began.

Hammond interrupted. "I know the fucking chronology. What exactly were you two men doing there in the first place?"

"Sergeant Brand just happened to be in the area on personal business," Wolper said. "We ran into him on the street. He had nothing to do with this. I take full responsibility."

Robin had to admire Wolper for loyalty to his subordinate, even if she still didn't trust Brand or buy his story.

Hammond seemed unimpressed. "Fine. Then I'll direct

my questions to Lieutenant Wolper. You were in the arcade with Dr. Cameron?"

"Yes, sir."

"I assume you had a good reason for bringing a civilian into danger."

Robin started to answer, but Wolper waved her silent. "It was an error of judgment on my part."

"Do you really think so?" Hammond asked with heavy sarcasm. "You're paid to exercise *good* judgment, Lieutenant."

"I'm aware of that, sir."

"If you thought Gray was in this area, you should have passed on the information to me. Investigating on your own initiative is bad enough. It's cowboy stuff."

"Yes, sir." Robin noticed the deputy chief's adjutant, whose badge identified him as Lewinsky, smirking at Wolper, enjoying his humiliation.

"Allowing a civilian to accompany you," Hammond went on, "especially a civilian who has already been victimized and who is personally known to the fugitive, was more than an error in judgment. It was potentially a catastrophe. If something had happened to Dr. Cameron while she was in our protective custody . . ."

Robin felt sure that Hammond was thinking about how it would have played in the media. His definition of a catastrophe was unfavorable news coverage.

"I understand, sir," Wolper said humbly.

"I hope you do. We'll have a fuller discussion of this matter when there's more time."

"Yes, sir."

"Meanwhile, you are to have no further connection with this investigation. Is that clear?"

"It's clear."

"I hope so, Lieutenant. I really do."

Robin spoke up at last. "Excuse me, Chief. Aren't you forgetting something?"

Hammond turned a cold eye on her. "What would that be?"

"We did find Gray."

"And lost him."

"We tracked him down," Robin persisted. "I had an idea of where he might go. Lieutenant Wolper helped me check it out. And we were right. Isn't that what's important?"

"What's important is following proper procedure. Without organization there is chaos."

"Did you hear that in a management seminar?"

Hammond straightened his shoulders. "Under the circumstances, Dr. Cameron, I would think you'd be less concerned with LAPD policy and more concerned with the recovery of your daughter." He cocked his head at a politely quizzical angle. "Or had you forgotten about her?"

Anger lashed her. She said the first thing she could think of. "You fucking pogue."

Wolper laughed. Lewinsky looked stricken. Hammond simmered, searching for a reply, found none, and spun on his heel to stride off, pursued by his adjutant.

"Nice use of the lingo," Wolper said.

Robin sighed. "I probably just got you in more trouble."

"Oh, yeah." Wolper smiled. "But it was worth it."

Wolper drove Brand back to the arcade, where he'd left his car. Robin sat in the backseat. No one said anything. The silence between them was thick and close, almost tangible.

Her cell phone rang. Gray again? Hurriedly she dug it out of her purse. "Hello?"

"Dr. Cameron?" It wasn't Gray. It was the criminalist, Gaines. "Your daughter had set up a password to protect her e-mail cache. I brought in someone from the computer crime unit to hack into the files. It turns out she *was* corresponding with this man Gabe, as her diary indicated. It's not clear if she actually met him or if it was just an Internet thing."

She kept her voice low, not wanting Brand, in the front seat, to hear. "Can you find out who he is? Trace the e-mails?"

"Let me have you talk to Pete Farber. He's our computer guy."

The phone was handed over to Farber, who started in on a technical explanation without any social preamble. "We have twenty-six e-mails generated by Novell's GroupWise software. The routing info indicates that the point of origin was the Los Angeles municipal WAN." He pronounced it like *ban*. "The IP address assigned to the user's computer is within a range reserved for the LAPD WAN—"

"Wait a minute." She lowered her voice still further. "LAPD?"

"Yes, ma'am."

"What is a WAN, exactly?"

"Wide-area network. Computers can be connected into a network of any size. If the network is small—say, all the computers in one office or one building—it's a local-area network, a LAN. If you start linking up LANs from different offices or buildings, you've got a WAN."

"And the LAPD has one of these WAN networks?"

"That's right. There are more than thirty-five hundred workstations in the LAPD, running the Novell NetWare operating system. Each LAPD station is a local-area net. The stations are linked together in a wide-area net, using high-speed T-one lines, mainly."

"And these e-mails were sent from within that system?"

"Right. GroupWise e-mail is used primarily for interoffice communication throughout the WAN, but the network does have Internet egress points—meaning it's possible for a user to send a message to someone outside the municipal net. That's what happened here."

"So just find out which user sent the e-mails—"

"It's not that simple. Any user can create an e-mail account under any name. The name 'Gabe'—no last name— is almost certainly an alias. The routing info tells us that the LAPD net was used, but to determine the specific workstation, we need additional information from ITA." He anticipated her question. "Information Technology Agency. The city agency that established the system."

"Then make them tell you."

"It takes time. We're trying to track down the administrator right now."

She bit back her impatience. "When you find him, will you know who sent the messages?"

"We'll know which terminal was used, that's all. It might be a terminal shared by various people."

"One way or the other, we're talking about a police officer?"

"Well . . . not necessarily a sworn officer, but someone on the LAPD system. It could be a clerical worker or, who knows, a civilian volunteer, a janitor, anybody with access to the terminal."

"But it could be a police officer?" she pressed. "The officers do use these terminals?"

"They do, yes, of course."

She thanked Farber, and when Gaines came back on the line, she asked him to keep her updated. "When we've traced the messages, you'll know," he promised.

The call was over. She put the phone back into her purse.

"What was that about?" Wolper asked from the driver's seat.

She couldn't give a truthful answer with Brand present. "A neighbor of mine. Calling to see if there's any news."

"It's better not to talk to friends and neighbors right now. You never know who'll start blabbing to the media or what they'll say."

She didn't answer. She stared at the seat in front of her, where Brand was sitting. She would never believe that Meg had been drawn to him in a personal encounter, but if he had created an Internet persona, perhaps passing himself off as a younger man . . .

She remembered Gray telling her that Mr. Cool was probably a cop. Was it Brand? She wished she'd asked how long Meg and Gabe had been exchanging e-mails. Had the relationship started before or after Brand became aware that he was likely to be selected as Robin's test subject? If it had started afterward, then maybe Brand had decided to get even with her by playing a sick game with her daughter.

She didn't quite buy it, though. Such a plan seemed too complicated, too subtle, for Sergeant Brand. Then again, she didn't really know him. And the messages had come from someone inside the LAPD.

Damn. She rubbed her head. Somehow things just kept getting worse.

"Headache?" Wolper asked. He'd been watching her in the rearview mirror.

"It's nothing."

"Not too late to take a trip to the hospital."

"No, thanks."

He shrugged. "Just asking."

At the arcade, Brand got out. "Nice to know who your friends are," he said in Wolper's direction. He glanced at Robin as she exited the backseat. "You too, Doc."

She stared back at him with cold, suspicious eyes. He walked off, not looking back. Quickly she slipped into the passenger seat beside Wolper. "Can we follow him, see where he goes?"

Wolper shook his head. "He knows my car. Under the circumstances, he'll be looking for it. I guess I should take you back to Parker Center."

She thought for a moment. "No."

"I told you, following him isn't an option."

"There's something else we can do."

"What is it?"

"We need to go to my office."

"Why? What's there?"

"The answer to my questions—maybe."

"The chief made it pretty clear that I'm to have no further involvement in this case."

"So you won't take me there?"

"Oh, I'll take you." Wolper smiled. "I just wanted to establish what a great guy I'm being."

She smiled back—her first smile in hours, she thought distantly. "Duly noted," she said.

"Then let's go."

He put the car into gear and headed east, toward the skyline.

Chapter Forty-six

It took Meg a long time to come back to herself. She felt as if she had gone away for a while, into a dream world of radiant peace.

She hadn't wanted to return. It was the moaning that had brought her back, a low, dismal sound like a foghorn.

She opened her eyes and found herself huddled on the bottom step of the cellar staircase, her handcuffed wrist suspended at shoulder height, her right arm wrapping her waist in a tight embrace. The flashlight still shone down from the landing, dimly illuminating the room.

A couple of feet away lay the man who'd tried to kill her, Detective Tomlinson, LAPD. He was still sprawled on his stomach, unmoving, showing no sign even of a rise and fall of breath. But he was alive. The moaning that issued from his open mouth was proof of that. Maybe he'd pulled free of the syringe before its entire contents could enter his bloodstream. Maybe he was big enough to absorb a dose that would have proven lethal to her. Or maybe he really was dying, but slowly.

She hoped not. She didn't want to take a life, even in self-defense. On the other hand, if he stayed alive, he might eventually awaken from his blackout or coma or whatever it was. And even if he didn't, Gabe or someone else was bound to stop by when Tomlinson failed to return.

One way or the other, she couldn't afford to be here. She had bought herself a reprieve, nothing more.

The cellar door was open. Escape was so close. The only thing holding her back was the handcuff on her wrist, the handcuff Tomlinson had claimed he would unlock.

She blinked with a new thought. Cops really did carry handcuff keys. And Tomlinson must have brought a key with him if he intended to move her after she . . . after he had . . .

She pushed away that idea. What mattered was the key. It had to be somewhere on his person. In one of his pockets, probably.

She moved closer to the unconscious man, as close as the short tether of the handcuff chain would permit, and reached out to the side pocket of his jacket. Some residual fear or distaste—perhaps the simple reluctance to touch a body that was so nearly dead—made her hesitate before actually slipping her hand into the pocket.

She shut her eyes and did it. Her fingers closed over something small and metallic—a coin, not a key. She dug deeper. More spare change. Nothing else. His pants pocket, maybe. She didn't want to touch him there, so close to his groin, his crotch, but then she remembered that she'd already had his private parts in her hand.

Somehow the thought made her smile, and the smile made it easier for her to explore this pocket also. She touched a wad of cloth, probably a handkerchief. A few crumpled dollar bills. That was all.

His belt, then. Sometimes cops wore keys and stuff clipped to a belt. She reached under his jacket, running her hand along the belt, feeling cracked leather, brittle and old, but found no keys, no equipment of any kind.

There was still the other side of his body to check, but she couldn't reach it. She grabbed the dead weight of his arm and tried dragging him toward her.

No use. He weighed easily two hundred pounds. With both hands free and the proper leverage, she might have been able to drag him. As it was, she had no more hope of shifting his position than of breaking the steel chain of the handcuff by sheer strength. And what if the key was in his vest pocket or the pocket of his shirt? She would have to turn him over, onto his back, an impossible task.

"So I'm screwed," she whispered.

Tomlinson groaned in answer.

There was one other possibility. The syringe.

She'd dropped it on the floor by her feet. Picking it up, she studied the slim needle as it caught the flashlight beam. She knew nothing about picking locks except what she'd seen on TV. It looked easy enough on cop shows.

Still, it might be possible to use the needle as a locksmith tool. Insert it in the handcuff's keyhole, try to jigger the thing open.

She gave it a shot, working the cuff on her wrist. She probed with the needle, having no clear idea of what to do.

How did locks work, anyway? She'd never even thought about it. Something about tumblers—or was that only the kind of locks they had on safes?

She was a moron. She didn't know the simplest practical thing. She had spent her time learning history and English lit when she should have been teaching herself street skills, survival skills. It was her mom's fault. If Robin hadn't sent her to that private school . . .

"Yeah, blame her," she whispered. "Real mature."

She struggled with the lock for what seemed like a long time. One thing was clear: The TV shows had lied. It was not easy to pick a lock. It was, as far as she could tell, impossible—at least without the right tools.

Finally she gave up. Her efforts had failed. She couldn't find a handcuff key in the detective's clothes, and she couldn't pick the lock. She couldn't do anything except wait for Tomlinson to regain consciousness and kill her, or for

Gabe to come back and kill her, or for some other bad guy to drop by and kill her.

The bottom line was that she was going to die. She had delayed her execution for a short time, but it was coming, and she was out of options. She would die in the factory, a dead place suitable for the dead.

Gabe had to get rid of her. And he was no angel. She knew that now. She knew how he'd used her. She knew how stupid she had been. She knew it all—too late.

Chapter Forty-seven

Gray circled the office building in the dark, his headlights off, only the parking lights shining. If there were cops staking out the place in a slickback, he needed to know it now, before he tried going inside.

Inside. He shook his head. Fuck, he must be a candidate for the puzzle factory to be even thinking about pulling this shit. Here he was, having just eluded the police back on the boulevard, and what was he doing to celebrate? He was cruising the corner where Doc Robin had her office, so he could commit a little after-hours B 'n' E.

Nuts. That's what it was. He wondered about himself sometimes. The people who thought he was crazy for killing high school girls had gotten it all wrong. There was nothing crazy about some good old-fashioned all-American blood sport. But what he was doing now, risking his freedom for a look in the doc's office . . . *that* was crazy, no two ways about it.

He was going to do it, though. Hell, he'd already decided. If he changed his mind, it would be like backing down from a fight.

He saw no black-and-whites in the neighborhood. No TV trucks either. He'd been worried that the newspeople might be hanging out here, but they'd gone. When he arrived, he'd seen the last couple of news vans hightailing it out of the area like they had a hot tip.

Where to stash his car was a problem. Couldn't leave it too close to the building. If any cops came along and saw it there, they'd know he was inside for sure. On the other hand, he couldn't park too far away. Might need to make a quick escape. Suppose there was an undercover car in the vicinity. He hadn't spotted any action like that, and he was pretty sure he could sniff a stakeout, but there was a chance someone was waiting for him to return to the scene. If so, he would have to run for it, and his wheels had to be close.

He compromised by parking the Firebird in the alley beside the building. He eased the car against a brick wall, maneuvering it behind a trash bin. The car was invisible from the street. Unless a patrol unit went down the alley itself, there was no way his ride would be spotted.

He left the car unlocked with the key in the ignition, ready to roll. Nobody was going to steal the fucking thing in the next ten minutes, and ten minutes was all the time he planned to spend inside the office building.

With the deputy's gun stuffed in his waistband, he headed out of the alley and crouched by the fence that surrounded the parking lot. He took a minute to suss out the area. If any watchers had eyeballed him driving into the alley, he would expect them to be moving in on him now. He saw no movement, heard no footsteps. More important, he got no sense of trouble. Sensing it—that was a street thing, a knack he'd picked up somewhere along the line. He knew when the boys in blue were around. It wasn't like the short hairs stood up or anything. He just knew.

He was willing to bet they weren't around now.

The fence was gated and locked at night, but it was more for show than anything else. There was no concertina wire on top, and any homeboy worth his spit could climb the thing without breaking a sweat. Gray went up and over, then quickly advanced, sticking close to the building's rear wall.

The parking lot was empty, the building dark. A few

lights burned in the upper windows, but none on the ground floor. He guessed that the place had been emptied out so The Man could do his Sherlock thing, collecting hairs and fibers and all that happy crap. These days cop work was more like fuckin' brain science, and there was something deeply wrong about that. The bad guys didn't use no lasers or microscopes, and the lawmen shouldn't, either. Ought to be a level playing field.

Brain science was the doc's turf. She was smart. Finding him at the arcade, now, that was friggin' genius. How the fuck could she have known he'd go there, when he didn't half know it himself? It was creepy, almost like she could read his damn mind even without plugging him into her machine.

He reached the back door and looked around. Still no movement. No shouts of "Freeze, police!" No lights snapping on, no Sam Brownes jingling with handcuffs and keys and batons and guns and Mace and rover radios.

The door was locked. He'd been expecting that, although optimistically he'd thought the door might be left unlocked at night because of the false security provided by the fence. He'd also hoped that even if there was a lock, it might be one of those corner-hardware-store varieties that he could defeat with his trusty screwdriver. No such luck. It was a nice solid dead bolt. With the right tools he might've tackled it, but he didn't have no tools so he had to go in another way.

It was no big thing. The ground-floor windows were unbarred. Leaving them that way was a risk in this part of town, but he guessed the egghead yuppies who rented these cubbyholes didn't want to sit staring at iron bars all day. Besides, the fence and the dead-bolted door probably made them feel nice and safe.

He picked a window at random, punched in the pane with his elbow, cleared away the clinging shards, and climbed through. He checked his back. The parking lot was still dark and quiet. If there were any bozos with badges around here, they were asleep on the job.

The office he'd entered was filled with computers and stacks of paper—an accounting firm or something. He made his way through the dark suite to the door and eased it open. The hall was empty. He saw no surveillance cameras. Easy pickings. He ought to come back sometime and rip off this place.

Doc Robin's office, on the opposite side of the corridor, was a few doors down. No problem spotting it. It was the one festooned with yellow tape warning POLICE CRIME SCENE—DO NOT CROSS. He ripped down the tape and tossed it aside. The door's simple spring latch was no problem. He shimmed it open, using the doc's own credit card. Poetic freaking irony.

Inside the waiting room, he shut the door and turned on the overhead light.

There was blood on the carpet where Gomer Pyle had bled out like a stuck pig. Stuck pig—that was a good one. The sound of his own laughter was startling in the stillness.

He went into the main room, the inner sanctum, the theater of cruelty, Dr. Cameron's House of Pain. The lab where he ran through mind mazes like a trained rat earning his cheese.

In here he left the lights off. It was always possible the LAPD was watching the windows. Anyway, he didn't need much light to find the file cabinet next to the desk.

Reading the files was a different proposition. He thought about carrying stacks of them into the other room, but that would take too long. He solved the problem by rooting around on the floor by the mind-fucking machine till he found the flashlight pen Doc Robin had dropped when she took that hit to the noggin. The light still worked. He was surprised the bag-and-tag brigade hadn't snapped it up—but now that he thought about it, he realized that most likely there hadn't been any of that nerd-squad action here, after all. The lawmen already knew who their suspect was. They didn't need hairs and fibers and fingerprints. They'd got him made, and the doc sure as shit hadn't said anything to change their minds.

It got him pissed all over again—being set up, framed, played like an amateur. He was a bona fide, genuine A-1 prime, government-certified serial killer, for Christ's sake. You didn't fuck around with a serial killer. It showed a lack of respect. And when you disrespected Justin Hanover Gray, you got payback.

He opened the top drawer of the file cabinet and beamed the penlight inside. One of Doc Robin's patients had fucked with him. The dude's name was in here someplace.

He started flipping through the manila folders in alphabetical order, checking each patient. The doc had said the guy was a cop who'd killed somebody. That ought to narrow it down.

There were no likely candidates in the As. He started on the Bs. Somebody named Barone—another con like Gray, but he wasn't no killer, just a rapist. Then there was a Berman, a paying customer with some problem called panic disorder, which Gray figured was a fancy way of saying the dude was a wuss. Billings, Jonathan. Blackmore, Katherine. Blythe, William. Brand, Alan . . .

Brand. That was the slick motherfucker who was playing this game.

He met all the criteria. He was her patient. He was a cop. And he'd killed a man.

Justifiable homicide in the line of duty, according to the official investigation. Gray figured that was bullshit. He didn't put any stock in what one cop said about another cop. All of them were busy covering for themselves and the department. They would never drop a dime on their buddy. Gray felt no resentment about that. Hell, he even admired them for it. They took care of their own.

He memorized Brand's address before replacing the file in the drawer. He'd already overstayed his welcome. Time to get back to his Firebird and pay a social call on his new friend.

Gray left the office. The door could not be locked without a key, so he just closed it, loosely reattaching the crime-scene tape. No point in advertising his visit.

He went down the hall to the outside door and cranked the handle, but the door wouldn't open. It was one of those locks that were key-operated on both sides. You needed a key to get out of the building. Goddamn fire hazard was what it was. He'd just have to go out through the window he'd used when he came in.

From an intersecting corridor came footsteps, rapid, closing.

He took a step toward the doc's office, but he didn't think he could hide in time to avoid being spotted. And the other office, the one with the busted window, was even farther away.

The stairwell. That was the ticket.

He stepped inside, careful to hold the door open a few inches so it wouldn't clang shut.

The footsteps rat-tatted closer. Now there were voices. A guy saying, "You really think this will work?" and some woman saying, "I can't be sure. It might."

Not just some woman. That was old Doc Robin herself.

Gray pursed his lips. Damn, he kept running into that bitch.

He was suddenly glad he hadn't taken refuge in the doc's office. She was headed there for sure.

"MBI can be helpful in recovering memories," she was saying. "If I relive the attack, I may be able to identify the assailant."

"Can you be sure the memory is accurate?"

"I don't know."

"Then this is just a big waste of time, isn't it?"

"If you have better things to do, don't let me keep you."

"Okay, okay, I'm only playing the role of skeptic."

"It suits you."

Sounded like the doc planned to tweak her memories with her brain machine—all so she could remember who clocked her. Gray thought it would've been a lot easier if she'd just trusted him, but it seemed she wasn't the trusting kind.

He wasn't too thrilled about how things at the arcade had ended. He was pretty sure the doc had kept him talking just to buy time till her police buddies showed up. It was a betrayal, and he didn't like betrayals. He had half a mind to step out of the stairwell and pop her and her boyfriend right now.

Problem was, he recognized the guy's voice too. It was the cop who'd yelled, "Police, freeze," or whatever Jack Lord bullshit he'd been barking. That guy wasn't likely to go down easy. He'd pull out his piece and start busting caps, and all of a sudden the hallway would be the OK Corral. Gray didn't think too highly of his chances in that kind of engagement. He stayed hidden.

The footsteps stopped. "Look at this." The doc's voice. "Door was left unlocked."

"Careless."

"Damn stupid."

The cop laughed. "You can't spell *slapdash* without LAPD."

Gray had to admit, he kind of liked that one.

When the voices had receded and the door had closed, Gray emerged from the stairwell. He went quickly down the hall to the accountant's office or whatever it was. He hoisted himself through the window, retraced his steps to the fence, and then it was up and over and back to the alley. He cranked the Firebird's engine and reversed into the street.

Alan Brand lived in Hollywood. Gray could be there in twenty minutes.

It was impolite to drop in without calling ahead, but he was sure the sarge would understand.

Chapter Forty-eight

Robin flicked on the overhead light in her office and took a look around. Her computers, left running after the attack, had powered down automatically to standby mode after an hour of inactivity. The MBI appliance was on the floor where Gray must have tossed it after unbuckling himself from the chair. She was glad the police hadn't confiscated the unit. She only hoped it hadn't been damaged in the fall.

"There's a kitchenette to your left," she told Wolper as she picked up the appliance. "You can fix yourself a cup of coffee if you like."

"I'd rather just get started."

"So would I, but the preparations may take a while."

Behind her, he entered the kitchen area. The small TV in the kitchen clicked on, and an announcer's voice told viewers to stay tuned for the ten-o'clock news.

She hadn't realized it was so late. Meg had been missing for nearly six hours.

Sitting in her swivel chair, she awakened the computers and turned on the appliance. She would have to run the diagnostics program to be sure that the ferromagnetic coils were working and were in the proper alignment. The program would take about fifteen minutes.

While it ran, she scrounged around on the floor for the two headset transceivers. The one she'd worn was all right, but Gray's headset had been broken when he had cast it aside. She had no replacement. She and Wolper would just have to talk over the loud clicking of the coils.

The electrodes attached to Gray's body had also been strewn everywhere in a tangle of wires. She swept them aside. There was no point in wearing the electrodes anyway. Wolper wouldn't be able to decipher the readouts.

On the TV news, the top story was under way: the ongoing manhunt for serial killer Justin Hanover Gray. Her name and Meg's had been kept out of the report. Gray was said to have attacked a psychiatrist working with him, killed a deputy, and kidnapped a teenage girl whose photo had been provided to the media.

She tuned out the news and considered the challenge of recovering her memory of the attack.

She was suffering from traumatic retrograde amnesia. No one really understood how memory worked, but most theories assumed that short-term memory had to be processed by the hippocampus, part of the brain's medial temporal lobe. A sudden shock to the brain, such as the blunt trauma that had produced her concussion, seemed to disrupt the electrical activity in the hippocampus and somehow prevented the short-term memory from being transferred to long-term storage. The memory most likely to be lost was that of the trauma itself.

The question was whether or not the memory still existed. If it did, and the problem was one of retrieval, then the MBI procedure might bring it to the surface in the same way that it liberated long-suppressed memories of childhood abuse and other traumas. But if the memory was simply gone, then nothing could reclaim it.

She was reasonably optimistic about retrieval. Most victims of concussion eventually recovered some memories of the event. How these memories were stored and how they were regained were two of the countless mysteries of the brain. Some experts postulated a dual storage mechanism—a kind of backup memory system that kept working even when the hippocampus failed. Other experts believed that hippocampal processing was only delayed by trauma, not prevented, and that even a short-term memory remained intact somewhere in the temporal lobe, ready to be consolidated into long-term storage when normal memory function resumed.

Nobody knew. When it came to the brain, what was known was vastly outweighed by what was unknown.

She decided to boost the output of the coils affecting both temporal lobes—the left, which processed memories of names and words, and the right, which handled memories of faces and other visual information. A strong low-frequency magnetic field over those areas would inhibit their activity and perhaps allow the relevant neural mechanisms to settle down and begin functioning normally after the agitation of the trauma.

The TV report was wrapping up as a reporter, live at the Hollywood cul-de-sac, repeated word of the failed pursuit. In midsentence he went silent. Wolper had turned off the set. He emerged from the kitchenette, carrying a mug of coffee.

"Hammond must be just loving this," he said.

His jocular tone infuriated her. "I don't give a damn about your office politics." She took a breath. That hadn't been smart or fair. "Sorry. I'm just . . . all wound up."

He came closer. "Do you really think you should be doing this right now?"

"I *have* to do this. Right now."

"Will it work?"

She sighed. This was the fourth or fifth time he'd asked. "I don't know. Let me work out the technical stuff, okay?"

Wolper drifted away. Robin concentrated on reprogramming the appliance's parameters. When she was finished, she checked the diagnostic results. All fifty-two coils were functioning normally. She exhaled a breath of relief.

"All right, I think we're ready to start."

Wolper joined her again at the computer console.

"Once I'm wearing the appliance," she said, "all you have to do is press the enter key. That will activate the appliance. I'll go into a trance. It should take five minutes or so. You'll see me getting relaxed."

She thought about telling him that she should not be allowed to stay under for more than thirty minutes, because the procedure's safety over longer time intervals had never been verified. She decided against it, not wishing to be pulled out just as she was on the verge of a breakthrough. She would remain in an altered state of consciousness for as long as it took.

"The MBI will be noisy. It makes a loud clicking sound. That's normal. Don't let it worry you."

"Why should I be worried? You're the one who'll be wearing this gizmo."

Robin didn't care for the term *gizmo*, but she let it ride.

"So what am I supposed to do," he asked, "besides watch you get your brain scrambled?"

"Your job is to ask me questions, the way you did in the interview room. Pretend you're taking a statement. Lead me through the events preceding the attack. My answers may be slow. It'll be like I'm on drugs or something."

"I've done a few interviews with drugged-up witnesses."

"There should be a point when I'm in position to see the assailant. That's the memory I need to recover."

"Even if you do remember, evidence like this will never be allowed in court."

"I'm not thinking about court. I just want to know where our focus should be."

Wolper studied her. "You already think you know where to focus. You're sold on Brand."

"What makes you say that?"

"You've been working with Gray for months. You want to believe he's clean. But he's not. A leopard can't change his spots."

She had no time or energy to waste on arguing. "There's

one other thing you need to know," she said. "The MBI process inhibits motor functioning. In other words, I'll be immobilized. It's natural. It doesn't mean there's a problem."

"Suppose there *is* a problem. Suppose you start spouting gibberish—more so than usual, that is. Or you start twitching and jerking—"

"The term is *seizing*. It's unlikely. If it happens, end the session."

"How?"

"Press the enter key again. Okay?"

"I think I can handle that."

"So are you set?"

"One more question," Wolper said. "Have you ever done this before?"

"I do it all the time. It's my job."

"I mean on yourself."

She'd been hoping he wouldn't ask, but since he had, she gave a truthful answer. "Only twice. For experimental purposes. And I didn't go very deep."

"Nervous?"

This time she lied. "No."

She settled back in the chair, her hands on the armrests. Eyes closed, she practiced taking slow abdominal breaths.

"I'm ready," she said.

"Then here goes."

The appliance came on. The sudden clicking of the coils was louder than she'd expected. She worried that she might not be able to shift into alpha rhythm while distracted by the noise.

But even as that thought occurred to her, she felt the peculiar distancing of her mind from her body, the strange numbness that told her she was being carried gently away.

She needed a fantasy environment in which to feel safe, and she chose a park in Ojai, an artists' community near Santa Barbara where she and Dan had often gone with Meg.

No, she couldn't think of Meg—not if she wanted to relax. Had to forget Dan, also. Too much baggage there.

She was in the park alone, untroubled, and it was a clear spring day. The breeze, laced with moisture from the Pacific a few miles distant, played over her skin and hair. The clicking of the coils receded. It became the chirping of crickets, the rustling of leaves.

In the park she settled down on the carpet of grass, sinking into the green, dewy shoots, letting sun and air envelop her. She was calm.

Wolper's voice reached her over the background sounds.

"It's been five minutes, Doctor. Are you relaxed?"

"Relaxed. Call me Robin."

"Okay, Robin. We need to talk about what happened here at your office a few hours ago. You were having a session with Justin Gray. Remember?"

"Yes."

"I want you to tell me how the session ended."

"It was . . . everything went dark."

"Before it went dark. Go back a few minutes earlier. Gray had the, uh, the helmet thing on. And I guess you were talking to him. Bringing him out of it?"

"Yes."

"So he comes out of the trance . . ."

"Yes."

"What are you doing right at that moment?"

She could see the scene playing before her closed eyelids. "Saving the session to a CD."

"And Gray?"

She heard Gray's voice in the background. "He's talking. Talking about his father. The way his father punished him." She heard the rustling of his jumpsuit. "And he's shifting in the chair. Restless . . ."

"What's happening now?"

"I'm labeling the CD. Writing with my pen." Bouncing circles of light over the letters she formed. "My flashlight pen."

"And then?"

Blackness. "Everything's dark."

"No, something happens before it all goes dark. Go back."

She reversed time, running it backward like a filmstrip. "Label the CD . . ."

"Right."

The light of the pen in her hand. Then—no light. "Dark. All dark."

"So you can't remember?"

"Can't . . ." This wasn't quite true. "Won't," she said slowly.

"Won't?"

This was odd. She needed to remember. But . . . "Don't want to."

"So you *do* remember. You just don't want to? Is that it?"

She didn't answer. She was trying to understand. Obviously some psychological defense mechanism was trying to protect her from reexperiencing the trauma. This was a good thing. It meant that the memory was there, retrievable, if she could overcome the mental barrier.

"Robin? Is that it?"

"Yes."

"Part of you remembers?"

"Yes."

"It's remembering right now?"

That sounded correct. "Right now," she whispered.

"Can you get in touch with that part of you?"

It was a good question, the proper question to ask, but she didn't know the answer. "Maybe."

"Will you try?"

"Don't want . . ."

"Will you?"

Her reluctance was irrational, but irrationalities could have as strong a hold as any rational conviction. Stronger, sometimes. She had to fight it, push past it.

"Robin? Will you?"

"Yes."

"What are you seeing now?"

The room wheeled around her. "I'm turning . . . turning in my chair."

"Why are you turning?"

"His voice. I hear it in his voice."

"Hear what?"

"Danger. A threat. So I'm turning . . ."

"Yes? You turn, and what do you see?"

"Dark."

Wolper sighed. "Everything's gone dark again? This isn't going to work, Robin. I'm sorry. It's a dead end."

He hadn't understood. She plunged forward in a rush of words. "The room is dark. I turned off the lights for the session. When I turn, I see the dark. Shadows. Movement . . ." She felt herself flinch and let out a soft cry.

"He hit me. I'm falling. I'm on the floor. He got loose, Justin got loose."

It was all happening again, happening at this moment, but in dreamy slow motion.

"You see him?" Wolper asked.

"Can't see. Too dark. Need to scream. Deputy's in the next room. If I scream . . . But his hand is on my mouth. He's leaning over me. There's light."

"What light?"

"The penlight. In my hand. It comes on. I see him. Right before he hits me again, I see him; *I see his face*."

"Is it Gray?"

"No."

"Is it Brand?"

"No."

"Who is it, Robin?"

"You. I see *you*."

She opened her eyes, and in the glow of the computer console Wolper smiled.

"That's right, Doctor," he said softly. "You saw *me*."

Chapter Forty-nine

After leaving Hollywood, Brand had driven into Newton Area, checking his rearview mirror to be sure he wasn't followed. He'd parked at the station house and gone inside, heading straight to his locker, ignoring the startled hellos from officers working the night watch.

There had been nothing in his locker except his uniform and his other gear. He'd gone over it twice, searching everywhere, until he was satisfied.

His house, then. It had to be in his house.

Back in his car, guiding the Crown Vic onto the freeway to make the crosstown run, he asked himself what the hell he was going to do. He didn't know.

This thing he'd gotten himself mixed up in was too big. Or maybe the real problem was that he was too small. The small fish always ended up as bait, snack food for the marlins and the sharks. He didn't have the clout and—he might as well face it—didn't have the smarts, either, to deal with his present circumstances. He was cornered, treed, sweating through his shirt, scared shitless, out of luck and out of moves.

God damn it, he hated his life.

The gate to his driveway was locked, as always. He got out of his car and opened it, then motored into the carport.

The gate was one gap in the bungalow's security. Would have been better to have an automatic gate that closed behind him as soon as he entered. Leaving it open until he closed it manually could allow an intrusion.

But he guessed he didn't have to worry about that now. When they came for him, they wouldn't be sneaking onto the property. They would come with a warrant, and he would let them in, because he would have no choice. And they would find what they were looking for.

Unless he found it first.

He turned off the engine, opened the car door—and was thrown back across both seats by the weight of a man's body atop his own.

In the glow of the Vic's ceiling light, he looked up into the face of Justin Gray.

"Hey, Sarge." Gray smiled. "You and me need to have a conversation."

Brand thought about the gun under his windbreaker, but Gray had thought of it first. He patted Brand down, unholstered the gun, and tossed it into the backseat, out of reach. "No tricks," Gray said.

"What the fuck do you want?"

"Like I said, I'm in a talkative mood. Hope you are, too."

"I've got nothing to say to you."

"We'll see."

As Brand watched, Gray depressed the cigarette lighter.

"Hey," Gray said. "I know you, motherfucker. You're the dude from the video place."

Brand was silent.

"You was chasing me—you and your friend. All official, with your guns out and shit. Two big men hunting the bad guy. Funny thing. You don't seem so big now."

"Neither do you."

"Oh, I'm big enough, Sarge. Why'd you set me up?"

"What?"

"You framed me for conking Doc Robin, snuffing the Deputy Dawg. Why?"

"I don't know anything about that."

"Right, right." The cigarette lighter popped out. Gray extracted it from the socket. "You're one tough mother, right, Sergeant Brand?"

Brand tried not to stare at the lighter.

"Brand," Gray said. "Now that's an interesting name. One of those names that means something, you know. Like, there's brands of cereal. And something that's never been used is brand-new. And then, of course, there's this kind of brand."

He pressed the burning end of the lighter into Brand's cheek.

Brand screamed, but no one heard it. Gray's hand covered his mouth.

The pain went on forever. Brand had never known there could be this kind of pain.

Finally Gray withdrew the lighter and pushed it back into the socket—all the way.

"That hurt, I bet," Gray said. "I know about shit like that. My daddy used to burn me with the radiator."

Brand couldn't answer. His eyes were wet. He was crying, maybe for the first time in his adult life.

"Used to brand me, I guess you'd say." Gray chuckled. "I don't got all night, Sarge. You wanna tell me what kind of game you crooked-ass cops are runnin' on me?"

He tried one more time to resist, not out of bravery but self-preservation. He was sure Gray would kill him if he heard the truth. "Nobody's playing any games."

"Pissing me off, Sarge." The lighter popped out again, recharged, and Gray grabbed it. It found Brand's ear, drilling partway into the ear canal, sending hot wires of agony straight into his brain.

Brand wanted to tell this man everything, but he couldn't stop screaming long enough to get the words out.

The lighter withdrew. The left side of Brand's head throbbed with pain. He thought his eardrum had been ruptured. Something oozed out of his ear and down his cheek.

He was crying again—big, racking sobs interspersed with shallow wheezing.

"Gonna talk?" Gray asked. His voice seemed far away. Brand figured he'd gone deaf in one ear.

I'll talk, he tried to say, but his mouth wouldn't work properly, and no sound came out.

Gray interpreted the silence as resistance. "Still holding out on me? Okay, then. Let's say I try putting this hot little number in your fucking *eye*." Gray popped the lighter back into the plug.

That did it. Brand recovered speech. "No, don't, I'll tell, I'll talk, don't . . ." All one flood of words, undignified and desperate.

"Knew you would. Gotta say I'm a little disappointed, though. I thought you'd take longer to crack. You ain't much of a man, are you, Sarge?"

"I'll talk," Brand said again.

"I got that." Gray smiled down at him. "So go on. Tell me a bedtime story."

He fought to control his breathing. He was deathly afraid that he would lose his voice again, and Gray would punish him for the pleasure of it.

"It wasn't me. I didn't . . . I wasn't in the office today."

"Then who was?"

"Wolper. He's the one. He's been dirty for years. I met him at the academy, worked with him on and off—"

"I don't want your bio. Who's Wolper?"

"Lieutenant in Newton Area. Where I work."

"You say he's dirty. Dirty how?"

"He takes payoffs."

Gray snorted. "What cop doesn't?"

"I'm not talking about a free meal at the taco wagon. I'm talking about major funds changing hands."

"Whose funds?"

"The Gs'. They're a street gang—"

"I know who they are. I keep my ear to the ground. San

Pedro Street Gangstas. They run a serious posse, deal an ass-load of drugs. Right?"

Brand nodded. "Right."

"You're saying this lieutenant, this Wolper, is tight with the Gs?"

"Has been for a long time. They pay him off every couple weeks. But lately he's been taking more chances. Getting bigger payoffs, I think."

"Son of a bitch got greedy?"

"I think it's his ex. She's always after him for money. Wants to send their kid to a special school or something."

"Yeah, blame it on the girl. I hear you."

"Whatever she wants, Wolper's pretty tapped out. He's doing things to raise money that he wouldn't have done before."

Talking wasn't so hard now. He was breathing almost normally. The pain in his cheek and his ear had receded to a spreading numbness.

"And what do the homeboys buy for their hard-earned cash?" Gray asked.

"Protection. Wolper's the watch commander. If he knows something is about to go down on his shift, he can deploy patrol units to other parts of the territory. Try and clear out the area where the action will be, give the Gs a better chance to get in and out. After the incident is called in, he can work it so the response is slower than it has to be and a little less organized. Nothing obvious. Just enough to give the Gs an edge."

Gray was watching, nodding. Brand felt a prickle of hope. Maybe he could give this crazy bastard what he wanted. Maybe Gray would let him live.

It was funny—a few minutes ago, he'd been thinking how much he hated his life, and now he wanted nothing more than to prolong it. Half-dead, disfigured—it didn't matter; he wanted to live.

"And there's other stuff," he added, trying to be helpful.

"Like?"

"Sometimes evidence goes missing from the storage rooms. A whole case has gotta be thrown out. Typical police bungling, everybody thinks. Wolper always shrugs it off. 'You can't spell *slapdash* without LAPD,' that's what he says."

He thought this was good—slipping in a little humor—and he was alarmed when Gray's eyes narrowed. "Wait a sec. Was this the asshole that was with you at the arcade tonight?"

Brand sensed a new danger here. He wanted to lie, deny it, but he was sure Gray would see right through him, and then the lighter would come out again. . . .

"That's right," Brand said. "That was him. He was escorting Cameron. If he hadn't been with her . . ."

But Gray wasn't listening anymore. He drew a gun from his waistband, yanked Brand into a sitting position. Brand looked at the gun, and the words *This is it* lit up in his mind like a neon sign.

"Slide over," Gray said. "I'm driving your car. Mine's got too much heat on her."

A reprieve. The psycho wasn't going to shoot him. Not yet.

Brand obeyed the order, risking a question as he slid into the passenger seat. "We going someplace?"

Gray tossed him a grin, and in that grin Brand saw a wildness, a ferocity that was almost inhuman. "Straight to the doc's office, Sarge—burning rubber all the way."

Chapter Fifty

Wolper wheeled the swivel chair close to Robin and stared intently into her face. "You really can't move, can you? Not a muscle."

To test the statement, he reached out with one hand and touched her face. She felt herself flinch internally, but her body registered no reaction. He dragged a fingernail lightly along her cheek.

"Amazing," he said, his voice low.

She willed herself to move. Lift an arm, twitch a finger, anything. It seemed like such a simple thing, the contraction of a muscle in response to a mental command, but now the communications line between her higher cerebral functions and her body had been broken, and there was nothing simple about it.

She wasn't tied down, wasn't encumbered in any way. She was free to get out of the chair whenever she wished, if only she could get her limbs to respond. She couldn't. She was paralyzed by the electromagnetic frequencies inhibiting her motor functions.

She had designed the MBI program to minimize the risk of seizure by suppressing motor response. Now she was trapped by her own technology.

He kicked the swivel chair backward and stood up. "I've

got to admit, Doctor, it makes things very convenient for me."

She noticed he'd stopped calling her by her first name. He had, in fact, been strangely reluctant to do so from the beginning. Perhaps he needed to depersonalize her, distance himself from his victim.

He got out of the chair and surveyed the room, taking a letter opener from her desk.

Cut my throat, he's going to cut my throat. . . .

But he made no move toward her. He looked up at the ceiling, then climbed onto the sofa underneath the smoke detector. With the letter opener, he began to pry the detector loose.

She knew, then. She knew exactly what he was going to do. She remembered his talk about throwdown guns, untraceable because the serial number had been eradicated. If he'd had a gun like that, he would have used it on her. He didn't—not with him, anyway. If he cut her throat or strangled her, he would get blood on himself or leave hair and fiber evidence.

But fire . . .

Fire would erase all evidence. Fire would reduce the room to ashes. There would be nothing for the crime-scene technicians to find.

The smoke detector had come loose. With the letter opener he cut the wires, then extracted the battery.

She tried to figure out how it had happened. Wolper and Brand were in it together. That was clear now. Together they had done everything they could to stonewall her. Brand had refused to show up for his session. Wolper had tried to talk her out of pursuing the case. When that failed, he sent her to the worst neighborhood in town, obviously expecting that she wouldn't risk the trip.

Still, nothing Brand said had implicated Wolper. And Wolper didn't strike her as the type to take undue risks out of loyalty to a subordinate. If Brand had taken the payoff from Valdez and then shot him . . .

But maybe he hadn't.

Wolper went into the waiting room, where he discovered a second smoke detector near the bathroom.

Robin thought back to the session. Brand had been resisting the MBI process. She remembered his fear of going into a trance—being hypnotized, as he called it. Of course he didn't want to be hypnotized when there were secrets he was afraid to reveal.

To overcome his resistance she had told him to report the scene in the parking garage as a spectator. He had reported witnessing a confrontation between a cop and Eddie Valdez. She had assumed the cop was Brand himself. What if it wasn't?

What if the cop had been Wolper?

In the waiting room, he slid an end table underneath the smoke detector and stood on it as he disabled the device. That detector was not wired into the AC, and all he had to do was remove the battery.

She replayed the session in her memory. Brand's voice, slow and thick, recounting the events.

"Eddie brings out the money. Thick wad, wrapped in wax paper, all taped up. Looks like a fat deli sandwich. Makes me hungry when I see it. I didn't have lunch that day—"

Her own voice, interrupting.

"Not you. You're the observer, Alan. You're only watching. Tell me about the two men. Eddie and the cop."

And Brand going on: "The cop takes the money, puts it in his coat. It doesn't print too bad against the material. Nobody will notice it there."

Every time he'd injected himself into the story, she had made him pull back and focus as an observer. It had never occurred to her that he might have actually been an observer all along. Maybe he had been making the pickup with Wolper—no, that made no sense; he had called in the report on his radio before entering the garage. He must have followed Valdez inside and stumbled on the transaction, watched from the shadows as it went down.

When Wolper realized he had a witness, he swore Brand to silence. More than that, he made Brand take the fall for the shooting, since Brand had already radioed that he was in pursuit of Valdez. Wolper, or perhaps others involved in the conspiracy, had finessed the shooting review so Brand was assured a positive outcome. Whatever discrepancies there were between the bullet that had killed Valdez and the gun Brand carried would have disappeared.

Finished with the smoke detector, Wolper went into the kitchenette. She couldn't see him without turning her head, and her head wouldn't turn, of course. But even over the clicking of the magnetic coils, she could hear drawers and cupboards being opened as he looked for flammable materials.

The conspiracy had all been covered up—until Brand started talking under the influence of MBI. Although he hadn't implicated Wolper, he had opened up the incident for a new investigation. Wolper had to take care of things before they went any further. She had told no one but him about her findings. He stalled her for a day with a bogus claim that he was going to review the case file on the Valdez shooting. Then he came after her.

At dinner she'd told him she was treating an inmate. She'd even said when her session with the convict was held. While the session was under way, Wolper must have entered the waiting room, made small talk with the deputy—and killed him with a knife or other sharp instrument when the man's back was turned. He came into this room, concealed by darkness, unheard because both she and Gray were wearing headsets. He would have killed her the same way he'd killed the deputy, then found a way to make Gray look responsible. Maybe he was planning to shoot Gray and then claim he had arrived early for his four-o'clock appointment. He would have been a hero—the off-duty cop who stopped a serial killer's rampage.

But Gray spoiled his plans. He had the screwdriver. He

used it to free himself from the straps. And when Wolper attacked her, Gray took him by surprise.

Gray really had saved her life. The blood on the screwdriver was Wolper's, not the deputy's.

Wolper had fled. He would have had to bandage his cut, dispose of any soiled clothes and other evidence. Then he returned to her office, feigning shock and sympathy. He had to return. He had to know how much she remembered.

He had taken a terrible chance. Suppose, when she saw him, her memory of the attack had instantly returned. He would have been finished. No more cards to play.

Except that wasn't true, was it? He'd had another card. The highest card of all.

He'd had Meg.

That was why she'd been taken. She was Wolper's insurance. His guarantee that whatever Robin remembered, she wouldn't dare talk. At the first hint that her memory was coming back, he would have quietly informed her that if she breathed a word, her daughter would die.

He had pretended to be concerned about her. He'd stuck close to her, handling her interview himself, chauffeuring her to Hollywood. He had needed to stay close so he could be sure she didn't start to figure out what was really going on.

Wisps of smoke drifted from the kitchenette. The smoke had an oily smell. She guessed he had poured cooking oil on the stovetop's electric burners and turned them on. The heat of the burners would ignite the oil. No doubt he'd put down paper towels and paper plates as kindling. It wouldn't take long for the fire to grow and spread.

Wolper emerged from the kitchen. "Clock's ticking, Doctor. But you already knew that."

He clapped his hands, a man satisfied with his work.

"To be honest," he added, "you should've been dead already. Would be, if Brand had come through. I told him to take care of you when you left Parker Center. Problem was, he wouldn't give me a commitment. Didn't have the stones. So when you went sightseeing, I had to play chaperon, make sure you stayed out of trouble. Then, surprise, Brand shows up at the arcade. Doesn't shoot you, though. He cuts and runs. And when I frisk him, what do I find? His off-duty gun—and nothing else. No throwdown."

He paused as if the significance of this statement were obvious. She just stared at him.

With a sigh, he explained. "You don't carry out a hit with a gun that can be traced to you. So if Brand wasn't planning a snuff job, what kind of bullshit game was he playing? I think he intended to warn you. He wanted to be a hero. I talked him out of that. Still, it was a close call. Too close. Lots of things have gone wrong tonight." He smiled. "But now I'm going to make everything right."

She spoke slowly, her voice dull and faraway. "They'll know it's arson."

Wolper shrugged off the remark. "That's not a problem."

He checked to be sure the windows were tightly closed. Already the smoke was getting dense, making her eyes water and her throat burn.

"Meg . . ." she whispered. She couldn't frame it as a question, but he understood her meaning.

"Don't worry about your daughter," he said. "She's a corpse."

The words made sense, but she wasn't able to take them in.

"We stashed her in an old bottling plant on South Central Avenue. I sent Tomlinson to take care of her."

Tomlinson. The detective who'd tried to talk her out of treating Brand.

Wolper looked briefly concerned. "Hasn't reported back. But he must've done it. She's a kid. How hard can she be to kill?"

So he wasn't certain Meg was dead. It hadn't been confirmed. There was a chance.

He read her thoughts. "Always hope, huh, Doctor? Good for you. Keep the faith. Me, I'm a realist, like I told you all along. You and your daughter are dead. Both of you."

He left, shutting the door to the waiting room, sealing her in to ensure a quicker suffocation.

The heat wasn't too bad yet, but the air was already fouled with smoke.

She still couldn't move. She would never move again. She would die in this metal chair. And Meg . . .

Meg was probably dead already. Even if she was somehow alive, Wolper would see to it that she didn't survive for long.

There was no hope for either of them, not anymore.

Chapter Fifty-one

Gray steered the Crown Vic onto the Santa Monica Freeway, eastbound, keeping one hand on the wheel. The other hand held the gun pointing at Sergeant Brand in the passenger seat. He was pretty sure Brand had been whipped into total submission, but it didn't hurt to be careful. A guy like him could come up with a surprise or two, especially if he had nothing to lose.

"Your file says you got, what is it, post-dramatic stress?" Gray asked over the hiss of the road surface.

"Post-traumatic. How the hell did you see my file?"

"I'm everywhere. I see everything. I'm like Santa Claus or God. I see when you are sleeping; I see when you're awake. . . . You never had no post-trauma stress, did you, Sarge?"

"I had the symptoms."

"Symptoms. Like what, as a for-instance?"

"Insomnia, anxiety, fatigue."

Gray glanced at him, then looked away. The guy was tough to look at, what with the circular scar of the lighter on his cheek and the oozing mess of his left ear. The right side of his face was untouched, but the left was a horror show. He was like that Batman comic book bad guy, Two-Face.

"Sounds like a case of the shakes to me," Gray said. "You

were shitting your diapers 'cause you thought you might get found out or maybe turned in by your good buddy Wolper."

"I was scared, yeah. I knew about what he was up to for a long time, but I was never, you know, directly involved."

"Till recently."

"Yeah."

"So it wasn't no post-traumatic whatchacallit. It was plain old fear."

"And maybe guilt."

"Ooh, your conscience doing a number on you, huh? You mean to say you ain't a complete scumbag?"

"I'm not sure what I am. At the arcade, if Wolper hadn't been there—"

"Yeah, you said something about that before. What would've happened if the lieutenant hadn't been hanging with the doc?"

That face of his was sort of fascinating, Gray decided. Two-Face wasn't precisely the right reference, though. It was more like Brand had partially melted. The Incredible Melting Man, that was it.

"I followed her and Wolper over there," Brand was saying. "I thought that maybe I'd come clean with her."

Gray smirked. "Maybe?"

"I'm not sure what I would've done. I mean, the thing is, they've got her kid, you know? I don't want that on my conscience. Not a kid."

"Who took the kid? Wolper?"

"No, I don't think so."

"So there's other cops in on this?"

"There are others, yeah. I don't know how many. I don't know how far it goes."

"This is a big fucking deal you got yourself mixed up in, Sarge. You really think you're smart enough to outfox all these other players?"

"No. I don't. I'm not smart."

"Gotta agree with you on that one."

Come to think of it, he wasn't sure there was an Incredi-

ble Melting Man. It was the shrinking man, right? Not melting. So maybe Brand was Darth Vader with the helmet off.
Or the Phantom of the fucking Opera.

"I tried to stay clear of it," Brand said. "I never wanted to
be part of the action. I'm still not really part of it. I mean,
Wolper figures I won't sell him out, but that doesn't mean
he lets me in on all the details."

"Did you know what was going down today?"

"Snatching the kid? No. I'm not even sure *they* knew. It
might've been improvised."

"How about the hit on Doc Robin?"

"I didn't know for sure."

"But you *kinda* knew, am I right? Be straight with me,
Sarge."

"I suspected."

"And you let it happen."

The scarred head turned in Gray's direction. "What, are
you lecturing me, for Christ's sake? I don't need any goddamn lessons from a guy who snuffs high school girls—"

Gray lifted the gun in his right hand, just enough to re-
mind Brand of its existence. "How about from a guy who
snuffs cops? You willing to hear a lecture from him?"

Brand settled down, cowed once more. "Fuck."

"So you were gonna come clean to the doc—maybe."

"I knew they still wanted to hit her. Wolper even called me
at home, tried to get me to do it. I let him think I might play
ball. But like I said, what I really wanted to do was—"

"Confess. Bare your soul. I got that. But you didn't."

"Cameron and Wolper saw me. I ran. I didn't want to face
Wolper. But he chased me down. He frisked me, found my
off-duty piece but no throwdown. So he knew I wasn't there
to whack her. I couldn't use a traceable gun for that job. He
must've figured I was gonna double-cross him."

"Which you were."

"Yeah, maybe. If Cameron and Wolper had separated.
And if I could've figured a way to do it so that I could warn
her and . . . well . . ."

"Save your own ass." This guy was a piece of work; he really was.

Brand seemed to hear the contempt in Gray's voice. "Survival is what it's all about," he said belligerently.

Gray almost smiled. *Yeah, Sarge*, he wanted to say. *Just look at you, with your Frankenstein face and your scared-rabbit heart. You're surviving real good.* But he let it pass.

"I hear you," he said. "How'd Wolper take it when he tumbled to you changing teams?"

"Told me not to even think about trying anything. Said if I tried to rat him out, he would see that the whole mess was pinned on me. Said there was already enough evidence to put me away if Robbery-Homicide ever decided to look at me close. I would take the fall."

"He planted some shit."

"That's what he told me. I didn't know if it was true."

Gray figured it probably was. That was the way he himself would have played it if he'd had to keep a weak link like Brand in line.

"Anyway," Brand said, "I had to assume he wasn't bluffing. I went to the Newton station house, checked my locker. Nothing there. Next place to look—"

"Was home sweet home. You would've torn the place apart looking for the stuff he planted. Wouldn't have found it, neither. Whatever Wolper laid on you was hidden too good for you to find. He wouldn't have told you about it if he thought you could sniff it out."

"Yeah, maybe."

No "maybe" about it, Gray thought. *This Wolper is smarter than you. He sees two steps ahead.*

"So you didn't say nothing to the doc?"

"I said what Wolper had told me to say—this bullshit story he fed me about how I was trying to redeem myself by assisting with your arrest. I'm not sure she bought it."

"She didn't."

"How do you know?"

"Because she's still trying to remember who conked her

on the noggin. Which means she thinks it might've been you. She's over at her office right now getting her brain dry-cleaned in that space helmet of hers."

"Alone?"

"Wolper's with her."

The melted-candle face turned toward Gray again. "If she remembers it was him—"

"He'll waste her." Gray nodded. "That's why we're riding to the rescue."

"So you're on her side?"

"I'm on *my* side."

There was a pause, and Gray figured Pumpkinhead was out of conversation. He was wrong.

"I don't get it," Brand said. "Why do you care about any of this?"

"Two reasons. One, I don't like being set up by any goddamn gangsta cops. And two, you assholes got the doc's daughter. You got Meg."

"You're worried about Cameron's kid? After you . . . I mean—"

"After I wasted five perfectly healthy teenagers with their whole lives ahead of 'em? I guess that's right."

"Doesn't make sense."

"I am a mystery and a conundrum, Sarge. I got layers. It's what makes me so goddamn fascinating. Now I don't suppose you know where Meg's been hid away."

"I don't."

" 'Course not. They don't tell you shit, right, small fry?"

Brand stared into the darkness. "Never thought they'd take the kid. Fuck, that's low. Should've expected it, though. It's like the fights."

This baffled Gray. "Fights? What fights?"

"The dogfights." Brand's voice was a low drone. "She probably thinks I go there for entertainment. That wasn't it. I went because that's what this city *is*. Whole fucking city's one big dogpit, and we're all caught in it."

Gray had no idea what Scarface was jacking his jaws

about. He skirted a Cadillac that was traveling too slowly in the fast lane.

"You're going to kill me," Brand said in the same low monotone. "Right?"

"What little birdie whispered that in your ear?"

"You're a killer. It's what you do."

"Maybe I'll go easy on you."

"You won't. You can't. You're the big dog in the ring. All you know is kill or be killed."

Leaving the Caddy behind, Gray eased back into the fast lane. "You might have a point there, Sarge."

"Kill or be killed . . ." Brand's voice trailed away.

"As mottos go, it ain't half-bad." Gray smiled, warming to his theme. "The way I see it—"

He had no time to finish. Beside him, Brand's right hand came up fast, and in it was a gun, a little snub-nosed job that had appeared out of nowhere like a magic trick.

Gray spun the wheel hard to the left, slamming the Crown Vic up against the guardrail. The car made a grinding noise and slewed across two lanes. Every horn in the world started blasting, headlights flying everywhere as the vehicles behind the Vic peeled around the car, some of them scraping the rear end and throwing new shudders through the chassis.

Brand, flung half-out of his seat by the collision, twisted around and fired the gun, and even though there was no way he could miss at a distance of two feet, somehow he missed anyway. He had time for only one shot, and then Gray squeezed the trigger of his Beretta.

He didn't miss.

Blood splashed him. He blinked it out of his eyes. Brand flopped and spasmed in the passenger seat, his butt-ugly face shredded like a Halloween mask. Gray snatched Brand's gun away before the cop fired it again in some kind of death twitch.

"You was right, Sarge!" he yelled over the ringing in his ears. "You *ain't* smart!"

He floored the brake pedal, stopping the car. A moment later, the engine died. Smoke rose from under the hood.

By now he'd conned what had happened. Brand carried an extra gun in his personal car. Kept it under the seat, it seemed. He'd been waiting for Gray to let down his guard. Nearly scored on that play, too. If Gray had been a split second slower, he would be the one barfing up his own brains right now. But he'd come through. He was alive, and the shit-eating, dick-stroking son of a black-eyed whore was dead.

"You hear me, Sergeant Fuck?" he screamed at the pale, shaking, faceless thing bleeding all over the other seat. "You're *dead!*"

Gray exploded out of the car. The freeway was backed up in the two lanes blocked by the slant-parked car. A frozen chain of headlights stretched for a half mile. The other lanes were clear, traffic whizzing past, leaving red comet tails of taillights.

Directly behind the ruined Crown Vic, some asshole in a green Volkswagen Beetle was tooting his horn and making faces through the windshield, pissed about the delay but too chickenshit to risk nosing around the obstruction.

Gray had never liked Volkswagens—he still thought of them as hippie cars—but he wasn't in a position to be choosy. He ran up to the door on the driver's side and rapped his gun against the glass.

"Out, motherfucker! Outta your clown car *now!*"

The jerkoff had stopped honking. He stared at Gray through the glass, not resisting, just plain paralyzed with fear. Gray knocked out the window with a swipe of the gun barrel, dusting the moron with crumbs of safety glass. "*Out!*"

It registered. The guy got out, Gray assisting with a tug that sent him tumbling to the asphalt. He jumped behind the wheel and swerved into the next lane, not giving a shit about the high speed of traffic or the flurry of horns and squealing brakes behind him.

With his foot stamping the gas pedal, he crossed the remaining lanes and took the next exit to the surface streets. Freeway would've been faster, but he couldn't stay on that road after jacking a ride and fleeing an accident. The Chippies and the city cops would all be after his ass, especially if Joe Volkswagen had made him as the city's most wanted fugitive.

He wasn't far from Doc Robin's digs anyway. He could make it there in another three, four minutes, even on surface streets.

He wondered what he would find when he got there— and whether the doc would still be alive.

Chapter Fifty-two

For Hammond, everything was falling apart.

They had failed to net Gray in Hollywood. The TV crews had been there to capture the debacle. That was bad enough. What was happening now was worse.

"I don't understand it," he said from the backseat as his driver chauffeured him and Lewinsky and Banner to the Hoover Street exit of the Santa Monica Freeway. "I just don't get it."

"Doesn't make sense," agreed Banner, sitting next to him. "Whole goddamn thing is spinning out of control."

Hammond gave Banner a warning glare. "No I-told-you-sos, Phil. I don't need any bullshit from you right now."

Banner frowned. "Just because this gamble of yours didn't pay off, you don't need to take it out on me."

"Why the hell not? I've got to take it out on somebody. Anyway, it's too soon to say it didn't pay off."

"Come on, Chief, it's a fucking catastrophe. We're talking Bay of Pigs here. We've got Sergeant Brand's car wrecked on the freeway. A DB inside that's probably Brand himself, and an armed carjacker ID'd as Justin Gray. It's a total meltdown."

"We don't know for sure it was Gray. The carjack vic

might've been seeing things. You know how unreliable eye-witnesses are."

"That's a pretty thin branch to cling to," Banner groused.

"Are you forgetting the chain of command here, Lieutenant?"

"I'm not forgetting anything. Including the fact that I warned you not to stick your finger in this particular pie."

"That's an I-told-you-so. I don't want to hear any I-told-you-sos, God damn it."

"Sir?" Lewinsky broke in. "We're here."

The car had come to a stop on the left-hand shoulder of the freeway. Hammond hadn't even noticed.

He stepped out. Cones and flares had been set up by CHP, cordoning off three lanes and forcing eastbound traffic over to the right. Highway Patrol officers stood waving flash-lights to direct the vehicular flow.

Brand's Crown Victoria—the plate had been traced to him by the first officers on the scene—lay crosswise on the road, straddling a lane division. The front was all crunched in and busted up, and the dented guardrail some distance to the west showed why. The rear of the car had taken some scrapes as well. Both taillights and one headlight were out. The engine was dead. The occupant of the passenger seat was likewise.

Hammond approached the driver's side and looked in, not touching anything,

It was Brand, all right. His face was largely gone, but his build and the dark windbreaker he'd been wearing in Holly-wood were still identifiable, although the windbreaker had changed color, having been dyed in a geyser of blood.

"It's him," he said as Lewinsky and Banner joined him. "Gunshot to the face. Where's the carjack vic?"

"First officer said a unit took him to Saint Vincent's," Banner reported. "He wasn't hurt, just shook up."

"Damn." Hammond shook his head. "I need to talk to him, confirm it was Gray. We got anybody at Brand's residence?"

"Hollywood unit is on the way," Lewinsky said.

"Maybe they'll find something that makes sense out of all this." Hammond took another look at the dead man in the passenger seat. "Somebody has to."

Chapter Fifty-three

During her hospital internship Robin had seen a few cases of smoke inhalation. She knew the smoke could kill her in a variety of ways. It could squeeze the oxygen out of the room, replacing it with carbon dioxide, leaving an inadequate supply of breathable air. It could irritate her respiratory passages until her airway swelled up and closed, choking off breath. It could poison her body with carbon monoxide, hydrogen sulfide, hydrogen cyanide—toxins that would render her unable to metabolize oxygen. Most likely, it would kill her in all three ways at once.

There was some consolation. She probably wouldn't burn to death. She wouldn't last that long.

The room was dark with smoke now. The overhead light was vanishing behind a sooty haze. Because Wolper had disconnected the smoke detectors, no alarm would sound until the smoke escaped into the hallway. It would take a long time for the fumes to seep through the door to her waiting room and the door to the hall. By then she would be dead.

Already she was coughing—the MBI current did not inhibit autonomic reactions like bronchial spasm—and her head pounded, and her eyes were watering from heat and toxic vapors. Soon her respiration would become troubled.

She would experience shortness of breath. She might begin to hyperventilate, an instinctive response that would only aggravate the problem. She would become light-headed, disoriented. Her eyesight would fail. She might go into convulsions, or slip into a coma, or drift off to sleep. That would be best. Dreamless sleep.

She was sleepy now. Even as the coughing grew worse, she seemed to distance herself from it. She might be leaving her body, a near-death experience—she'd read of those, had even talked to some critically ill patients who'd had such adventures. They had come back. She wouldn't. So it was not a *near*-death experience, was it? Just a death experience, that's all. What was it they always said? Go into the light. The light—

Darkness.

She blinked, coming back to herself. Everything was the same—smoke and heat, coughs racking her chest—yet everything was somehow different.

The overhead light. It was out. The clicking of the coils had stopped.

And she could move.

She leaned forward in the chair, testing her muscles, unsure what had happened, and then she was scrabbling at the appliance, pulling it off her head, letting it fall to the floor as she pitched headlong onto the carpet, climbed to one knee, and collapsed.

A new smell, burned rubber, filled the air. The insulation on the office wiring. The fire had burned through the wall, shorted out the wires, killing power to the lights and to the MBI gear. No power, no current—no current, no inhibition of her motor control, no paralysis. She could move again.

Couldn't walk, though. Lacked the strength.

Her coughs were savage, torturous. She spat up something like black goo. Mucus from her respiratory tract, dyed with soot.

She could barely see. Smoke everywhere and an orange flickering at the corners of her vision, the rise and fall of flames progressing around the perimeter of the room, inexorably sealing her in.

Her groping hands discovered her purse on the floor. It had been in her lap, must have been flung forward when she fell. Her cell phone was inside the purse, but she had no strength or voice to use it, and help could never arrive fast enough.

Still, the purse might help her. She unclasped it and thrust it over her nose and mouth, a makeshift mask. The air in the purse was stale but uncontaminated. She drew a deep breath, felt a little stronger.

With one hand pressing the purse to her face, she crawled forward. She reached the door to the anteroom. Raised her arm, searching for the knob, which seemed high, so high above her head, and slippery when she grasped it, the smooth metal resisting her efforts to turn it, until finally it yielded and she swayed backward, pulling the door open.

The lights in the waiting room were still on. That circuit hadn't failed. The room looked almost clear of smoke—a haven, a refuge. If she could get in there, cross the threshold, then she would be okay. She had to do it, even though her body insisted that it was time to curl up and rest, just rest. She had to keep going, for Meg—for Meg, for Meg—her mantra, her focus—for Meg.

She struggled across the threshold into the waiting room, fighting to catch her breath, recovering slightly. But already the smoke, a tenacious adversary, was crowding into the smaller room. She inched forward and encountered something dark and tacky on the carpet—blood—the deputy's blood. What was his name? Rains, Rivers? It seemed wrong that she couldn't remember.

She tried pushing herself to her feet, but her legs wouldn't carry her. Helplessly she fell onto the couch where her patients waited before sessions. A long spool of mucus, black and heavy, unreeled from her mouth onto the sofa cushion as she hacked out another series of deep coughs.

Her hands . . . she could see them gripping the arm of the

couch—the fingers so pale, almost bluish. Cyanotic. Insufficient oxygen to the extremities.

It was happening—death by asphyxiation, just as Wolper had said. She'd come this far. No farther. And Meg . . . she couldn't help Meg—couldn't do anything except cough and spit up black gunk and gasp out shallow, useless breaths and die. . . .

"Fuck, Doc Robin. You're a mess."

A hand on hers. Strength lifting her. Arm around her waist, propping her up.

Justin.

He hustled her out of the waiting room, into the hall, and laid her down on the floor, where she endured a final stint of bronchospasms that cleared out the last of the mucus. She was breathing again, pulling in oxygen and feeling it work. Her eyes focused. Her mind cleared.

"What are you . . .? How . . .?" Her voice was hoarse, every word a separate pain.

"It's the cavalry to the rescue, Doc. Just like in the movies, only I don't use no stuntman. Now let's get you outside."

He lifted her again. As she stood upright, she remembered the last clear thought she'd had.

"Meg . . ."

"What about her?"

"I know where she is."

"Yeah. Where's that?"

"Take you . . . I'll take . . ."

"Okay, we'll find her. No sweat. I'm on the job."

"Now. She's in trouble. It may already be too late."

"Then let's you and me get a move on."

Somehow she still had the purse in her hand. She used her key to open the rear door. Gray led her into the parking lot. She wondered how they would get out through the gate, which was locked at night, then saw that it wouldn't be a problem. On his arrival, Gray had rammed the gate with his car and popped it open.

He hustled her into the Volkswagen on the passenger side, then got behind the wheel and pulled away with a howl of tires.

The little car rattled, the hood loose after the collision with the gate. The VW must have been stolen, but right now Robin didn't care.

She noticed Gray watching her. "You okay, Doc?"

"I'm better. I'm all right."

"So where are we headed?"

"It's a factory on South Central Avenue. An old bottling plant."

"Wolper tell you that?"

"How did you know about Wolper?"

"Sergeant Brand told me. Right before he had an accident."

"Brand is dead?"

"Chill, Doc. It was self-defense. He pulled a piece on me. But only after he told me most of what I needed to know."

"But how did you put *any* of it together?"

"I'm smart, Doc. Not book-smart like you. People-smart. When a thing needs doing, I know how to get it done. Now what's the name of this factory?"

"He didn't tell me the name."

"What's the cross street?"

"He didn't say that, either."

"That ain't a lot to work with."

Robin moaned. "You mean we can't find it?"

"Hey, hey, keep it together. We'll ride south on Central Avenue till we spot the place, is all. Then we'll go in the same way the bad guys did."

"The bad guys." Robin looked at him, a new awareness taking shape. "You're not one of them anymore. You've changed."

"Changed my clothes, for sure. Changed cars a couple times too."

"Wolper said you would never change. He said a leopard doesn't change its spots."

"Cynical dude."

"Knowing we made a difference in our work together . . . it means a lot, Justin."

"Don't get all weepy on me, now."

"It means there's hope—hope for people like you. People like . . ."

"Like?"

Like my father, she almost said. "All the others. The ones behind bars. They don't have to rot their lives away. They can be reintroduced to society without risk. It's a whole new world."

"Don't go saving the world just yet, Doc Robin. Let's find your baby girl first."

Chapter Fifty-four

Detective Tomlinson was groaning again.

For a long time he'd lain silent, and Meg had been convinced he was in a coma or maybe dead. He had stopped moving, might have even stopped breathing. She hadn't been sure whether or not she should be glad he was so far gone. She didn't want him to be dead, but she sure didn't want him waking up, either.

Now he was stirring. The dose of heroin hadn't been enough to kill him, not when he weighed twice what she did. It hadn't even been enough to keep him out for the whole night.

When he was fully awake, he would take care of her. And it wouldn't be quick or easy—not after what she'd done to him, nearly killed him.

She tugged at the handcuffs still chaining her to the railing. All she accomplished was to chafe her wrist even worse than before. A warm ooze of blood trickled down her arm. Maybe if she pulled hard enough, she could slice her wrist down to the vein and then she would bleed to death. It was a better way to die than what he would do to her, that was for sure.

But maybe she could fight. She still had the hypodermic, empty now, but a weapon even so. She patted the pocket of her blouse, where she had stowed the thing after giving up on it as a locksmith tool. Just let him come close and with a little luck she could . . . she could . . .

She could do nothing. She knew that. He would be expecting a second attack. He would deflect it easily, take the syringe, and use it on her.

Tomlinson issued a grunt and started to rise.

She watched him in paralyzed horror. He thrust out both arms and pressed his palms to the floor, pushing himself up off the concrete. His eyes remained closed, his face blank. Somehow those details made it worse, as if she really had killed him and now he was a zombie rousing himself from the grave.

He was on his knees now. He swayed a little. His eyes opened. His head turned and he stared at her. His pupils were pinpoints of ink. The whites of his eyes were huge, horrible.

He lunged at her, and she screamed—

He fell on his side. The egg-white eyes were still open. He was breathing noisily, each rise of his chest accompanied by a wet suction sound. But he wasn't staring at her anymore. He was unconscious or semiconscious or something. In a stupor, anyway.

And he was close to her. Not lying on his stomach anymore. She could search the inside pockets of his jacket, maybe find a handcuff key.

She willed herself to squat next to him. Her heart was drumming in her ears. If he came to, she would be easily within his reach. But if he came to, she was dead no matter what, so it made no difference.

She touched the flap of his jacket, expecting him to rise at any second, as if the brush of her hand would be all the stimulus he needed. There was no reaction. She wished his eyes had closed. They unnerved her, open wide and gazing into the glow of the flashlight at the top of the stairs. She didn't like the way those round, almost pupilless whites caught the light.

With an effort, she peeled back the flap of his jacket and groped in the pocket. It was empty.

There was still the other pocket. That one was harder to

reach. He had fallen on that side, the jacket bunched up under him.

She snaked her hand under the flap and felt around for the pocket. Her hand moved over his shirt, filmy with sweat. She could feel the low tremors of his heartbeat.

She couldn't find the pocket, but it had to be there. She ran her hand over the outside of the jacket, and down low near his ribs she felt the shape of a gun, holstered to his side, a handgun with a long barrel. She thought about retrieving it, using it to hold him off, but it was mashed under his body, unobtainable.

The key was still her best chance. She risked pulling at the jacket, knowing that any movement might rouse him. She dug deeper into the folded fabric and finally found a slit, a cavity. Inside . . . something small and hard and metallic.

A key, the key she needed.

It was tucked at the bottom of the pocket, inside creases and folds in a narrow space too small for her hand. She tried closing two fingers over the key and easing it out. It slipped away. A second try, a second failure.

She reached for it again and only pushed it deeper into the pocket.

"Come on," she told herself. "Concentrate. Take it slow."

Good advice, but difficult to follow when her head was spinning with waves of dizziness and she had to fight off the desperate trembling of her muscles.

She dug into the pocket again, her fingertips brushing the key, now almost beyond reach. Carefully she snagged it between her fingers.

Breath held, she drew it out. Almost there . . .

It caught on a fold of the pocket.

Tomlinson moaned. She nearly panicked and let go, but somehow she held on. She jiggled the key back and forth to work it loose.

Another moan. The eyes blinking, not yet seeing her. He was still out, but coming around.

She resisted the impulse to tear the key free, aware that

she might lose her hold on it altogether. There would be no time to recover it again.

Tomlinson shook his head slowly, as if shaking off a long sleep. The slight movement straightened the jacket a little, and the key popped free.

She had it.

Clutching her treasure, she retreated to the railing. She jabbed the key at the handcuff on her left wrist. Couldn't find the keyhole. The light from the landing wasn't strong, and the keyhole was small.

"Fuck."

That wasn't her. It was him. His groggy voice, thick with phlegm. She glanced at Tomlinson, and his gaze met hers for an instant, flickering with recognition, then fading to blankness again.

She grabbed a shallow breath and narrowed her focus to the single problem of fitting the key into the keyhole.

"Fuck me . . ."

Him again. This time she didn't look back. If he was alert, she would find out soon enough.

She found the keyhole. Slowly, tentatively, in a process that seemed to consume many minutes, she rotated the key against the hole until it slipped inside.

A jerk of her wrist, and the key turned. The handcuff clicked open.

Free.

She tore her arm out of the cuff and ran up the stairs toward the open door, hoping there was a lock on it so she could lock him in—

And she fell sprawling on the metal staircase.

She thought she'd tripped. Tried to rise, couldn't.

Then she understood that he'd grabbed her by the leg, and he was holding on.

She spun onto her back. There he was, at the foot of the stairs, one hand clinging to her ankle while the other probed inside his jacket for the gun.

"You're dead," he told her in his raspy, croaking voice,

white eyes staring. Meg launched a kick with her free leg, booting him in the face. The impact punched him backward. He loosened his grip on her ankle. She tried to scramble up the stairs, but he was too quick. He already had her again.

She kicked a second time, missing him. He climbed on top of her legs to pin her down, and the gun was out, blue steel, shiny in the flashlight beam.

Click of the safety's release, the muzzle swinging toward her, and there was a gunshot, blood, Tomlinson dropping the gun as he slid backward onto the floor and lay unmoving amid a spreading maroon pool.

Meg didn't understand it. She lay on her back on the staircase trying to breathe, and then a tender hand was pressed into her own.

She looked up to see her mother kneeling beside her.

"Mom?"

"I'm here, Meg," Robin said. "It's okay now."

Chapter Fifty-five

Robin tried to keep the shock out of her voice. Her daughter was alive, and that was everything that mattered.

But, God, just look at her.

Her school uniform was dirty and torn, hair frazzled, eyes wild. Blood from the shooting had sprayed her all over. She looked like she had crawled out of a grave.

"It's okay," Robin said again. She hugged her daughter.

She and Gray had found the bottling plant after a slow, watchful drive down Central. They hadn't been sure it was the right place until they'd discovered the open gate and the police car. Gray had led her deeper inside the factory, where sounds of a scuffle could be heard.

Distantly she knew she ought to be shocked at the killing that had taken place nearly before her eyes, but she couldn't find the appropriate emotion inside her. The gun was still in Tomlinson's hand. He'd been about to kill Meg. Another second, and it would have been too late.

By shooting the man, Gray had saved her daughter. That was all Robin cared about. It was all that mattered.

She stroked Meg's hair and looked into her eyes. "Stay with me now," she whispered.

"I'm not going anywhere," Meg said.

Robin knew she still hadn't seen Gray. How would she

react when she recognized him? It would be another painful jolt to her system, already overloaded by stress.

But Meg could handle it. She was strong. Robin had never known just how strong until tonight.

"Let's get out of here," she said softly, "okay?"

Meg nodded. "Definitely."

Robin helped her to her feet. Together they climbed the stairs toward the glow of the flashlight that still rested on the landing. She remembered what she'd told herself as the fumes had started to overcome her: *Go toward the light.*

At the top of the staircase Meg raised her eyes, looking past the glow, and saw Justin Gray.

He stood there, watching the two of them with a cool, quizzical expression, the gun that had shot Tomlinson still held lightly in his right hand.

Meg drew back, making a startled, fearful noise. Robin tightened her grip to keep her from falling down the stairs. "It's all right," she soothed, "he won't hurt us. He's with us now. He's one of the good guys."

The gun swung in their direction. Gray smiled. "You sure about that, Doc?"

Robin shook her head, irritated with him. "Justin, stop fooling around."

But the gun didn't waver, and neither did his smile. "No foolin'. Looks like I'm sitting in the catbird seat now, wouldn't you say?"

"Mom . . ." The word from Meg was a tremulous moan.

Robin stared at Gray, unable to process what was happening, unable to think.

"Still think you're gonna save the world?" Gray asked. "I got news for you. This old world is long past saving. And us leopards don't *never* change our spots."

Chapter Fifty-six

After leaving Robin Cameron's office, Wolper stopped off at his mid-Wilshire apartment to pick up the packet of items he'd prepared long ago for just this eventuality. It was hidden in the bathroom wall, behind the mirror over the sink. He had to unscrew the mirror and take it down in order to remove the bulging envelope secreted in a cutaway section of drywall. Hidden alongside the package was a .22 pistol, untraceable.

He replaced the mirror and put away his tools before leaving with the package and the gun. Brand's home in Hollywood was only a short distance away. He made it there in under five minutes, spending the drive considering various ways to approach the situation.

He expected Brand to be home—probably taking his house apart one wall at a time in search of the planted evidence. Trouble was, the evidence hadn't been planted yet. That was what the envelope was for.

He didn't think it would be overly difficult to kill Brand. The man wasn't smart. He was easily manipulated, easily distracted. He only had to turn his back for a second and bang, a bullet in the temple, fired by the untraceable gun. He would wipe off the prints, put the gun in Brand's hand, and fire it again, leaving powder marks on Brand's fingers. The second shot would go into the ceiling. The crime-scene people would say Brand's hand had slipped the first time he fired. It wasn't uncommon. People got a little nervous when they were about to kill themselves.

Suicide was what it had to look like. Cameron had been right—the investigators would know that the fire in her office was arson. They wouldn't suspect Gray. Arson wasn't his style, and serial killers rarely varied their MO.

No, suspicion would fall on her newest patient, the emotionally disturbed Sgt. Alan Brand.

She had left with him, after all. That was how Wolper would report it to RHD. Wolper had driven Cameron and Brand back to the arcade, then left on his own because the D-chief had said he wanted him off the case. Cameron had said she would let Brand drive her to Parker Center. Only he hadn't taken her there. The two of them had gone to her office. It must have been Cameron's idea—she'd been trying to recover her memory of the attack. And she'd succeeded. She'd remembered that Brand had done it. Brand had felt there was no choice except to kill her. He'd set fire to the office and left her to choke on the fumes. Then he'd driven home and killed himself.

That was what had gone down tonight. Brand just didn't realize it yet. The victim was always the last to know.

When RHD searched Brand's carport, they would find evidence that he'd been mixed up in dirty dealings. The Valdez shooting wouldn't look so righteous anymore. That evidence would give him motive to attack Robin earlier today. He'd been afraid she would dig too deeply into his secrets and expose the dirt.

And the carjack attempt? Most likely it would be dismissed as coincidence. Even if someone guessed the truth— that a couple of homeboys who ran with the Gs had been hired to jack Cameron's Saab and mess her up, hospitalize her so she couldn't continue her therapy program—no one would pin it on Wolper. It would be Brand again. It was all Brand.

Brand, the mastermind. Wolper smiled.

It would work. It wasn't exactly the way he'd hoped things would work out, but as a backup plan, it was solid. He had all the angles covered.

Would have been easier if the carjacking had gone as planned, or if he'd succeeded in killing her this afternoon in her office. Would have been easier if Brand had agreed to pop Cameron in the video arcade, instead of wimping out and proving himself unreliable and therefore expendable.

What was the big deal about killing some nosy shrink, anyway? Weren't there enough shrinks in LA? Hell, Wolper would have iced her himself in Hollywood, except that having been seen leaving Parker Center with her, he would have been an obvious suspect. Would have killed her when she and Brand were in the car with him, if he'd felt he could trust Brand to play along.

That was the problem, though. He couldn't trust Brand. The man just didn't have the balls for this kind of work. And now he was going to pay for it.

Wolper parked on a side street so his car wouldn't be connected to Brand's home. With the envelope in his hand and the throwdown gun in his waistband against the small of his back, he walked the dark streets to Brand's bungalow. As he approached, he saw that the gate to the driveway was open and the carport was empty. Brand wasn't here.

He wondered about the open gate. Careless of Brand, especially in this neighborhood. It made things easier, though. He could walk right onto the property and plant the evidence, then wait for Brand to return.

There was no need to break into the house. The sign on the front lawn warned of a security system, and while many of those signs were phony, the name on Brand's was legitimate. No surprise. Cops saw a lot of craziness on the streets of this city. Off duty, either they migrated to the relative safety of the suburbs or they stayed in town and made their home a fortress.

Rather than tangle with the alarm system, Wolper decided to plant the contents of the envelope in the carport, among the paint cans and hardware supplies piled up along the side wall. He fished a pair of rubber gloves out of his pocket, opened the envelope, and began removing the assorted items inside. There were two stacks of hundred-dollar bills bound with rubber bands, some crystal meth and rock cocaine, a cell phone that had disappeared from an evidence room and had since been used to call an address in Newton Area that was a known hangout of the Gs, and, most incriminating of all, a floppy disk that listed payoffs and bank account numbers. The accounts had been opened overseas by an American using forged credentials. The American was Wolper himself, but no one could ever prove it wasn't Brand.

He considered the best hiding place. His gaze settled on a small tool cabinet with see-through plastic drawers. The bottom drawer was nearly empty. It would serve. He began placing the items inside, one at a time, pushing them toward the back to make them less visible. The plant shouldn't be too obvious, or Brand might—

"Police, put your hands up!"

The shout came from outside the carport. Squatting by the tool cabinet, Wolper turned as a flashlight snapped on, shining in his face.

"Hey, it's okay, I'm a cop, I'm a cop." He raised his hands, aware of the white latex gloves, shiny in the light, screaming of guilt.

"Put your hands up," the voice repeated. A young voice, tense and strained.

"They're up." Wolper kept his own voice cool. "I'm Lieutenant Wolper, Newton Area. Do I know you?"

The flashlight bobbed closer. Behind the beam a pale young face came into view. The cop's nameplate read BAKER.

"No, sir, you don't. You know him, Metz?"

His partner, Metz, took a moment to respond. "There's a Wolper at Newton station."

"He's me," Wolper said, rising slowly to his feet, careful to make no threatening moves. Both of the Hollywood cops had their guns drawn. "Or I'm him. However you say it."

"You got your ID on you?"

"Vest pocket."

"Take it out, real easy."

Wolper produced his ID case and flipped it open.

"Okay, Lieutenant." Baker nodded, but he hadn't lowered his weapon. "May I ask what exactly you're doing here?"

It was the obvious question, and Wolper was ready for it.

"I found Sergeant Brand's gate ajar. Came in to see if anything was wrong. Found the bottom drawer of this tool cabinet hanging open. I thought there might have been a four-five-nine. Pulled on some gloves so I wouldn't contaminate the scene. I found some materials that . . . well, they require an explanation."

He expected to be asked what he had found. But Baker surprised him. "Why did you come here in the first place?"

"Social call."

"At nearly eleven P.M.?"

"I'm a night owl." The guns still hadn't lowered, and Wolper began to be concerned. "Can I ask why you're here? Somebody call in a hot prowl?"

"No, sir. We were dispatched to Sergeant Brand's residence after his vehicle was involved in a crash."

This didn't make sense—a routine car crash wouldn't necessitate a visit to the victim's residence by a patrol unit—but Wolper didn't pursue it. There was another question of greater interest.

"A crash?" He gave a good imitation of concern. "How bad?"

"There was one fatality."

"Is it Brand?" Wolper asked, hoping the answer was yes.

"That hasn't been confirmed."

"Jesus." Wolper lowered his head for a moment. When he looked up, the guns were still fixed on him. "You know, you can holster your weapons, Officers. We're on the same team."

The cop named Metz spoke. "What were you doing by that tool chest?"

"I told you, I was looking for signs of a burglary. What I found was something else."

The bait had been offered a second time. Still they didn't take it.

"So you were looking in the drawer?" Metz asked.

"Right."

"That's funny, sir," Baker said. "See, we saw you from the driveway. We watched you for a minute or two before we called out. And it looked to us like you were putting stuff in the drawer."

"Did it?"

"Yes, sir. It did."

Wolper thought about how to play this. He decided to call on a little cop solidarity.

"All right, guys, let me level with you. I found some incriminating items in the drawer. I took them out to look them over, but I wasn't sure I wanted to be the one who found them. I'm not sure it's the kind of stuff that ought to be found. So I opted to put it back and walk away. I don't want to blow the whistle on a brother officer."

Now they would have to ask him to detail what he'd found.

They didn't. "What's the envelope for?" Metz asked.

He had seen the empty manila envelope, which Wolper had left on the floor.

"The items were in there," Wolper said. Instantly he regretted it.

"If you were putting them back the way you found them," Baker said, "why didn't you put them back in the envelope?"

"And if the items were incriminating," Metz added, "why would you conceal them?"

Cop solidarity wasn't going to work. These two wouldn't play ball.

There was another option. The throwdown gun was snugged behind his jacket.

It would be tricky. He would need to wait for the two men to lower their guard. They were both wearing vests. He would need to snap off two head shots fast enough to drop them before they could return fire. The shots would be heard throughout the neighborhood. He would have to run for it. A lot could go wrong in that scenario. Still, it might be his only chance.

He had to distract them. "I think we're losing sight of the big picture," he said. "I admit I wasn't exercising good judgment. The stuff I found . . . well, it rattled me. I've known Al Brand a long time. I never expected him to be involved in anything like this."

Come on, you bastards. Take the fucking bait.

"What is it you say you found, exactly?" Baker asked.

Finally.

"Look for yourselves," Wolper said. "I've gotta say it doesn't look good."

He stepped away from the tool cabinet, inviting the two Hollywood cops to check it out.

Hesitantly they advanced. The bottom drawer was still open. Baker shone his flashlight inside, lighting up the stacks of cash and the narcotics. "Holy shit, look what we've got here."

Wolper eased his right hand behind his back and grasped the gun. Two shots in quick succession—that was all he would have time for. Kill shots, both of them. Anything less than perfect shooting, and he was dead.

He waited for Metz to glance down at the open drawer. . . .

Headlights.

A car pulling into the driveway. Light bar on the roof twinkling. Another patrol unit. Two more uniforms.

He could never outgun four officers. Slowly Wolper let go of the gun, leaving it tucked in his waistband.

Baker and Metz were looking at him. "Your back bothering you, Lieutenant?" Metz asked.

"Muscle spasm. I get it sometimes."

The two guns were trained on him again. "I think we'd better pat you down, sir."

For a crazy moment Wolper thought about running. But there was nowhere to run. The two new arrivals were already getting out of their vehicle.

"I showed you my badge," he said. "I outrank the two of you, in case you hadn't noticed."

"Yes, sir, we're aware of that."

"Then let's not have any more bullshit about patting me down like I'm a goddamned criminal."

He turned, intending to walk out of the carport and get to his car and go. Go where? He had no idea. Just go.

Metz laid a hand on his shoulder. "Against the wall, sir."

Wolper wanted to resist, wanted to brazen it out, but already Baker and Metz were escorting him to the side wall of the carport, where he assumed the position like all of the thousand perps he'd busted. Baker found his off-duty weapon, holstered by his side, and Metz's probing hands discovered the throwdown.

"What's this, sir?"

The other two cops had reached the carport and were watching him without expression.

"Backup gun," Wolper said.

"No serial number," Metz reported. "This firearm is illegal."

"Tell us again why you came here," Baker said.

Wolper turned away from the wall to confront their hard faces. In that moment he felt the collapse of his future and all his hopes.

"I want a lawyer," he said quietly.

Baker nodded. "Yes, sir. I think you do."

Chapter Fifty-seven

"Justin," Robin whispered, "I don't understand."

Gray shook his head with a slow smile. "Then you're a lot dumber than I thought."

"Why would you save me, save both of us, if . . .?"

"If I'm still the baddest of the original badass bad boys? Think about it, Doc. Exercise that college-educated brain."

Her gaze flicked to Meg, huddled by her side on the landing.

Gray nodded. "You win the prize," he said cheerfully. "See, I wanted to find your darling daughter. Couldn't do it alone. But if we worked together, we had a shot. You helped lead me to Brand, and now you've brought me here."

Meg looked up at Robin. "You brought him?"

"I thought . . . he could be trusted," Robin said, her voice hollow.

She had thought so, yes. And she had *wanted* to think so. Wolper had been right about that. She had wanted to believe.

Meg straightened, defying Gray with her glare. "Why do you want me?"

"Shit, I been wanting you ever since you done sassed me outside your mom's office. I don't like sass in a sweet young thing. I mean to teach you not to disrespect Justin Hanover Gray."

"Go to hell," Meg whispered.

Robin pulled her close. "Quiet, Meg."

"Yeah," Gray said. "Pipe down; mind your mommy. You need to save your voice anyhow. You got a lot of screaming to do."

There had to be a way out of this. A way to escape—or summon help.

She thought of the phone in her purse. Carefully she slipped one hand inside.

"Was it . . . Was this your plan all along?" she asked.

He chuckled. "Fuck, no. I never planned to do no harm to you and yours. Figured I'd be too busy making the great escape. Things just happened, is all. I got set up, and that got me pissed royal, so I went on safari for the guys that done it."

She found the phone, but she couldn't dial it blind. Her fingers fumbled at the keypad until she found the large redial button. She pressed it.

"Somewhere along the line," Gray was saying, "it hit me how I could take care of two items of business at once. Teach those scumbag cops a lesson *and* get reacquainted with your daughter. Wasn't no grand plan. Just kind of came together for me."

She was fairly sure the call would go through—but who would she reach? She couldn't remember the last number she'd dialed.

"Got something on your mind, Doc?" Gray was staring at her.

"I just want to know what . . . what you intend to do with us."

"Like it's a big mystery? Gonna kill the both of you." He said it with a shrug. "But not till after I have myself some serious fun. A little mommy-daughter action is a whole new wrinkle for me. You know, I never did the nasty with them girls I snatched. Was always too looped to get it up. Ain't looped now."

Maybe hitting redial had been a bad idea. She still couldn't remember the last number she'd dialed. Was it Mrs.

Grandy? Or was it her own number at the condo, when she spoke to the SID technician?

No, that wasn't it. She'd used the phone once more—in the arcade. When she called Brand.

Perfect, just perfect. She'd placed a call to a dead man.

She had to try a different number. Hit O for the operator, maybe. She touched the clasp of her purse again.

"What're you reaching for, Doc?"

Gray had seen her this time.

"Nothing," she said.

"Gimme the handbag. Right now." He reached for the purse, and without pausing to think or to calculate the risks, she whipped it by the strap, smacking him hard in the face. He stumbled, and for a moment she was sure he would topple down the cellar stairs, but somehow he kept his footing and tore the purse out of her grasp. He pitched it away into the darkness beyond the flashlight's glow.

He was breathing hard. "Jesus, you're a pain in the ass."

The gun targeted her chest. She knew he was debating whether or not to fire.

"I'm sorry, Justin."

"No, you ain't. You're not sorry for nothing you did to me."

"I was always trying to help you. I wanted to make you better."

His face twisted. "I don't *want* to be better. When did you ever hear me complain about what I am? I been straight with you, Doc. I told you I like the silence 'n' violence. I like putting this old world into a world of hurt. You hear me? I made myself what I am. My parents didn't make me. Society didn't make me. *I* made me. I *made* Justin Hanover Gray. That's who the fuck I am. You never listened 'cause you didn't want to. You got your own motherfuckin' *agenda*. Wanna neuter me like a stray puppy? Declaw this cat? Ain't never gonna happen. I am the bad seed, Doc Robin. Deal with it."

"I never understood," she whispered, speaking only to herself.

There was no hope of reaching him. There never had been.

Chapter Fifty-eight

Hammond and Banner were standing near the wreckage of the car when Lewinsky returned from a trip to the D-chief's sedan.

"Okay," Lewinsky said, "it just came over the MDT." The Mobile Data Terminal was installed under the dashboard of every LAPD car. "A Hollywood unit is code six at Brand's house. They found Wolper there, by the way."

"Detective Wolper? In the house?"

"On the property. I don't know what's up with that. But another Hollywood car cruising the area found what could be the stolen Firebird."

"Could be?"

"License plate doesn't match. They ran the plate to a residence in Inglewood. Inglewood PD is on their way to talk to the owner."

Someone's cell phone started to ring. They ignored it.

"Gray could've switched plates," Banner said.

"I know that, Phil," Hammond snapped. "We all know it."

Banner was undeterred. "Gray could've ambushed Brand and driven off with him. Maybe he followed him from the video place in Hollywood."

"You think?" Hammond asked, his voice heavy with sarcasm.

"I'm just pointing out—"

"The fucking obvious. Good work, Columbo. What would we do without you?"

"Maybe I should stick to media relations."

"Maybe you should."

"You want me to get Susy Chen on the phone to cover this?"

"Shut up."

"It's a terrific story, Chief. Not only does the LAPD fail to find Gray, they actually let him kidnap and kill one of their own. I'll bet the public is feeling real safe now."

"You heard the chief," Lewinsky said. "Shut up."

Banner threw him a hard look. "Hey, that's original, Carl."

"You don't have to be such a goddamn prick. We need to work together and figure a way out of this shit."

"We wouldn't be in this shit in the first place if—"

"Don't say it," Hammond barked, "or you're back on traffic duty. And whose fucking phone is that, anyway?"

They looked at each other, then at the car.

"Shit," Hammond said.

He went around to the passenger side and fished the ringing cell phone out of Brand's windbreaker. He took a breath and pressed the OK button to accept the call.

"Yeah?" he said, wondering if he should try to sound like Brand or what.

No one was there. But there was no dial tone, either. He listened closely, the phone against his ear, his free hand blocking out the traffic noise.

Faintly he heard a man's voice, raised in an angry rant.

". . . a whole new wrinkle for me. You know, I never did the nasty with them girls I snatched. Was always too looped to get it up. Ain't looped now."

He knew that voice. He'd heard it on news clips of Justin

Gray's trial, which had been playing on the local news all night.

Lewinsky and Banner had reached him. "Who is it?" Lewinsky asked softly.

Hammond cupped the phone with his hand. "Gray."

Banner blinked. "You're shitting me."

"Yeah, that's right, Phil. April fool." Hammond checked the phone's LCD readout. "Brand's got caller ID. We can find out who placed this call."

Lewinsky had his pad out. "Give me the number. I'll do it."

Hammond listened again as Lewinsky moved away to use his cell phone, but now the only sounds on the line were distant, indecipherable noises. He heard a new voice raised in a shout. A female voice.

"Someone's with him," Hammond said. "A woman."

Banner shook his head. "Another victim. This is getting better and better."

Hammond turned to him. "You just don't fucking get it, do you? This is our break. We trace the call and we know where he is. Right now, in real time."

"Brand's still dead," Banner said morosely. "It's still a royal fuckup."

"Brand died in the performance of his duties. He's a goddamn hero. He led us directly to the whereabouts of the city's most wanted man and saved untold lives. Jesus, Phil, get with the program."

Lewinsky finished his call. "The call is being made from a cell phone—and it's assigned to Robin Cameron."

Hammond stared at him. "The shrink? Jesus."

"Maybe she's the one he's got with him," Banner said.

"Thanks, Phil, that never would've occurred to me." Hammond looked at Lewinsky. "Can we trace the call?"

"To the nearest transmission tower."

"We need a warrant?"

"Not if her service provider will cooperate. I've got RHD working it now. They'll call me when they get anything."

Hammond motioned to Banner. "Go tell these A-cars to get ready to rumble. We get a fix on this location, we're rolling."

Banner shifted his stance nervously. "Isn't that someone else's job? I mean, we're admin. Not, you know . . ."

"Not real cops? We're real cops tonight."

Banner, looking unhappy, headed toward the squad cars. Lewinsky's phone chirped. He answered, making brief affirmative noises and scribbling on his pad.

"RHD came through," he said to Hammond. "The call's being routed through a cell tower at South Central Avenue and Fourteenth Street. That's only a few blocks north of the freeway."

"The old commercial district," Hammond said. "Factories and warehouses."

"Right. Five minutes from here. We good to go?"

Hammond hesitated only a moment. "Let's do it. Let's nail this son of a bitch."

Chapter Fifty-nine

"'I never understood.'" Gray mimicked her, his voice raised in a falsetto. "You bet you didn't. You never got me at all."

He chuckled, an ugly sound.

"All that shit about my daddy burning me and belting me—fuck, yeah, he did, 'cause I was always shoplifting and setting fires and ripping off his cash. Okay, he wasn't no A-one parent. And my mama was a dumb ugly cow who never opened her mouth 'cept to stuff it with cheeseburgers and fries. They were a pair of low cards I drew, but fuck it all, I still don't blame them for the way I turned out. You're the one who's into the blame game. Me, I know my childhood sucked, and now I get to make other people's lives suck. Seems fair, don't it? What goes around, comes around. And now it's coming around to you, Doc. You and Meg."

Robin pulled Meg closer. "Don't do this, Justin, please."

"You don't tell me what to do, Doc-aroo. I'm the one running this show."

"Take me if you want, but not Meg—"

"Shut up."

"Please, not Meg—"

"I said, shut the fuck *up*!"

He struck her hard across the face, a ringing blow that sent her reeling backward into one of the old crates strewn on the floor. She fell on it, and the crate shattered, throwing up white whorls of dust.

In the passenger seat of his sedan, Hammond was on the dashboard radio.

"We're code two to the scene. Request Air Support at Central Avenue and Fourteenth. Have reason to believe the fugitive Justin Gray is in the vicinity. Tell ASTRO to look for a green late-model Volkswagen. Hold on." He turned to Lewinsky in the backseat. "How big a coverage area for the cell tower?"

"An urban sector's maybe one or two city blocks, that's all."

He spoke into the microphone again. "We're looking at a radius of one to two blocks."

"Roger that," the dispatcher said. "Air Fourteen en route, ETA two minutes."

"They'll beat us there," the driver said.

Hammond nodded. "But not by much."

Robin's head echoed with the punch. She tasted blood in her mouth. Her tongue seemed large and unwieldy.

She made an effort to rise, but fell down, coughing on dust and wood splinters.

Meg was screaming. Gray seized her by the hair and hauled her to the center of the room, where the two conveyor belts stood side by side under the skylight. He lifted Meg and flung her down on the nearest conveyor belt. The impact stunned her into silence. She lay on her back atop the rusted mechanism, the stars glowing down on her. She looked, Robin thought blearily, like a sacrifice on an altar.

"I been in stir a year without a taste of pussy," Gray said. "Got me a hard-on like a Louisville slugger, and it's all for you."

*   *   *

"Chief Hammond, Air Fourteen on tac one."

Hammond switched to the tactical frequency and heard the voice of the airship's observer.

"Air Fourteen. We have a visual on the Volkswagen. Parked in an alley in back of a large industrial site at Central and Pico. Second vehicle at the same location—one of ours, a slickback." *Slickback* was LAPD slang for a black-and-white police vehicle without roof lights. "No signs of occupancy in either car."

"A slickback?" Lewinsky said from the backseat. "Whose is it?"

It was easy enough to identify the car from the air. The last three digits of the shop number were stenciled on the roof, and the division number was similarly displayed on the trunk. But Hammond wasn't worried about the slickback at the moment.

"Forget the LAPD car for now, Air Fourteen. We're looking for a Caucasian male on foot. He's wearing a denim jacket and tan or brown pants." The carjack victim had given the description to the first patrol officers on the scene.

"Air Fourteen, roger. No visual on suspect. There's a means of ingress to the factory grounds—an open gate."

"Gray could be inside the building," Banner said, master of the obvious.

Hammond turned to the driver. "Bring us around to the back alley. We're going in." He switched from the tac frequency to the main comm channel. "This is Hammond, requesting Central Area patrol units as backup."

The dispatcher rogered him.

"We wait for the backup, right?" Banner asked nervously.

"No, we don't." As the car swung off the freeway onto Central Avenue, Hammond drew the pistol from his belt holster. It had never been fired on the job. "Lock and load, gentlemen."

*　　*　　*

While Robin watched, Gray thrust the gun into his waist-band, then climbed onto the conveyor belt. He straddled Meg, who lay unmoving, frozen by shock.

"Don't act like you never had none before," Gray said. "I told your mommy you ain't no virgin. Your cherry's been popped good. Am I right?"

From Meg, a whimper. "Yes."

Gray glanced across the room, meeting Robin's eyes with a smile of triumph. "Told you so. Your baby girl's a whore. Well, I know how to treat a whore." He unzipped his pants. "You're gonna like this, sweet thing."

Meg moaned. She still couldn't move.

But Robin could.

Her pain and shock had receded. Only anger and adrenaline remained.

Gray leaned over Meg, a jackal on a carcass. He wasn't looking in Robin's direction.

He didn't see her get to her feet, teeth gritted against a swirl of light-headedness.

She picked up a plank from the smashed carton. She advanced on Gray as his shoulders moved in the starlight.

"You want it, don't you, bitch? All you young cunts want what I got. It may be a little big for you—I'm what you call supersized—but I guarantee it'll fit just fine."

Robin lashed out with the plank. She caught Gray on the side of the head, and there was blood and a rip of flesh, and she realized there had been a nail in the plank.

He was howling as he swung off the conveyor belt, his face bleeding, penis hanging out of his fly.

She hit him again. He stumbled away.

"Meg, run!"

Shaken out of her paralysis, Meg scrambled off the conveyor belt and made a move for the exit. Gray darted in front of her to block her escape.

"There are other rooms in back," Robin shouted. "Hide there and don't come out no matter what."

She didn't wait to see if Meg complied. She ran for Gray and swung the board again.

He seized the plank by the edges, ripped it out of her hands, and threw it aside.

And he laughed.

The laugh told Robin that all this time he'd been playing games with her.

He liked games. He'd let her think she had a chance. But that was all over now.

"You're dead," he told her, his hand reaching into his waistband for the gun.

The chopper's Nightsun searchlight prowled the factory grounds, illuminating the vast expanse of the parking lot, as Hammond addressed his troops—Banner, Lewinsky, his driver, and four patrol officers from the crash site.

"All right, people, I want us going in prepared for anything. Gray's in there. He seems to have someone with him." He noticed Lewinsky on his rover. "Something up, Lieutenant?"

"Slickback's been ID'd, Chief," Lewinsky said. "It was signed out of Newton Area by Detective Tomlinson."

"Tomlinson? What the hell is he doing here?"

"Nobody seems to know."

Banner, looking more anxious than ever, drifted close to Hammond. "Chief," he said, his voice low, "you sure we don't wait for backup? Or for SWAT, maybe?"

"With the possibility of one or more civilians and a fellow officer inside?"

"I'm a media guy. I used to work Traffic. I didn't sign up for this."

"You're signed up now, Phil." Hammond raised his voice to address the group. "Move out."

Robin saw the gun in Gray's hand. At this range he couldn't miss.

She turned and ran. There was no place to hide in the

empty room, no time to get to the hallway where other rooms might provide concealment. There was only the open door to the cellar. She threw herself onto the landing.

Behind her, the gun boomed.

Was she hit? She didn't think so.

On hands and knees she crossed the landing. The flashlight, still resting there, spun and rolled against the door, shining into the main room, lighting up Gray as he bounded over the conveyor belt and sprinted toward her.

She picked up the flashlight and pitched it at him, a feeble gesture. He laughed again. She reached the stairs and tumbled down, colliding with something soft and fleshy, which was Detective Tomlinson, dead, his face shot away, and in his hand was his gun.

She pried it out of his fingers, and Gray burst through the door, and she raised the gun in both hands and fired.

Her finger worked the trigger again and again, muzzle flashes flickering in the cellar. She had never fired a gun in her life, had never even handled one, and she had no idea if she was hitting anything or not.

She pulled the trigger until the gun was empty, and then over the furious clamor in her ears she heard voices.

"LAPD, drop your weapon!"

The police were here. Better late than never.

She set down the empty gun. Slowly she pushed herself upright and climbed the stairs.

The wavering beams of several flashlights had found Gray on the landing. He lay curled in a fetal pose, groaning softly. Blood crisscrossed his body in a red skein.

As she reached the landing, the flashlights discovered her.

"It's me," she said weakly. "Robin Cameron."

Her own name sounded unreal, as if it belonged to some other person, or to a person she used to be.

The police didn't respond for a moment, giving her time to think that these officers might be part of the conspiracy too. If they were, then all her efforts had been wasted, and she and Meg were dead.

Then one of the men—Deputy Chief Hammond, she realized—came forward. "Are you all right?"

"I'm fine."

The statement struck her as absurd under the circumstances, yet somehow it was true.

"Call an RA," Hammond snapped to the man next to him, the one named Lewinsky, who'd been hostile to Wolper. "Call two—one for Dr. Cameron, one for him." His curt gesture indicated Gray. "What happened here, Doctor?"

She ignored the question. "I need to find Meg," Robin said.

"Is she here?"

"I sent her"—she waved toward the offices and hallways—"sent her to hide."

"Banner," Hammond said.

"I'm on it, Chief." The man named Banner left the room, following the glow of his flashlight down the hall.

Robin stepped past Gray and the two officers kneeling beside him on the landing. They seemed to be checking his vitals. As a doctor, she was in the best position to offer medical assistance, but she had no strength for it and, at the moment, no concern whether Justin Gray lived or died.

"What happened?" Hammond asked again.

"How did you find me?"

"Traced your phone call."

So hitting redial had worked. She stooped and retrieved her purse from the floor, then ended the call, breaking the connection.

"Doctor?" That was Hammond again.

"I shot him," she said, finally answering his question. "I shot Justin Gray."

"I can see that. Where's the gun you used?"

"In the cellar. Along with a dead man, Detective Tomlinson."

Hammond was bewildered. "You shot him too?"

"Gray did."

"What was Tomlinson doing here?"

"He came to kill Meg."

"This isn't making sense, Doctor."

"It will. I can't explain it all now. Wolper was part of it—"

"Wolper?"

"And Tomlinson and probably others."

"What possible connection could Tomlinson or Wolper have with Gray?"

"No connection. That's why they used him. He was the fall guy." She looked at the bleeding man. "He likes to play games, you know. This time, somebody tried playing a game on him."

Hammond shook his head. "I don't understand."

"It will all make sense. Later."

He seemed to accept this. She knew she should say more, but she was tired, very tired. . . .

Her cell phone rang. She wondered who it could be, and if she should even answer. Out of habit she fished the phone out of her purse and took the call. "Yes?"

"Dr. Cameron? This is Gaines." The criminalist. She'd forgotten about him. "Farber got through to the ITA administrator. We traced those e-mails to a specific terminal. Gabe is a police officer, I'm afraid."

Tomlinson, she thought. Or Brand.

"He works in the office of Deputy Chief Hammond. A lieutenant, name of Banner."

Robin stared at the phone, and then it had fallen from her hand, and she was running for the hallway, pausing only to grab the flashlight from the landing. She aimed the beam at the shoe prints stamped on the dust-coated floor. Two sets of tracks. Meg's—and Banner's.

Hammond and the other cops sprinted behind her, yelling questions she ignored.

This part of the factory had housed the administrative offices. She passed rows of doorless entryways. No skylight in here, but each office had a narrow window that let in ambient light from outside. Maybe Meg had found a way out through one of those windows. Maybe Banner hadn't found her.

But she knew this was an idle hope. The windows were too small to allow escape. Even if she had gotten out, Banner would follow.

He had to kill Meg. She could identify him as her kidnapper. He didn't know about the e-mail trace, didn't know he'd already been caught.

To save himself, he would kill Meg and make it look as if Gray had found her before tangling with Robin. Robin's testimony would contradict this version of events, but no one would listen to her. They would say that her memory had been altered by stress and trauma.

She could never prove otherwise. Memory, as she knew too well, was a tricky thing.

The trail curved into an intersecting corridor, ending at an office straight ahead. Robin ran to it, not caring that she was unarmed and unprotected.

In the office she found Meg huddled in a corner, staring. And Banner—sprawled on the floor, half-conscious, awash in his own blood. Imbedded in his neck was something slender and shiny.

A syringe.

"Little whore," Banner wheezed.

Robin slipped past him and knelt by her daughter. "Better watch yourself, Lieutenant. I shot the last man who called her that."

She hugged Meg and stroked her hair, while Hammond called for another ambulance.

Chapter Sixty

"Granola bars. Yum."

Robin studied her daughter for signs of sarcasm but found none. Meg seemed honestly contented as she sat at the kitchen table before a plate occupied by two unwrapped honey-oat granola bars.

"I seem to recall your showing a certain aversion to all things granola," Robin observed suspiciously.

Meg shrugged. "I've grown to love them."

"Since when?"

"It's an acquired taste."

Robin sat down opposite her. "So you ready for your triumphal return?"

"Definitely."

"There will be questions. And stares."

"I know."

Robin nodded. Although Meg's name had been kept out of the media, her friends knew what had happened, and friends always talked. In the six weeks Meg had been out of school—first recuperating in the hospital, then visiting her father in Santa Barbara, then traveling with Robin on an extended getaway to northern California—the word would have spread throughout the small social circle of the Gainesburg School.

For much of that time the school, which was on a year-round schedule, had been out of session—summer recess, they called it, though it lasted only a month. Still, nearly all the kids lived on the Westside, and they would have stayed in touch.

Now, with classes resuming and Meg's return expected, the entire student population would be waiting for her. Robin pictured them as vultures in gray-and-white uniforms. The image, she admitted, was probably unfair.

Meg saw her mother watching her. She smiled. "Don't worry, Mom. I can handle it."

Of course she could. She'd proven she could handle anything.

"Sorry," Robin said. "You're right. You'll be fine."

"Better believe it. Everything's copa—well, you know."

"Copacetic. You can say it."

"Even though it's *his* word?"

"He doesn't have a monopoly on it."

Meg finished the first granola bar and started on the second. "Any plans for today after you drop me off?"

"Nothing special." She hated lying to Meg, but she didn't want to talk about it.

"No patients?"

"In the afternoon. Morning's free."

Meg seemed to sense that this topic was going nowhere. "Happy with the new office?"

"It's a big improvement. Working there, I feel almost like an actual urban professional."

"You may need to start carrying a briefcase."

"Let's not get carried away."

The fire had rendered Robin's previous office unusable. She had no desire to remain there anyway. She had relocated to a building in the mid-Wilshire district, a safer neighborhood, but still within reach of downtown.

Downtown. The prison, she meant. The population of convicts who had served as her test subjects.

She wasn't treating any of them now. The loss of her

MBI gear in the fire had given her an excuse to suspend her experimental program. But new equipment was being made to order and would arrive soon. Then she would have to decide what to do with it. It could be used for purposes more prosaic than rehabilitation—fighting phobias, for instance. She wasn't sure if she would be satisfied with curing people's fear of spiders when millions of prisoners remained warehoused in jails.

Still, maybe the jails were where they belonged. All of them, forever. Lock them up, throw away the key.

She wasn't sure. Her old certainties had died on the night of Gray's rampage. She hadn't found any new truths to replace them. Not yet.

"Better get a move on," she told Meg. "Don't want to be late for your first day back. How would that reflect on me, your doting mother and unpaid chauffeur?"

"Badly."

"That's what I thought."

"Just let me brush my teeth. I intend to do a lot of smiling today."

Robin thought that was good. Her daughter was due a few smiles.

The Saab had been repaired and repainted. At first Robin hadn't liked driving a car that Gray had used. It seemed to be imprinted with his presence. Finally she'd taken it fifty miles up the coast with the windows open, the sea air whipping through. The trip had cleansed the car, expelling whatever psychic residue had lodged there.

She drove Meg the short distance to the Gainesburg School, where other parents were letting off uniformed kids with backpacks and bookbags. The scene appeared so normal, just a part of everyday life. And so it was, but Justin Gray was part of life, too. The miracle was not that the two parts ever intersected, but that they intersected so seldom.

"Mom? You okay?"

"Why wouldn't I be?"

"You've been kind of brooding and uncommunicative all morning."

"I'm preoccupied, that's all."

Meg made a move to get out of the car. She hesitated. "You're not worried about me, are you?"

"Going into the lions' den? Nope. I know you can handle it."

"That's not what I mean. You're not . . . well, you're not worried about me being on my own again?"

And screwing up like I did last time; Robin heard the un-voiced words. *Screwing up with Gabe.*

There had been many long talks between them on that subject, and Robin knew there would be many more.

"I'm not worried," she answered. "It's funny—I used to worry all the time. About you and me and . . . well, every-thing. Not anymore. Not since that night. What do you think that's about?"

Meg smiled. "Delayed reaction to stress? Post-traumatic dissociative depersonalization with delusions of happi-ness?"

"If it's a delusion, I'll take it. Get going now. Good luck."

"Won't need it," Meg said, leaving the car.

Robin watched her walk into a crowd of students who clustered around her. When Meg was lost to sight, Robin put the Saab in gear and drove away, checking the dashboard clock.

Her morning wasn't as open as she'd said. She had an appointment at ten A.M.

Downtown.

Gray was waiting for Robin in the interview room on the eighth floor.

It had taken him six weeks to recover from gunshot wounds to the groin and abdomen. Four bullets had hit him out of the sixteen she'd fired, emptying the Beretta's maga-zine. His condition had been critical for the first few days, but gradually he'd improved, and now he was healthy enough to be reinstalled in his old cell in Twin Towers.

The doctors had told Robin that Gray demonstrated a remarkable will to live. She hadn't been surprised. Whatever else he might be, Justin Gray was a survivor.

He was seated at the table, secured with handcuffs and leg irons. He smiled when the guards escorted her inside.

"What's up, Doc?"

She took the seat opposite his. The guards remained with them, standing silently by the door.

"How are you, Justin?"

"Took a licking, kept on ticking. Got me some fine scar tissue. It's like body art. I'd give you a look, but I don't think the Deputy Dawgs would appreciate me undressing in front of a lady."

"Probably not."

"You shot me up good, Doc. Regular Dirty Harriet, you are. Bona fide Jane Wayne."

"It was . . . instinct."

"Killer instinct." He said it with a smile.

There was silence, neither of them knowing what to say.

"Been watching the TV," Gray offered. "Nasty little conspiracy them crooked-ass cops had going."

"Yes, it was."

"That motherfucker, Wolper, and that other dude—what's his name?"

"Banner."

"Looks like they're ratting each other out. DA's playing one against the other to see who can squeal the loudest."

"That's about it."

"Couple of prize scumbags, ain't they?"

"Yes," Robin said. "They are."

Banner had begun manipulating Meg after meeting her at the awards dinner. He had a wife and a teenage daughter of his own, but he also had a secret obsession with young girls. He enjoyed impressing them by pretending to be a tough street cop, though he'd worked only Traffic and media relations. He'd had clandestine relationships with many girls, and Meg had been just one more, chosen at random, for convenience, not as part of any grand design. Only later, when Brand was assigned to Robin as a patient, did Banner begin to think about using his connection with Meg to gain leverage against her mother.

According to Hammond, Banner had tried to discourage him from taking over the manhunt. The reason was fairly clear—Banner hadn't wanted to be tied up with the investigation, because it meant he was unable to return to the factory and kill Meg. Wolper had been forced to draft Tomlinson for the job.

When the cell phone trace led Hammond to the factory, Banner became increasingly nervous. He knew that Meg would identify him instantly if she was somehow still alive. His last chance to silence her had failed when she saw him coming and ambushed him with Tomlinson's syringe.

"Buncha other assholes are implicated," Gray was saying, "but they're all low on the totem pole." He leaned forward. "You want my take on it? I say there's higher-ups involved, and they're getting protected."

He could be right. "I don't know," Robin said.

"That's how it always is. Fucking cops take care of their own. The big ones will walk away. Always do. It's the little guys that get it up the ass, every time."

"Are you one of the little guys, Justin? Are you a victim now?"

"Shit, no. Me? Never. Just telling it like it is. So why are you here, Doc Robin? Want me to take another turn as your lab rat?"

"No, Justin."

"Then what's the deal?"

"I wanted to ask you a question. It's something that's been on my mind."

"Ask away. I got all kinds of time."

"You killed Tomlinson with one shot," she said slowly. "He was all over Meg, and it was dark in the cellar—there was only one flashlight to see by—but you hit him on your first try."

"Damn, I'm good."

"You killed Brand with a head shot in the middle of a car crash."

"He was a foot away. No big thing to nail your mark at that range."

"Brand didn't nail *you*."

"I was faster."

"You were better."

He didn't deny it. "What's your point?"

"When I was diving into the cellar, you fired right at me. And you missed."

"Then I guess them two kill shots was just luck."

"You know what I think, Justin? I think you had no problem killing in self-defense or to save Meg. But when it came time to kill me, there was a split second of hesitation. A flicker of doubt."

Gray was quiet for a long moment. Then he smiled—not a warm smile, not friendly.

"Still wanna believe, don't you?"

She said nothing.

He leaned forward, his manner calm and conversational and wryly amused. "Doc, here's what happened. You whacked me on the head with that wooden board. Cost me a shitload of stitches, by the way—thanks very much. All that blood, it was running into my eyes, fucking up my aim. I was shooting blind."

"I see."

"But even if I hadn't been blinded, I still might've missed, 'cause I ain't no sharpshooter. Got lucky with Tomlinson, like I said. With you, I wasn't so lucky. And you know what else?"

Her voice was low. "What, Justin?"

"Every night I lie awake on my rack, wishing I hadn't missed you. I wish I'd put you down hard. You and your cunt daughter. I wish the both of you was dead meat, six feet under. That's the cold truth."

She nodded, taking this in. "All right."

"Not what you wanted to hear?"

"I thought we might have made just a little progress."

"No such luck. Got news for you, Doc Robin. That brain machine of yours ain't gonna save the world. And it sure didn't save my fucking soul."

"I guess I can't save everybody."

"You'll keep trying, I bet."

"Probably." She stood up. "Good-bye, Justin."

She took a step toward the door, where the guards were waiting.

Gray asked, "Is it your brother?"

She turned. "What?"

"You got a con in your family. That's why you're so hot to trot about this rehabilitation shit. When we were night-riding to your daughter's rescue, you almost let spill who it was."

"That's true. I remember."

"I'm betting it's your brother. Right?"

"My father, actually."

"Your dad's in lockup?"

"He died there."

"Huh." She expected a response, but he merely shrugged, absorbing the information without visible feeling. In his world, bad things just happened. That was life. There was no particular way to feel about it. "You say hello to Meg for me."

"She'll never even know I was here."

"Figured that. I'll be thinking of her, though. Look forward to seeing her again."

"You'll never see her."

She reached the door. Gray called after her, "Don't be so sure about that, Doc Robin. Keep looking over your shoulder. Someday I'll be there."

She looked back almost sadly. "I don't think so, Justin."

"Count on it." His head was lifted in adolescent bravado. "You hear me, Doc? These walls can't hold me forever."

Robin stared at him. "Yes, they can."

In his eyes, she saw that he knew it, too.

She turned, and the door shut behind her with a clang of solemn finality that rang in her ears as she walked slowly away.

Author's Note

As always, readers are invited to visit my Web site at http://michaelprescott.freeservers.com, where you'll find information on my previous and upcoming books, as well as interviews, personal essays, and an e-mail address.

Many thanks to my agent, Jane Dystel of Dystel & Goderich Literary Management, for her help throughout the writing of this book; to Miriam Goderich, also of DGLM, for valuable feedback and encouragement; to Tiffany Yates, for her expert copy editing; and to Doug Grad, senior editor at New American Library, for reading the manuscript with care and sensitivity. Thanks also to the sales and marketing professionals at NAL who manage the difficult job of getting the books into the stores.

Michael Prescott began his career as a screenwriter and freelance journalist. In addition to *In Dark Places*, he has authored five previous suspense thrillers. Currently at work on a new novel, he divides his time between the Arizona desert and the New Jersey shore.

You can contact Michael Prescott at his Web site: www.michaelprescott.freeservers.com

⊘ SIGNET   (0451)

Next Victim

By New York Times Bestselling Author

Michael Prescott

He calls himself Mobius—and he's a serial killer
who has eluded the FBI for years. Catching him
is an obsession for Agent Tess McCallum.

Her name is Amanda Pierce. She's on the run from
the feds—wanted for the theft of a military chemical
weapon. In an exclusive Los Angeles hotel, she
meets with Mobius. It's the last date of her life.

But for Mobius, it's the beginning of a new
life-and-death game. His opponent is
Tess McCallum. And the stakes are not one victim,
not two victims…but thousands.

0-451-20753-X

**Available wherever books are sold, or
to order call: 1-800-788-6262**

S808